worlds
apart

worlds apart

Jane CRITTENDEN

LAKE UNION PUBLISHING

Published by Lake Union Publishing, Seattle

www.apub.com

Amazon, the Amazon logo, and Lake Union Publishing are trademarks of Amazon.com, Inc., or its affiliates.

ISBN-13: 9781662509155
eISBN: 9781662509148

Cover design by Emma Rogers

Cover image: © janista © Marish © Chris WM Willemsen © Ellegant © avh_vectors / Shutterstock

Printed in the United States of America

Ian, Xanthe, Kenzie, you are my world

Chapter 1

AMY

Now

He's here.

I don't feel a rush of excitement. Nor a surge of blissful happiness. No swell of pleasure, not even a tiny sigh of relief. Nothing good registers in my brain or my body to encourage me to connect with this man. Instead, sharpness twists my chest and I think, *why now?*

Only minutes before, Shannon and I had been belting out a song that was playing on the radio in my empty café. She'd held the broom handle like a microphone and I twirled around her in my scarlet dress, a purchase she'd convinced me to make a few weeks before. I was still humming as we carried on clearing away the aftermath of the party and when I stuck my head inside the glass display counter to sweep up the cake crumbs . . .

He said my name.

I straightened up. But not because his voice set my heart aflutter or because I noticed his English accent, but simply because somebody, some *stranger*, called my name. And, like with all the customers who had come into my café that day to join our celebrations, I said, 'Hello'.

Now I properly see the man who stands in front of me and the second twist to my chest is so painful it obliterates the smile I had ready for this new customer.

'Amy?' he repeats. 'Amy Curtis? It is you, isn't it?'

He looks incredulous. Energy sparks his voice and instinctively I step back, the high heel of a shoe I'm not used to wearing grinding into Shannon's foot. She mutters a swear word and I shift slightly, letting my gaze stray away from him. Behind, the tables parade the post-party carnage and tangles of pink balloons sag and nod in the sea breeze that drifts through the open door. The radio is still playing but I can't hear the music any more.

Why now?

It already seems peculiar that, just this morning, I'd stood in this very spot, staring at the vacant tables and the glass display crammed with scones, sponges and cupcakes, voicing my doubts to Shannon that we'd sell it all. Then I'd unlocked the doors and the first group of customers trailed in, then the second, the third – and they kept coming, pouring in and jamming themselves on to the terrace outside. There were so many people that we got out our just-in-case fold-out chairs, and customers balanced cake and tea on their laps, spilling on to the beach with picnic blankets. Shannon and I had spun from customer to customer, smiling and laughing, and then – as with all great parties – it was suddenly over.

And he's here.

My eyes can't connect with his. They butterfly over him and land on the remains of the three-layer anniversary cake sitting on a table to his left. I'd baked a fruit cake for the bottom, carrot cake for the middle and then Victoria sponge, finishing the tiers with a coating of chocolate fudge. The *15 Years* I'd carefully iced to mark the occasion is now an unintelligible sticky scrawl, disappearing as fast as the years since I took over the café from Shannon's in-laws, when . . . *don't.*

I force myself to look at him. I recognise the tilt in the corners of his mouth. Not smiling, exactly, just *amused.* Then I lock on to eyes, hazel, just like . . . *don't* . . .

'It *is* you.' He grins and holds his arms wide as if he expects me to run around from behind the counter and jump into his embrace. 'I can't believe I found you.'

Found me?

He waves a folded newspaper and I catch a glimpse of my smiling face. 'I saw the article. I couldn't believe your café was just a few miles down the road from me.'

Down the road?

Shannon's still clutching the broom handle and suddenly springs back into life. 'See, Amy? I told you the whole of Auckland would know who you are now. How does it feel to be a celebrity?'

She squeezes my arm, tighter than is normal or natural, and laughs. The throaty sound usually makes me smile; it's shameless and loud with a hint of something naughty that always makes people glance in her direction as though they might witness something salacious. If anyone's a celebrity around here, it's Shannon, not me.

I glance at the identical newspaper article in a frame propped up by the till. Shannon had presented it to me just before the party ended. She'd let out a high-pitched wolf whistle to catch everyone's attention and gave an embarrassing speech about my achievements, which sounded like they belonged to someone else. In the photo, I'm wearing the same scarlet dress as I do now. I'm standing in the doorway of my café, holding a tray of red velvet cupcakes iced in creamy vanilla, my mouth stretched into a broad grin. Beneath the picture, five gold stars ring out. The critic described me as a 'Brit abroad with a genuine nostalgia for home'. Though, in truth, I've lived here for half my life.

'"Auckland's Best Baker",' Chris says, pointing the newspaper at me like a weapon. 'I knew you'd smash it one day, Ames.'

Ames. I flinch. The memory tears open the scar of all that's gone on before.

Chapter 2

Olivia

Then

Olivia stood alone in the corridor outside the classroom and stroked her hand down her hair; the right side, always the right side, that's just how it had to be. Murmuring voices drifted through the closed door as the class settled down for the lesson and chalk squeaked against the blackboard. Somewhere in the building, a door slammed. Olivia looked back down the stretch of corridor towards the double doors that had hissed shut behind her. An evil hiss, like a whisper, *you don't belong here*.

It'd only take a few minutes. She could fly through that door and be gone. Gone from this shitty sixth-form college and back into the freedom of real life. She hitched her bag on to her shoulder. Who was she kidding? Where would she go? The credit card her dad had given her would only last so long. Freedom didn't lie in that direction; freedom lay right here, behind *this* door.

So much for being on time. Her dad had promised to come with her this morning but, no, once the phone rang and she heard the urgent tone in his voice, she knew he'd ditch her for work. But stupidly she'd hung around long enough for him to say it to her face. And now he'd made her late. So much for staying invisible.

Olivia stroked her hair again and pushed open the door. A sea of faces swung towards her like one monstrous stare. Heat prickled her chest and crept up her neck. She was grateful she'd worn a black roll-neck.

Run.

No, this was the only way. Her only way out.

'Olivia?' The teacher greeted her with a faint smile and gestured for her to come in. She stood tall – though not quite as tall as Olivia – and wore her hair stretched back into a bun so tight her cheekbones leapt out from her face. An orange patterned scarf was knotted around her long neck. *She's like an elegant giraffe*, thought Olivia, and she began sketching a caricature of this teacher-creature in her mind.

'Find a seat, please.'

Olivia turned towards the prying eyes, skipping over everyone's faces in the childish way she had always believed made her invisible. Already the students had begun to turn away, taking advantage of the lull in the lesson to chat. A girl in the front row who wore a sticky layer of coral lip gloss locked on to Olivia. She smirked and whispered something to the girl next to her, who let out a bark of laughter. Olivia's face flamed and she willed an empty seat to make itself known.

'There's a space here!'

Olivia scanned the room but couldn't place where the squeaky voice was coming from. Then a girl with a fountain of blonde curls and a wide grin stood up at the back and waved her arms as though Olivia was blind. The class laughed and Olivia stared at her, instantly clocking her short, curvy frame and frantically looking around for another empty chair.

'Thank you, Amy,' said Giraffe, leaving Olivia no alterna-tive but to join the grinning elf. She set her mouth in a line and clumped between the desks. *She's a giant! What's with the ridiculous Morticia hair? Is it a wig? Is she a vampire? She looks bloody miserable!* The whispers had taken root in her head years ago and rolled on repeat in situations like this. The silence outside her head was just as excruciating as the other kids stared and compared her tit-less, oafish frame with the wafer-thin giraffe-teacher and this pretty pixie girl. Why had she ever thought she looked cool in her Doc Martens boots and mini skirt this morning?

'Class, this is Olivia, make her feel welcome.'

Amy was still grinning as Olivia slid behind the desk. She glanced at Amy's flowery blouse tucked into a blue denim skirt and grimaced. The hippy look was a style cliché she'd always hated – even Amy's feet were bare where she'd kicked off her wedges.

Olivia forced her mouth into a smile and folded all five foot eleven of herself into the chair. Amy leant towards her to say something.

'No talking, Amy,' barked Giraffe. 'In fact, Amy, you can start reading the play from page forty-five.'

Amy rolled her eyes but did as she was told. She began slowly, enunciating each sentence in a tone that was verging on sarcastic, which made Giraffe frown and Sticky Lips snigger again. Olivia pulled out the play and hunched further into the seat, praying the teacher wouldn't ask her to read next. She hated reading aloud but that didn't mean she didn't like to listen; the roll of Shakespeare's words had a lilt and rhythm that captured her imagination. They had purpose. They had meaning.

Today, the words on the page ran into one another and Olivia looked up and let her gaze roam around the room. She counted twelve boys – well, men, she supposed, now they were all approach-ing eighteen – and the thought made her head buzz a little. After a lifetime attending a girls' school, she'd got used to staring at rows of regulation blue blazers and smart ponytails, as the uniform instructed. Here, everyone dressed as they pleased, although a uniform of sorts was apparent in the mass of students wearing jeans, plaid shirts and baggy jumpers. Girls wore their hair loose, it seemed, but a couple of rows across she spotted a ponytail – on a guy! For a moment, Olivia imagined him walking into a shop to buy a packet of hairbands and smirked. His ponytail lay coiled between his shoulder blades like the chestnut brown tail of a playful puppy.

Olivia reached down and pulled out a small wire-bound sketch pad from her bag. She looked across to Puppy Boy and began sketching a caricature with round cheeks and a naughty grin, wagging a curly brown tail. He shifted in his seat and Olivia saw he wasn't looking at the play but scribbling in a notebook laid on his lap.

Amy's voice rose to a screech as she lapsed into a different character and a wave of laughter rolled across the class. Puppy Boy turned around and grinned at Amy, then his eyes rested on Olivia for a moment. Heat shot up her neck again, staining her cheeks, and in an effort to control the thrill of being noticed she scowled.

Not a puppy. Strong contours angled the guy's face and his eyes were an unusual medley of green and brown. Christ, she was swooning like the heroine in the play they were reading! The sharp lead in her pencil cracked, leaving a smudgy indent in the paper.

'Clearly Amy can't quite cut it,' snapped Giraffe. 'Chris, you read this section.'

Olivia looked up and saw she was pointing at Puppy Boy. He slid his notebook out of sight beneath his thigh and leant casually back in the chair. He looked as though he was about to begin reading, but instead he flicked another glance in Olivia's direction and winked. Amy sniggered but Olivia's eyes dropped to the play in front of her, heart hammering as she listened to the rich tones of his voice fill the classroom. She stared at the page until her eyes watered, running her hand down her hair over and over again. Then someone else took a turn to read and she found herself able to breathe again.

Slowly she looked up.

Chris.

Chapter 3

AMY

Now

'What are you doing here, Chris?' I finally manage to say, and Shannon stiffens beside me. The man standing in front of me is a faded version of someone I once knew as well as I knew myself. If I narrow my eyes, I could almost believe this is a trick. Like catching the person you miss most out of the corner of your eye when you're out somewhere, but as you turn, heart beating in excitement, the mirage dissolves and it isn't them at all.

Except this time, it really *is* Chris.

'I can't believe it,' he repeats and his mouth curves again, just ever so slightly, like something amusing is dancing at the corners.

I shut my eyes. Then I open them again. Chris is still here, waiting for what, I don't know. Well, I *do* know, but I can't think about it. I want to send him on his way, to tell him *he's too bloody late* and to get the hell out of here and never come back. Adrenaline fizzes through my veins but I can't quite shape the words out loud.

I feel Shannon's hand on my shoulder. 'I'm Shannon,' she says, her voice pleasant, but she doesn't stick out her hand or embrace him on the cheek, like she would if he was my friend.

'Chris,' he repeats, as if Shannon didn't hear me a moment ago. 'I'm an old . . .' We lock eyes for a moment. '. . . an old friend from sixth form,' he finishes.

I've wrapped my arms around my body and I squeeze myself. Somewhere in the recesses of my mind, a muddle of thoughts say Shannon won't understand that sixth form is college, and college in England is for older kids and not like the name they use for high school here. But I don't voice them to untangle the confusion, I'm thinking I need to take my heels off; there's a dull ache tugging at my calves.

'I'll make coffee,' she says into our silence, her green eyes flashing at me with concern. 'Sounds like you two have some catching up to do.'

I should be annoyed by her assumption that I'd want to spend a minute longer with this man than I have to. But there's no sign of the wolfish grin I've come to expect when I'm within touching distance of a guy that she deems available and with potential. Her dangerous smile is one that reveals the gap between her straight white teeth – and now her mouth is closed.

'This place is a mess,' I mutter.

'There's no rush,' she replies.

My gaze lands on Chris long enough to see his lips are still tugged up. I don't want to catch up. I don't want to talk – about anything. Shannon's shoulder-squeeze reassures me. I straighten up all five foot of myself – even taller today in these ridiculous heels. I stare at a spot of nothing over his shoulder, thinking, I could run upstairs, I could disappear into the kitchen, I could scream *Go Away – you're not wanted.* Or I could sit down and have coffee with him and nod along to whatever story he's going to spin me – and then tell him to jog on and get out of my life because *he's too late.*

I will not be a victim, so I push a smile on to my face. 'Let's go outside,' I say brightly, and move out from behind the counter, kicking off my shoes and yanking off my apron. I glance at the faded pattern of Bea's tiny handprints and then stuff it out of sight on a shelf.

Chris's eyes burn into me as I pad past him across the bare floorboards. I tug at the low-scooped neck of my dress and wish I was back in my usual shorts and T-shirt combo. Out on the terrace, a silver heart-shaped balloon emblazoned with *15* bobs on the rail where I tied it earlier. I walk past all the empty tables and sit down at the one with the best view of the ocean. The sun still shimmers high in the sky and the beach is scattered with families, couples and groups of friends. Nobody looks in a hurry to go home.

Chris settles himself down opposite me. He's wearing a green T-shirt and black board shorts and stretches out long legs in my direction. His tanned skin makes him look more like a Kiwi enjoying summer than a pale-faced Pom visiting from a British winter. I wonder how long he's been in Auckland and how this visit can be just a coincidence.

'Hey, Ames, do you remember the Aussie soaps we used to watch?' he says, and this time his upturned lips become a full grin. 'I always wondered if you'd become one of those bronzed, sun-bleached surf chicks and spend all your free time mucking about on a beach like this with your friends.'

Ames. I flinch. No one has called me that since I moved here. He makes my name sound as natural as when he said it the first time in an A-level art class all those years ago.

I notice a coffee stain on my dress, press my finger over the top to hide it. 'That isn't me,' I say, lifting my head to meet his gaze. 'That was *never* me.'

I'm biting back the rest of what I want to say, the words simmering in my mouth, and he looks at me curiously – am I hiding my fury that well? 'I wouldn't expect you to understand,' I say tightly. 'My life has been way too busy for lounging around on the beach.'

Chris glances at the café. 'So I see.' Then his mouth tips up – is he *amused*? 'How long has it been since we saw each other? It's got to be what – twenty years?'

Is this some kind of sick game? I don't need to count back the years and the date he speaks of is stamped as clear and lasting as a tattoo. But I'm not going to correct him. I'm not going to play his game.

'I never thought I'd see you again,' he continues. 'This is such a coincidence. I'm on secondment here.'

A coincidence? Heat flares but I force my tone to remain neutral. 'Really? Why did you choose Auckland?' I watch his reaction closely. He looks bemused rather than contrite and then a flash of something familiar in his expression makes my breath catch.

'Why not?' He laughs. 'I like it here. I might stay.'

Stay? Questions punch their way through my mind. But it's too late for answers because I already *know* the answers and I remind myself, *I'm not a victim*, and if I pretend to be friendly, he might be satisfied with this one visit, and he can bugger off back to where he came from.

'What do you do?' I'm surprised when a crystal-clear image of him pulling pints at The Fox back in England pops into my head – sticky carpets, ear-splitting rock music, the persistent fog of cigarette smoke.

'I'm an architect, in London.'

Chris must read my expression as encouragement rather than surprise. He smiles and talks quickly, explaining how he eventually got the A-level grades for university in London, how much harder the studies were than he imagined, and how he had to live at home and carry on pulling pints to pay the bills.

'There were times when I wish I'd done something different.'

He watches me and I think if he's looking for sympathy, he won't find any at my door. Then he shakes his head and the grin is back. 'It was worth the hard work – I love my job.'

Whispered words seep out from a memory I left buried years ago. They echo the picture he paints. We were building our future together; secrets shared in the heat and shadows beneath the covers, while the blaze of afternoon sun reminded us we should have been in class. 'You followed your dream,' I state, shoving the memory away. 'Whereabouts do you live in London?'

He looks at me oddly for a moment. 'I don't. I would've liked to, but, well, life doesn't always turn out how you expect, does it? I still live at home in Hillgate.'

'In the same house? Surely not the same bedroom?' A bark of laughter pops out. Now the memories are tumbling over themselves, and I can see his single bed squeezed up against the wall next to the wardrobe. The black-and-red diagonal patterned duvet cover, part of a set that came with matching curtains. His room seemed so grown up compared to my walls plastered with pop-star pin-ups.

He's laughing. 'No, not at my mum and dad's,' he says, shattering the image. 'I live in one of those terraced houses near the station. You wouldn't believe how much the town has changed. It's all pricey restaurants and slick wine bars now, and property prices are unbelievable.'

I look out across the beach towards the line of pōhutukawa trees. They're in the full glory of their crimson summer bloom, like they were all those years ago when . . . *Don't.* I focus on what he says; this town he speaks of is but a hazy memory of a life that feels like it belonged to someone else. He talks of a lifestyle I know nothing about and I wonder if this is a home he shares with a wife and family.

Shannon steps on to the terrace with a tray of coffee and sets it down in front of us. She lays out my favourite art deco coffee set – black with a gold trim – which right now looks faintly ridiculous.

'There you go,' she says, and I fully expect her to say something else, perhaps ask Chris a nosy question, but she doesn't, she just disappears back inside.

Chris picks up the coffee jug and takes a closer look. 'Nice,' he says.

This art deco set is one of many I've collected over the years and – along with my traditional cakes – is why customers visit time and time again. I made all the tablecloths from vintage fabrics I found stuffed in a box at the back of a second-hand shop, and in the centre of each table I always place a china sugar bowl with dainty sugar tongs.

Chris pours my coffee. I want to snatch it from his hand and pour my own. 'The Boat Shed,' he says, reading the name across the door. He gestures at the beach. 'Speaks for itself then.' He offers me the milk jug and I decline. He pours a splash into his own cup and then picks up the tongs and plucks a sugar cube from the bowl. The spoon chinks the china as he stirs and then he looks at the café again.

'You don't own the building, do you?' he says, running his eyes over the tatty weatherboarding and up towards my roof terrace, which has seen better days.

I shake my head but there's something about the way he's scrutinising the building that makes my hackles rise. 'Why? Is there something strange about that?'

'No, not at all.'

The Boat Shed was painted a vivid sky blue when Shannon's in-laws, Linda and John, took over the newly converted building all those years ago. Now faded, the paint looks dismal rather than coastal. Although the upkeep isn't my responsibility, I know the owners – distant and overseas somewhere – have no interest, so I've only got myself to rely on to make things right.

'Do you live nearby?' Chris asks, still stirring.

'Right here,' I say, pointing up at the rusty balustrade that surrounds the roof terrace. I can see my swing seat from here; it's our favourite place to sit at the end of the day . . . *Focus.*

He looks to where I'm pointing and frowns. 'Here?'

I bristle again. 'Yes, that's my flat, what's wrong with that?'

He shrugs and then grins. 'I can hardly talk – this is the first time I've lived anywhere other than Hillgate.'

Shannon comes out again, holding a tray of leftover cakes. 'Would you like one?'

I shake my head; my stomach is a bag of knots.

'For sure,' says Chris. 'I've always loved Amy's cakes.'

'*Everyone* loves Amy's cakes,' says Shannon, smiling, 'she's a legend around here.'

She puts the plate down and disappears inside again, and I watch Chris's hand hover over them. He selects a triangle of carrot and orange cake slathered in cream-cheese icing. *Does he remember?*

'Have you still got your little red recipe book?' He takes a big bite. It's been years since I interrogated people for their opinions on my recipes and it seems utterly absurd that I'm here, with Chris, sliding back into the old ways. 'I never could understand how you kept losing that thing when it was so precious to you.'

He laughs. But I don't want to fondly recall how many times I scuffled through my bag, or hunted through the kitchen cupboards searching for my precious recipe book – or that I still have it, tucked away in a box for safekeeping. Instead, I say tightly, 'I can bake most cakes with my eyes closed.'

Chris closes his eyes for a moment. 'Vanilla and orange . . .' he mutters, 'and cardamom.' He opens them again. 'This tastes exactly the same. Well, even better than I remember, but I guess you've had years to perfect the recipe.'

So he *does* remember.

And then I remember why he's here: his friendliness, his flattery, it's all part of the con to make me feel valued when his visit is not about me at all.

'A magic cake in a magic spot,' he continues, staring out across the bay. 'You've done really well, Ames. You're really lucky to be able to work here.'

Ordinarily I'd chatter on about how much I love having the beach as my home and my workplace. But – *luck?* His words blast through me. He doesn't know me or my life or how hard it's been to scratch a living. He doesn't know me at all.

'Not so much luck as hard bloody work,' I retort.

He smiles. 'Of course, that's what I meant. Fifteen years running a café by the sea. That would be a dream for most people and you've made it happen.'

I flush and shift in my chair. He sounds like Shannon.

We fall silent and Chris's gaze trails towards the beach. I snatch a glance at him. Why is he being so evasive? Why is he saying *nothing at all?* A black-and-white terrier bounces around the sand, its barks piercing the air as it calls to its owner to toss the ball. The dog scampers into the shallows and a greyhound sprints down the beach in pursuit, and they nudge together in the water chasing the ball and each other around and around.

It's not up to me to ask.

'You've kept your hair long,' he says, eyes on me again.

I don't like the way he's looking at me with that dopey half-smile.

'You don't look a day older.'

I snort.

'Hey, listen, it would be great if you could show me around sometime.'

Too much.

I start to get to my feet. 'Sorry . . .' Not sounding sorry at all. 'It's not a good time . . .'

'Of course, not right now,' he says, 'I can see you're busy, but perhaps when you next have a day off?'

I fold my arms and my eyes follow the sound of a baby on the beach, wailing for its mother. I watch her pluck him from the buggy, lock him into a sling on her front, adjust his sun hat, bob him up and down.

'Maybe your husband won't like you giving your ex the tour?' Chris says with a question in his voice.

'I'm not married.' *Not any more.*

'Your partner, your boyfriend, then.' His tone is neutral, but his eyes search mine for an answer.

I shake my head. I'm embarrassed by the intrusion, as though he's revealed me to be a sad, lonely spinster. Automatically, I glance at his hand: he's not wearing a wedding ring, but that doesn't mean a thing – not that I care whether he's single, married, or what.

'Well then,' he says, and I realise I've left myself vulnerable. 'Couldn't Shannon manage without you? It would be great to have a proper catch-up.'

I feel oddly pursued. Of course she could. But I can't do this. I can't. I don't want him here because I *know* why he's here and I want him gone.

He leans in close to me so that I can see gold flecks in his hazel eyes that remind me . . . *no.* 'This is crazy, what are the chances of us meeting again like this?' he says quietly.

For a moment I think he's going to reach out and coil one of my curls around his finger like he used to, and I press myself back into my chair. 'Chance? Is that what you really believe? And what's so important that we have to *catch up?*'

I'm gripping the chair to hide my shaking hands, but he doesn't take the bait. A frown replaces his smile. 'What else could it be? It's not like I knew where you lived.'

His lie crashes over me like a tidal wave and snatches my breath away. Because I know for a fact that he knew exactly where to find me, he just chose not to come. I'm trembling with the effort of holding back the jumble of accusations I've pushed down inside me. I won't give him the satisfaction of thinking I'm a victim and he's the controller.

I've done fine without him. I don't need him now.

My eyes are steel. 'Why have you come, Chris? I mean, why now?'

He stares at me for a beat, a flush mounting his cheeks. He jumps up and his chair clatters over. 'I'm here for a while,' he says with his back to me as he rights the chair. 'If you change your mind, drop me a text or call.' He scribbles his number on to a napkin, brushes his lips against my cheek and strides away.

My fingers creep on to my face, where the imprint of his mouth burns. I watch him cross the sand. I don't know who this man is, not really. I don't know where he lives, how long he's here, only that he *is* here – but he's too late.

Chapter 4

Olivia

Then

A squall of chair-scraping and raised voices filled the room as the teacher dismissed the class, but Olivia didn't join the rush to leave. She picked up the play and her sketch pad, keeping her eyes glued to Chris behind a curtain of her hair. She watched him lightly punch a Goth guy on the arm in greeting and the pair slouched out of the room, followed by Amy and a gaggle of friends. Amy shouted something as she disappeared through the door and Olivia heard the warm roll of Chris's laugh in response – and then the classroom was empty.

Olivia snatched up her bag and spotted a small red notebook on the floor near Chris's desk. Was this his? A swell of excitement rose up inside of her. She flicked through the book: the pages were filled with recipes neatly written in blue biro. Some of the ingredients were crossed out, with a ruler by the looks of it, and some of the notes in the margin were punctuated with question marks.

Olivia frowned. Did Chris like cooking? She slid the book inside the pocket of her black denim jacket. At the door, she hovered for a moment, rocking on her feet as she tried to see if Chris was among the groups of students chatting in the corridor. She wondered where she might find him and, if she did find him, what she'd say. She'd have to say *something*, she couldn't just hand his recipes back and say nothing, she'd look like a right moron.

Olivia headed towards the nearest door, which led out to a big lawn. Even though it was early October, the last of the summer sun hung on and students sat scattered across the grass eating lunch. If she slunk off to the back of the field, she could have a sneaky cigarette and see if she could spot Chris.

Olivia found a sunny spot away from everyone else and flung her jacket on to the grass. She tapped a cigarette out of the packet, lit the tip and took a deep, satisfying drag. She'd not listened to a thing in class this morning and she couldn't afford not to. She had to get it together; she couldn't fall apart now. Just one more year, that was all. Not even a year really. The exams would all be over by June. If she got her head down and studied her arse off, she'd be at Edinburgh University before she knew it. Away from this shithole town. Starting anew.

Olivia sucked on her cigarette again and glanced around at the groups on the lawn. She couldn't see Chris among them and even if she had, she couldn't think of anything more embarrassing than strolling over to a bunch of people she didn't know and handing the notebook to him. No, she'd suss out where he had his lessons and wait until she caught him on his own.

Olivia pulled out her sketch pad and a battered tin of charcoals from her bag. She let the cigarette dangle from her lips and started drawing, the image flowing from her mind down into her fingertips as if the two were talking a secret language and she was just the conduit. The tension from this morning dissolved and then, just as she was finishing, a shadow fell across her work.

'Don't let them catch you smoking here,' said a voice.

Olivia looked up and squinted into the sun. Amy stood over her, the light behind puffing her hair into a cloud of frizz.

'They go on and on saying students must use the smoking area,' she continued, waving her arm towards a fenced-in section around a large oak tree, 'but I've never actually seen a teacher out here on patrol, frogmarching smoking students back to where they belong.'

Olivia couldn't work out if Amy was joking or not, but before she could tell her where to go with her preaching, Amy had flopped down on to the grass next to her and kicked off her wedges. 'What you doing?' she said, looking over at Olivia's sketch pad.

Olivia whipped the pad close to her chest and Amy laughed. 'Is that your diary? Your innermost secrets and thoughts?' She laughed again and Olivia flushed. No one ever saw her drawings and she had no intention of changing that now.

Amy's grin loosened a little. 'Sorry,' she said, 'just a joke, I was actually wondering if you saw a red notebook when you left class earlier? I'm gutted. It must have slipped out of my bag somewhere and it's like, well, *my life*, I suppose.' The grin flashed again.

Olivia felt a stab of disappointment. Of course it was Amy's notebook. For a second, she felt like denying all knowledge and then imagined how she'd feel if she lost her sketch pad. She'd be mortified. She reached into her jacket pocket. 'Here you go,' she said, and felt strangely pleased when Amy's face lit up.

'Oh my God, thanks, Olivia! I thought someone had chucked it in the bin or nicked it.'

Olivia bristled. 'I didn't steal it. It was on the floor.'

Amy laughed again. 'Of course not!'

Olivia was beginning to realise Amy did a lot of laughing. It was a wholesome laugh; the sound that confident people made when they couldn't care less what anyone thought. She was clearly an annoying, glass-half-full kind of person. She probably spent her weekends doing charity work or something equally dull and square and *happy*.

Amy flicked through the pages of her notebook, which seemed like showing off. As though she was making a point and wanted Olivia to ask why the book was so important. Olivia thought she didn't care but a part of her *was* curious. Though she'd have gone mental if anyone flicked through her sketch pad as casually as she'd looked through Amy's notebook. God, how *embarrassing* for a stranger to see the caricatures she drew, it *would* be like having someone read her diary – if she ever wrote one.

But anyway, what was so private about lists of boring recipes?

'Thank God no one's scribbled in it or ripped any of the pages out,' Amy said, her fingers still turning the pages. 'There are some right bitches in English class.' Then something on one of the pages caught her eye. 'I thought that's what I needed to buy,' she muttered and flipped the notebook shut.

The girls looked at each other for a moment. Olivia wondered if Amy was expecting her to say something about her recipes, perhaps give her a cheery compliment, but she wouldn't, and then she wondered why Amy was still sitting there. A mischievous grin crept across Amy's face and she lunged forwards and grabbed Olivia's sketch pad off the grass. Olivia froze as she opened the pad.

'Hey, it's only fair, you've seen my recipes!' Amy laughed, and then stopped when she saw the thunderous look on Olivia's face. 'Sorry,' she said, but she was still smiling as she handed the pad back. 'I *am* only teasing. Your pictures are really good.'

Olivia's skin prickled hot, then cold, and she stuffed the sketch pad into her bag and stood up.

'Hey, don't go!' said Amy. 'I didn't mean to offend you, God, you rescued my baking bible! I'll owe you forever!'

Olivia began to walk away, feeling shaky and slightly sick. She didn't need this kind of *friend* in her life.

'I like the giraffe-teacher,' Amy called out. 'Is that Miss Hawkins? I've always thought she looked like a giraffe too. There's something about her neck, isn't there? It's so long and graceful, and her legs . . . God, I'd *love* to have long, skinny legs like that. Some people get all the luck.'

Olivia stopped.

'You know, I get it, I never show my recipes to anyone either, I should really know better. They're weirdly private, like a diary, you know?'

Olivia turned. Amy's wide smile filled her face and she searched for a flicker of something false. Something that would reveal the truth behind the conversation. But all she could see was a grin that plumped out Amy's cheeks and creased the corners of her eyes. *Squirrel.* A happy squirrel. Olivia felt something snag inside her and she walked back.

'Fancy one of my cakes?' said Amy, pulling out a plastic tub and flipping off the lid.

Olivia looked at the four fairy cakes nestled inside the box, each one set in a different coloured paper case. Four perfect curves of sponge topped with a whorl of piped buttercream icing and a rainbow sprinkle of hundreds and thousands. They were cakes you'd make for a kid's birthday party. Parties Olivia never had, and the children in her primary school class soon stopped inviting her to. These cakes were stupidly childish, but perfectly made, and Olivia felt the unfamiliar tug again. She sat back down and hugged her knees. Thank God she'd decided to draw Giraffe instead of finishing Puppy Boy – now *that* would have been embarrassing.

'Take one, then,' Amy laughed as she waved the box under Olivia's nose.

Olivia hesitated and then picked the cake in the red case. Amy watched closely as she took a bite. 'What?' she said through a mouthful of crumbs. 'Why are you staring at me?'

Amy leant closer. 'Do you like it?' she whispered, her round blue eyes watchful.

'Err, yeah, it's a cake, what's not to like?'

'But do you *really* like it? Is it the best fairy cake you've ever tried?'

What the hell was this girl on?

'Just shut your eyes a minute and savour the flavour.' She paused. 'I've got some secret ingredients in there.'

Was she coming on to her? Olivia put the rest of the cake down on the grass. 'I think I'll leave you and your weird cakes to it,' she muttered, scrambling to her feet again.

'Wait!' Amy almost shrieked. 'Sorry! I'm not a crazy head! Look, I'll eat one with you. Show you what I mean. I've been messing with this recipe for ages, trying out different flavours because I want to make the Ultimate Fairy Cake. That's why I was so distraught when I lost my baking bible. It's got everything written down. You're kind of like a taste-tester for me. I really want to know what you think.'

Olivia shook her head. She didn't need another mentalist in her life.

'Please?' Amy pressed. 'Look, how about I reveal the special ingredients and you tell me if you can taste them. I don't usually like to give away my secrets but—' She narrowed her eyes. 'I think I can trust you.'

'Why?' Olivia was genuinely curious.

'I've seen your sketch,' she said solemnly.

'And?'

'You want to keep your artistic secrets too.'

Olivia was about to fling back a barbed denial. The absurdity of this conversation was childish and irritating, but a grain of truth scratched at her denial and she flumped back on to the grass again.

'Go on then, I'll guess the ingredients, but I am *not* closing my eyes – freak.'

Amy laughed.

Olivia broke off a piece of cake and popped it in her mouth. She watched Amy's expression, expecting to see a frown of anxiety like she'd feel if someone was assessing her drawings. But her blue eyes shone and she nodded encouragingly as if Olivia were the one needing the reassurance.

'Vanilla,' Olivia said.

'And?'

'Coconut.'

'And?'

Olivia screwed up her eyes.

'One more?'

She opened them again. 'Nope, that's it.'

'Damn!' said Amy, laughing and falling back on to the grass. 'I'll have another practice tonight.'

'What was it?'

'Can't say,' Amy said, tapping her nose.

'I though you said you'd tell me your secrets?'

'Not all of them!'

Olivia flipped open her cigarettes and offered one to Amy. She shook her head and Olivia remembered what she'd said about the smoking area. She looked back across to the oak tree where students hung in groups. She thought she could see Chris in his black leather jacket, but he wasn't the only one in leather sporting a ponytail, and it was difficult to be sure from this far away.

'So how come you joined sixth-form a month late?' said Amy, her eyes closed to the sun.

Olivia sucked hard on the cigarette and let the smoke trail out of her mouth. 'I just did.'

'I'm not the only one with secrets, then?' Amy teased. 'Did you get a job and then change your mind? Was your summer holiday too fabulous to come home from? Have you made a miracle recovery from a life-threatening illness?'

Olivia snorted and sucked on her cigarette again. 'There's no secret,' she muttered.

'Well? Go on then, why?'

What could she say? She couldn't tell Amy the truth. She'd never tell *anyone* the truth.

'Come on, give me something. I've got all these questions bubbling up inside of me, but I'm trying really hard not to be nosy. Everyone says I'm nosy, my mum is *always* telling me I'm nosy, but how am I supposed to know the difference between being nosy and being curious? Or just plain interested?'

'Duh, perhaps because the person you're asking doesn't want to answer your question?' Olivia replied drily. 'Not everyone likes to spill their guts.'

Amy sat up and appraised her for a moment. 'Point taken,' she said with a laugh. 'I'm rubbish. I tell everyone everything so I kind of assume everyone else is comfortable doing the same.'

'Don't you notice how people react? You know, check out their body language?'

'What, you mean like the way you hugged your sketch pad to your chest?' Amy teased.

'Ha ha,' said Olivia. 'I mean smaller things, like someone dropping eye contact or turning away from you.'

Amy didn't reply for a moment. 'I'd not really thought about it like that before.'

Silence fell and Olivia found herself hugging her knees again. 'We had to move house,' she said. 'I made a mess of my lower-sixth exams.'

It's the truth – of sorts.

'Your parents flipped out.' Amy nodded enthusiastically.

'They say everyone leaves this sixth form with fantastic A-level results.'

'The teachers had better not be counting on me!' Amy laughed. 'I never wanted to do A levels, not in a million years. I'm only here because my mum's a complete control freak and I'm a complete coward. I want to go to cookery school and learn to bake professionally. Or get an apprenticeship in a fancy restaurant, surely there's no crime in that? My dream would be to cook, bake and run a restaurant, but she seems to think it isn't a proper job. God, she drives me insane. Look at these stupid shoes for starters.' She pointed at her wedges. 'She seems to think short arses like me have to wear heels all the time or we'll get nowhere in life. God knows why I listen to her. Actually, I do know why: because she buys me my shoes. I mean, what kind of person am I if I'm still letting my mum choose shit shoes for me when I'm seventeen? I've got to get a life.'

Amy flopped back on to the grass. 'I'm guessing you want to be an artist? Are you doing art A level, like me? God, tell me where's the sense in that? I'm not allowed to do home economics but I *am* allowed to do art.'

Olivia drifted. *What did she want to do with her life?* Or what did she *have* to do? She ground her cigarette butt into the grass. 'I'm becoming a lawyer.'

'A lawyer? But you're so good at drawing!'

Olivia tried to laugh but it came out like a croak. 'You've only seen one picture.'

'And it's bloody good,' said Amy firmly, fixing her with a clear gaze. 'Never give up on your dreams. We only live one life.'

Chapter 5

AMY

Now

I'm sitting on the edge of my bed and looking at the pink box beside me. My finger imprints have mussed the dust on the lid where I grappled to reach the box from where it was hidden on top of my wardrobe. It's slighter bigger than a shoe box, chosen because it was exactly the right size to fit everything in. Once I clicked the plastic lid shut all those years ago, I had to be sure it'd stay shut; I never wanted to look in here again.

The box hasn't been opened since that day.

I've never been tempted to open it. Not even when Bea and I finally managed to escape Mum's house fifteen years ago to take on the café and move into this flat. When I unpacked, I shoved the closed box on top of the wardrobe so Bea wouldn't find it and I couldn't see it, and it's been there ever since. I'd almost forgotten about it. Almost.

I trail my finger through the years of dust. Back then, in another life, I might have drawn an A entwined with C and three tiny love hearts in the right-hand corner. Now I trace Bea's name, then brush the letters away.

It's been twenty-four hours since Chris wandered into my café as brazen as hell and left a sharp imprint of himself in the shadows of my waking hours. I've tried to pretend he never came. I'm trying to hang on to the threads of my joyful mood, but the anniversary party is already fading.

Shannon must have noticed my plastic smile in the café this morning. She placed a firm hand on my back and steered me into the kitchen, saying she'd manage the till and serve tables. I didn't protest and so I've been out back and pulled every packet and box off the shelves to do a stocktake. At some point, I heard a customer ask to speak to me about making a birthday cake. When Shannon came to find me, I was crouched on the floor surrounded by bags of flour and sugar and it seemed too much of an effort to get up and speak to them. Shannon said nothing and made excuses for me.

Come to dinner, she'd said later as she backed out the door to do the school run. She's desperate to talk to me, no, *interrogate* me, but I'm not ready, not today, not ever. In fact, I don't even know why this old box is sitting on my lap. I push it back on to the bed and rub my hands down my shorts, where they leave a dusty grey smear. My bum aches from where I've been sitting on the kitchen floor all day and hunger growls. I head into the kitchen, throw some beans into a pan and stick a couple of slices of Shannon's leftover bread into the toaster.

My kitchen is a funny place, nothing like the café's industrial kitchen below. Cupboards crowd the walls and the room is so narrow Bea and I used to nudge hips and do a jig as we squeezed past each other. It's not a cook's kitchen. But then I'm not a cook, I'm a baker, as I remind my mother on a regular basis. Bea's the cook and the one who cursed the peeling worktop and ancient appliances yet still produced meals worthy of any fancy restaurant.

Until she upped and left me last month.

Bea's decision to go travelling has left me reeling. One minute we were squished together on the sofa while I helped her put together her university application to study food tech. The next, she'd turned eighteen and told me she was leaving. I don't know what she wants – and it hurts.

I stand at the sink spooning warm beans into my mouth directly from the pan, staring out the window. I miss Bea's cooking; her nagging me for a new oven; the songs we sang along to on the radio. I can't understand how I missed the signs. Why didn't I know she was so desperate to go?

Outside, fingers of an orange sunset crawl up the sky behind the island peaks. A motorboat bounces across the waves towards the horizon. My thoughts turn to Dad and *his* boat, and the first and last fishing trip we went on when he finally persuaded me to let Mum mind Bea. That evening, I'd tucked Bea up in her cot and snuck out of the bedroom, praying she wouldn't wake and leave Mum floundering.

Dad and I had puttered off into the twilight, dropped anchor and he showed me how to bait my rod and cast a long, even arc with my line. That evening we sat under a navy sky and talked about everything. Dad knew stuff about the big, wide world that had passed me by since Bea was born, and he pointed out the names of stars as they pricked one by one into the night. When we lapsed into silence, I let the hypnotic motion of the waves rock me into contentment and then I began telling him about the small details of my own little world.

I think about the pink box on my bed. I think of Chris smiling at me across the table yesterday. What would Dad make of all this? My throat constricts. I should know, but I don't. Soon after that trip, Dad was gone. He never knew Chris didn't come.

He'll never know he's here now.

I scrub my eyes and drop the pan into the sink and scour the insides until every trace of food has gone. Why now? I chuck the remains of my toast into the bin and run water over the plate and slide it on to the draining rack.

I stride back into the living room, where I can see a glimpse of pink through my open bedroom door. The box has been shut for seventeen years. I kick the door closed. The box can stay shut for another seventeen for all I care.

I slump on to the sofa and reach for my laptop. It's too early for Bea's email, the one she promised to send me every day, but I like to scroll back and look at the pictures she's sent. In one, she's grinning into the camera, her long limbs stretched out across the top bunk on a sleeper train in Thailand; then she's outside a beach hut, a hand shielding her eyes from the sun. My mind shutters through a litany of potential disasters – train thieves, bed bugs, and predatory men. In the latest photo, Bea's sitting astride a battered bike on a sandy track in Laos, grinning, jagged spikes of a mountain range visible in the distance behind her.

… by the end of the day we were covered in orange dust but the water in our hut ran orange too, so we cooled off in the river. Do you know, in the evening the local bus driver brought his bus into the water to wash it down too?? . . . We've got a guide, he's very smiley and his English is good, you don't need to worry, I'm in safe hands!

I can almost hear the laughter in her voice. I trace her pretty smile with my finger and a familiar thread of anxiety tightens my belly.

… I'm travelling with a friend!! She's American, bubbly, straight-talking and she's got a huge heart, she's great, you'd love her, perhaps you'll meet her one day . . .

In this photo, Bea's linked arms with the girl and they're wearing matching oversized sunnies that hide their eyes, hair scruffed up into topknots, Bea's damp curls escaping around her face. I'm relieved she's made a friend. She left New Zealand alone. I hope this girl knows more about the world than Bea does.

My eyes drift around the living room and take in the bookshelves stuffed with cookbooks and old cookery magazines, and the fat leather chair that has never been comfortable to sit in. The swing seat on the roof terrace lies empty and the evening sun pours through the doors. Auckland has been my home for nearly nineteen years. What do *I* know of the world? I've been on a plane – once. Because who needs to holiday abroad when everything you could ever want is right here?

I look back at Bea's photo and notice a hand clutching her waist – the rest of the body sliced conveniently out of shot. A boyfriend? She's only ever been on a few half-hearted dates. I frown and begin typing a reply. I'm about to press send and then I reread my message. I sound annoyed rather than interested and I hear Shannon's voice in my ear.

Let her go. She's eighteen!

I can count on one hand how many boyfriends *I've* had in my life – and one of those became a husband in a marriage that should never have happened. My gaze draws back to the closed bedroom door. I delete the message, shut down the laptop and go into my room.

It's pathetically easy to click off the lid – I think a dumb part of me hoped the box would've magically sealed itself. Inside lies a small teddy with a red satin heart sewn into its belly. I used to cuddle this awful thing to sleep, imagining I could still smell Chris in the folds of its fake fur. I throw it on the bed. It's sentimental crap.

A white envelope is next, crackling with dried petals that came from a single red rose. Another envelope; this time a folded piece of paper is inside with lyrics to a song I don't need to read because I know the words by heart. Then I pick up the red notebook, my baking bible, and a strip of passport photos slides out from the pages. Four snapshots of frozen happiness: Chris and I cheek to cheek; another with our eyes locked in a pose we must have thought looked romantic; then two with Chris cupping my face, our lips pressed together.

I snort. We look so serious. Yet back then we had nothing to be serious about. Nothing serious had happened to us – yet.

Chapter 6

AMY

Now

'Ready?' says Shannon, coming into the kitchen the following evening and sliding the broom back into the cupboard. She's hustled the last of the customers out of the door and swept up. We're supposed to be going for a walk, some sort of power walk, but I feel grubby and drained. 'Would you mind if we went tomorrow?' I say, untying my apron.

She fixes me with a look and my gaze slides away. It doesn't take a genius to work out why she wants my undivided attention. 'OK, OK, let's go then, but not too far, my legs are killing me.'

'Excuses,' she chides, wagging her finger at me. 'Don't you remember what you said? "Don't let me wriggle out of this, don't let me give you excuses" and on day one, what do I get? Excuses!'

Sea swimming is my thing, but Shannon has been trying to get me into running with some crazy idea that we could do a triathlon together. I made an offhand comment about a local event I'd seen and she leapt on the opportunity to drag me into her intense fitness regime. A regime that involves beach running, swimming, cycling, kayaking and the odd boating adventure with her husband, Grant, when his parents or I mind their kids. She's breaking me in gently and so tonight we're starting out with a 'power walk' – I guess I should be grateful she has such low expectations of me.

Despite the hour, the sun is a yellow ball of heat hanging behind a haze of cloud above three volcanic islands that rise up from the sea. Their triangular peaks stand proud in descending height, like a *proper* family, Bea used to say when she was young. She was too small to realise her words hurt me, but oh, how they did. Over the years, I'd tried my best to prove to her that we could be a family of two – I've never shaken the feeling that I failed her.

And now . . .

The tide is so low the water's revealed the line of rocks at the end of the beach that separate us from the adjoining bay. Shannon sets off at a pace that I already know I'm going to find hard to match. The soft sand is hard work on my calves and I'm bracing myself for the questions I know are about to come.

I remember there was a time when all I wanted to do was talk about Chris. Now I don't want to say anything at all.

'Are you OK?' Shannon says at last. Her tone is soft and careful.

'I'm fine,' I respond automatically. Because I *am* fine. I dealt with Chris and our relationship years ago. I've cried enough tears over him and this is just one of those weird coincidences that happen to people sometimes in their lives.

I lengthen my stride and begin to swing my arms as I walk. I'm quite enjoying the sensation and I feel some of the knots in my shoulders loosen.

'Tell me about Chris,' she says. 'I mean, tell me *everything*.'

To be honest, I'm surprised she's managed to withhold her curiosity for this long. I cast a sideways glance in her direction. She's not looking at me but at the rocky outcrop ahead of us, which we'll climb over to reach the next bay. This is one of the things I love about Shannon, she knows when to go in gently and when I need to be challenged.

She also isn't stupid, and I wonder what she made of Chris. I didn't know her when I first moved to New Zealand and in the years that I have, I've never mentioned him by name. She knows there was someone important in my life before I left, and it took years for me to get over him – of course she's probably pieced it all together.

'That was him, wasn't it?' she continues, eyes still on the rocks.

Him. It's all so ridiculous. Like I'm the lonely maiden who's been pining for my hero all this time. When, actually, I'm striding across a beautiful sandy beach, in one of the loveliest countries in the world, and I've got nearly nineteen years between Then and Now. I'm a woman scraping the fringes of forty, for God's sake, why is this such a fuss?

Still, I answer honestly. 'Yes.'

Shannon sighs. 'Oh hun, what a humdinger of a shock. The greatest love you ever had just strolled back into your life, that's a massive deal, ay?'

Greatest love. A tingle of memories zips up my spine but I push them away. 'It was good to see him,' I say, swinging my arms a little faster. 'It kind of put things to bed, you know. There was closure.'

I catch a flash of frustration in her expression that she corrects with a smile. 'Tell me about him, you can't leave me hanging!'

For a moment, neither of us says anything. I'm glad we're walking so I don't have to be scrutinised by her shrewd green eyes.

Shannon's tone softens again. 'Aren't you curious about what happened? Why he never followed you?'

Annoyingly, her words stab.

I shrug. 'What's the point? That was years ago. Nobody cares about that any more.'

'Nobody?'

We reach the rocks and I start scrambling over them, not really caring if I graze my knees. They're steeper and more slippery than I thought and, as we descend, I crouch so I don't break my neck sliding into a crevice. Shannon skips ahead of me, traversing each spiky edge like a mountain goat, and is soon standing on the other side waiting for me.

'This is beautiful,' I say, admiring the flawless sand stretching out in front of us. The bay is a perfect crescent and usually hidden beneath the high tide. To the right, the cliff face rises steeply and the line of a fence is just about visible at the top. Across the water, I can make out the hazy outline of the Sky Tower and a cluster of high rises in the city centre.

'Are you going to meet up with him again?' says Shannon, and I know I'm not let off the hook.

I shrug. 'Why? We caught up.'

'How long is he here for?'

'I don't know.' I don't *want* to know.

She glances at me, surprised. 'Really? I thought you'd—' She switches tack. 'Ah, you're hiding from him in the hope he disappears back into the hole he crawled from.' Her tone is light but her eyes are still on me.

'I'm not *hiding* . . .'

She swats me on the arm. 'Bull. You spent all of yesterday emptying cupboards and all day today cleaning out back. The customers have wondered where you've gone.'

I look down at the sand and concentrate on crushing the ridges left by the tide.

'You know, if he's only here for a short time, then you've got nothing to lose, ay? Why not have a yarn, then you'll have proper *closure*.'

She's trying to sound glib, but I hear the undertow and shrug, my eyes on the glistening water. It's tempting to take off my trainers and paddle my feet in the shallows where I know the sea will still be warm.

'Have you told Bea?' Shannon speaks quickly, knowing she's treading a fine line.

My skin prickles. 'No,' I say carefully. 'Why would I?'

'I guess it's good she's not here right now.' She stops and turns to face me. 'It makes things less complicated, ay? You've got a chance to sort things out in your mind.' She pushes her sunnies up on to her head and her green eyes swim in sympathy. This time I can't avoid her gaze.

I swallow hard. 'Sort what out?'

Shannon sighs. 'Come on, Amy, I know Chris is Bea's dad, it's pretty obvious after the things you've told me over the years.' She looks away for a moment and squints at the sea. 'Didn't he ask after her?' she says softly.

I think of the letter I gave to Dad to deliver. Then I think about the waiting. Waiting at home in England; waiting in my new home here in New Zealand. Waiting and waiting with desperation growing alongside Bea in my belly. I'd even picked up the phone a few times but in the long pause to connect I realised I couldn't bear to hear the coldness in his voice. Then one day I found the courage. I forced myself to wait for someone to answer, for Bea's unborn sake, but when his voice sounded down the line, I crumpled and hung up. Mum walked into the room, took one look at my face and shook her head as if to say, *I told you so* – and I never tried again.

A sob catches my throat. Then my face crumples and I'm wailing like a baby and Shannon's clutched me into a bear hug. I pinch my eyes shut but Chris's face stays with me. I see Bea's hazel eyes, the same curve in her lips, and grief pierces me like it did the day

I finally realised he wasn't coming for us. Bea's first birthday. The day I slammed down the lid on the pink box and shoved that part of my life away forever.

Shannon rubs my back like she would her kids. 'Come on, let's walk and talk,' she says.

My legs wobble and I'm vaguely surprised they still carry me when I place one foot in front of the other. Then, when we reach the next line of rocks, Shannon climbs up first and holds her hand out to help me. She pulls me towards her so we're inches apart.

'I don't want Bea to know,' I say fiercely.

Shannon studies me for a moment and then turns away, still gripping my hand to guide me around the rock pools, sidestepping patches of seaweed, and mussels and limpets clinging on for dear life. She's known us for ten years and been a supportive force throughout. Listening to Bea as she rocked through a roller coaster of emotions to learn how to live without a dad all these years. For me, as I navigated Bea's questions, which often caught me off guard and left me floundering for answers.

One day, when she was ten, she'd said: 'So if my dad isn't dead and still lives in the UK, then he doesn't love me.' We'd been crouching on the sand inspecting a shell and were in the throes of discussing if it was pink enough for our pink shell collection on the kitchen window sill.

'What?' Surprise pricked my voice.

Bea shrugged and wouldn't look at me, her eyes snagged on the three rocky outcrops – her island family. 'He doesn't love me, but that's OK, you love me, Shannon and Grant love me, John and Linda love me, Nana loves me.'

She held the shell up to the sky and I saw her swallow. 'I'm lucky, lots of people love me.'

My heart split that day.

Years later, it cracked wide open. Bea and I were on our swing seat, rocking together in the shadows of the summer evening. We'd just got back from a party in Shannon and Grant's garden to celebrate her sixteenth.

'I asked Shannon what she knew about my dad today,' she said.

I'd sensed this conversation coming, because it always did on her birthday and I stayed silent.

'Shannon doesn't know much at all, why is that? She's your best friend.'

I took Bea's hand and looped my fingers through hers. I'd always struggled to put the words right in my mind and now she was old enough to deserve answers, but how far should I go?

Bea shifted around to face me. 'Did you love him?'

I wanted to say no, he was just a fling, to make it sound like love was of no consequence, but it wouldn't have been the truth. I squeezed her hand. 'Yes, I loved him.'

'Did he ever love you?'

Tears swam in my eyes. 'Yes. Though it's so long ago, sometimes I wonder if we were just infatuated with one another.'

'Why have you never told me?'

Hurt crumpled her face and I knew I'd made a mistake. Why hadn't I told her that we'd loved each other? 'I suppose it was less painful to forget the person I loved than to keep resurrecting him,' I said slowly, my voice trembling as I realised how selfish I'd been. 'Perhaps I didn't want to examine the broken pieces of our relationship for answers.' Up above us, stars were beginning to prick into the velvety blackness and I wondered if Chris *had* ever thought about us. 'You know, looking back, I think your dad *did* love you, he was just too young and too afraid of the responsibility.'

Bea squeezed my hand and nodded. 'Thank you, Mum, that's what I needed to know.'

Now, Shannon comes to a sudden stop and turns to face me. 'Do you think hiding the truth is fair on Bea?'

Anger suddenly spills into the void that holds my tears and I snatch my hand away. 'He didn't care when I was pregnant,' I hiss. 'He didn't care when she was born. Why should he care now?'

Her gaze is steady. 'He was a kid.'

'I was a kid! He never came for us! So why now? Perhaps he's having a midlife crisis and full of regret?' I scoff. 'But he can't feel that guilty because he didn't ask me one single thing about Bea yesterday. He doesn't give a shit.' Tears blur the sea and sky together. 'I can't stand him, I don't want anything to do with him.'

Shannon grips my arm. 'Don't hate me for saying this,' she says quickly, 'but is there a chance he thinks that you left him? That you didn't want him to be part of Bea's life?'

I yank my arm away and my face shutters closed. How can she think this? 'I wrote and told him, Shannon, remember?'

Mum had gone ballistic when she found out I was pregnant. Their dreams to emigrate to New Zealand on the rocks because of my stupid 'mistake', as she so nicely put it. She kept saying he wouldn't want a teenage girlfriend with a baby and tried to keep us apart. Eventually I had to believe her, because she was right. I'd tried to tell him about Bea, but he'd sound distracted on the phone, he'd make excuses to avoid seeing me, so what else could I do but write him a letter?

For a short while, I'd been proud that Chris had thrown himself into revision to get the grades he needed to study architecture. I was torn between pressurising him to see me and leaving him alone, thinking if he knew about our pregnancy too soon I'd crush his exam success. But as time went on, his interest in me faded and Mum's words rang louder in my ears. Time was running out. They'd sold the house. The boxes were packed. Without him, without them, I had nowhere to live, no job – nothing but me and a baby.

'Mum and Dad would have emigrated to the other side of the world, and I'd have been left alone. All I could do was write to Chris and pray he felt the same about our baby as I did.' I suck in a jagged breath. 'I was naive to ever think an eighteen-year-old boy would be thrilled to know he was going to become a daddy.'

I scrub tears away with my fists. 'Don't you get it, Shannon? He made it clear he didn't want us. It was easier for him to pretend we didn't exist.'

Chapter 7

Amy

Now

Every morning this week, I've jerked awake remembering *Chris is in Auckland*. As I opened up the café, a hollow feeling of uncertainty settled, chest tightening as the day went on until the customers left, I'd locked the door and could breathe again.

Today there's a buzz of activity in the café, the terrace is full, and I try to shrug off my fatigue and allow the jubilant mood to be catching. I'm about to slide a piece of Victoria sponge on to a plate when I feel Shannon's whisper tickle my ear. 'Don't look now, but Chris has just walked in.'

Of course, my head snaps up and the sponge wobbles on the cake slice as I catch him sauntering towards me. He's wearing the same black board shorts as before, with a yellow T-shirt this time, mirrored sunnies hiding his eyes. He's got that annoying half-smile on his face again and I prickle. He's acting like he *knows* me, like he comes in here all the time; who would believe it's been eighteen and a half years?

Although I've been waiting for him to breeze back through the door all week, it's not because I *wanted* him to come, but because I assumed he would. Why has it taken him this long? What better things did he have to do than *see his child*? Never mind Bea isn't here, he doesn't know that. This man is selfish, a thoughtless pig, a bloody coward. Nothing's changed.

I glance down at the cake and try to manoeuvre it on to the plate, but I miss, and it plops on to the counter and bleeds jam – the same colour that's ripening my cheeks. I mutter a swear word and turn away from him to chuck it in the bin.

'Can you get me another slice?' I call to Shannon, not trusting myself a second time. Her glance flicks between me and where Chris stands at the counter, his face on full beam, my distorted reflection in the mirrored lenses.

She opens her mouth to say something, but I cut in. 'There's a queue,' I say, eyeballing him.

His grin fades a little and I straighten up, then, quick as a flash, his half-smile is back, and he pushes his sunnies up on to his head. 'Hello again and a very good morning to you too.'

His gaze holds mine for a beat too long and I catch the glow of happiness in his eyes. He is bold, he is fearless – and in a jolt I worry he's going to demand to see Bea right here, right now, in front of my customers.

I'm not ready.

Lucy, next in line, raises a carefully waxed eyebrow and rakes her eyes over him. New faces – especially good-looking males – are scant in our small beach suburb. I slide over to the till and Chris follows, sitting down at the table nearest me. He rests his foot on his knee and jiggles his leg.

It's annoying. *He's* annoying. 'It'll be a long wait,' I say, which isn't strictly true. Shannon and I are a slick tag team and can whip through a queue in a flash.

'I'm in no rush,' he replies, the grin back full blast.

I want to slap him.

'Skinny cappuccino to take away?' I say to Lucy, whose eyes are still glued to Chris. She's long limbed and finely chiselled, thanks to an inspirational yoga guru she met while travelling in India, apparently – although Shannon says it's because she got dysentery. Nevertheless, she's wearing the shortest of shorts and a cropped top that shows off her flat, brown midriff.

'Well . . .' she drawls, 'I think I'll have my coffee to stay today.'

She's also single.

What does that matter? Still, I can't help but glance at Chris to gauge his reaction and I find his smiling eyes on me still. Goosebumps tingle, a memory nudges, but I snort as I catch Shannon sticking a finger in her mouth, pretending to vomit, as she walks past and outside to clear tables.

'Aren't you going to introduce me then?' Lucy's eyes needle mine.

I don't reply and instead reach for the milk and pour it into a jug ready to steam.

'I'm Chris,' he volunteers.

Clearly, he isn't blind after all.

'Lucy,' she replies. 'How do you know . . . Amy?' She makes a face as though my name is something revolting.

Amusement dances around Chris's mouth as he waits for me to respond. My hand tenses around the jug. I want to wipe that stupid smirk from his face, and for a second, I consider hurling a live grenade into the room: *This is Bea's dad! He couldn't handle fatherhood, so he dumped us!*

'Amy and I are old friends,' he says.

'But *how* do you know each other?' she presses. 'I mean, you do *know* each other, don't you?'

A squeeze of anxiety tells me I'm not prepared for this conversation. Not at all. Steam blasts into the milk and I pretend I haven't heard. What do I say? What will he say? What do I *want* him to say?

Chris relaxes back into the chair. 'We went to sixth-form college together.'

I exhale and pour coffee into a takeaway cup – though I don't think Lucy will take the hint – and swirl in the milk.

'You're English!' she cries.

'*No shit*,' I mutter.

'How awesome, I love English men, they're so cute. How long are you visiting?' She tosses some coins at me, snatches up her cappuccino and slides into the empty chair opposite him.

I become still, ears pricked, aware that Linda, next in the queue, is waiting – and watching.

'I'm working in Auckland, I'm on secondment for three months.'

Three months? I do a quick calculation; he should be gone by the time Bea gets back. Once he knows Bea isn't here, there won't be any need for him to pop in uninvited. And anyway, he clearly isn't sticking around this morning, he's got a camera bag, he has plans. I snap back to attention.

'Earl Grey for two?' I say to Linda, who nods and presses money into my hand with a firmness that speaks of something else. I love Linda like I would a mother. After all, she *was* my mother-in-law for a short while and in many ways more of a mother to me than my own. Her capacity for sympathy, understanding and love are bottomless – and it reaches everyone. She gives me a soft smile and gently squeezes my fingers.

I glance over at Chris again. Lucy flicks her long hair over her shoulders and wheedles something about him coming to her next yoga class on the beach. He catches my eye and raises an eyebrow as if to say, *rescue me*. I smile, without thinking, and his face comes alive, pulsing another memory into my thoughts.

'You staying around here?' says Lucy huskily.

I strain to hear his answer as I fumble with the teacups and saucers. *It doesn't matter, he'll be gone by the time Bea returns.*

'Not far, near the ferry terminal.'

So close. I plonk Linda's teapot down on the tray and tea sloshes from the spout. I poke at the spill with a cloth, managing to knock one of the teacups over, which seems to fall in slow motion, and I scrabble to catch it but fail. The pretty yellow floral design – Bea's favourite – hits the floor and breaks into three jagged pieces and a sob of frustration sticks in my throat.

'Nice juggling,' says Chris, coming over.

'It's . . . one of my favourites,' I mutter.

He comes around to my side of the counter and crouches down next to me. 'Got some glue? I can fix that.'

I'm about to tell him to go away, to not be so presumptuous, but he's gently rolling the broken china over in his hand, examining it like a baby bird fallen from its nest. Up this close, heat radiates from his body and his familiar scent sends a twirl of nerves and confusion up my spine.

'Are you busy today?' he whispers quickly. 'Want to come out with me?'

I'm stunned and before I can even think of how to respond, a familiar voice booms out. 'Come on, Amy, we haven't got all day.'

Chris and I slowly rise up from behind the counter to see Linda's husband, John, looming in the doorway. I feel like I've been caught doing something naughty, my cheeks smart and I push away a lock of hair that's worked loose from my ponytail.

John cocks his head, studying Chris and I, then strides over. 'What's going on here?' he bellows.

He sounds rude but he's as soft as a cuddly bear – and loves a gossip. 'I dropped the cup,' I say, pointing to the pieces in Chris's hand.

Chris smiles. 'She was juggling.'

John chuckles. 'Is it one of your special ones, Amy? I can fix that for you.'

'Chris has already offered,' Linda interjects.

I whip around to look at her. What else did she hear?

'What a hero.' John's laugh bellows out. 'I didn't know Amy was taking on any more staff.' He scrutinises Chris again.

'He's on secondment from England,' Lucy pipes up. 'For three months.'

John glances at her. 'Into yoga, ay? Not a rugby man?' he says suspiciously. Despite the modern world we live in, John has a tendency to judge other males on the basis of whether they love the game or not. He will regale his rugby tales to any willing – and unwilling – audience. I sense the conversation might make a sharp detour in this direction if Linda or I don't intervene soon – and then Chris will never leave.

Chris's mouth twitches into a smile and he makes a point of looking at me while he answers John. 'No, no, I'm not into yoga.'

I'm not going to read between the lines but the twirl from before whips up my spine again, so I busy myself preparing another pot of tea with a fresh tea set.

'Actually I do like rugby,' he adds. 'And I'm working here as an architect.'

John's face lights up. 'Ah! You'll probably run into my son at some point, he's a planner at the council.'

Linda and I give each other a look. Grant's job is another of John's favourite topics, and although I have zero interest in the buildings that Grant's given consent to be constructed in our city, there's a chance Chris might. 'Don't let your tea go cold,' I say to John.

Linda pays and holds the tray out to her husband. 'Come on, outside now, Amy's busy.'

In fact, Linda's the last in the queue, for now, but I do need to clear tables.

'English, ay?' John continues. 'From London? You and Amy must *definitely* know each other!' His belly quivers at his own joke.

'Actually, they *were* at college together,' Linda says.

'No shit? You kids *do* know each other?'

Shannon comes inside with a tray piled with dirty crockery. I'd like to whisk it from her and disappear into the kitchen, but I can't leave John to blunder on. Plus, the quicker I serve Chris, the sooner he'll leave.

'Hey, Shannon, these two Poms know each other from home, what a coincidence, ay?'

She nods but concerned eyes land on me.

'When are you going to show Chris around?' John says. 'You need a day off, you've been working way too hard since Bea left, I'm sure your old friend would appreciate a tour.'

At the mention of Bea's name, my head snaps around to look at Chris, but his face is a mask and my stomach rolls in disgust.

'I'm free from midday,' Lucy says, standing up and tapping a French-manicured nail on her cup. 'I could show you around?'

'Chris has already asked Amy,' Linda says quickly, throwing me an apologetic look for eavesdropping.

Lucy shoots daggers in my direction and then steps close to Chris. 'You know where to find me,' she says sulkily and sashays out the door.

'I'm not sure whether this is a good idea.' Shannon watches me carefully. 'We're pretty busy today. What do you think, hun?'

John glances around the empty café. I'm about to point out that everyone's sitting outside when Shannon says, 'Quiet word?'

I scuttle into the kitchen behind her and exhale loudly once the doors have swung shut. 'Chris asked me to go out with him today,' I whisper. 'I don't bloody *want* to go. Did you see? He didn't react at all when John mentioned Bea. He's—'

Shannon touches my arm. 'I get it, this is a shitshow, but I was thinking when I was outside clearing tables, what if he wants to ask you about Bea? Perhaps you need to hear him out?'

'Why should I?' I whisper fiercely. 'I don't owe him anything.'

'I know, I just think—' She bites her lip. 'You've had such a stressful week, wondering and waiting, not knowing if he'll come back. And now you know he's going to be in Auckland until March, do you really want to be on edge the whole time he's here?'

Of course I don't, I'm wrung out already. But I also can't stomach the idea of spending any time with him when he's being so cold-hearted. But what if he keeps coming back? Makes a fuss about seeing Bea in front of my customers? Something clicks.

I should do this for Bea.

I sigh. 'OK, I'll go. I guess if things get heated, it's better we're away from here. I don't want an audience.'

I'm about to return when I remember something and fumble in one of the drawers. Back inside, Chris is standing where I left him, still holding the broken cup.

'Glue,' I say, pushing it into his hand. 'I'll be ready in twenty minutes.'

He looks surprised, then his face lights up. 'Great, I'll fix this now. Where are we headed?'

'What about the Sky Tower?' John booms as he strolls back in again.

I roll my eyes. 'Forgotten something?'

'Sugar,' he replies with a wink. 'Don't tell Linda.'

'Isn't there some on your table?' I say pointedly, but he ignores me.

'Beautiful day, you'll see for miles up there, and anyway, when was the last time you went up the Sky Tower, Amy?'

I shrug. Bea was probably eight or nine. We'd gone in the school holidays one summer, pretending to be tourists for the day and visiting all of Auckland's sights. I push the memory away. I don't want to think about Bea with Chris standing here.

'Shannon can hold the fort, can't you, love?' John says as she appears from the kitchen. 'Linda'll put her pinny on too.'

'And you'll watch the rugby,' I reply drily.

'John.' Linda's at the door and her tone is warning. 'Come *on*, Mac's arrived.'

He nods and points a meaty finger at Chris. 'In case Amy hasn't told you, I'm her father-in-law so no funny business or you'll be answering to me!' He roars with laughter. 'Only joking. You couldn't get Amy to answer to anyone. You kids have a good time.' And he lumbers back out to the terrace.

Chris runs a line of glue along the edge of one of the pieces of china. 'I've heard about the Sky Tower. You OK if we go there?' Gently, he presses the two broken halves together, holding them firm for a moment. He dabs glue top and bottom on the handle and pushes this third piece in place. The cup is whole again.

I'll go to the Sky Tower.

But I don't know if Chris's handiwork will prevent my cup from breaking again.

Chapter 8

AMY

Now

The ferry roars into life, the rotors churning the water as we slowly make our way across the short stretch of harbour between here on the North Shore and Auckland's city centre. Chris leans on the railings admiring the view, mirrored sunnies hide his eyes, but the familiar half-smile tugs his lips and I sense his excitement.

Anxiety creeps across my skin. When will he ask about Bea? What will he want to know first?

I'm grateful that the rumbling engine is making talk difficult, for now. Above, the sky's a clear cornflower blue and the sun's warming my cheeks.

My beautiful Bea.

I think about how many days I've missed like this with her over the years while I threw myself into turning the café into a thriving business. How, now, with the fifteen-year anniversary tucked neatly under my belt and my award-winning status announced to the city, I should be able to relax a little. As Shannon keeps reminding me: I am successful.

She also says Bea no longer needs me like she used to – is this why I've not heard from her for a few days? It's a truth I can't accept.

I slide a glance in Chris's direction. In the absence of him – *her father* – I cleaved Bea to me and we've been bound tight all her life. That doesn't dissolve overnight. As a child, she hung out in the café drawing pictures of cakes she wanted me to make that I pinned to the wood-plank walls. Of course, I baked every single one, bright rainbows coming to life with colourful sponges and vivid icing that had Bea laughing in delight. Later – many years later – she offered to cook dinner one night and from that day forward we fell into our routine: I'd collapse on the sofa after work and she'd present her latest dish. I'd wash up, she'd dry, then we'd settle down and watch TV together.

It's painful to know she'd planned this trip behind my back. It's worrying she's not been in touch. But now, with Chris right *here*, for the first time I'm relieved she's gone, and I tuck her to the back of my mind.

It's been a long time since I travelled on one of Auckland's ferries; I'm not one to roam aimlessly around the centre. Now I can see why so many people choose to commute to work this way. Speedboats criss-cross the harbour and a string of yachts scud towards Waiheke Island, white sails billowing, while beyond lies the great Pacific Ocean that separates us from the rest of the world.

I look over at Chris again. He's smiling at the harbour bridge, the salty wind pushing his hair upright so I can see strands of grey threading through the dark waves. The steel girders in the bridge glint in the sunshine and he follows their arc with his finger, like a little boy might do, then gets his camera out and begins taking photos.

My thoughts fall back to Bea again and the missing half of her childhood she never had with him.

I'm a tightly coiled spring. I don't want to be here. I don't want *him* to be here. I don't want to be waiting. Just like I did all those years before. Different now. This time I'll have to face the hideous moment he turns to me and demands to meet his daughter. But I'm ready. I'll uncoil in a flash so fast he'll retreat, he'll see my fury, he'll hear my comeback, and the coward he is, will think, 'I've made a mistake'. The scene is solid and faultless. I've played each possible scenario out in my mind.

Chris points at the bridge. 'I bet the view from up there is great,' he shouts above the engine.

My hair whips into my mouth and I drag it away. What's he waiting for? Why can't he just say what he's come to say and leave us alone?

He speaks again, but the wind snatches his words this time. Reluctantly I step closer. 'What?' I sound rude, I know, but I don't care.

'I'll have to walk across the bridge one day,' he repeats. 'I could get some great photos of the harbour from up there. Have you done the bridge climb?'

I shake my head. Bea hates heights.

He looks at me, lips curving at the corners, smiling but not smiling. He pushes his sunnies away and I catch the gold flecks in his hazel eyes again.

Bea's hazel eyes. The resemblance pokes my anger again. The memory stirs something else.

'Want to come with me?' This time he's grinning and I can't decide if he's flirting or it's a challenge.

I want to scream *no*, but I look away, shake my head. I'm already planning my escape. I'll stay on the ferry and cross back again. I'll tell him there's an emergency back at the café. Not that I need to give him an excuse. He can do his own bloody sightseeing.

He nods and slips the sunnies back on.

I remember something. 'You can bungy off there.'

He lets out a whistle. 'I have *got* to do that.'

Falling is all I can think about.

As the ferry docks, Chris is telling me about his travels around Indonesia en route to New Zealand, and I think *he got to travel, even without me*, and I can't find a pause in the conversation to tell him to carry on the day alone. He's still jabbering as we walk up the main street lined with souvenir shops crammed with New Zealand flags, sheepskin rugs, grinning sheep postcards, and all the other tat tourists think is symbolic of their holiday here. Chris asks questions about the city and I respond staccato, without elaboration, and ignore his puzzled expression. As far as I'm concerned, this is a one-way conversation.

We stop to cross a road. A flood of retired holidaymakers surges around us, eyes on an unseasonal All Blacks umbrella held high by their guide to hold their attention. Chris and I are nudged together in the crowd and he catches my arm as I stumble.

'You're very cool about all this,' he says.

We're standing closer than I'd like and he's looking down at me. Had I really forgotten how tall he is? I think of Bea's long legs. I push away the stir of old feelings.

'Cool about what?' I say, pulling off my sunnies to challenge his gaze but only seeing a distorted version of myself in his lenses.

Laughter ripples out of him and I tense. I hope he isn't going to ask questions with an audience at such close quarters. 'My point exactly,' he says. 'Aren't you just a little bit amazed by this—' He waves his hand between us, linking us together, as though we've picked up where we left off nearly nineteen years ago. He shakes his head, still smiling. 'I can't believe it, I really can't. I thought I'd never see you again.'

Pleasure warms his face and coats his voice and then he lifts his hand, and for a second I think he's going to touch my hair. But the crowd surges forwards to cross the road and we're jostled apart. Still I'm annoyed I didn't back away first, I didn't create the space between us – and that I felt a shimmer of something long ago buried.

We follow the tour group up the hill. 'So you're married?' Chris sounds casual but his change of tack startles me. He smiles briefly and then looks away.

'No,' I say, confused. And then before I can stop myself, I add, 'Are you?'

He doesn't answer straightaway. Then says, 'Yes . . . no . . .' and jumps back to his original question while I'm still processing his answer. 'Wasn't that your father-in-law at the Boat Shed?'

'John? No, I mean, he likes a joke, and sometimes he says stuff like that because he looks out for me. A father figure, I suppose.'

Chris throws me a puzzled look. 'Who is he then?'

'He's Grant's dad.'

He laughs. 'Grant's your partner, then?'

'My partner? No, not any more, he's married to Shannon.'

'Whoa . . .' He laughs again. 'This sounds complicated.'

I realise the situation sounds strange when the words are said aloud to someone who doesn't know me, *a stranger*. A smile twitches my mouth. 'Grant and I got divorced years ago, years and years ago. We weren't married long. Grant and Shannon are made for each other.'

The truth is, I was barely twenty when Grant and I threw ourselves into a whirlwind marriage in the hope it'd give us both what we needed in our lives. The trouble was we wanted different things. I was desperate for Bea to have a dad; I thought that was the right thing. And Grant? He needed someone who would wrap him in Forever Love and give him a brood of kids. I can be honest with myself now. I never truly loved him, not in the way a wife should love their husband, and I'm pretty sure he never properly loved me in that way either. But he adored Bea; he still adores Bea. He and Shannon are devoted to one another, they are one of life's true love matches that deepens with time and I'm truly happy for them. And I love their kids almost as if they were my own.

'Sounds like *your* marriage is more of a soap opera. You're either married or you're not. You don't sound very sure.' My voice is needle sharp.

Chris's jaw flexes and I'm annoyed with my tone and that I notice the familiar contours in his face haven't disappeared. I wonder if this is why he's come to New Zealand now, and I back off. I'm not interested in whether he's married or separated, or the workings of his marriage. This is not my concern. My concern is Bea.

We turn the corner and the Sky Tower looms up in front of us. 'Wow, people are bungy jumping off there too,' he says, pointing to a figure flying through the air, their distant screams getting louder as they hurtle towards the ground. I think about my own coiled body, waiting to spring undone.

'Crazy idiots,' I mutter.

'Fancy a go?' he says, punching me lightly on the arm.

I'm about to refuse, out of habit, I suppose, but the glow in Chris's eyes feels like a challenge. Then his expression becomes incredulous. 'Come on, don't tell me you haven't bungeed before? Isn't NZ where bungeeing was *born*?'

He has no idea what my life has been like.

'Why not? What happened to the adventurous Amy I used to know?' he teases.

She grew up.

She had your child.

'I didn't have a lot of time being carefree and *adventurous*,' I reply, my heart beginning to pound. 'Some of us had *responsibilities*.'

His smile slides away. I feel a sense of satisfaction even though I know what I've said isn't completely true. I could've come here and bungyed with Shannon, Grant or any of my friends, but there's always been the café, the baking, or something else. I could have tried to persuade Bea to join me when she turned eighteen, but she's always been a cautious child – lip wobbling on the climbing frame, taking up swimming to avoid the aggression of netball, refusing a school skiing trip to Christchurch. I knew how I felt being pushed by my mother. I'd never have forced Bea to do anything she didn't feel comfortable with.

Still, she managed to plan three months' travelling without my knowledge.

'There's supposed to be a fantastic bungy jump from a bridge in the South Island,' Chris continues. 'Wasn't it one of the first in the world? Have you ever been there?'

I shake my head and look up at the jump platform way above us. I feel like a disappointment. But I shouldn't care what he thinks.

'Why not? Amy who said she'd rather bake cakes and go travelling than go to university?'

He nudges me and I stiffen. 'I told you, no, no I haven't, I've done nothing like this before. Childish dreams about travelling couldn't happen for me, could they? We didn't *all* have the freedom to do what we liked.'

Chris pushes his sunnies on to his head this time and his eyes search my face. Unspoken words hover between us, waiting to be said out loud, and I suck in my breath, body tense, my bravado seeping away.

Say it.

Then something happens. He drops his gaze, shakes his head a little as if shaking the words away, and when his eyes land on me again his mouth has curved back into a smile. 'But there's nothing stopping you now, is there?'

My face is stony.

'Hey, I'm only teasing,' he says softly. 'Are you scared?'

'No, of course I'm not scared,' I snap. *I am petrified.* 'Heights don't bother me.'

Chris laughs. 'Let's do it then!' He grabs my hand and pulls me towards the entrance and to my surprise, I feel a flicker of excitement beneath the tumble of frustration and fury. The lift zips us to the bungy station and soon we're being briefed on what to do. Chris jokes with the staff and I listen as little doors of locked-up memories begin to crack open again.

'Amy?' A familiar young man with tangled blond hair appears wearing a branded bungy T-shirt and carrying our harnesses.

'Kieren,' I say, greeting Bea's old school friend. I'd forgotten he got a job here after they finished college. There's no way we'll manage five minutes without him bringing Bea into the conversation and my stomach flutters.

'What are you doing here?' he says.

'Bungy-jumping,' I reply, my smile tempering the sarcasm.

'Okaaay . . .' he says, yanking the straps tightly together. 'So, what made you decide to leap off New Zealand's tallest building today?'

I think quickly, picking up on Chris's cue from the café earlier on. 'I've brought Chris,' I say, waving my arm in his direction. 'He's an old friend from England, we went to college together.'

'Hey, like Bea and I,' Kieren says, smiling and handing him a harness. 'I hope we manage to stay mates for as long as you have. It feels like she's been gone ages, ay?'

Today, I barely register his wistful expression, which usually makes Bea roll her eyes and me smile behind my hand. Instead, I'm watching Chris and count the beats as I wait for him to ask me where his daughter's gone. But he's fiddling with his harness and, in a rush, I'm thankful that she's far, far away from him.

'Yes, ages for sure,' I reply, trying to keep my voice light. 'I can't imagine how long it's going to feel when she finally gets back.'

I shoot Chris another look but he's not meeting my eye. I want to shake him, tell him *She's not here! You'll be long gone by the time she's safely home.* But the nagging truth is I don't know that for sure.

'She seems pretty wrapped with what she's doing,' Kieren continues. A part of me wants him to keep talking to see if *he's* able to provoke a reaction in Chris, but on the other hand I want him to shut up. I don't want Chris to know Bea's whereabouts or for Kieren to let slip her return date. 'She's having an awesome adventure, I can't believe she's . . .' He crouches down to adjust the straps around Chris's legs. 'That tight enough, mate?'

My ears prick. Suddenly I realise Kieren may have heard from Bea even if I haven't, and I don't care what Chris overhears. 'What were you going to say? Has she emailed you recently?'

Kieren's face pinks. 'That comfortable, mate?' he says to Chris. 'You're all set now.'

But I'm not ready and I tug Kieren's arm. 'Is there something you're not telling me?'

He smiles. 'There's nothing to worry about, she's having such an awesome time, I'm jealous. Maybe the internet connection's dodgy. You know Bea, she wouldn't forget to email you.'

I nod slowly; my daughter has always been reliable. Though I think about the mobile phone I bought for her, still snug in the box and sitting on my living-room table. The man in the shop said it was the latest model and all the teenagers wanted one. I thought Bea would be pleased. But she said taking this phone

– any phone – wouldn't give her the *same experience*, whatever that meant. I should have been firm. I should have made her take it. Now emails sent from internet cafés in far-flung places are the only way she can communicate with me.

Kieren squeezes my shoulder. 'Right, I guess you're going first. Bea's always the first in our gang to jump.'

I stare at him and my stomach flip-flops. 'What? What do you mean? How many times has she done this?'

He colours again. 'Loads,' he mumbles. 'She's a bloody legend. No fear.'

I look at the platform projecting out from the tower; the toy city spread out below, ferries sliding through the harbour, the bays weaving around the North Shore coastline. My daughter has done this? More than once?

I'm suddenly conscious of how surreal this experience is. Being here, with Chris, in a city that's a lifetime away from where we grew up. I see a parallel world. One where I'm standing here with Chris about to do the jump – but we're teenagers, like Bea, and we're exploring the world together like we'd planned.

How does Bea fit into this picture?

How does Chris fit into our life?

Chris comes to my side. 'Do you want me to go first?' he whispers.

I imagine Bea somewhere in South East Asia harnessed to a makeshift bungy with no safety tests, inexperienced staff, teetering on the edge of a ravine. I gulp the air.

He touches my arm. 'You don't have to jump.'

'Come on!' Kieren shouts. 'Bea will be so proud of you! She'll be stoked when I email her. I'll have to send her a picture or she won't believe me.'

I keep gulping. Thinking of Bea. Thinking of Chris. Wondering what he makes of his brave, adventurous daughter, and his scared, unworldly ex-girlfriend.

I step forward and focus on the point where a line of dark-grey clouds skate the horizon. A storm is brewing. I open my arms wide. I'll do anything for my daughter. She is my world. And I leap into the unknown.

Chapter 9

Olivia

Then

The supermarket car park was busy when Olivia arrived one late Friday afternoon and she glanced at the clock on the dashboard. She'd have to be quick if she was going to have dinner ready before her dad came home. Not that he'd care whether there was food there or not. No, that wasn't fair. He'd care, sort of. He'd say thank you, shovel the food in, disappear into the front room and then be snoring in front of the TV by nine o'clock, leaving Olivia to clear up and crack on with the rest of her homework.

Olivia slid her Mini into an empty space. Not that the car was actually hers, not really, but her mum was hardly likely to come knocking to ask for it back. She pulled out her shopping list and marched up and down the aisles filling the trolley. She should have brought her Discman; this was so bloody boring. Instead, she distracted herself with thoughts of Chris.

Since that first day at college, she'd been keeping a careful but distant eye on him. When she'd walked into her first A-level art lesson with Amy, and clocked Chris laughing at something his drippy

Goth mate had said, she'd nearly had heart failure. What were the chances of sharing two A-level subjects with him? She quickly worked out that if she got to class early enough, she could hide at the back and covertly observe him through her long hair for as long as she liked without anyone noticing. Amy's constant jabbering was annoying, though – and had a habit of distracting the class too, inviting sarcastic comments from Chris. Things often turned into a verbal sparring match between them, until their teacher told everyone to 'simmer down'.

Olivia glanced at her list and grabbed a box of teabags from the shelf. Amy was a funny thing. Wired, like her crazy corkscrew hair. Unsurprisingly, it hadn't taken long for Olivia to get to know her. They'd fallen into step with one another when they'd worked out they shared quite a few lessons, and would often drift off to eat lunch afterwards and chat. Well, Amy did most of the chatting. She divulged her life story with ease, which suited Olivia as she felt part of their conversation without needing to reveal anything personal.

Over the weeks, Olivia had discovered Amy was an only child (like herself) and was totally obsessed with baking. She spent any free time she had in her kitchen and getting good grades was the last thing on her mind. She'd noticed Amy's face changed when she spoke about her mum, her eyes narrowing and her full, generous mouth seeming to fold in on itself. But when she talked about her dad, she couldn't look more different, like she'd been lit inside by a burst of warm sunshine.

The depth of these emotions felt alien to Olivia. When she thought about her dad – and especially her mum – she felt a hard flatness, a neutral equilibrium that tipped neither up nor down.

Olivia turned into the next aisle and was scanning the shelves for a can of baked beans when a familiar laugh rang out. She looked up to see Amy at the top of the aisle with a short, bald man – her dad? Olivia stroked the right side of her hair and busied herself with looking at the tins. Amy's voice drifted in her direction. She was chattering about which oats to buy for some flapjacks she was going to make. Olivia turned her head slightly and watched them through the curtain of her hair. The man was nodding and smiling and saying how lovely the recipe sounded and she should be sure to make enough for him to take to work to share with his staff.

'Yep, Dad, the more taste-testers I have the better,' she said.

Amy's dad put his arm around her. 'I'm very proud of you,' he said, obviously not at all bothered that someone might see him hug his daughter in public.

'Thanks, Dad,' Amy replied with a smile that *positively shone* and forced Olivia to look away again. She should go and say hello, but it felt intrusive to stroll up to them now.

'Do you remember me telling you about Olivia?' Amy's loud voice shot up the aisle again.

Olivia froze and then twisted her trolley around and broke into a run-walk, turning back to where she'd just come from. How embarrassing to be the subject of a conversation when they didn't know she was loitering nearby! Christ, they'd think she was a right nutter if they saw her.

'She's tried quite a few of my recipes.' Amy's voice floated over the shelves and Olivia wondered how crazy she'd look if she put her hands over her ears. 'I can't *quite* work her out, she's . . . *different* . . . but she pays attention, you know? She listens and she takes her time when she eats my cakes.'

Olivia smoothed her hair in fast, even strokes, and felt a familiar hot flush mottling her chest. She needed to leave *now*. This eavesdropping was *agonising*. Amy thought she was weird; she'd obviously been putting up with Olivia all this time. *Tolerating* her. But before she could move her cement legs back towards the entrance, Amy appeared.

'Olivia!' she cried. 'Your ears must be burning! I was just talking about you!'

Was she taking the piss? Olivia eyed her warily.

'I'm making some flapjacks and I was just saying to my dad – Oh! Yes, Dad, this is Olivia, Olivia, this is my dad.' Amy's arms windmilled as she spoke and Olivia noticed she was holding the red recipe book. 'I was telling Dad how you're my best taste-tester! God, everyone is *so bored* of me droning on about my cakes, but you . . .' She paused.

Olivia felt the heat shoot to her cheeks.

'Oh God.' Amy's hand flew to her mouth. 'Have I done it again? Have I been really selfish and forced my cakes on you too? Have you been too polite to tell me to bog off?'

Olivia didn't quite know what to say. She opened her mouth and then closed it again. The cutting remark that had been simmering below the surface dissipated when she saw Amy's dad smiling and shaking his head as though he was trying not to laugh.

'I'm Geoff, pleased to meet you.' He stuck out his hand and Olivia took it. His grip felt warm and firm and she could see where Amy got her wide smile and round blue eyes. 'I hear you're the number one taste-tester – very brave!'

Amy nudged him.

'Well,' he said, still smiling, 'there's been some interesting . . . *experiments*, let's say. Have you been subjected to any of Amy's weird and wonderful concoctions, Olivia?'

She loosened her grip on the trolley and felt her mouth relax a little, not quite a smile, but near enough. She shook her head. Christ, she must look so dumb.

'Don't be afraid to say what you think,' he said. 'It's the only way Amy will learn!'

'Dad!' Amy poked him again. 'You're being so rude! Those *experiments*, as you call them, were ages ago! You love my cakes now.'

'Yep, you're doing great, love,' he said and then patted his belly. 'I think she's trying to fatten me up!'

Olivia couldn't help but return his smile. His eyes had a twinkly look and even his crumpled beige suit seemed happy and relaxed rather than in desperate need of a press. He was so unlike her own dad, hunched shoulders in a crisp shirt (that she'd ironed) and a pinstriped jacket. Frankly, he was depressing.

'*Anyway.*' Amy rolled her eyes. 'There's nothing "weird" about these flapjacks,' she said, pointing at the ingredients in the basket. Then she noticed Olivia's full trolley. 'You shopping for your mum?'

Olivia hesitated and felt Geoff watching her. She nodded quickly. 'It's really boring, but someone's got to do it!' Her voice sounded high. *It wasn't a complete lie.*

'Olivia's driven herself here, haven't you?' said Amy and Olivia thought she detected a hint of pride. 'She's already passed her driving test and has got a really cute silver Mini.'

'Well done, Olivia,' Geoff replied. 'Amy's got a little bit of a way to go . . .' He chuckled. 'Like learning her left from her right, for starters.'

Amy laughed. 'I only turned seventeen in August! Give me a chance! You're supposed to be supporting me, not crushing my confidence!'

'Now, confidence is not something me or anyone could crush out of you, love,' he said, patting her arm. 'Focus is what you need.' He turned to Olivia. 'After you've dropped the shopping home, would you like to come over for dinner?'

Olivia looked at their matching apple-cheeked smiles and her throat unexpectedly constricted. *Of course I would, I'd love to come.*

'Yes, please come, then afterwards you can help me with the flapjacks!' Amy added.

Geoff snorted.

'All *right*.' She made a face at him. '*Watch* me make flapjacks. You'll have to close your eyes when I add the secret ingredients though.'

Geoff puffed out his cheeks, pretending to look sick, and a burst of laughter flew out of Olivia's mouth, sounding so joyful that for a moment she was surprised it came from her.

'Ignore him!' Amy said. 'So? Are you coming?'

Olivia hesitated. Dad could manage, couldn't he? Christ, he was a grown man and she was sick of seeing his hangdog expression when he came home. He needed to step up, grow a backbone, not drag himself around thinking he was the only one in the world with problems.

'Come on – it's Friday night!' Amy linked her arm through Olivia's. 'We're going to the DVD shop after this, you can stay and watch a film with us.'

Olivia imagined Amy's warm living room, low-lit with lamps and a big sofa that she and Amy would share, with her cheerful dad sitting in his favourite armchair. And Amy's mum? She wasn't sure how she'd fit into the picture. Amy didn't have anything good to say about her but still, she liked the idea of being part of this family for the evening.

Olivia opened her mouth to say yes, yes, she'd come. Then she pictured her dad pushing open the front door and calling out for her in the darkness and hearing nothing but his own voice echoing in the empty house. He'd sit in silence at the kitchen table with a plate of cheese and crackers. She gritted her teeth. She couldn't abandon him; it wouldn't be fair.

Olivia glanced at her watch. 'I can't this time . . .' she said. 'I've got to . . . well, I've got homework to do.' She sounded rude, she sounded lame, like she didn't want to come, and when she saw Amy's face fall, she vowed she'd make it up to her as soon as she could.

Later – much, much later – Olivia sat in the dark at the kitchen table with the casserole she'd made on the side parched to a crisp. In front of her lay a single sheet of A4 paper that she'd filled with utter nonsense in an attempt at her English essay.

Where was Dad? No key in the lock at the usual time. No phone call to say he'd be late. But then, why would he? She was nearly eighteen – an adult in his eyes – he didn't need to report to her or to anyone, but then neither did she.

Chapter 10

Olivia

Then

'You still coming back to mine?' said Amy a few weeks later. They were walking out through the main doors after their last lesson of the day. She'd been nagging Olivia to come over for ages, but Olivia had resisted. Surely if she went, Amy would expect to be invited back? And that was never going to happen. There was no way she could bring anyone home.

Olivia nodded. Amy could be very persuasive and, anyway, what was the point in sitting in an empty house every afternoon? She'd already done a ton of revision for her mocks this month.

'Is there an invite for me too?'

Heat shot to Olivia's face at the sound of Chris's voice behind them. He sounded close, achingly so, but she didn't dare turn around, not with a face like a tomato.

'No,' Amy said breezily.

Olivia dropped to her feet and unnecessarily fiddled with her shoelace, willing her colour to subside.

'Go on! Paul and I are *very* well behaved.' He laughed and Olivia wondered if he'd winked at Amy, like he'd winked at her.

'In that case, we definitely don't want you round, do we, Liv.' Amy looked down at her. 'You sound far too boring for us.'

For Christ's sake. Olivia straightened up and eyeballed Chris. They were a similar height and she felt a flicker of pleasure when he looked momentarily surprised. *Christ, he's gorgeous.* Her face threatened to flame again. *Take control.* She rummaged in her bag and pulled out her cigarettes.

'Got one for me?' Chris said, his lips curving into a smile. Olivia thrust the packet towards him and he flicked one into his mouth. It was only then she noticed Paul the Goth hovering behind him. She hesitated, then waved the packet in his direction too. He reached out, but the cigarette slipped through his fingers and fell into a puddle. He muttered something Olivia couldn't hear.

'Take another one,' she snapped. Christ, what was his problem? Cigarettes weren't cheap.

'Got a light?' said Chris.

'God, hurry up, we've got stuff to do.' Amy folded her arms.

'Like what?' he asked. 'Revision?'

Olivia held out the lighter for him to take. Instead, he bent his head, assuming she'd do the lighting for him. He was so close she could smell the leather of his jacket and a hint of citrus. Her hand trembled as she flicked the flint. Nothing. She flicked it again. Still nothing. *How embarrassing.* On the third time, the flame sparked and licked the tip of his cigarette. Chris inhaled and blew out a trail of smoke.

Amy grimaced and wafted her hands. 'I've got cookies to bake.'

'Cookies?' Chris burst out laughing. 'Are you two having a tea party?'

Amy rolled her eyes. 'Come on, let's go,' she said to Olivia.

Olivia didn't move. She lit her own cigarette and handed the lighter to Paul. She sucked in short, sharp bursts, finding the whole conversation both agonising and thrilling all at the same time.

'Is that your car, Livvy?' Chris pointed his cigarette at her silver Mini in the car park.

Livvy? She hated this version of her name. Her mum called her Livvy, like a little kid, but when Chris said *Livvy*, it sounded . . . sophisticated.

'Yeah, so what?' Amy replied.

Chris laughed. 'Chill! It's a cool car, I like it, that's all.' He looked at Olivia. 'When did you pass your test?'

Amy rolled her eyes.

'Last summer,' Olivia managed to say. After her dad threw a wodge of money at a string of lessons with a frizzy-haired driving instructor who smelt of dogs. It was only recently she realised that, after what had happened, he needed her to be able to drive as quickly as possible. Be independent.

Chris pounced. 'How many times did you take your test?'

'Bloody hell, it's not a competition,' muttered Amy. 'Don't tell me, you passed first time.'

He laughed. 'Of course, I've been driving for nearly a year now. I want to get a motorbike soon.'

'Good for you,' Amy replied drily. 'You'll be dead in a few weeks.'

'Oi, that's a bit harsh! So you don't fancy a ride on the back, then?'

She laughed. 'No way!'

'Olivia will, won't you?'

Olivia could see the challenge glinting in his eyes. For a moment they seemed to understand each other, and she felt a rush of pleasure. She nodded.

Of course I would.

◆ ◆ ◆

Olivia pulled up outside Amy's house and the girls got out of the car. A neighbour called a greeting and Amy wandered over and began chatting. Olivia waited, unsure what to do. This was clearly one of those friendly streets, or perhaps it was just Amy, she'd talk to anyone. She often flitted between groups of friends at college, her voice carrying down the corridors or across the canteen, punctuated with explosions of laughter. Olivia often stood waiting – just like this – unsure how to join in the conversation. It wasn't as though Amy excluded her, she'd always make introductions, but the names and faces all danced together. And anyway, Olivia didn't have time for friends. Friends let you down. The girl-group thing always ended in bitching and back-stabbing, something she'd learnt the hard way at her old school.

'Come on then.' Amy opened the front door and walked down the hallway, the low heels of her boots tapping against the black-and-white diamond floor tiles. Olivia knew she was expected to follow, but it seemed intrusive. What if Amy's parents were there? They weren't expecting her visit.

She glanced at the open door to her right and caught a glimpse of an armchair upholstered in a pastel pink-and-green floral fabric. The style wasn't Olivia's taste, but she guessed was probably straight out of Amy's parents' furniture shop, and therefore the latest trend.

'What you doing?' said Amy, tip-tapping back up the hallway. 'Do you want a tour? It's pretty boring. Just a house.'

'No,' Olivia replied, feeling guilty for some reason. 'Sorry, I was wondering if your parents knew I was coming over.'

'Pff,' Amy said, waving her arm dismissively. 'They won't be home for ages and, anyway, they won't mind you being here. They'd rather I have company.'

Olivia's eye caught a display of photos on the wall behind Amy.

'Oh God, don't look at them, aren't they hideous?'

The row marked Amy at different ages over the years. The last one was a family portrait, taken in a studio with a dark-green curtain as the backdrop. Amy sat on a stool in front of her parents, her dad's hands resting comfortably on her shoulders, their apple-cheeked grins a perfect match. Her mum, on the other hand, smiled as stiffly as her hair-sprayed blonde bob.

'Forget this, let's eat cookies,' said Amy, waltzing back down the hall, humming.

Olivia stood in the doorway. The kitchen looked immaculate. Varnished wood cupboards lined both walls and the empty worktop was made up of brown and cream tiles. The hob shone and the pine dining table in the middle of the room didn't have a litter of paperwork, like it did at Olivia's house. Perhaps Amy's mum had a cleaner.

'Sit down, make yourself at home,' Amy said, wrenching open cupboards and assembling the ingredients. 'God, make us a cup of tea, will you?'

Olivia filled the kettle and was soon sitting at the table watching Amy furiously mix the batter. Music blared from the radio and Amy hummed along, punctuating the songs with the lyrics she knew now and then, but otherwise saying nothing. There was something *comforting* about being here like this, with Amy, and before long the smell of baking filled the room.

Amy pushed a plate of cookies towards Olivia. 'OK, taste-tester, what's in these?'

Olivia broke the warm cookie in half and sniffed. Chief taste-tester was a role she'd grown to love. She looked forward to the cakes Amy brought to college and liked having her opinion listened to. Melted chocolate oozed on to her finger. 'Chocolate,' she said drily.

Amy rolled her eyes. 'Duh! And?'

Olivia inspected the inside and took another sniff. 'Some kind of nut. Hazelnut, I think,' she said, taking a bite. The cookie crumbled into an explosion of flavours that bounced around her tongue.

'Yep!' Amy grinned. 'And?'

'Orange.'

'Bingo.'

Amy's baking really was superb. It was lunacy that her mum hadn't allowed her to do home economics A level. Anyone with half a brain could see this was where her talents lay.

'Fancy going to the Zap Club sometime?' Amy said suddenly, her mind obviously on something other than cookies.

'Where's that?' Olivia replied, for once not giving a shit if she sounded like an uncool loser.

'Brighton. They're supposed to have a great club night on a Friday.'

Olivia shrugged. Clubs had never been her thing. Well, she'd never *actually* been to one to know for sure, but then she doubted Amy had either. She thought of Chris. He looked like the kind of guy who went clubbing with his mates every weekend. She'd been watching him these last few weeks, clocking the pub he went to sometimes at lunch and the direction he walked home from college. She thought about the way he'd leant towards her earlier to light his cigarette, the scent of his leather jacket mixed with the tang of citrus. She felt shivery just thinking about it.

Olivia wondered whether she should tell Amy. But when it came down to it, what *could* she say? It all sounded a bit juvenile to nudge Amy in the corridor at college and go, 'Cor, look at Chris's bum' – even though that was exactly what she was thinking.

She snapped back to now. 'Could do, I suppose,' she said. 'I could drive us.' Her dad wouldn't mind, she was pretty sure. He probably wouldn't even notice she'd gone out. 'Will your parents let you go?'

Amy snorted. 'No, probably not. Well, Dad would if Mum wasn't around, but Mum will definitely say no, she always has the last word.'

Olivia thought about the woman she saw in the photo. She looked brittle, but a photo didn't always tell the full story – she should know that more than anyone. 'What's the deal with your mum? Why's she so strict?'

'She's *old*, she's like, fifty-something. She didn't have me until she was much older than the other mums because she was too busy with the business. She's got no idea what it's like to be a teenager.'

Olivia didn't want to think about her own mum. 'So, how's that going to work? Persuading her to let you go to the Zap Club?'

Amy beamed. 'I'll say I'm staying at yours!'

Olivia flinched. *No way.*

But Amy obviously already had it all worked out.

Chapter 11

Amy

Now

My head is still swirling when Chris suggests we have lunch at the Orbit, the revolving restaurant in the Sky Tower. I've not eaten here before; I could never justify the expense, but I go along with the idea because I'm not really thinking about money or food or whether I'm hungry; my mind is saturated with Bea.

We're sitting at a table by the window with the blanket of Auckland city spread out below. The restaurant's rotation is imperceptible, yet our view constantly changes – like my baby daughter growing into a toddler, a child, a teen, a young woman, *a bungy jumper?*

The memory of a holiday we had together in the South Island springs forward. Bea was thirteen and we were hiking the coastal track in Abel Tasman Park. It was going to take us a few days. We carried our stuff, I taught her how to pitch a tent and each evening we'd swim in the sea. One morning we came across a swing bridge strung high above an inlet. I crossed first, looking down at the sparkling water in wonder, but when I reached the other side and looked back, Bea hadn't moved.

'I can't do it, Mum,' she'd shouted, clutching the sides of the bridge.

Even from this distance I could see she looked pale. I felt a pinch of worry. 'Sure you can!'

She shook her head. 'I can't.'

I didn't hesitate. I walked back, the bridge swaying gently beneath my feet, until I was standing in front of her. 'Do you trust me?' I said.

Fear glazed her eyes, but she nodded.

I turned around. 'Put your hands on my waist, keep your eyes on my backpack, and breathe in and out on my counts of three.'

We shuffled together across the bridge that morning, my voice ringing out above the water, keeping Bea steady, encouraging her forward, until we'd reached the other side.

A bungy jump? Do I actually know my daughter at all?

A glimpse of red flashes past the window with a muffled scream and Chris leans forward to follow the jumper's fall to the ground. 'That was such a rush,' he says. When he looks up, I receive the full force of his beam – and Bea etched into his features. 'Your daughter sounds brave. I'm not sure I'd be queuing up to jump again – at least, not just yet.'

His mouth curves into a smile.

My daughter?

That coiled feeling I thought had unravelled as I hurled myself off the Sky Tower ripples out of me as fast as a whip. '*My* daughter?'

Chris creases his brow and then his face softens. 'It's tough when you find out new stuff about your kid from someone else, isn't it? Especially something as terrifying as a bungy jump.'

I stare at him, my rage frothing and writhing. But all I see is concern – and confusion.

'Bea, she's your daughter, right?'

I'm suddenly falling again. Tumbling, twisting, scrabbling to hang on, and the sensation feels way, way more frightening than leaping off a building. Our recent conversations ticker backwards at high speed: *He didn't respond when I asked why he'd come; he thinks my responsibilities are towards my business, he didn't react when John mentioned Bea, when Kieren talked about Bea.*

The shock of the truth smacks me in the face.

Chris doesn't know Bea is his daughter.

Why doesn't he know?

I nod mechanically. I stare down the straight line of road that leads back to the ferry terminal and home. He doesn't know. *He doesn't know he's Bea's dad.* We're twirling the skies of Auckland and the truth revolves with me. I don't understand. I told him, I wrote him a letter, I made it very clear. None of this makes sense. I feel the urge to leap up, run back down the straight road, swim across the harbour and get back to my café, my home, where I know nothing has changed.

Except everything has changed.

The waiter appears at that moment and places our desserts in front of us. They sit like art on the plate: mine a complicated construction of meringue and lemon; Chris's a chocolate torte of some kind, decorated with a cerise-pink flower.

He points at the flower. 'Do you think I can eat that?' he whispers.

I can't look at him. 'Try it.' I poke at the meringue and lemon cream oozes out, making my stomach turn.

'Are you OK?' he says. 'Did the jump not agree with you?'

'No, not really,' I say. Isn't that the truth? I drag my fork around the plate.

He never knew Bea existed.

Why?

'Do you want to go home? I don't mind.'

I sip my water. I picture my tall, beautiful daughter with hazel eyes and chestnut hair like her dad's, idling on the swing seat next to me that evening she turned sixteen. *Do I have his eyes? His hair?* she'd said after we'd spoken. *Both.* Her questions gathered and spilled. *Is he tall? Was he handsome? How did you get together?* I'd filled her in, but I tried to keep my answers short because, what was the point?

Now there's a point.

Chris sits in front of me.

I could go along with this faux post-bungy sickness and walk away from him forever. Or I could pull myself together and give him a chance . . . to do what? Prove himself? I don't know what the right answer is – for Bea. But I don't have to make a decision yet. We have a whole afternoon together – if I want to.

'I'll be fine,' I say, pushing a smile on to my face. 'But I won't be jumping again. Once is enough for me.'

'Well, if you're sure . . .'

He's giving me an escape route and it's tempting to run but I've nowhere to hide.

I push my dessert to one side. 'I'll have a coffee.'

Shortly, our drinks arrive, and we stare out of the window again. Below is a hill with a scooped-out grassy crater at the top that marks one of Auckland's dormant volcanoes. Ant-like people crawl around the rim that's now a beauty spot in the middle of the city. I point this out to Chris and he asks me to name the other landmarks we see. I realise how much I love my city, and how strange it feels for someone to be so interested in the things I say.

Soon, Chris suggests we head to the marina because he wants to look at a new development there. I lead the way back down the hill, my mind still whirring, but I ask him about his job as an architect and the projects he's worked on. He becomes animated as he speaks, flashes of Bea spark now and then in the way he moves his hands, his smile. Still neither of us has spoken of the past. *Of before.*

He didn't get my letter.

He *didn't* abandon us?

My throat burns as I struggle to believe this new truth. How can it be possible? Dad would never have let me down. Never.

I bite back the instinct to ask him if he knew I wrote to him, if he had any idea what happened. But now the tables have shifted and it's up to me to talk about Bea, I'm paralysed with guilt, fear, indecision – my daughter should be told her father is here. But her emotions about him are fragile, and is he a man I can trust? It would be unthinkable to throw this news into an email. And what about Chris? I owe him the truth, of course I do, but I'm hesitant. Right now, Bea is my centre, like she always has been and always will be. It's been almost nineteen years since I've seen this man, I don't know who he is, I'd never push her into the arms of a stranger.

Chris and I walk around the marina and then I point to a bar with tables outside and surprise myself by suggesting we have a drink. I accept his offer to buy the beers and he returns with two bottles – no glasses – which suits me. A breeze tugs the umbrella above us and yachts rock on the water, sails flapping and chiming. I need to use this time wisely, find out what I need to know, fill in the gaps, because otherwise how will I know if he is good enough for Bea?

Chris is admiring the bridge again and taps the table with long fingers. Bea's fingers. The soft beat reminds me of something and carefully I unroll the memory in my mind. 'Do you still play the guitar?'

His gaze swings back to me. This time, with a different truth in front of me, I let myself feel the frisson of the past that's been nudging me since he first walked into the café. I swallow, unsure if treading this path is what I really want to do.

Chris blinks and relaxes back into his chair. 'No, not really, just a tinkering every now and then.'

'Really? But you were good.' I'd loved listening to him and my younger self swooned, embarrassingly, over the songs he used to play in private to me, but he doesn't need to be reminded of that.

'Do you remember those songs I used to play to you?' he says, as if reading my mind. 'I think I thought I was going to be a rock star!'

I colour slightly.

'And the awful lyrics I wrote!' He shakes his head, smiling, swigs his beer.

I think about his songs hidden away in the pink box. The box that's sitting in plain view on my coffee table, waiting to be picked over again.

'Terrible,' I agree, lifting the beer to my mouth.

'I can't believe the pub let Paul and I play music to a paying audience!'

I laugh. 'You weren't that bad, you did some good covers. Olivia and I used to look forward to coming to watch you.' The memory tugs a smile. Olivia and Paul. I've not thought about them in years. 'Did you stay in touch with Paul? What about Olivia? I wrote to her a couple of times, but then, I don't know, I guess we just drifted apart.'

Once, I thought Olivia would always be in my life, but like the rest of my years in England, she too is relegated to the pink box of dusty memories. Forgetting was the best way to move on after I realised she was never going to write back. She felt the distance in our lives before I did. She a law student; me a teenage mum – not that she ever knew. I nearly told her in my last letter, but Mum had done her job well; shame had settled solid and unforgiving and stifled the words.

Chris shifts in his seat. 'You wrote to Olivia?' He sounds surprised.

And you.

There's an awkward silence and then he speaks again. 'You wouldn't recognise Paul if you saw him now. He's gone all corporate, he's a hotshot accountant.'

I laugh. 'No way! Paul the Goth is now Paul the Accountant? I can't believe it. Have you got any photos on your phone?'

Chris pulls a mobile from his pocket and fiddles with it for a moment, then frowns and slides it away. 'Sorry, no.'

'What's Paul like now?' I say. 'I guess he doesn't wear make-up and earrings any more?'

'Nah. He got a job after uni as a trainee accountant and got away with the make-up and long hair for a while. Then the boss took him aside and told him he was good, really good, but if he wanted to go places, he had to smarten up. That advice made him a fortune. He runs his own accountancy firm now and drives a Porsche.'

I don't know what to say. Chris describes a life I know nothing about. This might have been my life, I suppose, if things had been different. I think about my anniversary party and how many people poured through the doors that day. I feel hopeful. I'm going to spruce up the outside, buy a smart new shade sail for the terrace, and follow up the request to supply outside catering to the marketing firm around the corner. I won't own a Porsche, but I'll be me, and I'll be happy.

'Paul and Olivia didn't stay together?' I say lightly.

Chris breaks into a smile and leans forward as if to tell me something, but then he stops, his eyes glazing over, and slowly sits back. In a flash, the smile's back. 'They were never really a proper couple back then, were they?'

I wonder if he means *like us*. Amy-and-Chris, the couple that everyone at college knew about. I think about our neat little four-some that last summer; Paul clutching Olivia's hand as if she might float away. Then, before, conversations Olivia and I'd have on the phone or holed up in my bedroom. She was keen on Paul from the start. Keen enough to talk me out of going to the Zap Club and persuade me that Rock Night at The Fox would be more fun. Keen enough to go every Friday. Paul seemed to be the one all over her, but that was Olivia's way, wasn't it? It didn't mean she wasn't interested. She never revealed to anyone how she felt, not even me. And looking back now, through adult eyes, it's a mystery we were ever friends.

'Sounds like Bea's having a good time abroad. Where's she gone?'

Chris's change of tack sounds casual, too casual, dangerous even, and my breath catches as I realise how close we're stepping towards the truth. Has he crunched the numbers? Has he worked out Bea is his? I turn over everything I've heard from him today and wonder if it's enough for me to feel certain it's the right decision for Bea. I don't know, I'm not sure. I think quickly.

'She's in Thailand, having a blast, for sure,' I reply truthfully, and carefully put my bottle down.

Chris's gaze meets mine.

He's worked it out.

'Did you have any other children with Grant?' he says.

My knee jumps up against the table, knocking over my bottle and spilling beer. Chris catches it before it rolls to the ground. I realise his assumption has given me a reprieve, an escape, a chance to shroud my world in deception – if I choose to.

'I'll get a cloth,' I say, standing. I tug my bag on to my shoulder and head towards the door but the urge to flee twitches my muscles again. I glance towards the harbour. I could walk out of here. Walk

85

away from all of this. Shut down my phone. Hide in the kitchen. Move away. Run, run, run. Until he gets the message. But this isn't about me. It's never been about me. And Chris is still waiting for an answer.

'Do you want another beer?' I call.

He nods, but looks wary, the way Bea's eyes used to dart over my face when she asked for more sweets, to stay up late, for permission to go to a party – will the answer be yes or no?

When I return, I move the conversation on, telling him about places he ought to visit while he's here, and soon we're back on the ferry. On the top deck, I point out Waiheke Island and suggest he goes on one of the wine tours over there. He takes photos and asks me when I last went, and I struggle to remember, it's been so long. There's a pause in our conversation and I think he might ask me to come with him, but he doesn't.

I don't know if I'm relieved or disappointed.

The ferry docks on the North Shore and we wander past the smattering of shops, closed now, until we stop at the corner where we part ways. I'm conscious of how close he lives to me – like our childhood homes – which messes with my mind and has me thinking about the past again. 'D'you know what happened to Olivia?' I say. 'I can't believe she was my best friend, we were so different.'

Chris draws out his camera and for an odd moment I think he's going to ask if he can take my photo. 'She's an artist,' he says, pointing it at one of the old colonial buildings on the other side of the road, now a restaurant.

My face lights up. 'No way! It's so good to hear she became the person she really wanted to be.' I'm about to ask more but as he moves the camera away, my joy evaporates. There's no curve in his mouth and his gaze lies somewhere beyond me.

A throb begins in my temple. 'What is it?'

Just ask me.

He pastes on a smile. 'I've just remembered, before, you forgot to tell me, did you have any other children with Grant?'

A gust of wind lifts my curls and I feel a floating sensation as they drift back down. I find myself slowly backing away, a twist of guilt and uncertainty tugging me back to the safety of home like a magnet. 'It's just me and Bea,' I say.

Chris nods, lifts his hand to say goodbye. 'See you again?'

'You know where to find me.'

As I walk back home, I roll over what I *haven't* said. I've not lied, I've not told a fib – and staying silent buys me more time.

A little later, I head out on to the roof terrace with a glass of wine and sit on the swing seat with the pink box on my lap. The sun is low in the sky, shooting splinters of orange and pink up towards the clouds. I lift the lid and pull out the teddy bear, the red notebook and the passport photos all over again.

Chris didn't get my letter. He thinks Bea is Grant's daughter.

I stare at our faces, crammed together for the tiny camera. Was I pregnant then? I screw my eyes shut and try to remember when we'd squeezed into the photo booth. Would it have made a difference if he *had* known? What would we have become? We might have travelled the world as we'd planned, with baby Bea propped up in a back carrier, Chris laden down with a rucksack stuffed with nappies. Perhaps we would've been happy to throw away our dreams and settle down into suburban bliss? My mind is a blank and I can no longer picture a fantasy scenario with the three of us together. All I see is me, full-bellied, barely more than a child myself, hunched on all fours on the hospital floor, sobbing and sweating and screaming his name as I push Bea into my world.

I press my fists into my eyes and try to imagine bringing up Bea without the black cloud of his absence that used to suffocate me at night.

I have to rewrite history.

To replace *He Never Came* with *He Didn't Know*.

My mind churns through the years, tumbling and spinning my emotions so I no longer know what is right or wrong, or true or false. I don't understand how this can be. I wrote Chris a letter. I told him about Bea. Dad delivered his letter. Is Chris lying? Why would he?

I stare at my empty glass and pour myself another. Then my phone bleeps and a photo of Bea pops up on my screen as if she knows I'm thinking about her. She's hosing down a baby elephant, her shorts and T-shirt soaked with her efforts, and her smile tells me all I need to know. She's happy and she's safe.

Check me out! she says. Emma and I are volunteering at an elephant sanctuary, isn't this little guy cute? He's my favourite, he's called Somsak, which means 'worthy'. It's so lovely that the people who run this place respect the elephants enough to make sure they're safe from the trap of horrible tourist rides.

I think of my day with Chris. Is *he* worthy? Am I denying her? Am I denying him?

She's mine.

She's his.

I type a quick reply, but I know she won't be waiting for a response. She'll have already left the internet café and disappeared back into the jungle with Emma, or someone, the boy with his arm around her waist . . .

I begin to put the things away and see a photo pressed face down at the bottom of the box. I peel it away and turn it over. Chris and I are standing in the doorway of The Fox. His arms are wrapped around my middle and I lean back into his chest. His head bends towards me and I remember he's inhaling the scent of my hair. I'm grinning and, like all great love stories, we glow in the shaft of the early evening summer sun.

I glow. Then I remember. I really am glowing because I'm pregnant and I'd planned to tell Chris later that evening.

Except I didn't.

Mum and I had an argument and my life spiralled beyond my control.

I scrunch up my eyes.

What happened to my letter?

I don't understand.

He should know he's Bea's dad, that Bea is his daughter.

He never knew I was growing our precious little girl. He didn't know I pushed her squalling into this world and lay in the hospital bed scared and fearful for her future.

Our future.

Just the two of us.

Chapter 12

OLIVIA

Then

'Look, Liv, they're baking cakes today.' Amy squashed her nose against the window of the home economics classroom to get a better look.

Olivia sighed. Art was starting in five minutes, she hated being late, plus she wanted to make sure she nabbed her usual seat at the back of the room. Still, she understood Amy's pain. She'd have gone mental if her dad had forbidden her to take art.

'Sometimes I really hate my mum,' Amy said fiercely. 'I could be in there right now and I'd have been the best student in the class. I'd have got an A grade.'

Olivia didn't doubt it.

'"Cooking isn't a proper A level and won't lead to a proper job",' she said, mimicking her mum's stern voice. 'What the hell does that even mean? She said I needed three A levels to get a uni place for teacher training and home ec couldn't be one of them – and then said I could do art! Where's the logic in that?'

Olivia didn't say she'd heard it all before; clearly Amy needed to vent.

'I can't believe Dad didn't stick up for me,' she continued. 'He is *so* wrapped around Mum's little finger. I keep telling them I don't want to go to uni, I don't *want* to be a bloody teacher.'

Nobody had cared which A levels Olivia took, or if four was one too many. It wasn't because she *wanted* to study four subjects – history and maths alone were intense – but there was no one to ask if art would be a good enough third A level to get a place on the law degree she wanted to do at Edinburgh. So she thought she'd better take English literature as well, just in case.

'Come on,' Olivia said, 'we'll be late.'

'What's going on in there?' Chris seemed to appear from nowhere and nudged himself between them, peering through the window.

Olivia's heart leapt as a heady cocktail of leather, smoke and citrus clouded around her. *Christ.*

Amy laughed and shoved him out the way. 'You're nosy, aren't you? It's nothing, I was just moaning that I'm not doing home ec. I'd rather be in there than going to art.'

'Really?' Chris looked genuinely surprised. 'Don't you like art?'

Amy shook her head. 'I don't hate it. I'd just rather be in there.'

'I love art,' Olivia interjected and then coloured. *What a childish thing to say.*

Chris didn't appear to have heard. He was still looking at Amy, who had her face pressed against the glass again.

'I wanted to take music,' he mused.

'Why didn't you?' Amy said.

'I want to do architecture. I had to take other subjects.'

'Wow, I've heard that's really hard. Years and years of study and training.'

'Come on, we need to go.' Olivia yanked Amy's arm.

Chris glanced at her, amused. 'Chill out, Alan won't mind if we're a few minutes late. He probably won't even notice we're not there.'

They both looked at Olivia and she scowled and marched off, all the while wishing she could *chill*, like Amy, and amble along the corridor with Chris, not giving a shit about being late. When she reached the classroom, the only empty desks were at the front next to Chris's weirdo Goth mate, Paul. Olivia slumped down next to him and shortly afterwards Chris and Amy strolled in, laughing about something.

'Is there something funny about my class?' murmured Alan, their teacher, perched on a stool in front of them. He was bald on top and what remained of his hair he wore in a ponytail. He began talking about the intricacies of portrait painting and Olivia's mouth twitched at the ceiling light beaming down on to his bald spot. She snatched up her pencil and began scribbling a cartoon of a tiny toy helicopter coming down to land on the shiny circle. Next to her, Amy caught sight of the caricature and laughed loudly.

Alan frowned. 'We're working in pairs today, drawing each other's portrait,' he said. 'You' – he pointed to Amy – 'can work with Chris. Olivia, you partner with Paul.'

What? Olivia dropped her pencil.

'I'll draw you first,' Chris said, turning to Amy.

Olivia wanted to shout, 'I'll draw you!' The truth was, she'd been drawing his portrait for weeks. Not stupid, childish caricatures, but careful pencil sketches she'd spent hours crafting while lying on her bed. She waited for Amy to say, no, you really must draw Olivia, but of course she wouldn't, would she?

'No way! I'm going first.' Amy's chair screeched as she shunted it around to face him.

Olivia stared at her back and disappointment sat hard and angry in her belly. Alan clicked his fingers. 'Come on now, get on with it, Olivia, Paul's waiting.'

Bristling, she turned to Paul the Goth. He stared openly at her through black kohl-ringed eyes, a black bob framed his white face and he'd penned his mouth into a black line. He rarely spoke and, when he did, no one could understand what he was saying because his mouth didn't seem to move, giving him the demeanour of a ventriloquist.

Amy's laughter rang out behind Olivia.

'Swap seats,' Olivia demanded, standing up and towering over Paul. *This was so unfair.* He raised a black eyebrow but did as he was told. Olivia's eyes narrowed as Amy wriggled in her seat and her curls bounced against her back. Chris was trying to keep a straight face while Amy drew him, but laughter crinkled his eyes and Olivia could see a smile itching to break free at the corners of his mouth.

What she would give to scrutinise his features with no shame or embarrassment, and she could have done that – if Amy hadn't sat in *that* chair. She should have hung back with them before the lesson, *she* could have made sure she sat next to Chris, *she* could have been the one drawing him now.

She flipped open her pad. 'Let's get this over with,' she hissed to Paul. Up close, behind the make-up, she saw his eyes were in fact bright blue, not brown as she'd first thought, and he had a band of blond regrowth running along the roots of his dyed black hair. She began defining his face with her charcoal, resisting the temptation to darken and elongate his pointy nose into the snout of a solemn raccoon.

Amy giggled and Olivia's head snapped up. The grin had broken through Chris's passive expression and Amy swatted him on the arm and told him to stop smiling. He let his mouth settle and even though he wasn't actually smiling any more, Olivia noticed his lips stayed tipped up – a smile of sorts – and she had to look away again.

Paul turned his head a fraction to follow Olivia's gaze. 'Keep still,' she barked, staring back at her drawing. She scratched at the paper and pressed her finger into the charcoal to smudge blackness around his eyes. Then she reached his ear and looked up to see them studded and laced with silver earrings. Her eyes wandered on to Chris again. Today his hair was loose and, this close up, she could see the ends were bleached a few shades lighter, as if holding on to the warmth of a sunny summer holiday.

He caught her looking and winked.

Olivia coloured. *Who did he think he was?* Paul snorted. She looked down at her drawing. The charcoal felt lumpy in her hand and she slammed the pad shut.

'Your turn,' she said, glaring at Paul. He studied her for a beat too long and she squirmed. He'd probably noticed her weird slanting eyes, which were neither blue nor green but some kind of muddy colour in between. She touched her hand to her chin, her *pointy chin*, then stroked her hair three times over. Her shoulders relaxed a little. At least she'd washed it that morning.

'That's better,' Paul muttered. 'Your shoulders are back where they're supposed to be.'

'What do you expect?' she retorted. 'This is weird.'

Paul flicked his gaze between her and the pad, his hand flying across the paper in confident strokes. Behind him, Olivia watched Chris draw Amy, his eyes fixed on her with an intensity that made Olivia's throat ache.

'You've got no chance.' Paul's voice wasn't much more than a whisper but the flame of shame that shot through Olivia's body told her she'd heard him correctly.

'What? What are you talking about?' she snapped.

'Them,' he said, without looking up. 'I mean, *him*. Absolutely. No. Chance.'

'Whatever. I don't know what you're talking about.'

'Don't be dumb, you're too clever for that.'

Olivia tried to ignore the thumping disappointment in her chest. Chris was bent over his drawing pad now, his hand moving in slow, tight circles, and she imagined him drawing Amy's curls. He looked up and his eyes raked over Amy's face and his smile slowly curved into a grin.

Amy fidgeted in her chair again. 'Are you finished yet?' she said. 'Show me!' She pounced for his drawing pad but he snatched it away.

'Nope, you'll have to wait,' he said, laughing.

Paul pressed his finger on to the paper and rotated it in circles to smudge the charcoal. 'Have you been to The Fox on a Friday night yet?' he said. 'They have live bands every week.'

'Sorry?'

'Are you deaf?'

Olivia flushed. 'I . . . no, I haven't.'

'You and Amy should come. It gets packed and it's a laugh.'

'Isn't it rock music, though?' She wrinkled her nose. 'Not my thing.'

'You should come!' Chris called over. 'You might like it! What do you reckon, Ames?'

Amy swivelled around to look at Olivia, her cheeks flushed. 'Sounds good, Liv, doesn't it?'

Olivia stared at her. She looked different, sort of warm . . . with a kind of *glow*. 'What about the Zap Club?' she said quickly. 'You've been going on and on at me for weeks about going there. I thought you were *desperate* to go. Oh wait, I remember now, you can't, your mum won't *let* you go.'

Nobody spoke. A red stain blotched Olivia's neck and her heart raced in a toxic mix of power and shame. Amy looked stunned for a moment and then she smiled, carefully.

'It's true,' she said, 'my mum *is* a nightmare.'

'Forget that place!' said Chris. 'It's shit, they only play house music on a loop. This is *real* music.'

Amy searched Olivia's face. 'It'd be cool to see some live bands, wouldn't it, Liv?' she said eventually.

Olivia stroked her hair and shrugged. She didn't really know what music she liked, but she'd be bloody stupid to miss out on a chance to spend time with Chris. *Anything could happen at the pub.*

Chris leant towards Amy. 'At least come and support us then,' he said. 'We're playing a set on Friday, aren't we, Paul?'

Amy snapped back to her usual sunny self and laughed. 'Well, that's settled then! What time are you picking me up, Liv?'

Chapter 13

Amy

Now

The following morning I'm icing a chocolate cake in the kitchen when I hear Shannon arrive, her flip-flops – her *jandals* – flapping faster than usual against the wooden floor. The saloon-style swing doors bounce open and she strides in, filling the kitchen with the scent of the freshly baked bread she's holding.

'Morning,' she says, putting the box down on the worktop.

I brace myself.

She rustles in one of the drawers and pulls out a bread board and knife. 'How did it go?' she says, beginning to slice one of the loaves.

I run the palette knife around the bowl to pick up the last of the vanilla icing. 'Good.'

'Good good? Or OK good?' she presses.

She's clever, is Shannon. She knows if she probes too much I'll clam up. But I'm clever too. I know how to give her enough to hold her at arm's length. I stroke the knife around the edge of the cake. The icing is thick and creamy and flecked with tiny black vanilla seeds that will enhance the richness of the chocolate. 'We had a nice time,' I say. 'We caught up on stuff and I quite enjoyed having a day off.'

'What sort of "stuff" did you talk about?'

'Our bungy jump.' I'm still churning through the shock of finding out Chris doesn't know about Bea and I'm not sure how to tell Shannon yet. I don't want to be judged. I don't want to be told what to do. *Plus, Chris thinks Grant's Bea's dad.*

Shannon barks with laughter. 'You did a bungy jump?'

I'm not surprised by her reaction. I can't believe I jumped either.

'Where? Off the bridge?' she says.

I shake my head. 'The Sky Tower.'

'You're crazy! What the hell brought that on?'

'Chris suggested it.'

She shoots me a look. 'Did he?'

I nod and pick up a small baking sieve, a pot of chocolate powder, and dust the top of the cake.

Shannon's still watching me. 'And Bea? What did he say?'

I push back through the doors, go over to the cooler and place the chocolate cake inside. I feel Shannon's hand warm on my shoulder.

'Oh hun,' she says.

I turn around but avoid her eyes; it would be wrong to accept her sympathy in the circumstances. I gesture to one of the tables and we sit down.

'Did you challenge him?' she says, her voice hardening.

I look down at the red and pink flower pattern in the tablecloth and push my finger into a crease. 'He doesn't know about Bea,' I say quietly. Saying the words out loud for the first time makes them rounded, real – and frightening.

Shannon sits back, confusion lining her face. 'What? He doesn't know he's Bea's dad? I don't understand . . .'

I shrug. 'He didn't get my letter, it makes no sense, but, really, he doesn't know. I mean, he realises Bea exists because we saw Kieren at the bungy, and you know what Kieren's like, he's still besotted with Bea and was talking about her trip, but somewhere along the line Chris assumed . . . he thinks . . .' My gabbling grinds to a halt. I need to be honest with her. 'He thinks Grant is Bea's dad.'

Shannon's mouth opens and then closes. Then she laughs, but it comes out like a squeak. '*What?*'

Suddenly, I realise how terrible this sounds. I jump up and smooth down the tablecloth on another table, straighten the chairs.

'And you didn't put him right?' she says, sounding incredulous.

For a moment I have the urge to snap, *this isn't your business, Bea is my daughter, not yours*, then I register the wider implications of Chris's assumption. My silence has drawn Shannon and Grant into this – and their two children.

Shame colours my face.

'You have to tell him! You can't let him think . . .' She gets up, shaking her head. She's not properly angry, not yet, but heat is beginning to sear her voice. 'What's Grant going to think? He'll be really upset. And John and Linda. This isn't right.'

'Why do any of them have to know?' I retort, fear making me jumpy and defiant. I want to hide behind this convenience for a little longer. I *need* this shield while I work through what's best for Bea. 'It's not like they're ever going to meet Chris, is it?'

Shannon comes to stand in front of me, her green eyes wide. 'Have you forgotten? John and Linda already have, yesterday, in here.'

I swallow and look over at the spot where John introduced himself to Chris as my father-in-law. A fatherly gesture, to fill the gap where my dad once stood. I look down at the table and the flower pattern blurs into pink and red smudges.

'You can't brush something as serious as this under the carpet! You can't pretend your conversation with Chris never happened!' She steps closer. 'You can't hide the truth from Bea forever,' she whispers fiercely.

Her words bite, but I refuse to look at her.

'Don't you at least owe it to Bea?' she presses, her voice rising as if I can't hear her. 'What if someone like Kieren finds out you've been saying Grant is her dad and she thinks that really *is* the truth? It only takes one email for everything to blow up.'

I close my eyes, picture Bea's shocked face. I open them again. It's a stretch, and unlikely. 'Please,' I say, properly looking at her. 'I know this isn't right, but I need to buy a little time.' My head is stuffed with memories and conversations and I can't unravel it all. I don't know what to do. 'I didn't tell Chris an outright lie. He just assumed and I . . . didn't correct him.'

'You need to get this sorted,' she hisses, emerald eyes flashing, and she marches back into the kitchen to escape me.

Shannon and I limp through the day; I can't remember a time like it. She's loyal to the core and I understand how much I've hurt her, betrayed her even. I know my untruth will hurt Grant too – if she decides to tell him. She won't hold back for long. Maybe she won't hold back at all; their marriage is rock solid.

I'm outside stacking up chairs and wiping down tables, getting ready to close, when I look up and see Grant striding towards the café. His job at Auckland Council's planning department keeps set hours and it's unusual to see him here at this time of day. My heart sinks, I wonder if Shannon's already told him, and he's come to have it out with me.

'Grant, hun,' she says, coming out of the kitchen and planting a smacker on his lips. She laces her arm through his and squeezes him to her. 'What a lovely surprise! Are you taking me out somewhere nice?'

He looks pale beneath the freckles that dust his cheeks and she notices and pulls back. 'Is everything all right?' she says. 'Are the kids OK?'

'Yes, love, they're fine,' he replies, but his smile is tight. 'I want to speak to Amy.'

I wonder if Shannon's thinking what I'm thinking. Has my ugly lie already begun to spiral? But why would he leave work early to confront me? And how would he know anyway?

Grant gestures for me to sit down and I do as he asks because I sense he'll insist if I don't.

'I'll get on with closing up then,' says Shannon, moving away.

'Love, you need to hear this too.' He grasps her gently by the elbow and steers her into the seat next to me.

We both stare at him and a giggle bubbles up inside of me. Grant has always been a serious sort of man and today I feel like a naughty schoolgirl facing the headmaster. I look away and bite my lip, wondering what I have to laugh about.

Grant sighs. 'I heard some news at work this morning.' He pushes his hand through a tuft of golden-red hair. 'I was in a planning meeting. The owners of your building are selling up. They've submitted a resource consent application for the Boat Shed to be demolished, with a design for a new café and retail outlet to be built in its place.'

I feel like I'm standing on the other side of a glass wall watching him, my face pressed close, straining to hear the words. 'What? I don't understand. I'm getting a new café?' I glance at Shannon.

She's staring at her husband, face like marble. 'Shit,' she breathes.

Grant reaches across the table and places his hand on mine. I stare down at the freckled skin and fine, sandy hairs. 'No, the design and the consent application is so the owners can improve the value of the building and its sale price. The buyers don't have to take you or your business on.' He pauses. 'You've got to think about your home, Amy, too, where you're going to live.'

I swear I can already hear the roar of the bulldozers outside. Grant's words smash through me as if the walls of my café are already being torn down.

No business; no home. What am I going to do?

Shannon and I part shakily, which thankfully hides our lingering fallout from Grant. After I've locked up, I pull on a swimsuit and head down to the sea, trying to get my head around his announcement. Ordinarily, I love my evening swims when the sea is still warm and I can wash away the frenzy of work, but today I drag myself through the water, my mind heavy with Grant's bombshell, churning over the decision to tell Chris about Bea – or not.

My eye catches the three rocky outcrops rising up from the horizon – Bea's island family – and my mind rolls back to when she was small and pointed to the tallest one. *Why can't I see my daddy? Doesn't he love me?* Back then, I'd said he lived too far away to reach us.

Now, he lives in the same city – streets away from me.

Would he love her? Could he love her? *Never the way I do.*

I don't stay in the water long and as I walk back up the sand, I find myself stopping in front of Mum's house. It's one of ten or so that back on to the beach, hers a white modernist-inspired slab of architecture that crows above the old bungalows either side of her. I hesitate for a moment, it's rare for me to drop by – Mum isn't the kind of person who likes to be surprised – but I have an urge to tell her Grant's news. She runs a real estate firm in the city, she *knows* people, there's a chance she could help. I shake my head at my own stupidity. *Who am I kidding?* Mum has never helped me with anything.

Then I think about my letter that Chris clearly didn't receive. Is there a chance she might know what happened? I'm doubtful. Dad promised he wouldn't tell her I'd written to Chris and he promised to deliver the letter for me. But he's no longer here to ask – and she is.

I pull my towel tighter around me and go through the gate, where palms stand sentry either side. A thicket of bamboo lines the path leading to a white stone terrace outside a wall of glass doors. There's no doubt this is prime land and a stunning place to live, no matter what I think of the modern box Mum built in place of the bungalow here before.

It was always Dad's dream to emigrate to NZ and Mum only agreed once she knew I'd be safely at uni. Dad whooped and punched the air when they won the bid to buy the old bungalow that backed on to this beautiful sandy beach. The restoration project became his pride and joy.

Then he died.

Mum tore the old place down without a second thought and built *this*. I don't know how she lives with that on her conscience.

As I come closer to the doors, I see Mum standing at the kitchen island in the open-plan room. She's holding a glass of wine and staring at a piece of paper lying on the worktop. Her blonde bob curves smoothly against her cheek and her mouth is a familiar thin line. Age folds her face. She's getting old, she *is* old – well past retirement and still obsessed with selling commercial space as hard and fast as she did when we first moved here. After Dad passed away, I thought she might slow down, realise that life was too short, but instead she threw herself into building the house and then back into work.

Mum's work clothes – a cream shift dress and glossy nude tights – unconsciously mimic the room she decorated in careful layers of ivory, white and gold. Abstract art, curated by someone else, hangs on the living-room walls, and I know if I run my finger along the open shelves that separate the two spaces, there'll be no dust, simply a collection of featureless sculptures staring back at me. My own home is chaotic by comparison – loveable and liveable.

Although the door is open, I tap gently on the glass. 'Mum,' I say, suddenly feeling uncomfortable about turning up unannounced.

She looks up, eyes roving over my swimsuit and towel. 'How unexpected,' she says, sounding like I've interrupted her from something important.

I can see her mind ticking over. God forbid I shed sand on to her clean white floor, but I bite my tongue as nothing satisfying comes from being sarcastic to my mother.

'Sit down.' She ushers me back outside towards a chair on the terrace. 'I'll get you a robe.'

I do as she asks, and now I'm here, I wonder why I came. There's no point telling her my business is about to be ripped apart because she'll only tell me I'm complaining. And if I ask her about the letter, I'll have to reveal I wrote to Chris – and admit he's here, in Auckland, *now*. Mum always made it clear how much she hated him.

I should have some answers ready, arm myself against her reaction, even though I don't know what her questions will be or what I need to say. The last time I had to justify Chris's existence, Dad was around to smother the flames of our argument and I don't know if I can deal with her fury alone.

I am not eighteen.

I remind myself to focus on Bea and what she needs, not dwell on my own concerns.

Mum returns with a bottle of wine, two glasses and a fluffy white robe, which I shrug on, silently grateful. 'Have you heard from Bea recently?' I ask, surprising myself. I thought her email yesterday would've reassured me, but I still feel uneasy. Perhaps I'm being unfair on myself – her father is in Auckland and has no idea of her existence.

The truth rattles my heart.

'She emailed a photo yesterday,' she replies, pouring me a glass of wine without asking if I want one. She slides it across the table. 'The one with the elephant. Did she send it to you too?'

Mum pins me with her dark eyes and I nod and sip my wine. It's cool and crisp and the heat of the alcohol floods my empty stomach, reminding me I haven't eaten in a while.

'What's the matter?' She frowns at my expression. 'She sounds like she's having a fantastic time.'

'I don't know, she's not written me a proper email for a while.' I hear my voice constricting into a whine.

'You can't expect her to email you every day,' she says snippily. 'Honestly, I'm surprised she's had this much contact with us.'

'She promised.'

'Don't be silly,' Mum snaps. 'She's not going to write you a lengthy account of her every move, she's eighteen not eight, they're all selfish at that age. Believe me, she's not going to be worrying about you or me and what we're doing or thinking.'

Her words sting. Even after all these years, I don't know if what she says is deliberate but it's definitely not harmless. I've heard these words dressed up in different ways at different times, accusations gathering momentum that can't ever be forgiven. It's only with the resilience of time that I manage to stay silent.

'This is a fantastic opportunity for her,' she continues. 'She's seeing the world. She'll come back a completely different person, and better for it, too.'

Her presumption annoys me. She never wanted me to go travelling with Chris. Or learn how to bake professionally. What's different now? But this is old stuff, old, old dreams, and I don't bother to explain how I feel. And anyway, the subject is closed now as far as she's concerned.

Mum sips her wine, her face impassive, and I have no idea what she's thinking, I never have – apart from that one time. Then, her face drained of colour and fury exploded into a slap around my face.

I'd been celebrating Olivia's birthday with lunch in the pub with Chris and Paul, and floated home on a high to get ready to carry on in the evening. When Mum announced I'd been spending too much time with Chris, and I had to stay home and revise, I'd flipped and hurled my pregnancy bomb into the room. Of course, it was never the way I intended to tell her and Dad. But I truly thought Chris would be by my side all the way. I loved him and he loved me. Our baby was meant to be. I doubted nothing and no one. Chris would be my hero.

I was dumb and naive.

Dad had steered me away from Mum's icy anger and walked me down to the local park with my arm tucked through his. He found an empty bench in the children's playground and showed me my future.

'Is this the life you want, Amy?' he'd said, gesturing to the children dangling off the monkey bars, demanding to be pushed on the swings. 'This isn't a trick question and you may not even know the answer yet. You have to understand there's no right or wrong and it's nobody else's decision but yours. But you also have to under-stand the responsibility you're taking on. This isn't a whim, or for fun, or to please a boy. This is the big one. This baby will be your responsibility for the next eighteen years. For the rest of your life.'

I embraced that responsibility, I absorbed myself in that responsibility, I committed myself to that responsibility – and I still *long* for that responsibility.

'I saw Chris yesterday,' I blurt, suddenly having the childish urge to see Mum's perfect world come crashing down. 'We spent the day together.'

Mum wears her mask well. For a moment I think she's going to pretend she doesn't know who I'm talking about. Then her eyes dart left, right, and a line pinches her forehead. I am triumphant. I can't imagine she thought either of us would ever lay eyes on him again.

'Is that so?'

My eyes narrow. Did she know he was here? Did someone see us out the other day and report back? It's possible. Mum has always had her informants – that's what has kept her company going for so long. She has made it her business always to be the first to know everything in this small city. Mum is the mistress of silences and I'm annoyed at my own impatience. 'Well? Aren't you going to say anything else?'

'What else is there to say?' she says, topping up her glass.

Heat fires through my veins. 'Did you see us together? Did you know?'

She looks steadily at me. 'No, Amy, I didn't see you. I didn't know you'd seen him.'

I watch her carefully, sure she's hiding something, and swiftly switch tack. 'Why doesn't he know about Bea?'

Mum startles, revealing a crack in her mask, and I power on. 'For years I thought he'd come for us – for Bea, at least – and now he's here and he doesn't know anything about her. I wrote to him!

107

I told him about Bea! I gave Dad my letter and I told him not to tell you.' My voice cracks. A rational part of me is still surprised that the pain of losing Chris cuts the way it did back then. 'I don't understand what happened.'

Two circular spots of red bloom on Mum's cheeks but she remains silent.

I scan her face but she won't look me in the eye and then, slowly, I begin to see the answer to the question I've not yet asked. Shaking, I get to my feet, shrug off the robe and pick up my towel. 'You knew about my letter,' I say furiously.

Mum's gaze touches on mine and she nods, ever so slightly.

For a second, my breath is sucked away. 'And you didn't think it was important to tell me that Chris never received it?'

She stares at me. Her mouth moves but nothing comes out.

I curl my lip in disgust – and Dad's absence tears through me like a knife. There's no answer she can give me that I want to hear and I turn away and run back down the path to the beach and to my home.

Chapter 14

Amy

Now

I've bumbled through this last week, furiously baking most evenings and spending the days throwing my energy into the café. I'm ignoring the fact it'll all be gone soon, and I'm ignoring the fizz in my head that Mum has always known Chris never received my letter.

He sent me a text following our bungy jump to tell me how much he'd enjoyed seeing me. I'd kept my response light and then another one popped up a few days later. This time he told me he was going on a guided walk over the Auckland Harbour Bridge on Saturday, and did I want to come? I'd been in the middle of baking a lemon drizzle cake and impulsively responded: *Sounds good but I'm working.* I was, but I also need time to think, to let the shock settle, to work out what's right for Bea, the café, *my life.*

I've never missed Dad more than I miss him now. He'd have the answers. He'd never have betrayed me. Mum must have discovered my letter before he delivered it or suspected something and confronted him. Either way, she forced him to stay quiet. Poor Dad, he must have felt terrible.

Now it's Sunday and I've gravitated towards my other family – Shannon, Grant and their kids, Reuben and Kira. We're on the beach sitting under a gazebo that Grant's expertly secured into the sand. I can see Mum's house from here, the white box sticking out above the line of pōhutukawa trees. She'll probably be in the garden under the pergola, laptop open, avoiding the sun, avoiding the sand, avoiding the sea. I've never seen the point of her living by the beach.

'It's not the end,' Grant insists, digging a channel for Reuben to run his truck through. We've been talking about the Boat Shed being destroyed – at least, that's how I put it – but I'm not expecting him to have the answers, at least not ones I want to hear.

'I've spent years building my business,' I repeat, annoyed that the words lodge in my throat. I'm lying on my front watching Shannon and the children playing at the water's edge. Kira's splashing about in the shallows and Reuben's collecting shells to decorate his track. Shannon's not mentioned my subterfuge since Grant came to see us that day. She's been sensitive to the shock of me losing my livelihood, putting her own concerns about losing her job aside – and, since I haven't seen Chris in a week, there's been no reason to worry.

'You could easily start again somewhere else,' Grant repeats, sitting back on his heels to look at me. His face is shaded from the sun with an All Blacks cap, but I swear his freckles are still multiplying. 'Perhaps it's time for a change.'

Shannon's not within earshot to rescue him and I wonder, unkindly, how she can bear his blundering and blindness to other people's feelings.

'And where do you propose I do that?' I demand, pushing myself upright and brushing sand from my arms.

'Business in the city centre is expanding and there're still empty units that need filling. If you set up over there, you'd have heaps of breakfast and lunchtime trade.'

'And why would I want to give up this' – I sweep my hand across the beach – 'to work in a box with the traffic roaring past?' I huff and Shannon strides back towards us. She looks fantastic in a polka-dot green bikini and Grant obviously thinks the same because he can't take his eyes off her.

'Uh-oh, what gems of advice are you offering Amy?' she says, catching my stony expression as she collapses on to a towel beneath the gazebo.

'I suggested she set up a café in the city,' he says mildly.

'That again.'

'I want to be by the beach. I can't stand the city. It's too busy.' A whine I don't like comes into my voice. 'What about Shannon? She'll lose her job, too, don't you care about that?' I can't imagine her not being by my side. I couldn't have made the café what it is without her.

'Well.' He darts her a look.

Shannon's eyes are sharply trained on the children by the water. 'I don't want to leave either,' she says. 'But I don't know what choice we have. If we had the money, we'd buy the building, ay Grant? But I'd probably still knock it down and build something else.'

I'm stunned. I always thought Shannon loved the old Boat Shed as much as me. I know work needs doing but its history, the faded charm and my memories are all part of the fabric.

'It could be renovated.' Shannon skims my face. 'In winter it's pretty chilly inside, ay?'

I prickle. 'But the terrace is lovely! Customers love sitting out there.'

'But if we had new windows and a new roof, we'd get more winter trade. I was stoked to have so many new customers come to

111

our party. We want them to carry on coming, in winter too. Give them somewhere pleasant to sit inside, more windows, bigger windows perhaps, so they can still enjoy the view.'

'You're talking like a developer,' I retort. 'Our café has character!'

Grant snorts. 'There's a big difference between character and decay.'

'What do you know?' I shoot.

He shrugs.

'Come on, say it, what's on your mind?'

He sighs. 'Open your eyes, Amy, it's time to let go and move on. This is pointless talk. The building will be demolished before you know it. Take control and do something about it now, don't wait to be thrown out. You've got a fantastic business, a great reputation, and the award is really well timed. Now's the time to make the move while everyone in the city knows who you are.'

I can't respond without saying something I might regret so I get up and go to the children by the water.

'Having fun?' I say, lowering myself into the shallows. Cool water ripples over my legs and I listen to Kira chattering about the game they're playing. Reuben makes the sound of an engine as he pushes a yellow tractor through the wet sand, and I nod and murmur in the right places. My anger begins to ebb away. I don't know what the answer is yet. But I do know I don't want to alienate my friends just because I don't like what they say to me.

They're watching me from under the gazebo like concerned parents. Shannon's brow is furrowed and Grant mouths 'Sorry'. I want to fight this decision that's been made. But I have to be realistic. I have no means to do this. Grant's right. I have to take control.

A wet hand slips into mine and Kira looks at me. Her eyes are the same clear blue as her father's and her cheeky grin is all Shannon. I'm not alone and I need to remember this.

◆ ◆ ◆

We spend the afternoon together but, in silent agreement, we don't mention the café again. Shannon talks about Bea and her travels, and all the exciting places she's visited. My mind is on how I'm going to pay her university fees when she returns, and where the hell we're going to live, but I say nothing except grumble about her lack of contact.

'You'd have thought she'd have emailed me again by now,' I mutter. 'I hate not knowing where she is – *who* she's with.'

'Psshhh,' says Shannon, waving her arm dismissively and coaxing the kids out of the sun and under the gazebo with a snack. 'She'll be having such an awesome time. No offence, but she won't be thinking about her boring old mum. No one that age cares about their parents. Frankly, I'm green with envy, I'd love to visit all those places.'

'Would you?' says Grant, patting sand into a mound for the sand palace he's building for Kira. 'I didn't think you wanted to travel.'

'Well, I didn't, not when I was young, but it'd be great to show the kids the world, ay?' She starts to rub sun cream on to Kira's shoulders. 'I'm surprised you've never taken Bea back to England, Amy, to show her where you were brought up.'

I snort. 'There's not much to see back there. Rain and gloom, where's the fun in that? Besides, when have I ever had the money for that kind of holiday?'

'I miss Bea,' says Kira, wandering over to Grant and eyeing his work. 'She makes awesome sandcastles.'

'Really, chook?' He laughs and tickles her. 'You sure about that? Well then, in that case I'm the chief at finding the best shells.'

Kira grins – 'Race you!' – and she shoots off down to the shore with Grant and Reuben in tow.

I smile as I watch them and Chris slides back into my thoughts. I think about my letter that contained a parallel life Chris was never given the chance to be part of – because of my mother and her decision to control my life. It makes my chest feel tight.

'Look, this thing about Grant being Bea's dad—' Shannon begins.

'I know,' I interrupt. 'I'm going to phone Chris later and tell him there's been a mistake.' I'm not sure if I am, but it sounds like the right thing to say.

'No, don't do that, it might sound a bit . . . strange. You don't want him working things out for himself, do you? Not until you're ready. I've been thinking about it. I mean, I suppose it wouldn't really matter if no one saw Chris again. But then I thought, why *aren't* you seeing him again? I mean, he's Bea's dad! You can't just let him wander into your life and back out again?'

'I know for sure that Chris never got my letter,' I say quietly, squeezing a handful of sand, then letting the grains trail out through my fingers. 'I won't forgive her, I'll *never* forgive her.'

'Who are you talking about? Your mum?'

I nod and tell Shannon the story. 'When I confronted Mum, she knew about the letter,' I finish. 'She's known all this time that Chris had no idea he was Bea's dad and she never told me.'

Shannon frowns. 'Did she tell you what happened to the letter?'

'Mum always controlled Dad and she wanted to control my life too,' I hiss. 'I was a disappointment. She didn't want me shacked up at eighteen. She took it from Dad to punish me for getting pregnant.'

Shannon sighs. 'You know what this means, ay? You have absolute proof that Chris *never* knew about Bea.' She watches me, her green eyes round with concern.

She's right. However angry I might be with Mum, Chris has nothing to hide, it's only *me* that carries a secret – a lie – and now

I have no reason to withhold the truth from him any more. I feel dizzy with the enormity of what this means.

She touches my arm. 'What are you going to do?'

A flutter of panic beats inside my chest. 'Bea's missed out on so much, but he's still a stranger, isn't he? I don't know him at all.'

'It's a bloody shock for sure,' she nods. 'You know, perhaps it would be a good thing to get to know him a bit? Before Bea gets back?'

'I can't tell her, not while she's away.' My heart pounds. 'But I can't tell Chris before I've told her either.'

'Hey, hun, slow down, give yourself time to get used to the idea, you don't need to rush any decisions.' Our gaze falls on Grant and the kids crouched down by the shore, poking in the sand. 'But if Chris is here for a few months,' she says softly, 'you *do* need to tell him you made a mistake letting him assume Grant is Bea's father, ay?'

I nod. 'Of course.'

Kira catches us watching. She jumps up and races towards us, swinging a bucket. 'Look, Mummy, look, Amy, look what we found!' she cries.

We both peer into the bucket and make appropriate cooing noises as we pick over her treasure. Soon we're all decorating the sandcastle and then someone's shadow falls over us and we look up to see Chris standing there.

'Hi,' he says, smiling.

I scramble to my feet and Shannon says, 'Hey, Chris, how are you?' as though he swings by the beach all the time.

A flush creeps into my cheeks. I'm conscious of how I must look, poured into a swimsuit that I'd told Shannon made my boobs look big, and she'd laughed and said that was the point, and insisted I bought it anyway. I crouch down to look for my T-shirt and find it stuffed under my bag, covered in sand. I shake it out and tug it over my head.

'Fabulous day,' he nods. It's hard to tell who he's looking at behind the mirrored sunnies.

'Roasting,' I reply, flapping my T-shirt to let in a non-existent breeze, re-tying the hairband that holds my hasty gathering of curls. I wonder briefly whether Chris has come looking for me. But that's stupid. It's a hot day. Everyone goes to the beach when it's warm.

'I've just been to the café,' he says by way of explanation. 'I thought you might be open today.'

I shake my head. 'Not on Sundays.' Mum thinks I'm mad to be shut on the weekend, says it makes no business sense, but when else can I hang out with the kids?

'Hey, hi,' says Grant, standing and shooting me a questioning look. Of course, he's never met Chris, and Chris still thinks my untruth is *the truth*. I glance at Shannon, and she must be thinking the same thing because her eyes widen.

'This is Reuben and Kira,' she says quickly, gesturing to the children and hopping to her feet. 'My husband, Grant.'

Grant wipes a sandy hand on his board shorts and they shake hands. But before Grant can say anything, Shannon grabs his arm and calls to the kids, 'Come on, let's go splash in the sea with Daddy!' They don't need asking twice and race off towards the water with Shannon practically dragging Grant behind her.

The hint is loud and clear, even though neither of the men have a clue what's going on. Chris looks at me, his mouth curled in amusement. 'What was that about?'

I cross my arms and hope the embarrassment burning my face could be mistaken for the heat. It's as though Shannon's set us up to have a private chat so I can ask him on a date.

'Nothing,' I say, shaking my head. Then I remember his plans to walk across the bridge yesterday. 'How was the climb? Get some good photos?'

'Loads – too many! Auckland's such a beautiful city, always sunny, never seems to rain.'

I look up. Tufty white clouds cling to the blue sky and I smile. 'It does, but often it's windy so we might have a downpour and then the sun's back out. I don't miss Hillgate's dreary grey days, that's for sure.'

'You don't call it home any more? Hillgate, I mean?'

I shrug. 'My whole adult life's been here, so this feels more like home than anywhere.' I don't add that *Home will always be where my daughter is.* Though that isn't true any more – at least, not for now.

We watch Shannon and Grant standing in the water, holding hands with their kids and swinging them high over the waves. They squeal in delight and Chris smiles. 'Cute family.'

It occurs to me I know so little about this man, this grown-up version of the boy I once knew so well. He briefly mentioned a wife, but what about children? Where are they? Did he leave them behind too? I think about Shannon suggesting I get to know him better. 'Have you got kids?' I say quickly, and the loose sand beneath my feet feels like it might give way. *I'm not ready.*

I'm taken aback to see sorrow etched in his face. I'm not sure what to say. Doesn't he have kids? *Couldn't* he have kids? Does he think he missed out on being a parent?

Does this change anything? Everything?

Kira screams and it breaks the moment as we both instinctively glance in her direction. Reuben's kicking water in her face and Shannon's telling him off. The scene catapults me back to the reason she's left us here alone.

'Hey, I bet the little ones are missing their big sister,' Chris says.

Shame flowers as I realise how far I've let this assumption go, and how easily one misplaced word from him could confuse and upset the children.

My mouth goes dry. 'Yes, but not in the way you think. Grant's not Bea's dad.' I dig my foot into the deeper, cooler part of the sand and curl my toes tight.

Will he do the maths? Work out the truth?

Chris throws me a glance, but I can't read his expression behind those damn mirrored sunnies. He looks back at the family unit. 'You assumed . . . I didn't explain properly,' I mutter.

'Right.' He shrugs. 'You don't have to explain, it's none of my business.'

I hear him.

You don't owe me anything.

Chapter 15

Olivia

Then

Olivia peered through the gap in her bedroom curtains. The street-lights glowed in the dark and next door's Christmas lights pulsed red and green. She pressed her face against the glass, looking as far up the road as she could see, but the path was empty; no sign of her dad yet.

A car appeared and crawled towards the house opposite. It pulled onto the driveway and a tumble of kids got out. Olivia watched the mum wrestle them inside and then the Christmas tree lights sparkled to life in the living-room window. She wondered what her Christmas would be like; it couldn't be worse than last year. Her mum had promised she wouldn't drink and for a small, hopeful moment, Olivia thought she might stick to it. She'd decorated the house, wrapped presents and even managed a huge food shop on Christmas Eve.

Then, Christmas morning: 'What's this?' Her dad pointed to three champagne flutes filled with something orange on the decorative breakfast table.

'Just a little something special for us all on this special day,' her mum twittered.

'It's just orange, right?' Her dad sniffed the glass suspiciously.

Olivia's mum's hands fluttered as she tried to ride out the questions and a familiar sinking sensation rolled Olivia's stomach. Like the day she'd found her mum and Pete in her parents' bed. A ghoulish tangle of naked flesh, Pete gripping her mum's hips, pumping into her, eyes closed, his face stamped with an expression Olivia hoped she'd never see again.

She'd wanted to close her eyes, too, but they were stuck wide open. She'd wanted to scream, but nothing came out. But more than anything she wanted her dad to roar, to run at them, to drag them apart and tell them to stop. He said nothing. He turned away, walked back down the stairs, out of the house and into his car, then she heard the snarl of tyres on the gravel.

It was all her fault.

They were supposed to be going for pizza after the cinema. But Olivia had convinced her dad to come home so they could have a takeaway with her mum.

Next door's Christmas lights sputtered into darkness for a few moments and then began flashing again. Olivia looked back down the road – still no dad.

The house sounded horribly silent and she reached out to press play on her CD player – then changed her mind. She could whack up the music and no one would complain. But what if she didn't hear her dad come home? What if he came upstairs to say hello and caught her getting ready to go out? She doubted he'd say anything, but because nothing was clear any more, she wasn't prepared to take the risk. He might suddenly spring into heavy-handed father mode and demand she stay home and revise.

Not tonight.

Olivia eyed the white carrier bag next to her bed. For a moment, she wondered if her dad would question the transaction on the credit card he paid off every month. She could say the purchase was for new shoes for college; he wouldn't ask to see them. She opened the box and took out a pair of black leather thigh-high boots with spiky heels. She tugged them on, zipped up the sides and stepped in front of the mirror. She could see the outline of her bra beneath the chiffon blouse. She tugged the front a little lower to reveal the black lace trim. *Better.* Let them look, let *him* look. She slashed red lipstick across her mouth.

Ready.

Olivia's car had been an unexpected outcome of that *sickening* afternoon. Not long after, her dad had reappeared in a taxi to pack his things. He'd rooted through her mum's handbag, grabbed the car keys and driven off, while her mum shrieked obscenities after him. Olivia had never seen him so determined. She was secretly quite proud. Then later, when he'd found this place to rent, he'd pushed the keys into Olivia's hand and said the car was all hers.

Tonight, the Mini meant freedom. No sneaking around required in this house. She could do what the hell she liked.

Olivia was about to start the engine when a tap on the car window made her jump. *Dad. Christ.* She opened the window.

'Hi, love, off out somewhere nice?'

Olivia zipped her jacket to her chin.

'Amy and I are going to the pub. The Fox has a rock night on tonight.'

'Sounds fun. Is Amy a new friend from college?'

She nodded. 'She's in my art and English lessons.' *And if you'd been a bit more interested in my life, you'd already know that.*

He yawned. 'Meeting anyone else?'

'Yeah,' she muttered.

'Ah!' Her dad suddenly became alert. 'Boys?'

Olivia eyed him warily. He was smiling as though it was a great joke that she might be meeting a boy. Christ, she was seventeen – only a few months off being eighteen – it wasn't like she was off to a stupid school disco in the hope of a slow dance with the boy she fancied.

'I'm glad you've made some new friends.'

Friend. Just the one. Though maybe after tonight she'd have another *friend.* Chris.

'Look after yourself, sweetheart. Going to the pub with friends can be great fun but stick together and keep an eye out for boys that . . . well, you know . . . just stay *safe*, love, that's all.'

He reached out as if to touch her, then pulled back. Olivia looked away. *Stay safe? What the hell did that mean?* She reversed carefully off the drive. *Did he think she was going to have sex?* She looked at him, standing on the doorstep. *Did he think she was a slut like her mum?* He waved as she pulled away. *He didn't notice my boots.* And soon she was navigating the roads towards Amy's house.

The Fox was tucked away on a country lane just outside the town. Olivia had heard that for years it had been nothing special, just another old pub with low beams, sticky brown tables and thread-bare stools, veiled in a haze of cigarette smoke. Then they'd started Friday Rock Night, never asked anyone for ID, so word had spread and now it seemed every teenager in the area had adopted The Fox as their favourite end-of-the-week haunt.

Amy pushed open the door, releasing the shrieks of a singer dancing wildly on a makeshift stage on the far side of the pub. The woman swung her long blonde hair back and forth, and a sea of bodies moved rhythmically to the beat in a blur of black, denim and leather. Olivia smiled, the energy was electric, but Christ, they'd never find Chris and Paul in that mob.

Amy headed for a corner of the bar furthest from the dance floor where there were two empty bar stools and sat down. 'Oh my God, Liv, you look amazing,' she said, eyeing Olivia's outfit. 'A proper rock chick!'

Olivia glanced at Amy's flowery blouse; the strap of the cloth bag pressed between her breasts, accentuating their voluminous shape. She pulled her jacket closed across her non-existent cleavage, suddenly thinking of a whole list of reasons why wearing a see-through chiffon blouse was a bad mistake.

Amy grinned. 'Paul's going to love you in those boots.'

Olivia bristled. 'Paul? What do you mean?'

She laughed. 'He *so* fancies you!'

What?

She laughed again. 'So, what're you drinking? Beer? Vodka?'

'Duh, Coke, I'm driving.'

'Oh yes, of course.' She frowned slightly. 'I might have a vodka and orange . . .'

Olivia wondered how often Amy went to the pub. Not that Olivia had ever been a regular anywhere herself. Drinking had never been her thing. 'Have a snakebite and black,' she suggested, thinking about the drinks she'd heard kids at college talking about.

Amy made a face. 'Sounds horrible. Is that the purple drink?'

'It's beer, cider and blackcurrant. You'll probably like it.'

Amy turned to order. 'Isn't that Chris behind the bar?'

Olivia looked over. He had his back to them, his shoulders broad in a black T-shirt. She felt her breath catch.

'Chris!' Amy yelled, waving. 'Serve us next!'

He turned and lifted his hand in acknowledgement. Olivia whipped off her jacket and tugged down the front of her blouse.

'Paul must be here.' Amy spun around on the stool and searched the room. 'Have you seen him yet? He's probably moshing in the crowd over there.'

Chris appeared in front of them. 'What can I get you ladies?' Hazel eyes rested on Amy, then Olivia, then back on Amy. Olivia saw his gaze drop briefly to Amy's chest and bounce back up again.

'Snakebite and black,' said Amy, grinning. 'Coke for Olivia, she's driving.'

'Decided to come, then?' Chris called as he went to grab a pint glass.

'Seems we're the last in college to know about this place. We're obviously not cool enough!' Amy shouted back, just as the singer finished her set. Her words rang out and a man-boy with long greasy hair at the bar snickered, but she appeared not to notice. 'I didn't know you worked here, I thought you said you were performing tonight?' She pointed to the empty stage, where the crowd had begun moving back towards the bar.

'I am.' Chris splashed blackcurrant into the top of Amy's pint and placed it in front of her. 'We are – me and Paul – a bit later.'

'Where is he?'

Chris laughed. 'There.'

Paul loped out of the crowd towards them. He'd tied his hair back and a sheen of sweat smudged the kohl around his eyes. Something in his face changed when he caught sight of them, and his black lips twitched briefly into a smile.

'You came,' he said, staring at Olivia.

She didn't respond. God, he thought she'd come tonight because he'd asked her, how *embarrassing*.

'I was just asking Chris about your band. Who sings?' Amy said, glancing between them.

'Me usually, but Paul sings a bit too.' Chris filled a glass with Coke. 'He plays the keyboard. I play the guitar.'

'Is it your own music?'

'Nah, just covers, but it's a laugh.' He placed Olivia's drink in front of her. 'Is that all?'

Olivia fumbled in her bag for her purse. Was she supposed to ask them if they wanted a drink too? She got out a note. 'Do you guys want a drink?' she muttered.

'Not for me, thanks,' said Chris. 'Paul will, won't you, mate?' He grinned.

Paul shook his head and fished into his pocket. 'No, it's OK, I'll get my own.'

Olivia pinked. 'I can buy you a drink . . . I have enough money.' She pushed the note towards Chris.

'Oh my God, this snakebite drink's a pint,' said Amy, suddenly noticing the glass in front of her. 'I'll never drink all that!'

Chris dropped Olivia's change into her hand and leant on the bar so his eyes were level with Amy's. 'Can't your little frame handle all that booze?' Sarcasm laced his voice but the amused curl in his mouth said something else. Icy fingers crawled up Olivia's spine.

'Hey, there's nothing wrong with being small,' Amy retorted, grinning.

He laughed and straightened up. 'Nope, there's nothing wrong with being small at all.' And he walked away to serve another customer.

The three of them were silent and Olivia watched Amy's eyes flit around the bar, coming to rest on Chris, once, twice, three times, like a butterfly selecting the best nectar. Was Chris Amy's type? She didn't think so, but who *was* Amy's type? She'd gone out with a guy in the summer term last year, she'd muttered one day when they'd passed him in the corridor at college, which was more than Olivia had done, but he'd looked pretty nondescript.

'I need the loo,' Amy said abruptly, sliding off the stool.

Olivia was about to follow, but Amy was already pushing through the crowd, greeting people she knew and then disappearing into the throng. She sensed Paul's eyes on her again and felt a mixture of irritation and embarrassment.

'Enjoying the music?'

'I've only heard one song,' she replied crisply.

'You look great.' His eyes focused on a spot behind the bar. 'I like your top.'

Olivia crossed her arms and shifted her weight on to the other foot, conscious she stood taller than Paul tonight in her heeled boots. She looked over to the bar again. Chris was on the far side talking to a customer, then Amy appeared and his face creased into a smile. He said something that made her throw her head back and laugh, then someone shouted for him to serve and he moved away again.

'Chris and I are playing next,' said Paul.

Olivia sipped her Coke and wished Amy would come back. She was so much better at small talk. 'So . . . you play the keyboard?'

'Yeah. We've been jamming together since we were about twelve. We write songs too, but . . . well . . . we're not ready to share them with the world just yet.'

Olivia nodded and noticed Amy had slipped behind the bar and was leaning against the wall next to the optics. She was having some sort of animated conversation with Chris, her hands chopping the air around her, while he nodded and poured measures.

The crowd at the bar began to close in around Olivia and Paul, and someone jostled against her. She teetered for a moment and Paul grasped her arm. 'You look amazing,' he whispered. This time his eyes searched hers out, the blue of his irises clear and sharp within the monochrome make-up. But before she could pull away, he let go. 'Got to get sorted for our set,' he said. 'Come and stand at the front?'

Olivia nodded. Then, just as he was about to get sucked back into the crowd, she reached out and tugged his arm. 'You need to fix your make-up.'

Paul's fingers grazed his cheek and he smiled. 'Thanks.'

Soon, the girls were standing by the stage and the audience surged around them, infusing the air with energy and anticipation.

'Good chat with Paul?' said Amy, nudging Olivia. 'Did he love your boots?'

Olivia shook her head. 'Relax, I don't fancy him.'

'Chris thought your boots were incredible.' She gulped back the last of her pint. 'Actually, I was a bit jealous.'

Pleasure rippled through Olivia and she stood a little straighter. *He noticed.*

'I'm just going to stick this on the bar.' Amy disappeared into the crowd with her empty glass just as the lights dimmed. Chris and Paul ran on to the stage and plunged headlong into a Nirvana song and the crowd roared in recognition, throwing themselves around to the beat, forcing Olivia to join their rhythm or be pushed to the floor. Adrenaline surged through her veins, and she grinned as she watched Chris fling himself around with his guitar, Paul pounding the keyboard.

'Good evening, everyone,' Chris announced as the song came to a close. 'Now for something different. This is one of our own.'

The crowd stilled and Olivia looked around, wondering where Amy had got to. Chris began plucking the strings of his guitar, the notes linking together, intensifying, and resonating with the rich tone of his voice. He looked up and caught Olivia watching and they locked eyes. She flushed and for a moment it was as though everyone else had faded away. He was singing the lyrics to her, they tingled every cell of her body, sending her into a spin of pleasure.

A poke in Olivia's side jolted her gaze away and Amy threw her a grin before looking back at the stage. Her face glowed in the light and Olivia saw that Chris's eyes were locked on Amy – *still* locked on Amy. She swallowed and pushed her way back through the crowd and out the door, letting the cold winter evening cool her burning cheeks.

Chapter 16

Amy

Now

'Promise me you'll give this a chance?' says Shannon. She's driving us towards the new port development where Grant thinks I should begin my next business venture. I'm a reluctant passenger but what other options do I have?

'Grant may be a lot of things,' she continues, 'but he knows a good business opportunity when he sees one.'

Outside the window, an army of grey industrial buildings line the highway. I catch glimpses of colourful shipping containers stacked up on the quayside and, beyond, the sun glitters on the water. It does nothing to raise my spirits. This part of the city has always seemed depressing to me.

'I haven't told Grant that Chris is Bea's dad,' says Shannon, swinging past traffic at a speed that probably isn't legal. 'You know Grant, he hasn't a curious bone in his body, so if I've told him Chris is your old school friend, then he's your old school friend.'

'Thanks,' I say, grateful for her loyalty, especially after the untruth I let Chris believe. I'm relieved we're straight on that now, but I wonder if Grant's already pieced everything together. Years ago, way before Shannon, when we were still married, he'd asked me if I was in touch with Bea's dad. I knew if he was going to be her father figure I owed him a proper explanation, except my shame still felt raw.

'He might have worked it out,' I say quietly. 'I've never mentioned Chris by name, but I told Grant I'd made a mistake with a boy I'd gone to school with.'

Shannon nods. 'I suppose so. He hasn't said anything to me, but then that's not his way.'

'Don't tell him,' I say urgently. 'I know I shouldn't make you hold stuff back from him. I just need . . . a bit more time.'

'Why? Chris seems like a really nice guy. Genuine, I reckon. I don't know why you're being so suspicious. He and Grant had a great time watching the rugby the other day – Grant's quite taken with him. Talk about chalk and cheese.' She laughs.

Shannon had asked Chris to join us that afternoon on the beach. He'd got stuck into the sandcastle-making and afterwards Grant had insisted he watch the game in a local sports bar with him. As well as rugby, they'd bonded over work, apparently. Grant can be a planning bore but then Chris is passionate about being an architect.

'You think so?' I reply, looking back out the window at the port. Shannon's right. Chris *has* been nothing but nice, friendly, warm, interested in everyone, and yet . . . something still niggles.

'God, anyone who plays with my kids is a winner in my book,' she says. We turn off the highway and head straight into the heart of the industrial zone, passing estates of identical bland concrete buildings. 'Grant said Chris has a daughter,' she says softly.

My heart jumps into my throat.

Bea has a half-sister?

130

I think back to the lines of sadness drawn across his face when I asked him if he had kids. 'He didn't say, why did he tell Grant and not me?' I murmur.

Shannon indicates left and pulls into a car park that's almost empty. 'I didn't know anything about it until this morning because Grant thought I already knew. He was very vague. You know what he's like, he didn't ask for any details.'

Shannon pulls up the hand brake and we look at each other.

'Bea's got a half-sister,' I whisper.

'What are you going to do? She'll be back in a couple of months. Will Chris even be here?'

'He said he was here for three months,' I say slowly.

'Bea's back in March, ay?' Her breath whistles out. 'They *might* not cross paths, but they could.'

When I think of Bea flying into my arms at the airport and imagine Chris surfacing alongside me, I don't see a happy ending. All I picture is her face folding into confusion, crumpling into tears when I confess and anger striking.

I can't do this to her. 'Perhaps it's a good thing.'

'She's got a half-sister, Amy!' Shannon's voice shrills. 'It's one thing burying your head in the sand for years because you thought Chris didn't care that he had a child, but now, well, it's a completely different story. Chris is right here. He never knew about Bea and now there's a sister out there for her. Neither of them have had a chance to love Bea. You can't keep on lying to yourself.'

I'm stunned for a moment and then my fighting instinct kicks in. 'I'm not lying!'

Shannon's eyes are like lasers. 'Aren't you?'

'No, Chris has never asked me who Bea's dad is, so I've never lied.'

We get out of the car in silence and I look around at the tall grey buildings that square off the car park. I'm struggling to see how my café could thrive in this dismal place; how I could entice customers to come here. I don't know what Grant's thinking.

Shannon's still looking at me and I know she hasn't finished. 'You're not thinking about Bea, you're thinking about yourself.'

My heart stings. *Am I?*

'How can you say that? I've *always* put Bea first, *always*. Why do you think I've come here? This dull, lifeless place . . .' I throw my arms wide. 'I'm not stupid, I know I have to move. I know I've got to *do* something otherwise Bea and I are going to be homeless and I'll be skint and she won't be able to go to university.'

Shannon sighs, her frustration disappearing as fast as it came. 'I'm sorry, I shouldn't have said that, of course you do. I'm just imagining how different Reuben and Kira's life would be without their daddy.'

'That's not fair,' I say, quieter this time. 'I didn't have a choice.'

Shannon places her hands on my shoulders. 'No, but you have a choice *now*. You can put things right.'

We stare at each other. She's right, she's *nearly* always right, but that doesn't mean I'll give her the satisfaction of knowing it. A smile smooths her face and she tucks her arm through mine. 'Come on, let's not talk about this now, let's see what Grant has in mind.'

I groan. 'Really? Which monstrous building is it? Why the hell would anyone want to come to a café here?'

She marches me towards a pair of steel doors and pushes hard to open them. The foyer is deserted, and she clatters up a metal staircase while I trail behind her. As I approach, I hear her talking quietly to someone on the landing above, but I can't see who it is. I round the corner and see Mum standing outside a frosted-glass door. She's wearing her work uniform, a pencil skirt and jacket, and suddenly I know what's going on. This is one of Mum's commercial properties and she's trying to flog it to *me*.

'Hello, Amy.'

My hackles rise but before I can say anything, Shannon begins to gabble. 'It's a great place, Amy. I know outside looks a little . . . soulless' – she shoots Mum a look – '. . . but when you come in and see—'

'Come and see, the view is fantastic.' Mum's best saleslady smile cracks her mask. Am I the only one who notices it never quite reaches her eyes? That she pastes on this expression when she's trying to win people over?

'I'm not coming in.' I sound like a teenager and hug myself with my arms. I *look* like a teenager.

Shannon darts to my side and loops her arm through mine. 'Please?'

Mum's smile strains. 'You may as well come inside, you're here now.'

I feel the weight of my responsibilities and the options I don't have. Mum senses a splintering in my stubbornness and flourishes the keys, and I let Shannon nudge me inside. Then I'm being hustled through an empty office space and up another flight of stairs into another empty room, smaller this time, but encased in a huge wall of glass.

'Far out,' breathes Shannon.

I feel as though I'm flying above the harbour.

Mum springs into life. 'This will be perfect,' she states, as though it's a done deal. 'The whole building is already rented out and the other two are nearly at full capacity. They're small businesses but there are ten companies in each building and between ten and thirty employees per company. You'll have no trouble finding customers, there's nowhere else for people to go.' Sales pitch over, she hands me the keys. 'Take your time,' she says, and disappears out of the room.

I spin around. 'What? That's it? Her spiel is over and she's gone?'

'She doesn't want to pressurise you,' Shannon says.

I can't be bothered to argue the point and look back at the view instead. The back of the building is angled away from the port, so you see the harbour rather than shipping containers and huge fishing trawlers. There's a glorious view of North Head on the North Shore and, to the right, distant views of Waiheke Island.

I imagine how many tables I could fit into the space and where I could put a serving counter. Could it work? I'm not sure. There's more to consider than the view. 'I need to think about this.'

'Chris likes it,' Shannon says, sneaking me a glance.

'What?'

She shrugs. 'Grant showed him the photos.'

'When?'

'Oh, I don't know, I think they bumped into each other at a meeting.'

'What's it got to do with Chris?' I'm a little indignant.

'Grant thought he'd be interested from a design point of view and, you know, you and Chris are *old friends* and all that.' She smirks. 'He didn't mean any harm. I think he thinks Chris might be able to persuade you to agree.'

I huff. 'I don't know why he'd think that.'

'Chris actually seemed genuinely interested. Quite excited for you, Grant said.'

I eye her suspiciously. 'And?'

A grin creeps across her face. 'He's quite a catch, ay?'

We look at each other, then I'm shaking my head and we're laughing and I think, yes, he's still good-looking, and he's been nice, and what's really stopping me from telling him about Bea?

Later that evening, I'm back in the Boat Shed kitchen, about to make flapjacks, when my eye catches the framed newspaper article hanging on the wall. A line jumps out, the one that remarks on my café being *in desperate need of a facelift*. I'd always meant to make plans to improve the building but now it's too late. It won't be long before this place is flattened to the ground.

I think about the glass room and the views I saw today as I pull together the ingredients. Then I flip back to when we first arrived in New Zealand, when Grant's parents, John and Linda, still ran the Boat Shed, and made tiny baby Bea and I feel so welcome. Dad encouraged me to come here every day. He knew I needed the company while he and Mum worked – and I didn't know what else to do. I'm sure he'd have spent all his time with us if he could, but he'd promised Mum he'd build the real estate business with her. That was the deal, he said, otherwise she wouldn't have agreed to move to New Zealand.

But they didn't expect me to trail along.

Or Bea to arrive in their lives.

Nor Dad to have a heart attack.

I pour oats into a bowl and dip a warmed tablespoon into the syrup jar so the liquid slides off. Flapjacks were Dad's favourite bakes, though I can't take the credit for this recipe as it's Linda's – with a few adaptations of my own. I sprinkle in grated coconut and a teaspoon of cinnamon.

I wonder what might have become of me if my parents hadn't bought their house on the beach just along from here. If John and Linda hadn't owned the café back then. If I'd never met Grant. If we'd never married. The business had been like a wedding present, I suppose, although my in-laws had never said it in so many words.

What might have become of me and Bea if Chris had received my letter?

I press the oat mixture into the tin and slide it in the oven. Dad would have been pleased with their gift. Though I'm not sure what he would have thought about my marriage to Grant. Dad liked him well enough, he was pleased I'd found someone to date so I could be me again for a while and not just a mum.

Getting married hadn't been the plan. Dad's death crucified me. Mum retreated. Grant became my rock. I'd congratulated myself on picking a husband who was my friend, and I forced all memories of the fizzing excitement I'd felt with Chris aside with the realisation he wasn't ever coming for us.

A tap on the café door breaks my thoughts and I pop my head out of the kitchen to see Chris standing on the terrace.

He's handsome.

Shannon's words jump into my thoughts and I feel strangely flustered as I walk towards him and see his face break into a grin.

'I've brought picnic tea,' he says holding up a bag as I open the door.

I smile, surprised, but disappearing into the evening with him feels . . . *like a date?* I point to my apron, the one decorated with Bea's tiny handprints. 'That's very kind, but I'm baking . . . I've got to tidy up . . . get ready for tomorrow.'

'That won't take all night, will it?' he insists. 'What've you made? Smells lovely.' He's already closing the door behind him before I've had a chance to respond.

'Flapjacks,' I reply, briefly wondering whether Dad would encourage me to let Chris back into my life – for the sake of Bea, for *his* daughter, if nothing else.

'Can I help? To speed things along? It's a lovely evening. Too nice to be slaving in the kitchen.'

Chris's mouth tilts and I find myself beckoning him to follow me. He leans back against the counter, chatting about his day and asking about mine, watching while I tidy the ingredients away.

When I pull out a stool to reach the high shelves, I wave away his offer of help, then fill the sink to wash up. He asks for a tea towel, and we stand side by side in silence for a while with the fluorescent strip light humming above us.

A shared chore.

Would this have been our normal life these last nineteen years, if he *had* received my letter?

Chapter 17

AMY

Now

We're sitting on a picnic blanket at the top of North Head, another magical viewpoint in this City of Sails. We've finished eating Chris's simple picnic of crusty brown rolls with local ewes' cheese, washed down with a rosé from a vineyard on Waiheke Island. It's as if *he's* the local and *I'm* the tourist – and I'm strangely flattered by his efforts.

'*Amy Curtis, Auckland's best baker*, no question,' Chris mumbles through a mouthful of flapjack, quoting the newspaper article.

'Such a charmer,' I respond drily, but I'm smiling.

'Always,' he says with a wink. 'But seriously, sweet but not sickly, crumbly not concrete, these flapjacks are amazing.'

I'm about to say this is Linda's recipe, adapted with ingredients from a long-ago recipe I wrote in my baking bible when we were in sixth form. But I'm not sure if this conversation is going to lead me somewhere I don't yet feel ready to go.

Chris looks as though he's going to say something else, but then fiddles in his bag and pulls out a camera tripod.

The mount where we sit is another of Auckland's dormant volcanoes that rise up from the corner of the North Shore peninsula. If I stand and rotate, I'll see Bea's island family out at sea, the long road wriggling back to where we've just come, the bridge, and the city centre across the harbour. My eyes pick out the boxy new development in the port and the expansive glass in the building where I'd stood earlier today looking over to where we are now. The words are on my lips to ask Chris his opinion, but Grant's already done that for me and anyway, he doesn't need to hear anything more about my troubles.

Chris fixes the camera into place and points it towards Bea's island family.

The irony doesn't escape me.

'Have you always run the café? Did you ever give teaching a go?' He takes a lens out of his bag and twists it into place.

I hug my knees to my chest and look down at the blanket as I consider how I can answer this question. The fabric is a classic red tartan and one I've had since Bea was small. The stitching is coming away along one of the edges and I pick at the loose threads. 'No, I never became a teacher,' I reply carefully.

'Jeez, how did you persuade your mum that you didn't want to go to university?' He laughs. 'Has she improved with age? How are your parents?'

Of course. He doesn't know Dad has gone.

'What do you think?' I say, making my voice sound light. 'Mum's still a pain. She's still meddling in my life. She still works all the time.'

'I thought she'd have retired by now. I remember she seemed so old compared to my mum.' He smiles. 'Or perhaps we were we just very young.'

Silence falls and I wonder if memories snag his mind like they do mine.

'She's in her early seventies,' I say. 'I keep telling her to retire . . . I mean, what's the point in working all the time and never relaxing? Look at where we live.' I throw my arm wide. 'We're so lucky but Auckland's wasted on her, she never goes anywhere.'

'Didn't they have a furniture shop before? Is that what they do here?' he says, rotating the lens.

'No, she owns a commercial real estate firm in the city.'

Chris falls silent for a moment. 'Really? Which one?'

'Very unimaginative – City Real Estate,' I say, getting to my feet. 'Can I have a look?' He moves aside and I see he's framed the three spiky silhouettes, now darkening against the golden sky.

Daddy, Mummy and Bea.

I have to tell him.

It makes me wonder again about Chris's daughter. He's said nothing and it feels too personal to probe because he'd have told me if he'd wanted me to know. And anyway, if I start asking too many questions, won't that encourage him to ask me about Bea?

A flock of seagulls appear above us, cawing and twirling as they eye the remains of our picnic. I step away from the camera and busy myself with tidying up before they plunge down and have a feast of their own.

'Do they live near you?' Chris says, back behind the camera again.

For a moment, I forget what we're talking about. 'Mum does – too near.' I laugh, but it sounds strained.

'Just your mum?' He turns around. 'They're divorced? I'm sorry to hear that.'

Goose pimples prickle my arms. I cram the last of the rubbish into the bag. 'No, it isn't like that,' I say, my gaze falling on the island family as I realise I've not had to say these words out loud for a long time. 'Dad died.'

◆ ◆ ◆

Bea was one when Dad had a fatal heart attack. Sometimes a song, a smell, or a glimpse of something familiar in someone catches me and his death feels like it happened just yesterday. Mum found him. Dead in bed. There was no spectacular chest-clutching, no dramatic collapse in the street, no slumping on to his desk in the office, incidents that might have given someone – anyone – time to administer first aid or call an ambulance. He slipped away in the night. Breathing one minute. Grey and cold the next. Like someone blew out his flame.

Later, Mum said he'd been feeling tired, said he had indigestion, and I'd shouted at her for working him too hard, for not telling him to take some time off, for not forcing him to see a doctor, *for not doing anything.*

I find myself telling Chris the story. Except I'm not actually telling him, he just happens to be a person sitting next to me, listening to my words spill into the warm air. He says nothing and I'm grateful – platitudes ring empty. At some point I pause, then I feel the warmth of his hand on mine as if he's urging me to carry on. But I can't say anything further because that'd mean saying I saw Dad lifeless in his bed too. Because I still lived with my parents. Because we couldn't afford to live on our own. Because I had a baby to care for.

Dad, Bea and me. We were a close-knit trio.

Dad always came home from work in time to cook tea for us and that last evening together was no different. He loved being part of Bea's journey of food discovery. He experimented with different flavours and textures, laughing when she made a face, and laughing even harder when her eyes caught his and her little mouth opened like a bird for more. Back then, Mum's modern palace hadn't been

141

built. Our home was Dad's cosy bungalow that he was lovingly putting back together.

The evening before Dad died, I'd been walking on the beach with Bea snuggled and dozing in a papoose strapped to my front. A gust caught the air and whirled sand around us so I draped a muslin over her sleeping head and turned back towards home. At the gate, the wind had wedged sand underneath and I struggled to push it open. Bea woke and pulled the muslin from her head, laughing, and we played a game of peekaboo. I remember feeling happy; perhaps I'd accepted Chris wasn't coming for us.

The wind funnelled us through the back door into the narrow galley kitchen. Dad stood at the stove and came forward to kiss Bea on the head and me on the cheek.

'Ready to eat?' he'd said.

Dad had already laid the table in the dining room for the three of us and I slid Bea into her highchair. He placed Bea's bowl in front of her before I'd had a chance to fix her bib. Her hand darted out and she stuffed a handful of spaghetti into her mouth. Pieces of pasta and brown sauce flicked on to her new red cardigan and she banged her hand on the tray in pleasure.

I frowned and Dad laughed. 'Use your spoon.'

Giggling, Bea threw another handful towards her mouth. Dad grinned and pushed a spoon into her hand.

'Stop laughing,' I snapped, getting a cloth. 'She thinks it's a game.'

I pulled her bowl away and she whimpered as I briskly wiped her hands and face. I was never going to be able to get the stains out of her cardigan and this was one of the better ones I'd found in a sale. I tugged on her bib, glaring at Dad, who just smiled, and made faces at Bea to distract her until she could dive back into her tea.

The rest of the evening followed like every other. Dad bathed Bea and read her a story, and Mum returned home from work just in time to say goodnight.

Sometimes I pick over the details of that evening to see if there were any signs. Did he complain of chest pain? Of feeling dizzy? Surely I'd remember? Dad wasn't young, he worked full-time, he helped me every single evening.

I drove him into the ground, not Mum.

Chris and I sit quietly staring out across the ocean. I don't speak again until the tightness in my chest loosens and my memories fall back to where they belong.

'Have you seen the row of houses with gardens that back on to the beach, near my café?' I say eventually. 'They were all bungalows at one time – there's still a few original ones left – Mum flattened theirs and built the big white box in its place.'

Chris glances at me. 'Really? The one that cascades down the hill?'

I crack a smile. 'Cascades? Listen to you with your fancy architect-speak.'

'What a place to live,' he breathes. 'I envy the architect who was commissioned to design that.'

'Mum said he was the best in Auckland.'

He laughs. 'No surprise there. Only the best for your mum.'

Ordinarily, I might have bristled at someone criticising her – whatever disparaging thoughts I have of my own. But Chris . . . he was there, he remembers the tough times I had with her, that *we* had with her.

'What about your mum and dad? How are they?' I say hesitantly. Looking back, I don't remember much about them. They were at work during the day – except that one time. A snapshot of me hiding under Chris's duvet springs into my head and I bite my lip to hide my smile.

Chris looks at me. 'What?'

I shake my head, but a giggle begins to fizz out.

'What's funny? My parents?' His smile tells me he's not cross.

'Nothing! I was just remembering the first time I met them . . .' I let my sentence trail and then the penny drops.

He laughs loudly. 'Yeah, probably not the best way to meet my parents. Did we really think Dad wouldn't notice the big hump in my bed in the middle of the afternoon?'

'Less of the big!' I say, lightly knocking his arm.

We'd snuck out of college and disappeared back to his empty house. His parents had returned home unexpectedly and obviously heard us upstairs. His dad came up and rapped on the door but didn't bother waiting for an answer – I'd dived under the duvet.

Chris is still laughing. 'I pretended I'd just woken up, like that was believable. God, Dad gave me hell after you left – though only because I'd bunked off college.'

'Do you remember your mum calling up and asking what was going on?' I giggle again. 'I thought she was going to come in too. Talk about the walk of shame afterwards. Your dad gave me such an evil stare, he must have thought I was a right slut!'

Chris suddenly stops laughing and I feel my face turn crimson. I've repeated the word Mum hissed at me all those years ago when she discovered I was pregnant.

Chris places his hand over mine again. 'You were never a slut, Ames.'

Chapter 18

Olivia

Then

'Chris said they've got some new bands playing on Friday,' said Amy, pressing her finger into the last crumbs of lemon cake on the plate. She'd come up with another spectacular recipe after college and Olivia had struggled to pinpoint the magic ingredient, much to Amy's delight.

'Yeah, he said,' Olivia replied. See? It wasn't as if Chris *only* spoke to Amy, he talked to Olivia too. In art, she'd made sure *she* was in the seat next to him this time, although, rather annoyingly, Amy had sat on his other side. Still, it wasn't a bloody competition.

Was it?

'I reckon this is my favourite cake.' Olivia popped the last piece into her mouth. The lemon icing was the right side of sharp and the cake was light and moist because of the ground almonds. 'Do you think your mum will let you go again on Friday?'

Despite Olivia's childish running away incident, she'd gone on to enjoy the rest of the evening. Outside, the cold had slapped her back to reality. It was obvious as the evening went on that Chris was a massive flirt, he adored his audience, whether it was Olivia, Amy or the crowd that cheered them after the set finished.

Amy frowned. 'Don't see why not, you dropped me home on time.'

'What did she say when you came in?'

'Nothing, she'd gone to bed. Dad was dozing in the chair.'

'Do you think he noticed you were pissed?'

'I only had three pints!'

'You didn't stop talking all the way home.'

Amy smiled. 'What about you? Are your parents all right about you going out again so close to the mocks?'

Amy had assumed Olivia's obsession with revising was driven by her parents. Olivia hadn't said otherwise – not exactly lying – and anyway, often Amy talked so much, she didn't always listen and so she'd let her fill in the gaps.

'Oh God, they're not going to let you go, are they?'

Olivia let out a brittle laugh, because it was funny – who was going to stop her? 'Yeah, I'll be able to go, I'll just do double revision this week.' A truthful answer. She needed A grades.

Amy scanned her face. 'You don't really talk about your parents,' she said, frowning slightly. 'Not even to complain about them.'

Olivia floundered. Christ, how could she respond to that? *My dad's never home and my mum's a whore . . . an alcoholic.* Somehow, admitting her mum had a drinking problem seemed to suggest that whatever she did wasn't her fault. *Like fucking my dad's best mate.* She couldn't help it, she was drunk! She'd fix the 'problem'. Except it couldn't be fixed. Her mum's recoveries never lasted.

'Sorry!' Amy held up her hands. 'I'm being nosy again, aren't I? I get it, you messed up your exams so it's best to get your head down so you don't get any grief from them. And when you do that, they leave you alone and let you have a life, right?' She frowned again. 'Did you get kicked out of your last school?'

There were many, *many* times Olivia wished she had. To have stuck two fingers up at the bitches in class and walked away from their whispers about her mum, stirred into the school by their snotty mothers who'd fed them their poisonous gossip.

'No, I wanted to leave,' she admitted. 'I needed to start somewhere new.'

Amy was properly looking at her now. 'You said when I first met you that you moved house,' she began carefully. 'You said you *had* to move.'

Is that what Olivia had said? That she *had* to move? Amy had been listening all along. She looked down at her plate and stroked her hair. The urge to tell Amy about her mum, and what she'd seen, what her *dad* had seen, swelled up inside her. She opened her mouth, but nothing came out.

Amy's eyes rounded. 'Shit, sorry, Liv, I shouldn't have asked, I'm interrogating you.' She patted her arm awkwardly and took their empty plates to the sink, clattering them about in the water. Olivia grappled around for something to say to change the subject. She glanced around the kitchen – it looked like a food bomb had gone off – and instead got up and began to wipe up the sticky mess of sugar and flour strewn across the surfaces.

'You do want to come on Friday, don't you?' said Amy.

Olivia handed her the mixing bowl to wash. She thought so, but she didn't want to be stuck with Paul or spend the evening watching Amy and Chris flirt with one another – or anyone else they came into contact with. She could see now they hadn't really singled each other out, it was all in Olivia's head.

'Is that why you've made my favourite cake?' Olivia retorted. 'To butter me up so I'll drive? It's what you do when you're trying to cajole your mum into agreeing to something, isn't it?'

Amy spun around, her face pink. 'God, Liv, I don't *expect* you to drive me . . .'

Olivia thought her tone had sounded teasing. 'I was joking! Of *course* I'm coming and I don't mind taking you.'

Amy's face broke into a grin. 'Brilliant! It'll be fun and, anyway, I think Paul's keen for you to come.'

'Shut up!'

'Could be worse.'

Could be Chris.

Amy wandered back to the table, leaving the dirty dishes soaking in the soapy water. She picked up her red notebook and began humming along to a song on the radio as she scribbled something down.

Olivia stuck her hands in the water and began scrubbing the bowl, which reminded her of home. She glanced at the clock above the kitchen door. 'Hey, I've got to go,' she said. *Time to make Dad's dinner.* 'I've got English revision to do.'

'God, I wish I could be motivated like you. You'll easily pass the mocks.' Amy was still writing. 'Anyway, what *is* the time?'

'Five.'

'Shit, I'd better clear this up before Mum gets back and goes nuts.'

'I'll help.'

'No, don't worry, I know where it all goes.'

As Amy opened the front door to let Olivia out, a middle-aged woman with a blonde bob strode up the path towards them. Olivia recognised Amy's mum from the hall photo.

'You must be Olivia,' she announced, looking directly at her. 'I'm Susan, pleased to meet you – at last. Amy's talked a lot about you.'

Amy rolled her eyes.

'Are you off home? I guess it'd be too much to hope that you girls have been revising these last couple of hours?' She wiped her thumb across Amy's cheek to remove a trace of flour.

'Mum!' Amy swatted her hand away. 'Don't freak out. In fact, don't go in the kitchen or you *will* freak out. I'm just clearing up.'

'Are you revising tonight, Olivia? Amy tells me you're a diligent student. I hear you're encouraging her to put some effort in.' Her face softened into a smile.

Olivia eyed the cream blouse she wore with frills down the front, tucked into a pencil-thin navy skirt. A caricature slipped into Olivia's mind. *Poised and groomed like a poodle.* No, that wasn't right, she didn't have Amy's curly hair. *The proud stance and sleek tresses of an Afghan hound.* 'Yes, yes, lots of revision to get through,' she replied, with a slight squeak in her voice.

Amy grinned. 'Olivia's going to be a lawyer, aren't you? She's doing four A levels. She's mega clever.'

Olivia stared at Amy. Surely this conversation wasn't helping her? Then Amy mouthed 'Friday' behind her mum's back and mimicked a steering wheel.

'Er, yes, I'm off to revise. Amy is too. We're . . . we need to get ahead of ourselves because there's a Christmas gig at the pub on Friday we want to go to.'

Susan glanced at Amy. 'Is there now?'

She nodded vigorously.

'I'll be driving again, Mrs Curtis. I'll drop Amy back at eleven thirty, like before.' Olivia thought she sounded like a creep, but Susan didn't seem to notice.

'That's very kind. Your parents don't mind you going? Of course, you won't be drinking.'

'Oh God, *no*, Mum, Olivia doesn't drink, not at all, not ever.'

Olivia shook her head and began backing down the steps. 'I've got to go,' she said. 'See you tomorrow, Amy.'

In the car, Olivia glanced in the rear-view mirror just before she pulled away. Amy stood with her arm linked through her mum's and waved. Amy said she hated her mum, but clearly it wasn't to the depths that Olivia hated *her* mum. Her throat tightened. By the time she'd reached the end of the road, tears were running into themselves and she pulled over and banged her fist on the steering wheel. Why hadn't she listened to her dad that day?

It was her *fault he'd seen what he saw. She'd blown their family apart.*

Chapter 19

OLIVIA

Then

Later that week, Olivia found herself sitting alone on a bench in the college grounds. The clouds hung low and heavy with rain, and she pulled up her hood and took out a sketch pad. Amy was at home with a sore throat, so Olivia could savour the solitude of lunch break and spend a blissful hour scratching out caricatures with no interruptions. Just like she used to at her old school, except there she'd had to hide her sketch pad inside a magazine. It had only taken one person, that one time, to snatch the pad away and wave it around to a cacophony of jeers to make sure Olivia kept her work private.

Sixth form was different. You could be anonymous and no one gave a shit.

From the bench, Olivia had a direct view of the smoking area and contemplated wandering over to have a cigarette. But she thought she could see Paul under the oak tree – no Chris – and didn't want to give him any reason to think she was following him around.

'Livvy!' Her stomach flipped at the sound of Chris's voice behind her and she snapped her sketch pad closed. What would happen if she didn't respond? Would he call her name a second time? She opened the pad again, to a blank page, and began drawing long lines of something and nothing.

'Livvy?'

Olivia still didn't look up. Instead, she focused on the toecaps of Chris's Doc Martens boots just inches from her own. Slowly she slid her eyes upwards, taking in muscular thighs in tight jeans, swallowing at the sight of his crotch and leaping on to his leather jacket. Her eyes rested on the sweet curl of his mouth for a moment. He looked amused.

'You OK? Lost in your own world. How's it going?' Wind snatched at his hair and he tucked it unsuccessfully behind his ears.

Chris towered over her and Olivia felt . . . *protected*. No Amy. No Paul. They were in their own vacuum. She pushed the hood away and the cold bit into her flushed cheeks. 'Sorry, didn't hear a thing.'

'Jeez, it's cold, fancy going to the pub to warm up?'

Christ. Yes, yes!

'Sure.' She stuffed her sketch pad into her bag. 'Where – The Crown?'

'Yep, come on or we'll run out of time.'

Chris grabbed Olivia's hand and pulled her to her feet, flushing her body with happiness. They slipped easily into a conversation about their art A level coursework, with Chris asking most of the questions and laughing at some of the dry remarks Olivia made. She felt something inside of her unfold.

As they turned on to the high street, rain began to fall in thick drops and Olivia pulled out an umbrella.

'Let me under, I'm getting soaked.' Chris pressed himself close to her and she inhaled an intoxicating cocktail of citrus, leather and the unique scent of *him* that made her pulse race. They were a similar height, *she could just turn her head . . . her lips could graze his . . .* She wondered what he'd say if she looped her arm through his. It'd be natural, right? That's what friends did.

'Did you enjoy Friday?' he said. 'I mean, *really* enjoy it?'

His breath felt warm against her cheek. Olivia turned her head a fraction and her eyes fell on his lips again, that amused smile, what did it mean? She looked away, nodding. She'd loved the energy of the music and had really got into moshing with the crowd.

Careful, he's a flirt.

'I saw you getting stuck in on the dance floor! Hey, how about coming to Black Jacks on Friday? I'm not working and fancy going somewhere different. Do you know it? It's a club in town.'

Olivia's body tingled. *Was he asking her out?*

They'd reached the pub and a car sloshed past, sending an arc of muddy water in her direction. Chris pulled her away. 'Nearly got you,' he said, still holding her arm. 'What do you think? I mean, we could all go. You, me, Amy and Paul.'

You and me?

Amy and Paul.

Olivia fumbled to close her umbrella. *Christ. Play it cool.* 'I'll think about it,' she said.

'Great!' Chris pushed open the pub door and bounded over to a table near the bar. Paul was there with the rest of their college mates, all nursing pints. 'Did you get one in for me?' he said to no one in particular and plonked himself down on an empty stool.

A wedge of disappointment settled into Olivia's stomach.

'Here.' Paul pushed a fresh pint towards Chris and stood up. 'Can I get you a drink?' he said to Olivia.

She felt a flicker of gratitude and then one of the idiots at the table let out a soft wolf whistle and another one snickered. She spun away from their wolfish eyes and stalked over to the bar. *What on earth was she thinking? What was she doing here?*

'Coke, please,' she said to the girl serving.

'Here, let me,' said Paul and before she could protest, he paid.

Olivia pulled out her purse. 'I've got money,' she said stonily.

'It's a Coke, Olivia, don't sweat it.'

'You don't have to babysit me.' She yanked off her coat and stirred the ice in her drink with a straw. She didn't have to leave. She'd show them. She could enjoy a drink in the pub on her own.

'I'm not.' Paul glanced over his shoulder. 'Ignore them. They're puerile.'

She snorted. 'Why do you hang out with them, then?'

'They're all right really. They think they're being cool acting like that in front of a girl. They'd shit themselves if they ever had to speak to one.'

'And you don't? Shit yourself when you talk to me?'

He stared at her. Blue eyes all intense again. 'Do I look scared?'

Olivia smiled a little. 'No.'

'Did Chris tell you about Black Jacks on Friday? He said he was going to.' He took a swig from his pint. 'Fancy it? It's a big venue and they've got a good line-up.'

Chris *didn't* ask her out? Was Paul asking her out, then? Or did they both want her to go?

'What about Rock Night?'

Paul shrugged. 'We go to The Fox all the time and Chris has got the night off.'

Olivia stroked the side of her hair with the flat of her palm. She stroked it again. Amy might not be well enough. Her mum was bound to say no because driving into town wasn't the same as staying local. But Olivia could go on her own with them, couldn't she?

Chris ambled over with his pint. 'So, what do you think? Has Paul charmed you into coming? Black Jacks this Friday?'

154

He tugged a crumpled packet of cigarettes out of his denim shirt pocket. He offered them around, lit up and then blew a couple of smoke rings towards the ceiling. He looked questioningly at Olivia.

She turned back to her drink and let her hair slide over her face. 'I'm not sure.'

'How's Amy? I've not seen her for a couple of days. Is she ill?'

Olivia stiffened. She detected a thin and slightly strained tone in his voice. 'She's got a sore throat,' she muttered.

'Perhaps we should rearrange to the following Friday so Amy can come?' Chris glanced at Paul. 'I can swap shifts with someone.'

Olivia pushed her drink away and pulled her coat back on.

'Hey, where you going?' Chris said.

'Just remembered something.' She moved towards the door.

'See what Amy says?'

Olivia didn't reply and stepped back out into the drizzle, remembering too late that she'd forgotten her umbrella.

'Olivia.' Paul stood in the doorway holding it out to her.

She reached out to take it from him and felt the tips of his fingers graze hers. 'Thanks,' she said, and turned away.

Later that evening, Olivia lay on her bed with her eyes closed. The conversation with Chris earlier that day hummed around her. She wanted to lock in his voice when he'd called her name. Resurrect that heady scent of his. Feel his arm jostling with hers beneath the umbrella.

The jangle of the phone ringing next to her bed shook her thoughts aside. 'Hello?'

'How are you?' Amy's voice croaked down the line.

'Fine, but you sound awful.'

'Oh God, my throat is so sore, I can't talk for long. Tell me what I missed today. I've been waiting for you to call.'

Olivia imagined Amy sitting at the bottom of the stairs huddled in a pink fluffy dressing gown, the coiled cord stretched taut from where the phone was fixed to the wall. The day marched through her mind, but she couldn't think of anything or anyone except Chris.

'Nothing really,' she muttered.

'Give me something!' croaked Amy. 'I'm dying here.'

The line hummed in the silence. Amy usually led the conversation, bouncing from one subject to another, and Olivia scrabbled around for something interesting to say.

Chris.

She screwed up her eyes. 'I saw Chris today.'

'And? So what? You share art and English with him, big deal.'

'Yeah, well, we chatted . . . in the pub at lunchtime.' Olivia's mind whirred and her heart began to beat a bit faster. 'He asked me if I wanted to go to a gig with him. In town.'

The line hummed again.

'Oh, right, like a date?' Amy sounded flat.

'Not sure.' Olivia chewed the skin around her thumbnail.

'Who did you go to the pub with?'

Did Amy sound annoyed? It was hard to tell, but she shouldn't lie. 'Chris.'

'Right, well, listen, I do want to hear all about it, but I feel like shit. I'm going to bed.'

The phone clicked dead and Olivia dropped the receiver back in its cradle. She'd meant to tell Amy the whole truth, she really had.

Chapter 20

Amy

Now

Mum's expecting me for dinner. She phoned and summoned me earlier and *of course* she can't be refused – though a hopeful part of me still thinks she might want to apologise.

I'm already late. But I take my time to wipe away the last of the cake crumbs and coffee smears from the outside tables, then I stack the chairs.

Threads of dusk are beginning to weave through the sky above the ocean, deepening the clouds to purple. In Bea's world it's still lunchtime and I wonder where she's eating and if she's sitting safely out of the searing sun. An email from her appeared yesterday – another photo of her on another beach that could be anywhere – the one-liner said, Having a fabulous time! Xxxx.

Her messages have become shorter, more vague. Has something happened? Or is my imagination running wild? Is it time to listen to what everyone else is telling me and accept she's breaking away from me?

I wander back inside and reach for my bag. My eye catches the letter that arrived this morning, which I shoved on the shelf between the teacups and saucers. I don't want to read it again. I know the words by heart. The cold, hard facts echo exactly what Grant told me. The Boat Shed will soon be crushed to a pulp and replaced with something shiny and new. I flick off the light switch and leave.

Outside, the terrace is empty, so when Chris materialises from the shadows I stifle a shriek. 'God, what are you *doing*, creeping up on me like that?' I'm laughing, my hand on my chest feeling the hammer of surprise and delight.

'Sorry.' He grins. 'I meant to come earlier, see if you wanted to go for a swim, but I got held up at work.' He clocks my bag. 'Where you off to?'

I make a face. 'Mum's, she's *invited* me to dinner.'

He raises an eyebrow. 'She doesn't usually have you over?'

'Hardly,' I mutter. 'Walk with me?' He nods and we fall into step as we cross the sand. Gentle waves ripple the sea and the breeze is a welcome balm. I know I'd much rather feel the cool water washing over my skin as I swim than manage a strained evening with Mum.

I give Chris a sideways glance. A snap image of us in the water together tingles my senses and his mouth twitches. 'Looks too good, doesn't it? Got time for a dip?'

'Are you a mind reader?' I laugh. 'No, I can't, I'm late.'

'All the more reason, your mum's already annoyed, what difference will it make?' His mouth curves in amusement.

Is he flirting with me?

I glance down at my shorts and T-shirt – I had no intention of dressing up for Mum. 'I haven't got my togs.'

'What's wrong with skinny dipping?' Chris's eyes dance over mine and in a flash I'm trying to remember what underwear I put on this morning.

I can't believe I'm even *considering* this.

In a snap, I've unzipped my shorts and whipped off my T-shirt, leaving him gaping and me laughing as I run down to the sea. He's quick behind me and I realise he's been wearing board shorts all along. 'Cheat!' I cry, moving into the deeper water to cover myself.

We paddle about and I try not to notice his bare chest – clearly, good genes and sport have been his friends over the years. His playful grin stays steadily focused on me and begins to unspool something familiar, and unfamiliar, so I duck beneath the water to block out the feeling.

When I resurface, Chris has gone and for a moment I'm confused. Then I jerk as his hands suddenly grip my thighs, propelling me upwards, making me shriek as I fly out of the water and sink under again. I bob back up, laughter tearing at my chest, salty seawater and giggles bubbling out of my mouth and nose.

'Sorry,' he says, holding his hands out, grinning, not sorry at all.

I slap water at him. He does the same and then we're circling one another, laughing, me diving out of his reach as he jumps forward to catch my legs again. It's stupid, it's fun – what is this?

'I better go,' I say eventually, catching sight of the lights glowing on Mum's terrace. 'Mum's going to be furious.'

Chris smiles. 'Nothing changes.'

We wade back out of the water and back to where we left our bags, and Chris offers me his towel. I'm suddenly conscious of standing in front of him in damp underwear but he's averting his eyes and I drag mine away from his body, rubbing myself down and quickly dressing.

'Your mum's going to wonder what you've been up to,' he says with a half-smile, glancing at the damp patches around my boobs and crotch.

A shiver skates my skin that's nothing to do with the air temperature.

'You're not going to tell her you were with me, are you?' Chris's face has become serious and I feel the mood shift.

I shrug. 'Probably not. Look, I better go, give me a call?'

He nods and I feel his eyes on me as I make my way up to Mum's gate. I give him a wave before I disappear up the path, and as I come close I see the outside table's laid and she's waiting at the door.

'You're late,' she announces and disappears. Like last time I came, she returns with a robe, which I take but don't want. 'You got distracted.'

I flush. I wonder if she was watching Chris and me in the sea, but she doesn't comment, which in Mum's world probably means that she did.

'The fish is overdone,' she declares. I follow her into the kitchen and slide on to a bar stool while she pulls a tray out of the oven. She slices open two foil parcels, releasing a buttery garlic smell. Red snapper. Dad's favourite.

'How was your day?' I say, coiling my damp hair up into a scruffy bun.

'Busy enough.' Mum scrutinises my face. 'You're working too hard, you look exhausted.'

I'm tempted to mutter something about the pot calling the kettle black but I'm tired of this repetitive tirade and I don't have the energy for a fight.

Mum pours us both a glass of wine. From inside my bag, my phone bleeps and I scrabble for it, hoping the message is from Bea. Chris's name flashes on the screen and I glance at his text. He tells me he forgot to ask, did I want to go to a gig on Friday night? My stomach jitters. *A date? Like something we'd have done together back in sixth form.* I'm not sure, I need to think. I drop the phone back into my bag.

'Was that Bea?' Mum asks, opening a drawer and taking out plates.

I shake my head. She doesn't need to know I've been spending time with Chris – not yet, anyway.

'Have you told Bea that Chris is here?' she says. Her voice has an edge to it.

'No, why would I do that? An email isn't really the best way for me to tell my daughter there was a fuck-up years ago, that her nana intercepted the letter I wrote to her father to tell him she existed, but he never knew and oh, by the way, he's here right now and might like to meet her.'

My sarcasm hangs thickly between us but Mum carries on moving around the kitchen, loading dirty dishes into the dishwasher and wiping the surfaces as if I've not spoken.

'The fish is getting cold,' I say pointedly.

'It would change everything,' she says eventually, watching me closely.

I look over towards the door I've just walked through, and back along the path lined with whispering bamboo. I imagine myself running across the sand, plunging into the sea and pounding through the waves until I reach my Bea.

I don't want Bea to change. I want Bea to stay *my* Bea.

I carry our plates out to the terrace and Mum brings the wine in a bucket filled with ice. The outside light is bright but the blind darkness that surrounds us makes me feel like we're actors, centre stage.

'How is business in the café? Thriving, I would imagine.' She glances at me, presumably eyeing my *haggard* face again as though this marks my inability to cope. I know her question isn't really a question because she isn't interested in my answer – I figured that out a long time ago. My usual response is vague because it's just easier that way but, this evening, her question reminds me of all I'm about to lose.

'What does it matter? The Boat Shed's being taken away from me.' I shovel a forkful of fish into my mouth. I chew and chew, but my throat tightens and I can't swallow. I force down a gulp of wine and it burns my throat.

Mum dabs a napkin to her lips and appraises me. 'That's not strictly true, is it? You know you can recreate the café somewhere else.'

A moth buzzes hopefully against the light bulb and I hear the waves thundering on to the shore. A horrible thought suddenly occurs to me. 'You knew the development was going to happen ages ago, didn't you? Before you brainwashed Shannon into showing me . . . that awful *box* at the port, and you didn't think to tell me?'

'Of course I knew,' she replies crisply.

I'm angry she can still make me feel so disappointed. Then something else clicks. I'm so, *so* stupid. 'You're selling the Boat Shed building for the owners, aren't you?' I whisper. 'You're going to profit from my loss!'

'Don't be dramatic. There've been rumours about a new development on the site for years. But this is the first time it's come to anything concrete. The sellers mean business this time, Amy. They've got planning consent for the building to be demolished and replaced.'

My knife and fork clatter to my plate. 'How could you know this and not tell me? How could you even be *involved*? Have you forgotten? This is my business! My home!'

Mum sighs. 'Amy, I *am* telling you, that's why I asked you to come here tonight.' She spears a piece of lettuce. 'There was nothing to be gained from telling you until we knew the full facts.'

'We? Who's we?'

I'm taken aback when Mum flushes, her usual composure fractured for a moment. Her mouth works the salad; her dark eyes focus on a spot somewhere to the left of my head, then they snap back to me.

'What I'm saying, Amy, is you can't give up just because you don't like change. The development includes a design for a new café. You need to put together a proper business proposal so you're ready to approach the new owners when they come on board – before anyone else does.' She pauses. 'If you need help, you only need to ask.'

Her offer sounds like veiled criticism and if I accept, she'll only point out more of my failings. I drain my glass and the surge of alcohol propels words out of my mouth before I know it. 'I've been spending quite a lot of time with Chris. I was late tonight because I was with him.'

Mum's fork pauses on the way to her mouth. The teenager in me inwardly delights as her lips snap closed into a thin line.

'We had a *really* good time,' I press, watching her closely. Her fork starts moving again, scraping the plate. 'It's been *really* good catching up.'

Finally, she looks at me. 'There's something else I wanted to talk to you about tonight,' she says.

It's as if I'd never spoken. Fury gathers inside of me and I slosh the last of the wine into my glass until it reaches the top. 'Go on then,' I say, taking a swig and swallowing. 'Say it.'

'I've seen Chris too.' She fixes me with another of her unreadable stares.

I gasp. I don't understand.

'There's no easy way of saying this, Amy. He came to the office. He works for the architect practice who've drawn up the plans for the new development.'

Blood pounds in my ears and my mouth goes dry. I grapple back to the conversations I've had with Chris – on our picnic, just now on the beach. It makes no sense, she's meddling again. Didn't she do enough of that nineteen years ago?

'He's a different character these days,' she muses. 'I'd never have imagined he'd become an architect. He's a talented man, he knows what he's doing.'

'I don't believe you,' I retort. 'He would've told me.'

Her eyes hook mine again. 'We'll sort this out, Amy,' she says briskly. 'Before Bea comes home. His secondment comes to an end just before she gets back, he'll be gone before we know it.'

Chapter 21

Amy

Now

I propel my arms through the water and a sharp knot pulls at the muscles between my shoulder blades. I should be at the café getting ready for the day. But when I stood on my roof terrace this morning, I thought about the string of potential buyers Mum paraded through my life this week, poking at the corners of everything I thought was mine, and the glassy shimmer of the sea beckoned.

Today is the day I take charge of my life. John and Linda will soon arrive at the Boat Shed to hold the fort while I take Shannon to see a café over on one of West Auckland's wild beaches. Apparently, it isn't much to look at – but then my café is nothing to look at either. I can't say I particularly love the volcanic black sand out west – in my opinion, the beaches don't have the glory of the golden sand here – but if I want the beach to remain my back garden, what choice do I have? The cost of property around the North Shore bays has spiralled in recent years, fuelled by the return of travelling Kiwis and overseas investors swamping the market with their American dollars and British pounds. And I think I've found one place I can actually afford.

I increase my stroke, snatching oxygen each time I turn my head, my lungs burning in protest. Perhaps it's a miracle the Boat Shed has remained mine for this long. I don't want to give it up, but everyone around me is giving up, telling me it's time to move on and start afresh. Nobody understands how much I love the worn wood of the kauri floorboards, indelibly marked with decades of feet, and the way shards of sunlight greet me through the cracks of the old window shutters every morning. I swear I smell baking, even when I'm not baking, permeating the walls, warming my heart – along with the customers who bring their smiles with them every day.

Then there's my flat to think of too. I can't imagine living anywhere else. Shannon thinks I'm mad to find charm in the peeling kitchen worktops and the salty sea air that seeps through the windows in winter. The gentle rock of my swing seat, those glorious views, where else could I be – me?

My arms begin to tire, and I slow. Once again, my mind drifts back to Mum's words, delivered clipped and curt a few evenings ago. I'm no longer stunned to discover she's the real estate agent for the owners – what did I expect? But to hear that Chris is involved in the new development? Fury has punctured my initial shock. How can I tell Bea now that Chris is her dad? What would I say? *Your dad's a liar. He can't be trusted.* I kick hard across the last stretch of water and reach the rocky outcrop where, not so long ago, the tide was low enough for Shannon and me to clamber over to the next bay.

I haul myself up on to a flattish section and think back to when I told Chris that Dad had died. That evening, a tiny piece of the old me – the me I'd carefully tucked away – unfurled a little and I started to feel . . . what? I don't know. A connection? No, too strong. A shared history, I suppose. Then our flirtatious play in the sea. Bloody childish. Was he secretly laughing at me? Naive Amy and her crappy café that's only fit to be bulldozed?

Before all this, Shannon said there was nothing to dislike about Chris, and for a moment, I was beginning to see what she meant. I went home that evening and stared at my photos of Bea and imagined how she might look standing next to Chris: two tall, slim figures; tousled heads; speaking in that careful, thoughtful way they do, shot with a sharp sense of humour. Bea would enjoy his company – like I have this last month.

But now?

I roll the stiffness from my shoulders. He should have told me he was working on the development. Quite clearly, Mum's wasted no time letting him know she's revealed his little secret. He's left voice messages and sent texts, but I don't really want to listen to what he has to say. I've more important things to sort out, like my livelihood, *my life*.

I stare back at the beach. A lone runner breaks into a sprint near the water's edge, narrowly missing being knocked over by an excitable dog. Further on, my towel is a red dot on the sand and I'm reminded of how far I've swum. I slide back into the water and feel encouraged by the light wind that nudges me gently along. And while I swim, I make a decision. I don't care about Chris's ambitions. I'm sure Shannon will agree we can make this other café work. It'll be a change, a big change, but isn't that what everyone's been telling me I need?

I head towards the shore and soon my feet touch sand. As Mum said, Chris will be gone before Bea gets back and everything can return to the way it was.

'You ready for us?' John bellows as he ambles into the café later with Linda. He pauses at one of the tables and launches into a conversation about fishing with a man he may or may not know, and absently pets his black Labrador. Linda swings into place behind the counter, still the pro, even though it's been years since they ran the Boat Shed. We greet each other with a warm hug and then I catch Mum coming through the door and frown. John draws her into his conversation and I clock her casual slacks and flat shoes.

'What's she doing here?' I say sharply to Linda.

'Your mum's offered to help,' she replies, pulling a floral apron from her bag and tying it around her waist.

This is one mystery I can't fathom: how Mum, Linda and John can be such great *buddies*. Being around John and Linda is like being wrapped in a warm, cuddly jumper, but Mum's company can only be compared to wearing a starched shirt you're fearful of creasing. I could just about stretch to understanding their friendship when Dad was alive because he'd buffer Mum's caustic remarks but, without him, I don't get it.

Linda's warm hand is on my arm and she leans in close. 'Let her help,' she murmurs. 'Don't make a fuss.'

Mum's laughter shrills out at something John says and I roll my eyes. She can be so fake. 'She's only here to nose around, to find reasons to help her sell the place,' I whisper furiously. 'I wouldn't put it past her to run the sales pitch by my customers.'

Linda locks eyes with me. 'Or she's here to help her daughter out.'

Mum walks over to the counter and we greet each other warily.

'We were just talking about the building out west, ay?' Linda says, nodding at me.

I don't want to tell Mum anything, but I can't ignore Linda.

'What's it like?' says Mum.

'I'm not exactly sure,' I say slowly. 'The realtor said the building's empty and has only just come on the market, but apparently it used to be a café.'

Mum nods. 'Sounds promising. Does it come with accommodation?'

'No,' I snap. 'I'll work it out.'

'Didn't you say there's a place nearby with sea views that's available to rent?' Linda interjects. 'You said it was cute and not expensive and perfect for you and Bea.' She turns to Mum. 'Amy's done her homework.'

Shannon's arrived and is outside on the terrace talking to a customer, so I disappear into the kitchen to grab my things. I hear John's bellowing laugh and Mum's trill again and push the doors open a crack to see what's going on. The three of them are gathered around the counter. Linda says something low I can't catch, and Mum flings her hand over her mouth to control another bout of laughter.

A hollow feeling grows in my stomach. I just don't get it.

'You ready?' Shannon calls.

I go back into the café and Linda smiles. 'Take your time, love, the three of us are happy to be here all day. Make sure you have a proper look round. It's a big decision.' She pulls me into another tight hug. 'It'll all work out,' she whispers.

Mum pats my arm as I pass and I feel her eyes follow me out the door. I'm still not convinced Linda's right about her wanting to help but I put this behind me. Soon, I'm driving Shannon and I out west, listening to her chatter about the dance class Kira has just begun. The suburbs begin to thin, then the road climbs and, for a moment, we're high enough to see the dense green forest of the Waitakere Range, with the sea a grey line in the distance. I realise how far this place is from where I know. But I remind myself this

169

is the point. I can afford to run a business here. I can afford to live here. It's a fresh start.

'It's quite a long way,' Shannon murmurs as the road dips down again. Dense bush thickens the edge of the roadside as we wind our way down through the forest to the beach, and in some places the trees are so tall they form a canopy above us.

I feel far from home.

'Have you phoned Chris back?' says Shannon.

'No,' I say, glancing at her, but she's looking out the window. 'Why would I?'

'I thought you might have calmed down by now,' she replies, a hint of mischief in her voice.

'He *lied* to me, Shannon. I'm not really interested in what he has to say.'

'Lied,' she murmurs. 'But *did* he lie to you?'

We've had a similar conversation before. Once Mum told me that Chris worked for the architect firm who'd drawn the design for the new development, my thoughts turned to Grant. Of course, because of his job, he knew too, and I was livid, but he'd quickly calmed me down as he'd assumed Chris had already told me.

I sense Shannon's sympathy slipping. 'It's like you want to find fault with him. I mean, did you specifically talk to him about losing the café and how you felt about it?'

'That's not the point though, is it?' I bristle. 'I wasn't about to whine on about my problems. He should've told me his firm were working on the development.'

'But what could he have said?' she muses. 'Perhaps he was as shocked as you when he discovered the project he was working on was your café and flat. All a bit awkward really.'

'He had loads of chances to say something . . . but didn't.' I'm angry, but I realise I don't really know what I wanted Chris to say.

'You sound . . . disappointed,' she ventures, shooting me a glance.

I keep my eyes on the road. 'Disappointed? In what?'

She's about to say something else when we emerge from the forest on to a stretch of road high above the beach. Below, a huge expanse of ocean churns over in great, white, foamy waves.

'Wow,' says Shannon. 'I haven't been here in ages. I'd forgotten how arresting it is.'

I pull over into a viewpoint and the wind yanks at the door as I get out. The roar of the sea and the elements clamour around us; salty spray stinging our faces and whipping our hair. We absorb the turbulent scene and watch kite surfers spring and dance across the waves. The stretch of black sand laid out below is like a different planet from home. I trace our route as it curves down the hill towards an enclave of old timber houses and a scattering of new, modern homes. At the end of the road, next to the beach, is my new café – I hope.

'I love it,' I say, drawing in a deep lungful of salty air. For the first time, I feel a sense of hope.

Shannon looks at me carefully. 'It's pretty spectacular.'

We climb back into the car and I drive slowly, scanning the houses as we pass. Most are simple bachs – seaside holiday houses rather than places lived in all year around, wood cladding rubbed raw by decades of harsh coastal weather.

The car park by the beach is almost empty except for a ute and a van with a dent in the door, and I guess we've arrived before the realtor. We wander on to the sand and I notice a derelict hut close to the rocks. It looks like it's seen better days and my heart sinks a little.

'Is that it?' says Shannon, nodding towards the hut.

I make a face. 'No, it can't be, it must be up there,' I say, pointing to another road that leads away from the beach.

A smart black car pulls in and soon the realtor is by our side and we're shaking hands. He looks young, too young to be doing this job, and his black raincoat flaps in the wind as he rattles off facts about the property. I'm standing with my back to the hut and slowly it dawns on me that this is the building he's talking about.

'Shall we go and look?' he says, walking towards it without waiting for an answer.

I exhale. I knew the building wasn't going to be shiny and new, but even from this far away I can see the structure is rotten. As we get closer, I notice the door is swollen with damp and the realtor hesitates when I ask to go inside.

'I'm not sure . . . this property is for sale to be demolished and replaced,' he says. 'I don't think it's safe enough to go inside, we don't have approval.'

Demolition. I seem to be sleepwalking through the same story. I can't afford to knock anything down and start again. But I haven't come all this way to give up, so I go to a window. A thick layer of salty grime coats the glass and I rub gently to peer inside. It's not huge, but bigger than I imagined. Shannon and the realtor are watching me.

'Can you give us a minute?' I say to him.

He nods and walks back towards his car, pulling his coat around him.

'What are you thinking?' Shannon says, sounding concerned.

'The price is good. I can afford to run a business here. I think we could really turn this around,' I say brightly. 'It's smaller than the Boat Shed but it wouldn't cost as much to repair. I could get a bank loan.'

Shannon nods but her lips form a straight line and I know she doesn't agree with me. I realise with a jolt that Chris would know what to do. He'd have the professional vision to strengthen my argument. 'It'd be a lot of hard work as we'd have to do most of the renovation work ourselves,' I say, warming to my theme. 'It'll mean not paying ourselves for a bit, but we could factor that into the loan. I wouldn't want to leave you short.'

Shannon is still quiet and looks back to where the realtor is sheltering inside his car. Other than the kite surfers, we haven't seen another soul since we arrived, but it's wild out here today. I'll need to be prepared that trade will be quiet when the weather's not so great.

'I like the solitude,' I say, throwing my arms wide and enjoying the sound of the sea roaring around us. 'And it's energetic! The change will be good for us.'

'Amy,' Shannon says finally. 'I can't do this.'

'Why? It wouldn't take that long. We'd be up and running before you knew it.'

'No, it isn't that.' She shakes her head. 'I can't work with you in the new café.'

I frown. 'Why not?'

'I'm pregnant.' She laughs, but her green eyes watch me, laced with anxiety. 'Grant and I have decided it's best if I take some time out until we get used to running around after three kids.'

'Wow . . . Congratulations . . .' I falter. 'The café will be too far away, won't it?' I feel myself start to gabble. 'What am I thinking? You couldn't work here and take the kids to school. Let's take Mum's café in the port. It makes much more sense. You could bring the baby to work! The customers will love it.'

Shannon presses her hand to mine; her fingers feel icy and damp. 'Amy, it won't work,' she says softly. '*You* need to decide where to set up your new café. I'll be here to support you, but it has to be your choice, not ours.'

I feel like I'm spinning back to where I started, and Shannon tucks her arm through mine and squeezes me close.

Chapter 22

AMY

Now

'I can't believe you're having another baby,' I say.

After a morning being blustered by the wind, in contrast Shannon and Grant's garden is bathed in sunshine, such is the fickle weather of this coastal city. I'm still reeling at their news. I thought Shannon might have let on, told me they were trying, perhaps. But, no, not a hint, not a whisper.

The three of us sit beneath a pergola, thickly weaved with grape vines, a strew of weekend papers on the table in front of us. Kira and Reuben chase each other around the paddling pool with water pistols, shrieking.

'I know, we're mad, huh?' Shannon grins at Grant. 'Three little munchkins, what were we thinking?' Grant looks up from the sports section and leans over to brush his lips across hers. He places his hand on the curve of her tummy and smiles gently. It's an intimate moment and ordinarily I wouldn't mind, they've always made me feel part of their family, but today his gesture pricks a little. Another baby. Three children.

Am I jealous?

I'm shocked the thought has even entered my head. I've never been jealous of them. I think of Bea miles and miles from me, forging her own path in life. My precious Bea. Life wasn't meant to turn out like this. It's not as though I've lived like a nun all these years and haven't tried to find that special someone, who I might have wanted to have a child with one day. But there came a point in every one of those relationships when they couldn't accept that Bea would *always* come first.

'I'm really, really pleased for you,' I say and, to prove my point, I get up and give them both another hug. 'Are you going to find out the sex this time?'

Grant darts Shannon a look. 'Well . . . I thought that'd be a good idea . . .'

'Nope, we're not!' She flicks his paper with her finger. 'It's lovely having a surprise. It's not like it makes a difference. Girl, boy, who cares?'

'It'd help me get the nursery ready,' he mutters.

'God, such a traditionalist! We'll paint it green or yellow, like we did for Kira and Reuben.'

'But then when Kira was born you made me decorate it pink,' Grant points out. 'I'm just saving myself the trouble of doing the same job twice.'

Shannon rolls her eyes and makes a tsk sound to close down the conversation. I laugh. We all know she'll get her own way. I look over at the kids and Kira catches my eye and runs up, pointing her water pistol at me. Her blonde hair sticks to her face and water drips down her yellow swimming togs. Her expression is defiant, and I'm reminded of Bea at that age.

My Bea will never be that age again.

Kira lowers the plastic gun. 'Are you sad, Amy?' she says, frowning. 'I miss Bea, do you?'

I press my mouth into a smile and push a wet tendril of hair behind her ear. 'Of course I miss her, but she'll be home very soon.' It's been three days since she last emailed. I've shoved my phone deep in my bag to stop myself checking for updates.

Satisfied, Kira runs off and sprays her brother. He responds by dumping a bucket of water over her head and she starts to cry. Shannon goes over and bundles Kira's wet body into her arms. 'Reuben, come on, be gentle, she's only little,' she calls, and rubs her briskly with a towel.

'You're going to be a big sister soon,' I say to Kira. She nods, her thumb wedged in her mouth.

Shannon looks concerned. 'I'm sorry to desert you, Amy, I know the timing isn't great. I was looking forward to getting stuck into a new business with you, but I promised myself if I got pregnant, I'd stop working and focus on the baby and the kids for a while. It's been a manic few years juggling, and I can't keep relying on John and Linda for help.'

Grant flips the paper down. 'Come on, Shannon, we talked about this,' he says, sounding exasperated. 'Amy can manage, she knows things are going to have to be different.'

I'm expecting Shannon to respond to Grant's outburst with a barbed comment, but instead she smiles and touches her tummy. 'I know, I know, it's just that being involved with a new business is an exciting time. Think of all the possibilities that come from starting over again!'

'Exciting?' I venture slowly. 'That's not how it felt this morning.'

'Forget that,' says Shannon, dismissing our disastrous visit with a wave of her hand. 'That hut sucked.' She laughs her big throaty laugh and the sound teases a smile out of me.

'Yeah, it was a dump,' I admit. 'But I'm sure *something* could be done, couldn't it? I just need some good advice on how to renovate the building and attract more customers.'

Shannon gives me a look and I know what she's thinking. 'No,' I say, holding up my hand. 'I'm not talking to Chris about it.'

'But . . .' She shakes her head. 'No, you're right, don't talk to him about it. It's beautiful out west, but you'd be going bush. It'd be as depressing as shit when the weather's crap. You'd never have any customers.'

She's only voicing what I already know but still the words sting a little.

'Where's next on your list?' she says brightly.

I sigh. 'I don't know, I'll have a look online tonight.'

'What about the place at the port?' Grant says, putting down the newspaper again.

Shannon nods vigorously. 'Yes, yes, the place at the port is perfect! You've got a customer base who'll be gagging to spend their money on breakfast and lunch and coffee and cakes. What's not to like?'

They both look at me expectantly and I suspect a conversation like this had gone on before I arrived. 'It's not right,' I say firmly. 'It's not me. I'll find somewhere.'

Kira wriggles out of Shannon's arms.

'Don't sit on it for too long,' Grant says. 'You might miss out.' He stands and stretches. 'Hey, I forgot to say, Chris is coming over later. We're going to watch the game this afternoon.'

Shannon and I look at him. *What?* Chris is the last person I want to see. Shannon doesn't look too pleased either.

'When did you two get so friendly?' I mutter, and go over to the paddling pool where Reuben's playing. I hear Shannon ask Grant why he's sprung this visit on her. He mumbles something and I look up and see Kira barrelling towards me. She leaps feet first into the water, sending a wave on to my T-shirt. She laughs and jumps up to give me a wet hug, and just like that my irritation evaporates.

Soon I'm sitting in the paddling pool in my shorts and T-shirt, letting Reuben dump buckets of water over my head and Kira drive a toy car up my arm. When Grant wanders over, we're all giggling and Reuben turns the bucket on him. We play with the kids for a while until Shannon calls them inside.

Grant and I stay sitting in the cool water like giant kids. 'Give Chris a chance to explain himself,' he says, pushing a slick of sandy hair away from his forehead. 'Not everyone is out to get you. You've got to let go sometime.'

I swirl my hand in the water, creating an eddy for a plastic boat. I think about the dates I've had over the years, mostly engineered by Shannon and Grant, who've clearly been analysing me from the sidelines. *Is that how they see me? Am I uptight?*

'You of all people know how hard it is, this parenting lark.' Grant sweeps his arm towards the house. 'And you've done it all on your own. Surely everyone needs a bit of love in their lives? Don't you think it's time to start trusting again?'

Love? What's this talk of love? Grant's words wedge thick in my mind. I know he isn't referring to us, but instead he's talking about the blind dates and double dates that have gone nowhere, and the relationships that seemed promising at first, but petered into . . . what? There was Brad, then Scotty, guys I still see around, now happily married with kids. I liked Brad for his zesty outdoor spirit and Scotty for his wit. But at some point, in both relationships, something changed: talk of weekends away, holidays abroad, moving in. It was always the same, they wanted more of me and less of Bea.

'You've been getting on well with Chris.' Grant searches my face. 'You've known him for a long time, haven't you? Since school?' He smiles softly at me. The ghost of the conversation we'd had about Bea's father, years ago, hovers between us. Of course, he's figured out that Chris is Bea's dad. *He knows.*

I turn away and wipe my palms across my cheeks, pretending I've splashed water in my eyes.

'Give him a second chance,' he says. 'If only for Bea.'

Later, Reuben pleads with us to load up the water pistols and have a water fight. The three of us chase the children and each other around the garden and soon we're soaked through. Shannon wraps Kira and Reuben in towels and I flop on to the grass and let the heat dry my clothes. The sunshine against my eyelids reminds me of summery sixth-form days out on the field, where Chris and I would lie on the grass pointing out clouds shaped like animals. I smirk and think I must remind him of this memory – then I remember I'm supposed to be angry with him.

I wonder if I still am.

'Any more news from Bea?' Shannon calls over.

I sit up. She's rubbing sun cream on to Reuben's face and he scowls and darts from her grasp. 'Not for a few days,' I reply. 'She'll be home soon enough and she can fill in the gaps for me then.' The distractions of the afternoon have stopped me dipping into my bag to check my phone and now Shannon's reminded me, the urge is back. I'm about to get up when Chris appears at the door with Grant behind him. I freeze as the conversation we'd had in the paddling pool earlier comes rushing back. *Will he tell him?*

Chris steps into the garden. He's wearing the annoying mirrored sunnies again, but his smile is friendly. My hand creeps up to touch my hair, flat and sticky around my face. I realise I'm staring and quickly say hello, and all I can think is *Shannon and Grant both know Chris is Bea's dad.* What a bloody mess I've created.

'Watching the rugby then?' I find myself saying, desperate to stuff the silence with pointless words in case Grant says something that's going to rip everything apart.

'Been having a water fight?'

I pull at my damp T-shirt, sure my bra must be on show through the white fabric, and then fold my arms. Shannon hands me one of the kids' towels and I hold it, unsure what to do. Wrapping it around my body feels like I'm drawing attention to the problem, so I drape the towel awkwardly around my neck. I look like I've just come back from a sweaty workout.

'Where are you watching the game?' I say.

'Yes, where *are* you watching the game?' Shannon's eyes bore into Grant's again. He avoids her gaze and catches Kira as she runs past, pushing her sun hat firmly back on to her head.

'At the sports bar in the city,' Chris says, blundering into a conversation I'm pretty sure Grant hasn't had with Shannon yet. 'Grant says it's the best place to go, right, mate?'

Grant mutters something and Kira wriggles away, leaving him exposed to Shannon's wrath. She flicks her head towards the door and he follows her inside with the children trailing behind, demanding ice cream.

'You've dropped him right in it,' I declare.

'Whoops.' He smiles and shrugs.

The sun's still blazing and now we're alone I don't know what to do. I've been so focused on Grant spilling my secret that I'm not really thinking about the showdown I thought I wanted to have with Chris about the café. Not that here is the time or place. I could demand we go somewhere and have it out in private, but I realise I don't know what I'd say. What can I say? Just because he works for the architect practice on the project doesn't mean he has to tell me his business. This secondment to New Zealand is like one long, fun-filled holiday for him. I'm just an old acquaintance who happens to have helped him fill a few bored days. Why would he care what happens to me or my café?

'It's hot.' Chris moves into the shade of the pergola. He pulls off his sunnies and looks so intently at me that I turn away. 'Why haven't you returned my calls?' he says. 'I wanted to explain what happened.' His words are as frank as his stare, and I'm reminded of Bea again.

I pour us both a glass of water, lukewarm from the sun. I weigh up what I want to say. If I tell him I'm angry – that he let me down – it'd be the truth, but he'd probably think I'm mad. He has no reason to be loyal to me. A thick tension hangs between us and I can hear the children arguing inside about who's going to have the last strawberry ice cream.

I challenge him. 'I've been busy. You know, looking for another place to run my business?'

Chris gazes into his glass. 'I suppose Bea must be coming home soon,' he murmurs, surprising me. 'You must want everything sorted out before she gets back.' He looks up again. 'It must have been difficult seeing her leave. Saying goodbye.'

My throat tightens. His eyes seem to be filled with other words, words I can't hear, and for a moment I think they're going to spill from his mouth, but instead he gulps back some water.

What's he trying to say? I pull out a chair and sit down. Has he worked it out?

Breathe. Focus.

'When did you find out my café was being demolished?' I refuse to let my mind wander. 'Did you know when you first came to see me?'

Chris exhales and then nods. 'I saw the article about you in the newspaper and I put two and two together,' he says slowly. 'God, I didn't really know what I was going to say when I saw you – I hadn't seen you in nearly nineteen years! Then, when I turned up,

181

you weren't exactly friendly, and anyway it seemed like a pretty shitty thing to do. To say, hi, I haven't seen you in a while and, by the way, I'm part of the development team that's going to knock down your café.'

He puts the glass down and the tightness in my throat hardens to a lump.

He didn't really come looking for me.

'Then when you agreed to have the picnic with me, I planned to tell you then, I really did, but you said your mum owns City Real Estate and that really threw me. I knew we had a meeting with them, and that made me wonder if she'd already told you I was involved and that's why you were so arsey with me the day we did the bungy jump.' He shakes his head. 'But you seemed different that evening… and I bottled it. I didn't want to bring it up, and then when you started talking about your dad, I couldn't just . . .'

'What?' I press.

'. . . You were upset, you needed to talk, it wasn't the right time to tell you.'

I'm about to say, *And when was the right time?* But I catch myself. I sound like an angry girlfriend.

'It must have been weird seeing Mum again,' I mutter instead. 'Did she recognise you at the meeting?'

He laughs. 'Yes. She looked a bit shocked though.'

'Caught off guard. Ha, that's a new experience for Mum.'

'She recovered herself quickly and when she said she needed to tell you herself about me being part of the development team, I realised you didn't know. When you didn't return my calls, I guessed I'd annoyed you, but I wanted to tell you I was sorry, I *am* sorry, I should've told you right from the start.'

I slump back in the chair. When will Mum stop meddling in my life? 'It doesn't matter.' And it really doesn't. The only thing that matters is finding new premises and a place to live. 'You were in a difficult position.'

'It does matter,' says Chris quietly. 'I've upset you.'

I'm mortified when the lump in my throat swells, but I push down the mixed feelings with a swallow of water. 'Mum's the one who's upset me,' I say, attempting a smile. 'She's bloody irritating and had no right to say that to you.'

We catch each other's eye. 'Nothing's changed, then?' he says, and this time I smile properly.

The chattering sound of the TV drifts through the open door and Chris glances at his watch. 'Hey, do you want to come to the game with us?'

I make a face. 'No, rugby's not my thing.'

'What *is* your thing?' he says curiously.

For some reason, his question makes me blush. 'I like swimming. In the sea.'

'Do you paddleboard? I'm going to give it a go after work one evening. Fancy coming?'

I see the contours of Bea's face in his earnest expression, and I exhale. 'Sounds fun,' I say with a nod.

'Ready?' Grant steps back into the garden and beside him, Shannon is glacial.

Chris glances at me and back at Grant. 'Why don't we stay here and watch the game on TV?' he suggests.

Grant's face falls but Shannon instantly thaws. 'Great idea!' she says. 'You two can do a barbie afterwards.'

Chris laughs. 'I think we can just about manage that, can't we, mate?'

The two men go inside and Shannon looks at me. 'Friends again?' she says with a wink.

I roll my eyes. 'Don't even think about it,' I say.

She comes a little closer. 'So when *are* you going to tell Chris about Bea?' she whispers. 'It's taking every ounce of my willpower not to blurt it out to Grant and anyway, he's divine, and it's so obvious you two are made for each other.'

'Shannon!' I cast an anxious glance back inside. 'And anyway, Grant *knows*.'

She looks at me in surprise. 'Did you tell him?'

I shake my head. 'Like I thought, he remembered our conversation. He's done the maths.' It's only as I say this out loud that I realise how frighteningly easy it could be for Chris to leap to this conclusion too.

I look back inside. Chris is sitting on the floor in front of the TV with Reuben, pointing at the screen and telling him something about the game. Kira's perched on Grant's lap, her face still sticky pink from the ice cream.

'He's tall, dark and handsome,' whispers Shannon close to my ear, laughter tracing her voice. 'He's kind, funny and thoughtful. What more could you want?'

'Stop it,' I say, gently pushing her away.

She laughs and strolls back inside.

Shannon and I spend the rest of the afternoon playing with the kids in the garden and chatting, while Grant and Chris watch the game. The pair go on to make dinner, grilling burgers and sausages in slick tandem, much to our amusement – Chris patiently letting the children help him put together a salad. After a run of kids' TV programmes that we all watch together, Shannon tells the children it's time for bed.

'Amy, please can you read me a story?' says Kira from beneath the crook of my arm. I get up and catch Chris watching me from the armchair across the room. Before I can react, he looks away, and Reuben bounces over to him.

'I want Chris to put me in bed,' he states, folding his arms.

Grant laughs. 'Fine by me, mate.'

I smile and pad through to the bedroom the children share, with Kira swinging my hand. She's already in pyjamas, and she springs into bed and points out the book she wants me to read. I can still hear Reuben cajoling Chris, and I plonk myself down on a cushion between the two beds and wait. Reuben wears a triumphant grin when he appears with Chris at the door. I tuck him in, but Chris stays leaning against the door jamb as I read. The children giggle softly as I make up funny voices for the characters and then I'm done and turn off the lamp, leaving the glow from their night light.

''Night, kids,' I whisper, giving them both a kiss on the cheek.

'And a kiss from Chris,' says Kira sleepily, lifting an arm towards him. He comes over and crouches down, kisses his fingers and touches them to Kira's cheek. The gesture is so sweet and simple it twists my stomach. And although my tight throat tells me I'm sad, I know it's also shame corkscrewing around and around inside of me.

He'd have been like this with Bea.

'Do you have a little girl like me?' she murmurs.

Reuben sits up. 'Or a little boy like me?' he asks hopefully.

For a moment there's silence in the darkened room and I wonder if the children are holding their breath, like me, as we wait for Chris to reply. I can't imagine what he might say – I'm burning with curiosity, but I like to think I've respected his privacy. He must have his reasons for not talking to me about his daughter. And how could I have pressed him for information, but refuse to talk about my own?

Chris straightens up. 'I had a little girl once . . .' he says softly, '. . . but she's not so little now.'

Reuben slumps back on to the pillow with a huff and Chris leans over and gently touches knuckles with him. 'She liked climbing trees when she was your age, and kicking a ball around in the garden – and eating lots of ice cream.'

I think of Bea and how much she liked doing these things as a child, and a creepy feeling trails up my spine. Does he mean *Bea*? Crazy thoughts begin to twirl and dance. I try to catch Chris's expression, but the night light casts his face in shadow and, besides, he's not even looking at me.

'Bea still likes playing tag rugby with me,' says Reuben grumpily. 'And *she's* a grown-up big girl.'

The sound of Reuben's voice is like a dart of sense penetrating my madness and I shake my head, annoyed with myself. *What am I thinking? Chris is not a stalker.*

'That must be fun,' he says. 'I bet she can't wait to play with you when she gets back.'

'What's your big girl's name?' murmurs Kira, her eyes already closed.

Chris turns and looks directly at me. 'Her name is Gemma.'

But I still can't read the expression on his face.

Chapter 23

Olivia

Then

'What a complete shitshow,' said Amy, tugging a pink bobble hat over her curls as she pushed open the college doors.

The cold bit into Olivia's cheeks. She wasn't sure she'd done that well in the mock English lit exam either. She'd written loads, but whether her essays had answered the questions was another story.

'Hey, Amy! Olivia!'

The girls turned and Chris jogged towards them, his breath funnelling in white clouds. Butterflies danced around Olivia's stomach.

'Nice hat,' he said, nodding at Olivia's black beret. 'Very French.'

Did he really think so or was he taking the piss? She narrowed her eyes.

'How did you find the exam?' His gaze hopped between the two of them and settled on Amy.

'Fine,' said Olivia quickly. 'What about you?'

Chris was still looking at Amy.

'Rubbish!' she said brightly. 'I'm winging it, I need to get my head down before we do the real thing.'

'Blimey, you're leaving it late.'

Amy pulled out a plastic box with her latest creation inside. 'Everything I want to do is right here.'

'Been baking *cookies* again?' he smirked.

Olivia expected Amy to flush but she laughed. 'You'll never know,' she said, tucking the box under her arm.

'You're feeling better, then. Livvy said you had a sore throat.'

Shit, Olivia knew what he was going to say next. She'd not got around to fully explaining to Amy what had happened at the pub and now the conversation was hurtling towards her like a car crash.

'Livvy told you about Black Jacks, right?' Chris continued. 'We were going on Friday but—' He grinned and shrugged, as if his shrug would fill in the rest of the sentence. 'Fancy coming this Friday? I'm not working. I changed my shift.'

Olivia lit a cigarette and took a long drag. He looked like a little boy, eyes all round and eager, like Amy was an amazing birthday present. *One he couldn't wait to unwrap.*

Again, Olivia expected Amy to look flustered, but instead she threw her a quizzical glance as if to say, *what the fuck?* 'Yeah, I suppose,' she replied. 'Though am I supposed to have heard of Black Jacks?'

'Didn't Livvy explain?'

They both glanced at her and Olivia dragged on the cigarette again. 'You were ill, I forgot,' she muttered through a stream of smoke.

'Three or four bands perform each Friday. You know, proper bands, not like me and Paul.' Chris laughed. It was a warm, mellow sound, rich with promise. 'We had a brilliant laugh last time. You'll come, right?'

Amy glanced at Olivia. 'With Liv and Paul?'

Liv and Paul? She didn't want to be *Liv and Paul.* She wanted to be *Chris and Livvy. Livvy and Chris. Chris-and-Olivia.*

'I don't know,' Olivia muttered.

'Aw, come on, it'll be fun!' said Chris.

Try harder.

He turned his attention back to Amy. 'You're free, right? I'll get my dad to drive us, then I can have a few beers. What d'ya reckon?'

Christ.

'I'll drive,' Olivia snapped. 'Paul doesn't live far, does he?'

He grinned. 'You're a star, you can pick him up on your way to me.'

Olivia ground her cigarette butt with the heel of her boot. 'I've got to go,' she said, going over to her car. 'Do you still want a lift, Amy?'

Amy hesitated long enough for Olivia to feel something slip between them. She yanked open the door, got in and started the engine.

'Wait a sec, Liv!' Amy flipped the lid off the box and held it out to Chris. 'Not cookies, it's carrot cake, try it.'

Chris picked out a triangle and tried to balance it in the palm of his hand.

'Have the box,' she said. 'Give it back to me tomorrow.'

He licked cream cheese icing from his fingers. 'Thanks, Ames, tastes great.'

Amy ran to the car and Olivia pulled away; she wanted to get home, *now*.

Amy turned on the radio and began humming. Olivia could almost hear her thoughts whirring and wasn't surprised when she said, 'I thought you said Chris had asked *you* to the gig.' Before Olivia could think of what to say, Amy carried on. 'I didn't realise he wanted *me* to go with him. I clearly wasn't listening when you phoned last week, God, I'm such a doughnut. He did ask me out, didn't he? Like a proper date? He said something about getting his dad to take us, before you offered, so that would've been a date, wouldn't it?'

Olivia was about to say no, he didn't just want *her* to go, he wanted them *both* to go, but she bit her lip. The painful croak had finally left Amy's voice and she sounded more cheerful than she had in days. 'You weren't up for talking much,' she muttered. 'Anyway, I didn't think you'd be that bothered.'

'I'm *very* bothered.' Amy giggled and Olivia glanced over. Her cheeks were flushed the same pink as her bobble hat. 'He's pretty lush.'

Olivia felt like slamming on the brakes, bundling Amy out of the door and telling her to make her own bloody way home.

'Paul's pretty good-looking underneath all that make-up, isn't he?' She grinned.

Was he? Olivia hadn't really noticed. His make-up was just part of who he was – though, thinking about it, the kohl emphasised the blue of his eyes, even if they were a bit intense. He had a gentleness about him that was *reassuring*, she supposed, but not boyfriend material. She didn't fancy him. He wasn't her type.

Chris was her type.

Olivia pulled up outside Amy's house.

'Now I've got to figure out what to wear,' Amy said. 'I know it's not exactly *a date* but, still, if Paul's going, it's a bit like a double date, don't you think?'

'No!' Olivia spluttered. 'It's not a double bloody date.'

'I won't leave you with Paul,' Amy replied, casting her a side-long glance, 'if you don't want me to.'

'Chris asked me to Black Jacks first, you know,' Olivia said in a rush.

Amy's face froze and Olivia felt a momentary snatch of satisfaction.

'Did he? Oh, I thought . . .'

'Don't you remember? I said on the phone. I told you he'd asked me to the pub at lunchtime *and* he asked me to go to Black Jacks.'

Confusion creased Amy's face. 'I *thought* that's what you said, but then I . . .'

Olivia waved her hand dismissively. 'Come on, it doesn't really matter. What matters is getting your mum to let you go. Now, get a shift on, I've got to get back to revise.'

Olivia had already eaten beans on toast and was looking at her maths revision when she heard her dad's key in the lock. He plodded in, kissed her briefly on the head and dumped his briefcase on the table. He picked up the post and leafed through the letters.

'Do you want a cup of tea? Anything to eat? I can make something,' she offered. At least he'd remembered to phone and tell her he'd be late home tonight.

'I grabbed a sandwich,' he said, opening the fridge and surveying the contents.

Olivia put the kettle on, and her dad filled his plate with cheese and crackers and drifted into the front room. The soft burble of the TV floated through the open door and she wondered if he was in the mood to chat – though she didn't know what they'd talk about. She could hardly tell him about Chris. About the way she'd treated Amy. But she could talk to him about her English lit exam. He liked reading; he read on the train to work. If she talked through the exam paper with him, he'd probably know if she'd done all right.

Olivia hovered in the doorway. Her dad's eyes were shut. 'I had my English mock today,' she said quietly.

A low snore rumbled through his mouth and she watched his chest rise and fall for a moment. He didn't need to hear her troubles; he had enough of his own to deal with.

Chapter 24

Olivia

Then

Frost dusted the front garden of Chris's house at the end of the cul-de-sac and twinkled beneath the streetlights. Olivia stopped the car and switched off the radio but left the engine running. She was bang on time and wondered whether to knock for him or beep the horn. She tapped a black-lacquered nail on the steering wheel; her mouth felt dry.

A cat appeared, eyes like shiny pebbles in the glow of the headlights, then the front door of the neighbouring house clicked open and someone came out with a bag of rubbish, pausing briefly to look at her car. Olivia cut the engine.

A Christmas tree sat in the parting of Chris's living-room curtains and above she saw a dim light at the window. Had he forgotten she was coming? Her hand hovered over the horn and then she remembered the neighbour staring and unclicked her seat belt.

For a moment, Olivia wished she *had* taken the more obvious route to collect Paul and Amy first. What was she going to talk to

Chris about in the car? Would she be able to concentrate with him sitting so close to her?

She got out; a sharp wind whipped through her satin camisole and she pulled her leather jacket closed. The doorbell chimed and straightaway a light went on in the hallway. Olivia stroked her hair twice and then the door opened, revealing a lady with shoulder-length wavy hair the same chestnut brown as Chris's.

'Hi?' his mum said with a puzzled smile, her greeting sounding like a question.

'I've come to pick Chris up,' Olivia mumbled.

The lady's smile deepened. 'Of course. You look freezing! Come in.'

A bass beat thumped through the ceiling and Olivia blinked in the brightness of the hall light. She caught sight of herself in the mirror opposite. She looked ridiculous: smudged kohl around her eyes and a red slash of lipstick. Where the hell was Chris? She didn't need to be standing here making small talk with his mum. He was the one who'd said seven thirty. Why wasn't he ready and waiting?

'I'm Sarah, and you are . . . ?' She looked at her quizzically. 'Chris never tells me anything.' Her laugh tinkled; she sounded kind. 'No, that's not true. He said he was going to Black Jacks to watch a band with friends, but he didn't say who.' She glanced at the car keys in Olivia's hand. 'You're the driver tonight, then?'

Olivia nodded. 'Yes, I always drive.' Then grappled for something else to say. 'I don't drink!' Christ, she sounded desperate to be believed, like she was lying.

'Of course not!' Sarah tinkled again. 'Are you at college with Chris?'

Small talk, I hate small talk. Where the fuck was he? 'Yes,' she replied, stroking her hair.

Sarah nodded and Olivia realised she still hadn't introduced herself.

'Listen to me chattering on, you probably want to get going. Chris is rubbish at being on time. Go on up to his room and tell him to get a move on.'

Olivia stared. Upstairs? *To his bedroom?*

'It's the door at the end of the landing, though' – she pointed to the ceiling – 'it's not hard to work out which room is his.'

Music pumped behind the door and Olivia stroked her hair a couple more times before turning the handle. A hot, fuggy smell of man-sweat mingled with stale cigarette smoke and the citrus tang of aftershave filled the room, a jolting reminder of when they'd huddled together under the umbrella. Chris had his back to her and was crouched down air-guitaring to a song she didn't recognise. She grinned, watching his bum gyrate in tight black jeans, then he jumped around and spotted her. She laughed as he straightened up, brushed his hands down his thighs and switched off the hi-fi. The room fell silent.

'Hi,' he said, pushing loose strands of hair from his face. 'Is that the time already?'

'Yep, we're late.'

'Shit! Are the others in the car?'

He didn't wait for an answer and thumped off down the stairs.

'Are you going to introduce me to your . . . friend?' Sarah was still in the hall and had a big smile on her face.

A warm glow spread through Olivia. *His mum thinks I'm his girlfriend!*

'This is Livvy.' He shoved his arms into his leather jacket and a crushed box of cigarettes fell out of the pocket.

'Christopher!' Sarah reached for them, but Chris pounced first and stuffed them away.

'Chill, Mum, we're late, see you later.' He grabbed Olivia's hand and tugged her down the steps and she tottered giddily, caring less about breaking an ankle in her boots than his firm grip.

'Where are they?' he said, glancing into the back of the car. 'I thought you were picking them up first?'

'Getting them now,' she said, dragging on her seat belt and starting the engine.

'We're kind of going back on ourselves, aren't we?'

Olivia had already thought he might ask. 'Paul said he'd walk round to Amy's.' Only a little fib: she'd suggested it and he hadn't objected.

Olivia tried not to think about Chris's body filling the front seat and the halo of heat radiating off him. He fiddled with the radio, stopping on a song he liked, and began drumming his fingers on his thigh. 'I wonder why Paul went around to Amy's?' she blurted.

Chris glanced at her. 'What do you mean?'

'I could've picked him up on the way here. He didn't *need* to go there.'

Chris looked out into the night and Olivia noticed his knee starting to bounce. 'Yeah, it's a bit weird.'

Olivia went through her mental checklist of conversation starters she'd planned. 'How long have you and Paul been in a band?' she said.

'We started having guitar lessons together when we were about twelve. We mucked about with music in our free time for ages. Paul really got into the keyboard and then, when we were fifteen, we badgered Paul's dad to get us a gig at the working men's club.'

Olivia took a left turn. 'I thought you were brilliant.'

Chris smiled. 'Thanks. We enjoy playing but we don't play as often as we'd like because of college and stuff.'

'Is music what you're going to do? You know, after A levels?'

He laughed and shook his head. 'Nah. I'm not that arrogant! I'm going to uni. I want to be an architect. What about you? What are your plans?'

'Me?' The traffic lights changed to red. People rarely asked her what she wanted to do. 'I'm going to be a lawyer.'

'Really?' He sounded surprised. 'I'd have had you down as doing something creative.' He waved vaguely. 'You know, you've got great style, your drawings are amazing and, well, you look like someone who'd be comfortable doing something arty.'

He coughed.

Was he embarrassed?

You've got great style.

The lights changed to green. 'Art's a bit flaky, isn't it?' she replied. 'Nobody made a million quid drawing pictures.'

'Except Van Gogh.'

'Not true. He only sold one painting when he was alive.'

'Really? That's a bit harsh. His family must be minted now.' Chris flicked radio stations. 'Is being loaded really important to you, then?'

Christ, she sounded mercenary. 'No, that's not what I mean, I'm unlikely to make a million as a lawyer either. I'm being metaphorical. Money buys you freedom, doesn't it? You have more choices in life.'

Chris nodded. 'True. I don't want to be stuck here for the rest of my life.'

'Got to get the grades though. Architecture's a long slog. What, seven years of study, isn't it?'

'Yeah, but I'm having a year out first. I'm going travelling before I have to knuckle down. That's why I'm doing loads of shifts at the pub. To save up.'

Olivia stared into the blackness of the night. The only thing important to her, so essential for her future, was becoming a lawyer. Her world suddenly felt very small and very boring. 'Where will you go?'

'Everywhere,' he said. 'I'm going to get a round-the-world ticket. Australia's top of the list – all that space and sun!'

Olivia glanced at him. He tapped his fingers on his thigh again, a smile playing around his mouth. 'What, like an episode of *Home & Away*?' she said.

Chris laughed. 'Yeah, that'd be right, all those sexy bronzed surf chicks.'

'Can't wait, I suppose?' she said, turning into Amy's road.

'Nope, nothing's going to stand in my way.'

Chapter 25

Olivia

Then

Chris drew them into the throbbing heart of Black Jacks among a mass of heaving black leather and shiny piercings. The building looked as though it had been an old theatre: a domed roof arched high above them and thick black curtains hung across the stage. Smoke swirled around the dance floor, and flashing lights picked out dismembered arms and legs jerking in time to the music.

As Olivia followed Chris to the bar, she felt Amy's fingers loop through hers so they wouldn't lose each other in the crowd. Faces thick with make-up – boys, girls, whoever – glanced at them as they passed, the rotating lights catching silver hoops and studs in ears, noses, eyebrows, lips. Olivia remembered her face in the mirror in Chris's hallway. She'd got it right after all, she looked the part. She just needed the piercings. Perhaps her belly button? Could she do that? Flash off her flat white belly?

The crowd pressed in as they got closer to the bar and Amy let go of Olivia's hand. Light fingers touched her waist instead and she twisted around to see Paul behind her. She brushed his hands away and searched for Amy, then saw her, pushed up next to Chris, who'd manoeuvred himself to the front of the queue. Olivia surged forwards to join them.

Chris took their drink orders and Amy squeezed Olivia's hand. 'You look so cool,' she shouted, her eyes flitting around the room. 'I look a right dork.' She grinned cheerfully and plucked at the strappy mini dress she wore over black leggings.

From this angle, Olivia had an eyeful of Amy's generous cleavage – which meant Chris did too.

'Do you like my new boots?' Amy clutched Chris's arm for balance so she could lift her leg to give Olivia a closer look. 'I needed something, you know, for tonight. There's no *way* I'd get away with thigh-high boots like yours, my mum would go *mental*, but I couldn't wear my wedges, could I? D'you like them? I know they're the same as yours, but Doc Martens are Doc Martens, right?' She laughed.

Olivia looked down at her boots. Would her dad go mental if he knew? He never went mental about anything.

Chris handed around the drinks.

'Let's stand over there by the stage so we can see the bands.' Paul's breath tickled in Olivia's ear, making her jump.

'Christ, Paul, you scared the shit out of me,' she said. 'Where?'

He pointed to the side of the dance floor that had yet to fill up.

'Good idea,' shouted Amy.

Paul laced his fingers firmly through Olivia's and she let him tug her towards the stage. She sensed the crowd's energy growing and felt a streak of excitement. When they reached the dance floor, she pulled her hand away and Paul shrugged off his jacket. 'I can't be bothered to queue for the cloakroom, I'll dump our coats over there, no one will see them.'

Olivia handed hers to him. His eyes lingered on her black satin camisole for a moment and she ducked her head away, hiding her smile. Clearly, her choice had the desired effect. She just needed Chris to notice too.

Where were they? Olivia glanced back towards the bar. People were still pouring into the venue and the crowd had swelled. There was no way she'd find them now.

Suddenly, the room went dark. The audience cheered, then fell quiet. Someone whistled. Olivia glanced at Paul and they grinned at one another. A cone of light clicked on, illuminating the lead singer at the microphone, and slowly he began to strum his guitar, the pace increasing in time with the drummer, and then the whole stage lit up and the crowd roared.

By the time the first band had finished, Olivia had given up trying to figure out where Chris and Amy had got to. Thank God Paul hadn't deserted her. He'd gone to the bar and bought drinks and promised not to move when she had to join the mile-long queue for the Ladies during the interval. She'd danced next to him, a little self-consciously at first, and then she'd let him drag her into the heart of the dance floor where they moshed until they were both slick with sweat and laughing.

Now, though, with the music finished, the harsh overhead lights on, and the floor sticky with beer and littered with fag butts, the magic had evaporated. Paul's hair hung in greasy strands and black rivers of make-up ran down his cheeks. Olivia imagined she looked the same.

'Where are they?' she said as they rescued their coats from where they'd left them.

'There.' Paul pointed to the dance floor, now almost empty.

Two familiar figures stood pressed together, arms wrapped around one other, and a bolt of anger shot through Olivia. They should be *embarrassed* with so many people still milling around, glancing over at them. They were so *obvious*. But neither Chris nor Amy was looking at anyone else. They stared at each other with stupid grins on their faces. Olivia swallowed. She was caught in a hideous nightmare in which she knew how the tragic story ended but couldn't do anything to stop it. She swallowed again. Damn her dry throat from all the singing. She tore her eyes away and kept swallowing and swallowing, fumbling in her pocket for her cigarettes.

'Well, there we go,' Paul said, lighting one and passing it to her.

Olivia sucked hard. 'What do you mean?' she snapped, wrenching on her jacket.

Paul cocked his head towards *them*. Olivia knew she'd regret looking, but the scene unravelling before her had an irresistible pull. She watched Chris reach out and cup the back of Amy's head, his hands tangled in the curls of her hair. She tipped her face towards him, her mouth parted in full bloom, and she kissed him softly, then deeply, making Olivia's heart beat in desire and heartbreak all at the same time.

The moment should have been hers.

Chapter 26

Amy

Now

It's the weekend again and I've had a busy morning that's disappeared in a flurry of customers, adding to takings that have been climbing steadily since I won the award – the irony isn't lost on me. I've shut early and I'm sitting on the swing seat on my roof terrace. Mum's marching another troop of potential buyers through here this afternoon and I don't want to hang around to watch them pick through my life.

I've arranged to have Reuben and Kira here for tea and a sleepover to give Shannon and Grant a break, but with an empty afternoon stretching before me, I plucked up the courage to call Chris. I asked him if he wanted to go paddleboarding.

The sea sparkles in the sun with barely a ripple, ideal for my first paddleboarding experience. Bea's the expert, though, and now I'm wondering why I never found the time to get her to teach me. I couldn't see she was leaving me, she's always been by my side, and I thought we had forever to do everything together. But she grew wings and I didn't notice, then flew away to explore the world.

Just this morning the email I've been waiting for finally arrived, containing a few more sentences than before and a photo of a sunset over an empty beach. Although she tells me she's been jungle trekking and kayaking, it's an itinerary delivered in staccato, and I sense the empty space between the lines. I wonder what she's *not* telling me. Is she in trouble? Has she run out of money? I'm pretty certain she wouldn't hide this from me – yet she's hiding something.

I think of the man's arm wrapped around her waist in the picture she sent before. Perhaps he's the one standing in the shadows of her silence? The idea fills me with a twist of pride and dread. Boys – boyfriends – were never high on Bea's agenda and now she's exposed to a whole planet of worldly-wise boys when her life has always been so . . . narrow.

Shannon keeps reminding me she's having the time of her life. I guess she is, isn't she? *She's a woman*, I remind myself.

Was I a woman at eighteen?

So now, as I go back inside, my mind rolls back to Gemma, Bea's sister. This faceless girl has been on my mind all week. It's an exhilarating feeling mixed with apprehension – and an irrational stab of jealousy for her mother. Anxiety flutters again. How old is she? Chris said *she's not little any more*. What did that mean? Nine? Ten? Thirteen? Fifteen? Did Chris jump into the arms of another while I struggled on here as a teenage single mum? I wonder how I can approach this conversation without encouraging him to ask the same questions of Bea. It's selfish and I'm a hypocrite but I have the urge to know everything about Gemma before I tell him about Bea.

Suddenly, I'm uncertain what this afternoon might bring. Chris isn't just a filler for my time today. Something's unfurling inside of me and it can't be ignored.

Bea and Gemma are sisters.

As though my thoughts have summoned him, Chris appears, striding along the path with a paddleboard gripped under his arm as if this is the kind of activity he does every day. Perhaps it's the excitement I see in his pace or his enthusiastic wave when he spots me, but familiarity strikes hard. And as I shut my front door and walk slowly down the stairs, I'm thinking of Bea, and I'm thinking of Gemma, and I realise I have to tell him the truth.

But now I'm terrified about what he might say.

We greet each other with a peck on the cheek as natural as any friends. The scratch of his bristles grazes my skin where he hasn't shaved this morning and I pick up a familiar scent that stirs my teenage senses.

'Perfect conditions, huh?' he says, pointing at the ocean's glassy flatness. The tide is low and the sea is so shallow that people are standing way out, playing ball games in the water. 'Even if we fall off, it won't be deep.'

'Hey, speak for yourself, I won't be the one falling in.'

He grins and we dump our stuff on the beach. I turn away to peel off my T-shirt and snatch a glance over my shoulder at him. His back is honey-coloured from the sun, muscles defined in smooth skin, and I feel a flicker of something dangerous and look away. *What am I thinking?*

We wade through the water until it's waist-high for me and Chris holds the board steady. 'Ladies first,' he says.

I concentrate on pulling myself on and try not to stare at his bare chest inches from my face. Then I realise it's quite tricky and so I fling a leg over and drag myself on to my knees. He laughs at my clumsiness and I giggle too, and although the water looks calm, the board is rocking.

'Go on then, stand up.' He smirks but his face isn't unkind. 'I'm holding it.'

'You'd better be.' Carefully, I put one foot forward so I'm in a lunge and I'm aware how inelegant I look and stifle another giggle.

He hands me the paddle. 'Stand straight, it'll help you balance.'

I wobble on to my feet, push myself to standing and Chris whoops in delight. I grin triumphantly.

'Ready? I'm letting go.' He steps away and I feel the board loosen beneath me as it's released to the sea. Instinctively, I clench my core to stay upright. Crack this and I'll be as toned as Shannon.

I stroke the paddle in the water, cautiously at first, and the board bobs along. I grow taller, pushing the paddle more quickly, and it's exhilarating, and again I wonder why it's taken me so long to do this. Then, as I get closer to the edge of the rocky outcrop, I realise I don't know how to stop, or turn, and a jet ski bounces past, flinging waves in my direction and I'm falling, the water stunning me – and then I tip upright.

Chris is at my side. 'You OK?'

I'm only chest deep.

Laughter bubbles up, tugging my mouth and cheeks and bursting out in a gale of pleasure. Chris smiles and I realise he's not wearing the mirrored sunnies and I can see the crinkles at the edges of his eyes. I feel another rush of pleasure that he's here, with me, after all this time, looking the same but different, and that makes me laugh even more, and then we're both laughing about nothing and everything – what else matters?

After a while, we head back to the beach and stretch out on our towels. Chris pulls a couple of beers from a chilly bag and offers me one. He snaps off the lid and clinks his bottle to mine.

'Well done,' he says. 'You're pretty good.' His curved lips tell me he's teasing.

'Better than you,' I retort, enjoying the cold beer sliding down my throat.

'Says who? I'm not the one that fell in.'

'Only once! I was going faster than you.' I smile behind my bottle.

We fall silent and I gaze around the beach, idly wondering if there's anyone here I know and whether I care if they see me hanging out with Chris or not. We seem to be surrounded by other couples, towels laid side by side like us, mirroring, perhaps, how they share their bed at night. Nearby, a dark-haired man strokes sun cream on to his girlfriend's back, then leans forward and grazes his lips across her shoulders.

My eyes wander on, taking in the families at play in the sand. Sometimes I wonder how my life turned out like this – Bea and me in the micro-family I created. I'd always hoped I'd have another child, a sibling for Bea, because I know how difficult it was to grow up alone. No one understood how it felt to live with my parents – *with my mum* – not even Chris. It was only Olivia who understood, but even that was short-lived. No one remembers Dad the way I do. There's no one to share silly childhood stories I hear siblings repeat to one another long into adulthood. So to *know* Bea has a sister is exciting and terrifying in equal measure. I must ask Chris about Gemma, but I don't know how to shape the words when he's been so unwilling to talk about her.

I glance over at him. His eyes are closed and I let my gaze roam over his body. I take in his six-pack and follow the line of hair that disappears beneath the waistband of his shorts. A rush of memories come tumbling forward of me running my hands over him and reaching for the belt buckle on his jeans that first time . . . I feel light-headed, like a teenager all over again, and drag my eyes away. *Stop.*

Sparkles of sunlight dance across the surface of the sea. Is Chris lonely? Is that why he suggested we go paddleboarding? Am I just someone to fill in the time while he's living here? And why did I suggest he come over today? Am I lonely too? My eyes fall back on him again. I feel greedy and want to keep looking, keep staring, and soak up every little detail. *I shouldn't, I can't* . . . but I could, oh yes, I *know* I could, I really, *really* could.

No. *No.* I force some deep breaths. I shouldn't be thinking like this, and as if Chris can sense me watching, he opens his eyes and sits up.

'Not long until Bea's home,' I say quickly to hide my staring, and before I've really thought whether this is the right conversation to have. Though there's a chance talking about Bea might tease out something about Gemma.

He slips on his mirrored sunnies.

Damn.

'I can't wait to hear about the places she's been to in Thailand,' I begin to gabble. 'She's been kayaking, elephant rides, boat trips, she's been having the time of her life. I never thought she'd leave me and then, before I knew it, she was gone.' A stupid lump lodges itself in my throat. Why am I harping on about this? 'Though I'm beginning to realise how important it is she's having these new experiences. New Zealand is so far from the rest of the world.'

Chris watches me carefully. 'You know, that's the most you've ever told me about Bea,' he says. 'I kind of assumed you'd found her being away difficult and that's why you didn't really want to talk about her.'

His comment smacks me in the face and a wave of guilt washes over me. In hiding Bea from him, it's like I've made out she doesn't exist, and that awfulness breaks my heart. I scan his expression – has he worked it out? Is he waiting for me to reveal the truth?

'I've *really* missed her, but she'll be home in a couple of weeks,' I say, my heart starting to beat a little faster. 'Will you still be here? I mean, I remember you saying you were away for three months?'

Chris turns his gaze towards the sea. 'I'm here for another four weeks,' he says softly.

For some reason I feel a squeeze of disappointment at the idea of him leaving and I think I see a shadow wash over his face. But perhaps I'm transposing my own feelings on him. Perhaps he's thinking about Gemma, about missing *his* daughter.

'Why don't you talk about Gemma?' I say curiously.

Chris looks startled for a moment. Then he sighs. 'I should have told you more about her,' he says.

I shrug. 'You don't have to.'

He falls silent again, then frowns, and I wonder if that's all he's going to say.

'Have you got a photo?'

He rubs his hand down his face and I feel like I've overstepped the mark. Then he recovers himself. 'Not on me. I haven't got my wallet.'

I appraise him for a moment. 'Tell me something about her then.' I'm coiled with anticipation. 'What's she like? Who does she take after, you or . . . her mum?'

Does she look like Bea?

Chris pushes his hand through his hair and his mouth slackens into a line. It's like I'm seeing him for the first time. A flush of desire shoots through me again, pricked at the corners with jealousy as a jumble of new and old feelings come tumbling back. Why did I ask? I don't want to hear about his estranged wife. She's bound to be leggy and gorgeous.

'Gemma's tall, with long dark hair,' he says slowly, his gaze back on the sea. 'She's beautiful.' Then he exhales noisily and his voice picks up pace. 'She wants to study photography. I'm not sure it's right for her though.' He looks at me as though I might have the answers. 'She's very shy. Photography is a competitive business, I'm not sure she's got the confidence to sell herself. I've been encouraging her to think about doing something broader, something in design, perhaps, with photography as part of the course.'

All the time Chris is talking, my brain is whirring, calculating that Gemma must be fifteen or sixteen, and that he didn't hang around long to find a new girlfriend, *a wife*, and then I realise he's gone quiet and he's looking at me, waiting for me to stay something.

A strange laugh pops out. 'Chris!' I exclaim. 'What's happened to you? Don't you remember how much I fought my mum against becoming a teacher? She wouldn't let me do home ec A level and all I ever wanted to do was go to cookery school, and now you're doing the same thing to Gemma! Don't stop her from following her dreams.'

He stares at me for a moment and slowly begins to smile. 'Says you, fretting over Bea being away. Isn't wanting her at home by your side the same thing? Perhaps you're not letting Bea follow *her* dreams either.'

Aren't I? Then a terrible thought pops into my head. 'I don't think I even know what she dreams of doing,' I say quietly.

'Does any parent? Did we ever tell our parents what we *really* dreamed of doing?'

I feel the air thickening around us. Back then, I'd thought my dream, my reality, was being with him and having a family together – but I can't say that.

Can I?

My heart begins to pound. 'Chris . . .' I begin, just as he starts to speak. We both stop. 'No, you go first . . .' I urge.

His eyes lock on to mine. 'Why did you leave me?'

'Leave you?' I repeat dumbly. 'I didn't leave you . . . you . . . I thought you didn't want me.'

His face crumples briefly and then he composes himself. 'What makes you say that?' he says cautiously.

'I . . . I wrote you a letter, explaining . . . everything. You didn't reply or try and contact me.'

He frowns. 'A *letter*? What are you talking about? I never got a letter from you. I thought . . . we thought you . . .' He puts his head in his hands.

'We? Who's we? What did you think?' I say, confused.

Slowly, he lifts his head. 'Olivia and I, we were worried. We came to your house to talk to you but, God, I don't know, one minute you were there and the next minute you were gone. I didn't know what the hell had happened. You went and moved to the other side of the world!'

We stare at one other as the words sink in and despite the sun searing my skin, a coldness creeps down my spine and I feel a familiar twist of pain in my chest. It's like the scar he left behind being ripped open, except now I wonder if he's been carrying a scar like mine all this time.

Chris thought I left him? Mum wouldn't let Dad give him my letter. Deep inside, the anger still simmers, but right now I'm weary of the conflict between Mum and I. This is all so long ago, perhaps the letter isn't important any more.

'I'm sorry,' I say, unsure exactly what I'm sorry about. Just that I am so, so very sorry. My throat aches as my parallel life spools in a blur through my mind. I've let Bea down. Oh God, I've let Bea down.

Chris leans towards me. He twists his fingers through mine. His skin feels warm – and safe. 'I'm sorry too,' he mutters.

I stare at our entwined hands, suddenly afraid to look him in the eye. This is the moment, I must tell him, *now*. I can give Bea what she's always wanted – a father, a sibling – but Chris will be furious. I pull my hand away and give him a watery smile, but before I can voice the difficult words, I hear a shout.

'Amy!'

We both turn to see Reuben and Kira running across the sand towards us, Shannon following with their overnight bags.

My secret will have to wait.

Chapter 27

Amy

Now

'Chris!' Reuben shouts later from the roof terrace, where I've set up a plastic sandpit. I asked Chris if he wanted to stay for the afternoon and now he saunters over dutifully to join in Reuben's game. I'm in the kitchen with Kira, who's standing on a stool at the counter, puffing as she squeezes cookie dough mixture in her hands. I glance over at Chris; we're playing happy families and a pang of sadness shoots through me.

Kira pokes me with a sticky finger. 'Like this, Amy?' she says. 'Am I making it right?'

I sift a little more flour and help her roll the dough into a ball, showing her how to break off pieces and make smaller balls, then flatten them and place them on the baking tray. I speak quietly, my ears pricked and listening to Chris chatting to Reuben, making the appropriate car noises and asking questions about the game. It strikes me that he's probably missing Gemma as much as I miss Bea. I wonder how he's been able to leave her behind. Surely

Gemma must be coming for a visit soon? I make a mental note to ask him later.

Later. He hasn't said how long he's staying today – and I haven't asked.

I slide the cookies into the oven and help Kira untie the apron and wash her hands. She yawns and I glance at my watch. 'Let's put a cartoon on before tea,' I say. 'Reuben, time to come in now.'

Reuben trails in and Chris lifts him up at the sink so he can wash his hands. He picks up the DVD I've left on the side and offers to put it on while I clear up. Shannon's words fly into my mind. *He's kind and thoughtful.* I wash the bowl and think about how much I've laughed this afternoon. *He's funny.* I wipe the cloth over the counter and remember how he looked lying on the beach. *He's tall, dark and handsome.* I could turn around and check for myself, but the jittery feeling I've had all afternoon tells me I know the answer already. I decide to take another peek anyway, but Chris is leaning against the door frame watching *me*. My face flames.

'What are you making the kids for tea?' he says. 'Can I help?'

I yank open the fridge to hide my burning face inside, and start pulling out cheese, ham and salad. 'Nothing exotic. Shannon gave them a meal at lunchtime so she said a sandwich would be fine.' I gesture vaguely towards the kids, but I don't trust myself to look at him in case he sees the longing written on my face. I should never have allowed my thoughts to get carried away on the beach. It's unleashed a crazy urge that's dangerous, exciting and downright inappropriate with Kira and Reuben here. 'Thanks for asking though.'

Chris doesn't move and it occurs to me he perhaps wants to go home. He's probably had enough of this weird afternoon playing mum and dad. 'Oh,' I say, putting down the knife. 'You don't have to hang around. God, you didn't need to stay this long! You've probably got things to do.'

We stare at each other for a moment, then he glances over at the kids and back at me. 'Well,' he starts, 'I haven't got plans, I can stay . . .' He shrugs and looks at the kids again. 'But I can go, if you'd rather. I mean, I'm kind of gatecrashing.'

Kira shrieks, 'Don't go, Chris! We don't want you to go!' Reuben's eyes are glued to the TV and she turns and shouts in his face. 'Tell Chris you want him to stay!'

Reuben jerks at her voice and drags his thumb from his mouth. 'Don't go,' he mumbles.

'I guess that's settled!' I say brightly, and I turn back to the sandwiches, but my hand shakes when I pick up the knife.

'Can I sleep here tonight?' says Reuben a little later, bouncing up and down on Bea's bed.

'I want to sleep there,' Kira pouts.

I laugh. 'Not if you're going to argue.' I turn to Chris. 'When Bea's here, the three of them sleep on the floor.'

'On the big blow-up bed,' Reuben adds. His faces creases into a smile as he realises something. 'I could have the big blow-up bed all to myself!' He turns to his sister. 'You can have Bea's bed,' he says solemnly, and she shrieks with delight.

'Let's wash the sand off before we get into PJs,' I say, crouching down to rummage in their bags. The kids run off to the bathroom and I follow. It's still damp in here from my shower this morning and I stand on tiptoes to push open the tiny window set high up on the wall. The children leap about beside me, yanking off their sticky clothes, and I swirl bubble bath into the water.

'Shall I fix us something to eat?' says Chris at the door.

I've not thought about dinner; obviously, I wasn't expecting company. 'Sorry, there isn't much in the fridge, but there's pasta in the cupboard.' I lift Kira into the bath first, then Reuben.

Chris disappears and for a moment I panic when I think about the framed photos I have of Bea dotted around the living room – even though he's had heaps of time to notice them this afternoon. I fight the instinct to push him into the kitchen so he doesn't linger over them while I'm not looking. But that's stupid. And anyway, what's he going to see? A collection of photos framing my beautiful daughter at different ages in different places. *Lots of kids have chestnut-brown hair.*

I reach for the shampoo and catch sight of the pale-blue tiles on the walls, the grout lined with black mould. I wonder why I've done nothing to update the bathroom over the years except change the lino and fit a new shower curtain. I think about the chipped Formica counter in the kitchen and the walls that haven't been decorated in years. I wonder what Chris thinks of my scruffy flat. I wonder what my home says about *me*.

I sponge the children's bodies and the scent of apple soap fills the room. Reuben flaps his hands forwards and backwards in the water to create more bubbles. This was always Bea's bedtime routine. When she was small, she'd coat my face in a bubble beard and call me Mummy-Daddy.

I can hear Chris clattering around the kitchen and for a second I let myself imagine that this is what family life might have been like for us: Chris, me, Bea . . . and maybe even a brother or sister. Tears threaten again. I suddenly have the urge to tell him about every single one of these stories and the life he's missed with her. Bea will be home soon. The timing is right. I'll be there to support her, and we can take the slow steps to draw Chris into her life.

'Out now,' Kira demands. I lift her into my arms, rub her down and pull a nightie over her head. Soon they've both said goodnight to Chris and I've kissed their warm cheeks and carefully pulled the door to. I pause before going back through to the living room, aware that butterflies are spinning around my stomach.

We're alone – sort of.

Through the open doors, I see Chris has laid the table on the roof terrace. The moment feels strange. Is this a romantic meal or domestic routine? Couples eat together every day, all over the world, except we're not a couple, partners or married – but we have a daughter.

'Pasta?' Chris calls from the kitchen, flourishing his arm wide as if he's serving me oysters. 'I used the tomatoes you had on the windowsill and some of the Parmesan in the fridge – I'm sure there must be a fancy Italian name for a dish like this.'

I laugh a little nervously and carry a jug of iced water outside. Right now, I wish I had a bottle of Sauvignon Blanc stashed in the fridge. I could do with knocking back a glass or two.

We begin eating and, of course, because I've not had to cook, the simple food tastes delicious and I tell him so. A breeze has picked up, tugging the flat sea into white ribbon waves. The golden sand glitters as the sun descends and people pack up to go home.

My view. Thoughts land on the buyers that traipsed through here today, standing where we sit, rubbing their hands in glee at the wonderous scenery.

'You know, I've lived here for fifteen years, and not once have I been bored of this view,' I say fiercely. 'I feel like it belongs to me. Waiting for someone to buy this place is torture. I don't want to leave, but another part of me wants the sale done so I can move on.'

Chris lays down his fork. 'Grant said you'd looked at somewhere in the port.'

I'm mortified when tears spring into my eyes and I get up and stand by the railings. Black paint flakes off the metal and I push at the broken pieces with my finger. 'I know everyone thinks this place is a dump. But I *love* it. It's not just a business. It's *my* business, *my* life, my history with Bea. Everywhere I look, I see the shadow of her as a toddler or a ten-year-old or a teenager. I can't leave those memories behind.'

My voice breaks and the tension that has been gathering in my chest since this afternoon suddenly loosens into sobs, becoming a display of everything I could lose. I feel Chris's hand touch my shoulder and then gently he turns me around and draws me into his arms. His body's warm and his scent jump-starts the teen memories again, striking sparks in a place that's been cold and forgotten for too long.

I tip my head back to look at him and he pushes my tears away with his thumbs. For a moment, our eyes lock. Then, slowly, we move closer to one another until our lips connect, gently at first, then deepening, our kissing igniting a fire that flames me with a desire that's both new and familiar, rash and reckless, and nothing else matters – I just wish Reuben and Kira weren't sleeping here tonight.

Chapter 28

OLIVIA

Then

Olivia trailed the aisles of the supermarket with a shopping list, but her trolley was still empty. She picked up a packet of biscuits and stared at the label. It had been months since *that* Friday. Weeks and weeks of watching the *Amy and Chris Show* play out on a loop at college, until she wanted to scratch her eyes out.

Now Amy waltzed out of class with Chris, her hand slid snugly into his back pocket, his arm slung around her shoulders, looking like the dream-team couple that everyone envied.

'Hey, Liv,' Amy had called over her shoulder that first time, 'coming to the canteen with us?'

Olivia had trailed along with Paul in tow like a pair of gooseberry saddos with no other mates to hang out with, because that was the truth. They'd slipped on to the bench opposite the happy couple and Olivia just *knew* from the way they sat glued to one another – and the stupid way Amy wriggled – that she was letting Chris crawl his fingers beneath her skirt. To Olivia's horror, tears flooded her eyes and she'd dropped her head and begun stroking her hair. *Breathe. Act normal. Walk away.* Slowly, she'd stood up, desperate for a fag.

'You coming, Paul?' she'd said, pasting on a smile.

He nodded and sprang out of his seat so fast Olivia thought the bench might topple backwards.

Then, another time, Olivia spotted Amy in the corridor without Chris. But it didn't take long for her to drag Olivia to the smoking area so she could bask in attention from them both. Olivia had smoked cigarette after cigarette, wanting to tear her eyes away, to leave, yet stuck with a fierce yearning to stay close to Chris. She'd watched them through narrowed eyes: him, leaning against the oak tree, arms wrapped around Amy; her, so short she'd had to stand on tiptoes to kiss him. How ridiculous. Olivia's mouth would have been perfectly in line with his. Every. Single. Time.

Now, Olivia stared down at her shopping list. The days had fallen into a boring routine of college and homework, with the odd visit to Amy's house – when she wasn't with Chris. Even Friday Rock Night had lost its shine. But she had to remind herself that in six months' time she'd be living in halls at Edinburgh University. No meal-planning; no cooking, if she didn't want to. No Dad. No Amy . . . *no Chris.*

Chris had told her he wanted to go to Manchester University. That wasn't too far from Edinburgh, was it? Olivia could visit him. She doubted his relationship with Amy would last – who wanted a girlfriend when they were at uni? She could be Chris's *special friend.* Olivia smirked. His *fuck buddy.* She liked the sound of that version of herself – cool, sexy, mysterious and in complete control of her life.

But then again, Amy and Chris might still be a couple.

Olivia shoved the biscuits back on the shelf and crushed the shopping list in her hand. She couldn't be bothered. She couldn't be bothered with any of it and walked away from the empty trolley. She should be out buying clothes, having a pub lunch with a friend – *with Chris* – not dragging around the supermarket like a dried-up old spinster.

She strode down the aisle and squeezed through a gap between two trolleys. A lady with dark hair turned as she passed and then her face collapsed into surprise. 'Olivia,' she said, clutching a can of baked beans to her chest as if Olivia might steal them from her.

Mum?

No, remember you call her Jeanette now.

Olivia stared. Gone was the clumsy make-up and knotted shoulder-length hair. Instead, an elfin cut shaped the planes of Jeanette's cheeks and a thick fringe emphasised the slant of her cat's eyes – Olivia's eyes. Beneath her raincoat, she wore a short green smock dress and a pair of brown leather boots. She looked . . . *trendy*, although a little seventies, but it was more than that. Jeanette's smile seemed softer somehow, as if Olivia was viewing her through the haze of a soft-focus lens.

She looked down into Jeanette's trolley. Clearly, she'd not made it to the booze aisle yet; she'd probably pick up the bottles just before she paid, in case she bumped into anyone she knew. Olivia knew her tricks, hiding them under a giant multipack loo roll, then a long explanation to the checkout girl about a party that night and how necessary it was to stock up.

Olivia had nothing to say and walked on.

'Livvy,' Jeanette called after her.

But she kept moving, stroking the right side of her hair over and over again and ignoring the tap of her mum's boots behind her.

A hand cupped her shoulder. 'I'm so happy to see you.'

Olivia shrugged her off and increased her pace, *onwards and away, far, far away*, past the curious stares and towards the exit. She marched blindly across the car park, trying to remember where she'd parked. Panic mounted as she imagined the tap, tap of Jeanette's boots and she gulped at the air, pushing back the tears.

Jeanette was shopping. *She was buying food.* When did she ever care about something as trivial as that? A flash of her sprawled naked on the bed with *him*, that disgusting man, popped into her head.

Perfect hair, perfect make-up, food in the trolley.

She's in rehab. Again.

Olivia had heard it all before, yet for one fractured second, she thought, *What if . . .*

'I'm not going to make you any promises,' Jeanette had said once.

Said twice, said three times.

'Not because I don't want to,' she'd pleaded. 'I just don't want to let you down.'

Olivia knew the patter.

'I've got a job! I'm working at the hair salon again!' she'd say.

Olivia weaved through the car park, her blurred vision desperately combing the rows of cars. *If she's got a job and she's in rehab, why hasn't she called me?*

Later that afternoon, Olivia was lying on the bed sketching another portrait of Chris when a car pulled on to the driveway, making her sit up and pull aside the net curtain. Amy sat at the wheel of her dad's battered Ford, laughing. The car began to roll backwards and Geoff wrenched on the hand brake. He wagged his finger at her and began laughing too.

Chris must be working; Olivia was the next best thing. But still she felt a shimmer of pleasure and ran down the stairs.

'Hi, Olivia,' said Geoff, getting out of the car. 'My God, I wasn't sure we'd get here in one piece.'

'Oi!' Amy shouted as she got out. 'I heard that.'

'Had a few problems with the hill starts, didn't we?'

She grinned. 'Shut up! You're just a rubbish teacher.' She opened the boot and pulled out a carrier bag. 'I hope you don't mind me dropping in out of the blue, Liv. I needed some driving practice, so I suggested to Dad that we came here.' She held up the bag. 'I've brought ingredients to make a cake – what are you up to?'

Olivia thought about the abandoned trolley, her mum's surprised face, her homework – and Chris's portrait under her pillow. 'Nothing,' she said with a shrug.

'Give me a ring when you need collecting,' said Geoff, getting back in the car.

The girls headed inside and Amy dumped the bag on the work-top. 'You home alone?'

Olivia nodded. 'Dad's playing golf.'

Once, Amy had asked about Olivia's mum, but she'd changed the subject and Amy had not asked again. Somewhere along the line, an unspoken arrangement had settled between them.

Amy flicked on the radio and began to hum to the music as she flitted around the kitchen finding bowls and spoons. She unpacked the bag and was soon pressing butter and sugar together with a wooden spoon. Olivia's thoughts kept twisting back to Jeanette, and then she realised Amy had been unusually quiet. 'I saw my mum today,' she said.

Amy looked up.

Olivia averted her eyes and stroked the side of her hair. 'I don't call her Mum,' she murmured. 'I call her Jeanette. She's cut her hair. It's really short. It actually looks all right.'

'Where did you see her?'

'Supermarket.'

Amy tapped an egg on to the side of the bowl to break it. 'What did she say?'

'Nothing. I didn't speak to her.'

She began mixing again.

'She didn't have any booze in her trolley. I think she's in rehab.'

Olivia had never told Amy about her mum's drinking. But Amy didn't flinch, or stop what she was doing, or look surprised, or say, *You never said!* She just nodded. 'That's good . . . isn't it?' she said carefully.

Olivia went over to the sink and began rinsing the dirty bowls. 'It doesn't mean anything,' she said, clattering them together on the draining board. 'She's been there before. She never sticks it out.'

'But she might. This time.'

'Yeah, right.' Amy didn't understand. She'd *never* understand. Booze controlled her mum and that was a fact.

'What you going to do?' Amy said.

'Do? What d'you mean?'

'Are you going to meet up with her? Properly, I mean?'

'No, why the hell would I do that?'

'Well . . . she's still your mum . . .'

'So what? You hate your mum too, don't you? She just happens to live in your house, so you have to see her every day. I mean, if she and your dad were divorced, would you choose to spend time with her?'

Amy's face paled and she stopped stirring. 'I don't *hate* my mum,' she said quietly. 'She's annoying and controlling but she's still my mum, and my parents do actually love each other in their own weird way.'

Shame flooded Olivia. 'Sorry,' she muttered. 'It's just . . . difficult . . .' Amy didn't know the half of it, but Olivia didn't want to go there now. She just wanted to focus on being with her and having a nice afternoon – without Chris. Not psychoanalyse the shitstorm that had consumed her life.

Later, the girls were sitting at the table with cups of tea and slices of Victoria sponge oozing jam and cream. After the silence of earlier, Amy's chatter had gone into overdrive. 'Come out with Chris and me tonight,' she said. 'You need cheering up. We're going for a Chinese.'

'No way, I'd be a right gooseberry.'

'Ask Paul then, he'll come, won't he?' She slid her a sidelong look. 'He definitely will if *you* ask him.'

'I'm not asking him! He'll think it's a date.'

'He *so* fancies you! Chris said.'

'But I don't fancy him! He knows that, we're just friends.'

'So you're going to sit at home all on your own and feel sorry for yourself.' She laughed. 'Come *on*. It's Saturday night.'

Olivia shook her head and took another bite of cake.

Amy went quiet again.

'Chris's mum and dad are going away for the weekend,' she said softly, running her finger through the last bits of jam and cream.

The cake turned sickly in Olivia's mouth.

'We're going to . . . you know . . . *do it* . . . it's the big one, Liv,' she whispered. 'Chris wants us to be alone so it can be . . . special.'

That's why Amy had been so quiet this afternoon.

Olivia tried to swallow. She reached for her tea but the cup was empty, so she stood up and filled a glass with water. 'Right,' she said, looking out into the garden.

'Is that all you can say?'

Olivia turned. Amy's eyes gleamed and she wasn't sure if she was angry or emotional. 'It's your decision. You obviously know what you're doing.'

'Do I? Do I know what I'm doing? I *think* I know what I'm doing.'

'You're not exactly going to get arrested. It's not illegal to have sex when you're seventeen.'

'That's no help!'

'What do you want me to say?'

'I don't know! Do you think I should? I absolutely want to, I really, *really* do.'

'So what's the problem?'

'Well, it's a big thing, isn't it? I've never done it; he's never done it.' She frowned. 'At least, I don't think so . . . Oh God, I never thought about *that*. Suppose he isn't a virgin? Is that a good thing or a bad thing? I can't bear to think about him having sex with anyone else. But then at least he'd know what he was doing. Imagine if we did it and it was shit? Don't they say it hurts the first time and it's usually awful? What if I don't like having sex with him?'

'I can't believe you don't know if he's a virgin or not,' Olivia scoffed. 'Wouldn't that be kind of a critical conversation to have before you make a decision like this?'

'I suppose.' Amy pressed her finger into the crumbs on the plate. 'What would you do?'

'I wouldn't do it.'

'What? Why not?'

'Knowing what your mum's like, it wouldn't be worth the consequences if she found out. You'd be grounded for life.'

'True, but then how'd she know?'

Olivia smirked. 'You can hardly disappear for the weekend, can you?'

Amy made a face. 'I was going to say I was staying here with you . . .'

'*What?*'

'I know it's a big ask.'

'What am I supposed to say if she phones?'

'I'm sure you can make something up!' Amy said brightly. 'Look, I'm not being funny, but you don't know how it feels to be like this with someone . . . I don't think I can hold out for much longer.'

Christ.

Olivia thought quickly. 'I'd have to *really* love the guy.'

'Seriously?' Amy laughed. 'You're so old-fashioned!'

Olivia didn't laugh.

'Only joking! I know what you mean, I'm the same, and I *do* love him, Liv, I really do.'

A rod of anger shot through her. Since *when*? 'You sound like a cliché. "I'm so in love",' she replied sarcastically. 'What d'you know about love?' She cocked her head. 'No, don't tell me, he loves you too, how bloody convenient.'

Amy stared at her. 'What's your problem? Of *course* Chris loves me.' Her smile looked a little uncertain.

'He's just said that because he wants to have sex with you! Can't you see that? Then he'll dump you and be on to the next naive girl.'

'Chris wouldn't do that!'

Olivia shrugged.

'Would he?'

'You know him better than me. What if you get pregnant?'

Amy laughed. 'I'm not that stupid!'

'It's not just you that has to be responsible.'

'Jesus, you sound like my mother! Chris isn't an idiot. He's already said he'd use a condom. And anyway, I'm thinking about going on the Pill, but then there's all the side effects and stuff. Plus a condom is best for STDs . . .'

Olivia snorted. 'I don't think you need to worry about AIDs, especially if Chris is a virgin. That is, *if* he's a virgin.'

'Don't . . . I can't think about that.'

'Sounds like you've made up your mind, then. Just don't tell me any of the gory details.'

Amy laughed. 'Why? You're my best mate, I tell you everything!'

Olivia turned back to the window. 'Because it's gross!' she hissed. 'And it's private and . . . *wrong*.'

And because I can't bear to picture him doing things to you that I want him to do to me.

Chapter 29

OLIVIA

Then

After Amy had gone, Olivia pushed a pile of laundry into the washing machine and began making the evening meal. The routine was automatic, but today she hacked into onions and sawed at the carrots, making thick rounds that would take ages to cook.

Christ, was she really nearly eighteen and this was the extent of her Saturday night? Cooking for her dad. Doing household chores. She thought about Amy going out for a Chinese with Chris – and the planned shag fest. What a fucking nightmare. Amy and Chris were *in love*. In lust. Whatever. Amy had made her mind up and there was nothing she could do about it.

Olivia heard keys in the front door and her dad called out a greeting. He ambled into the kitchen and sat down in his usual chair at the table. He looked expectant. Did he have to sit in the same seat every single mealtime? Christ, it wouldn't hurt to help out either. Olivia slammed a plate of food down in front of him and he looked at her in surprise.

'Everything OK?' he said.

'Fine,' she snapped.

He eyed her warily as she clattered pots together in the sink. 'You not eating?'

'I'm not hungry.'

'Are you going out tonight?'

'No.'

'Why not? Isn't Amy around? And those boys you go out with to the pub?'

Olivia thrust the pan around the sink and water sloshed on to the floor. 'I'm too busy to go out, aren't I? I've got washing to do, the bathroom to clean, the hoovering *and* the food shop.' A tide of emotion steadily rose within her. 'Someone has to look after you, don't they? Someone has to be the skivvy round here. No other fucker is doing anything to look after this house.'

'Olivia!'

She spun around. 'What? Olivia – what? So I swore, so what? I'm pissed off, that's why. Really pissed off. I don't drink, I don't stay out late, I study hard, I do everything for you, and I may as well be invisible. You didn't even ask me about my mock results!'

The shriek of her voice lingered for a moment and then she tossed the dishcloth down, ran up to her room and threw herself on to her bed. Sod him. She wanted him to be a dad. To *do* something. *Anything*. Instead of dragging his miserable face around and expecting everyone to feel sorry for him. She wanted him to stand tall and proud, to give her a hug and tell her everything would be all right.

She pushed her face into the pillow, sobbing, and then the phone began to trill on the bedside table next to her. She bunched the pillow around her ears, but still the phone rang on. Why didn't her dad answer it downstairs? It wouldn't be for her. She'd just spent the afternoon with Amy, no one else knew her number.

But what if it was . . . Chris?

Christ! Was she ever going to learn? He *loved* Amy; he was going to be having wild sex with her the minute they could be alone.

The ringing stopped. Perhaps the call had been Paul? Would he have been brave enough to ask Amy for her number? She'd made it clear she wasn't interested in him but, still, hanging out with Paul for the evening was better than lying on her bed crying like a kid. The shrill sound started again and Olivia snatched up the handset. 'Hello,' she said flatly, wiping her eyes.

'Liv, it's me.' Amy's voice sounded strange, strangled.

Olivia sat up properly. 'You OK?'

'Yes. No . . .' Amy sucked in a shaky breath. 'Mum and Dad have just sat me down and said . . . they said . . . they're moving – emigrating – to New Zealand.' She began to cry quietly.

Olivia pictured Amy twisting the phone cord around and around her fingers. 'What? That's a bit sudden. When are they going?'

'Mum says they've been planning it for ages. Apparently, Dad has always wanted to live over there and now's the right time. They didn't want to tell me before just in case they didn't get the visa. But the visa came today. Oh God, Liv, you should have seen the look on Dad's face. He was glowing, he's really excited about it. I kind of ruined it. I was so shocked, I flipped out and Dad's face crumpled. I feel really mean now. This is his dream and I've spoilt it for him.'

'How did they expect you to react? When are they going?'

'Not right away. They're going to wait until I go to uni. They say I'll be busy doing my own thing, living my own life, and I can come and visit them in the holidays.'

'But you're not going to uni.'

'I know.'

'You need to tell them.'

'I know! But then what if they decide *not* to go to New Zealand? Mum won't leave me here if I haven't got a plan and I'd feel awful if I ruined it for Dad.'

'What are you going to do, then?'

'What would you do?'

'Duh, get a proper plan together! Work out exactly what it is you want to do. Do you want to go to cookery school or get an apprenticeship in a restaurant? If you give your parents a clear idea, then they'll feel happier about leaving you. Amy, this might just be the get-out clause you've needed! You'll get your own way after all! Go for it, we only live one life, right?'

'Yes!' She went quiet for a moment. 'Chris and I have been talking about having a year out together and going travelling.'

Olivia didn't say anything.

'There's nothing wrong with that, is there? We'll have our A-level results and Chris will defer his uni place at Manchester. Then, we were thinking, I can get an apprenticeship up there. I'm sure there'll be plenty of restaurants I can apply to.'

Olivia gripped the phone. She wouldn't be his *fuck buddy* then.

'Olivia? You still there?'

'Yep.'

'So?'

'What?'

'Is that a good plan? Do you think my parents will go for it?'

The emotional tide flooded back. 'Maybe,' she croaked, trying to hold back a fresh wave of tears. 'I've got to go now.' She replaced the handset and pushed her face back into the pillow.

Chapter 30

Olivia

Then

Olivia watched Chris sling his rucksack over his shoulder and the key slide out of its pocket. Ching! The metal bounced on the wooden floor, unheard and unseen by the stampede of students intent on getting out of college and on with their weekend.

Olivia darted out of the way, following the key with her eyes as it spun across the floor, shunted this way and that by oblivious feet. She thought she might lose sight of it, then, by sheer luck, someone's foot caught the tip and propelled it towards her so all she had to do was stop it with her foot.

She looked down. Chris's front door key.

She looked up again and watched the *happy couple* disappear through the doors, Chris's arm pulling Amy so tight to him they looked like one being that could never be separated. The doors swung shut and they were gone.

Olivia looked back down at the key. Unzipping the side pocket on Chris's rucksack, where she knew he kept his key, wasn't something she'd planned on doing in art earlier. Although she couldn't deny the rising fury she felt every time Amy giggled or they whispered to one another, pointing at the clock every five minutes as it inched towards home time.

Tonight was *The Night*. The start of the weekend that Amy had been longing for.

By chance, Olivia's pencil had rolled on to the floor. When she'd bent down to pick it up, Chris's bag was within easy reach. So, just like that, she'd slid open the zip and sat back in her chair, her heart pounding. No one saw.

And anyway, she didn't purposefully *take* the key, it just – fell.

Olivia bent down and picked it up. She didn't need it, she wasn't expecting to find it, but now she had it, it seemed like serendipity. She could already see how things would play out. Amy and Chris were probably running out of the college entrance, hand in hand, desperate to get back to Chris's empty house as soon as possible. Oh yes, Olivia knew all the details. She'd dug her nails into her palms when Amy divulged the plan, forcing Olivia to be her alibi if her mum phoned. What could Olivia say? She just had to remind herself to nod in the right places.

The lovebirds would soon be marching up the hill, swinging hands and smiling at one another. They'd arrive, Chris would shrug off his rucksack and reach into the pocket for the key, grinning his lopsided grin and never taking his eyes off Amy. His fingers would grope and fiddle inside the empty space and he'd have to drag his gaze away from her and search a bit harder until the entire contents of his rucksack were laid out on the ground.

Olivia opened her satchel and pulled out a small purse. She dropped the key inside and zipped it tightly closed. She kissed the purse and put it back in her bag.

234

Later that evening, Olivia lay on her bed, waiting for Amy's call that she was certain would come very soon. The phone remained silent and she picked up the receiver, half expecting to hear the trill of Amy's voice on the other end.

Amy *would* call. She'd be desperate to tell her about the disaster that had gone on that afternoon.

Olivia looked at the key lying on her dressing table. She'd rushed upstairs after college and flung it down as if it burned her fingers. Shame flared briefly and she'd yanked open the drawer and pushed the key inside. What had she done? She'd done nothing bad. She'd just made things . . . difficult. Then she remembered how Amy and Chris had looked, nestled together, energy in their step, desperate to be back at his, desperate to be naked in bed.

She'd taken the key back out of the drawer. Nicking Chris's key might stop them today, but it wouldn't stop them forever. They'd find another way to . . . *fuck*.

The phone rang and Olivia snatched up the receiver.

'Wow, were you waiting for me to call?' Amy sounded giddy – not annoyed, not frustrated, but *excited*.

Olivia had the urge to slam the phone back down.

'You'll never guess what happened this afternoon!' she trilled.

Olivia's stomach rolled over.

They'd done It. How?

She reached for the radio and music blared into the room. 'I can't guess,' she muttered into the phone.

'What?' said Amy, laughing. 'I can't hear you! Turn the radio down!'

Olivia fiddled with the dial, annoyed by the magnet of her own curiosity. She lay back on the bed and flexed her feet forwards and backwards, unpainted nails and pale feet a stark contrast against the purple duvet cover.

'We got back to Chris's house and he didn't have his key, can you believe it? It'd fallen out of his bag.'

Olivia's skin prickled. 'Wait a minute, are you at home? Can't your parents hear you?'

'No! I'm at Chris's house, duh!'

'But I thought you said you couldn't get in?'

'We couldn't! That's what I'm trying to tell you! I thought I was going to cry but then Chris said he'd see if the downstairs loo window was open. The side gate was locked so he jumped over and it was, thank God, but tiny! Chris was way too big to squeeze through so he told me to have a go, can you imagine? Me and my big boobs and big butt. He shoved me through. We couldn't stop laughing, I must have looked so ridiculous.' She paused. 'God, I hope he didn't notice how massive my arse is.'

Olivia felt light-headed. God, her toenails looked awful. She sat up and tucked the phone under her ear and reached for the nail polish – Orchid Black, an almost perfect match to her duvet cover.

'Do you think he noticed?' Doubt laced Amy's voice.

'Probably.' Olivia stroked polish on to her big toe: centre, side, side.

'Thanks!' She laughed a little uncertainly.

Olivia ran the brush over the next toenail and admired the glossy purple. 'Where's Chris?' she said suddenly. 'Does he know you're talking to me?'

'Of course! He can't hear anything though, he's in the shower.'

Nail polish plopped on to Olivia's foot and she wiped it away, leaving a purple smear like a bruise.

They've definitely done It.

Amy's voice dropped. 'We'd have been gutted if we couldn't get in. I love him so much, Liv. I can't believe he loves me as much as I love him.'

Olivia closed her eyes and slid the phone out from under her chin and rocked her head from side to side to release the crick in her neck. She began to mouth along to the lyrics of the song on the radio and contemplated whacking the sound back up. She put the receiver back to her ear. 'Great,' she said flatly.

'I know you said you didn't want to hear the details, but—' Amy's voice became all breathy. 'Oh God, Liv, we've had a *great* time, I don't know what I was worrying about.'

Olivia laid the receiver on the bed this time – another coat of polish? Or was one enough?

'Liv? Are you still there?' Amy's voice sounded tinny and distant.

Olivia picked the phone up again. 'Listen, I've got to go.'

'Liv.' Amy's voice softened. 'Are you OK? You've been a bit, well, off, recently.' She sighed. 'I know I've been caught up with Chris and haven't been around as much. I'm sorry.'

Olivia looked at the key on her dressing table. 'I'm fine. Hey, I found a key on the floor after art today, do you think it might belong to Chris?'

Chapter 31

AMY

Now

'Did you have a good time, kids?' says Shannon when she arrives at my flat the following morning. She's wearing a snug vest top that matches her green eyes and emphasises the swell of her pregnant belly. She crouches down and sweeps Reuben and Kira into a hug and the children respond in a tumble of words that make her laugh. 'What was that? Did you say Chris was here?' she says.

Kira nods. 'He had a sleepover as well.'

Shannon straightens up and looks at me with the widest wolf-ish grin I've ever seen and breaks into a burst of throaty laughter. 'Did he now?'

My face pinks. 'No, he didn't!' I protest, but my grin is almost as wide as hers. I shake my head. 'Seriously he *didn't*,' I repeat. 'He stayed for dinner and went home.'

'Okaaay,' she drawls, unsuccessfully trying to hide a snigger behind her hand. 'Kids – go and get your stuff.' They run off to Bea's bedroom and Shannon grabs me, her face inches from mine. 'What happened?' she whispers, her eyes dancing.

She's so close I can detect a trace of mint chewing gum on her breath. 'None of your business,' I say, but I'm smiling.

'Did you get foxy?' she whispers.

'Shannon!'

'Come on!'

It's a stupid conversation, like we're teenagers, but the frothy feelings that jump around inside me feel exactly like that. 'Just . . . kissing. Well, lots of kissing.' Until late into the night, when I reluctantly pushed Chris out the door because he couldn't be here when the kids woke up.

She claps her hands together and laughs but before she can say anything further, Reuben and Kira barrel back into the living room and the doorbell shrills on the café door below.

'Amy!' comes a shout from down below.

The children race out on to the roof terrace and peer through the railings. 'Chris! Auntie Susan!' Reuben cries, and he runs back inside. 'Shall I open the door?'

'Chris,' Shannon repeats with a wink, 'and your mum?'

I'm as confused as her. Mum and I have shared few words since she admitted she was handling the sale of the Boat Shed; I've kept out of her way when she's turned up with prospective buyers. I've got more important things on my mind and my mood is far too buoyant to be dampened by her sour company. And as for turning up here with Chris? God only knows what *that's* about. He'd said to me as he left last night that he'd be back as soon as Shannon had collected the kids, and here he is. But entertaining my mother was not in the plan.

'Come on, kids, time to go,' says Shannon as she gathers their things. 'Lovely sundress.' She grins again. 'Don't worry, I'll steer your mum away. I'll invite her for a coffee. You don't need her cramping your style today.' She bursts into another peal of dirty laughter and the three of them clatter off down the stairs, with Kira asking Shannon why she keeps laughing, and her replying, 'Because I'm *so* happy'.

I stand at my front door, running my hands down my dress as I wait for Chris to appear around the corner. The fabric is a floral pattern with yellow roses and something I've had in my wardrobe for ages, but felt was too dressy to wear for no reason at all. But today, I *like* that I have no reason to wear it. I'm proud of the way it shapes my cleavage and nips in at the waist, I feel good. And I don't want Chris to think I live in shorts and T-shirts – even though I do.

The sharp clip of Mum's heels sound on the stairs below, followed by Chris's heavier footsteps. My heart sinks. Shannon's persuasive tactics haven't worked and suddenly I feel stupid standing here in this ridiculous dress, and I don't need Mum pointing this out to me. She appears with Chris behind her and as they climb the last flight to my door, I step back to let them in. Mum brushes a kiss on my cheek and Chris shrugs his shoulders, telling me this was not in *his* plan either.

The three of us stand silently in the living room, looking at one another. Mum is in her 'weekend' clothes – navy slacks, a crisp white shirt and pumps – and for once I'm the one who feels overdressed. I don't want to ask her to sit down, let alone make her a coffee. I can't think of one good reason why she'd be here. All she's done is ruin things for me. She's responsible for Chris and I being apart for all these years; for Bea not growing up with her dad; for my home and my café being snatched from under me.

'I bumped into your mum on the beach as I was coming over,' says Chris by way of explanation, and then he surprises me by moving to my side and taking my hand. 'Shall I make some tea?' he asks.

I shake my head. 'We've got plans, haven't we?' I say pointedly.

Mum's eyes rove over the hand-holding and then my dress. 'Perhaps I should have phoned first,' she says.

Was that an apology? We both know she never phones, she's always turned up when she feels like it because she assumes I'm always available.

'Was there something you wanted to tell me?' I'm sounding rude, but a part of me is pleased with my ability to stay calm this morning, because isn't this how Mum always speaks to me? Impassive. In control.

Chris edges away from us. 'I'll be outside,' he mutters, and goes on to the roof terrace to sit on the swing seat.

'What is it?' I hiss. 'What do you want?'

'I was coming over to apologise,' Mum says, pulling out one of the dining chairs and sitting down.

I watch her warily, unsure how to respond. She looks down at her folded hands and then up at me. 'I'll get to the point. I should have told you at the start that the owners wanted to sell the Boat Shed building,' she begins. 'I should have said that they'd hired me to do it for them.' Her hands twist in her lap. 'It wasn't fair for you to find out about the sale through Grant – or for me not to tell you I was involved. Goodness, I'd have been cross if the situation were reversed.' She lets out a brittle laugh. 'I thought telling Shannon about the vacant premises at the port might have been some way of improving the situation.'

'You mean so you wouldn't feel guilty.'

She smiles a little. 'I suppose so.'

We're silent for a moment.

'It wasn't about me profiting from your loss,' she continues. 'I thought selling the old building would help give you the push you needed to expand and improve your business.'

I open my mouth to retort but she's quick to carry on. 'What was that place like? In West Auckland?'

'A dump.'

'That must have been disappointing.'

I swallow down the anger that rises and make a noncommittal noise. I blank out what she says and focus on Chris. He must sense me watching as he turns and mouths 'OK?' and I nod in reply.

'It was a rotten hut. It needs rebuilding and I just can't afford to do that.'

'Remember what I said, Amy, about helping. If you really like this place, we can sit down and work out a business plan.'

I study her closely and watch her mouth work itself into a strained smile. I don't quite know what's going on – it feels like she has something else on her mind. But she doesn't say anything more and, anyway, I'm anxious to get rid of her. I want to hang on to the swell of excitement I'm feeling with Chris being here.

I mutter a thank you and say I'll think about it, then Mum gets to her feet.

'I'll let you get on with your day.' She glances at Chris. He's rocking the swing seat back and forth. The rusty hinges squeak, reminding me of last night and our quiet laughter as we paused in our kissing, thinking the creaking might wake the kids.

I catch Mum staring at me. She looks like she's going to speak, but instead she brushes her lips to my cheek and calls out a goodbye to Chris. I watch her disappear down the stairs and wait until I hear the café door close. Behind me, I sense Chris approaching and I slowly shut my front door. Then he's right behind me, his breath tickling my hair and his hands circling my waist, jump-starting the flutter of anticipation I've had all morning into something far more electric. He buries his face into my hair and inhales.

I think about the photo of us outside The Fox standing together, just like this, and I lean back into his chest.

Now we're alone.

I close my eyes and a thousand thoughts come marching into my mind. Me, squeezing through the downstairs loo window in his house, and how I shook as he undressed me, which I'd tried to laugh away, and he'd silenced with fluttery kisses that made me shiver all the more. Then my thoughts jump back to now, and all the things I don't want to think about, and instead I let the heat and wanting in the press of our bodies muffle them into silence.

Slowly, I turn around. I tip my face up to his. Intensity burns in his eyes, matched by my own, and his mouth moves towards mine. I pull away and grin, gently prodding him backwards towards the sofa. He laughs as he collapses back on to the soft cushions and then lifts me up by my waist and pulls me on to his lap, making me squeal.

Instantly, my laughter evaporates. We stare at one another, and a skitter of excitement and nerves skates across my skin as I trace my finger around the shape of his lips and reach down and kiss each dancing corner. I pull back and he inhales sharply. He runs his hands through my curls, reaching for me again, pulling me towards him. Our mouths crush together and his hands glide along my bare thighs beneath my dress and cup my bum. I tug at his T-shirt and our kisses deepen. Then we're fumbling with each other's clothes in a familiarity that isn't familiar at all and, as we move together, I feel a rush of sweet release I remember so well.

Afterwards, I lie on Chris's chest and listen to his heartbeat slow to a steady thrum. Then, as the shimmering haze of the moment begins to lift, a confusing twist of pleasure and anguish washes over me.

What have we done?

Chapter 32

OLIVIA

Then

Olivia stood in the kitchen in her dressing gown, staring at her dad's scrawl on the back of a sealed pink envelope.

Happy Birthday love! Sorry, there's been a work emergency! Have a great day and I'll be back as fast as I can.

Olivia saw her day dissolve in front of her. He'd promised to take her to the National Gallery, where there was an exhibition she'd wanted to see for ages. He'd even booked afternoon tea at the Savoy afterwards. He'd said he wouldn't play golf. But golf masked as work. *Networking*, he called it. Why couldn't he have just said no? He had plans to take his daughter out, she was turning eighteen – such a milestone! And he couldn't *possibly* spend the day without her because it wouldn't be long before she'd be gone – and then he'd hardly see her at all.

Olivia slid a purple-painted nail beneath the flap of the envelope and pulled out the card. A huge '18' decorated the front, neatly sidestepping the humility of having to wear a badge, which, in a parallel universe, would have been her mum's idea of a hilarious joke. She laid it face down on the table and clicked on the kettle. It was only ten o'clock; the day was already stretching into an eternity.

Happy-bloody-birthday.

The phone on the wall shrilled and Olivia reached for it without thinking.

'Hello?'

'Hi, love, happy birthday.' Jeanette's voice filtered down the line.

Tears instantly pricked Olivia's eyes, much to her annoyance. *Hang up, hang up, hang up.*

'Livvy, darling, I know you don't want to talk to me, I understand that. But just give me a minute.'

'How did you get our number?'

'I phoned your dad at work and he said—'

'What? Dad *gave* you our number?'

'He's not a monster, Livvy, he knew I'd want to speak to you on your birthday.'

Cheers, Dad.

'Darling, I don't want to annoy you, it's your special day.'

'*Annoy* me?' Olivia snarled. 'Is that all you think you've done?' She clenched the handset. She didn't need to listen to this. Especially not today. Yes, it was *her* special day and she didn't need anyone ruining it.

'I'm sure you've already got plans,' her mum began to gabble. 'I thought . . . well, if you haven't got plans, you might like to come out for lunch with me. I mean, I want to take you out to lunch, but if you're busy, I understand . . .'

Olivia scrubbed angrily at her eyes. A day all alone? Or lunch with her mum? There was no contest. 'I'm busy,' she hissed and hung up the phone. What was her dad thinking, giving Jeanette their number? Some birthday this was turning into.

The phone rang again and she snatched it up. 'I don't want to speak to you and I definitely don't want to see you!' she yelled.

'Whoa,' said Amy. 'You don't sound like you're having the best birthday *ever*. What's going on?'

'Oh, hi, sorry, I thought you were my mum.'

'Oh right, wow. What did she say? I mean, apart from wishing you happy birthday?'

'She wants to take me out to lunch.'

'Uh huh – and?'

'And – what?'

'Isn't that a good thing?' Amy ventured. 'Oh wait, you can't cos your dad's taking you out, isn't he?'

'Nope.'

'What do you mean – no? I thought he was taking you to some fancy hotel in London for afternoon tea?'

'He's gone off to golf. Some work thing.'

'That's out of order, it's your eighteenth!' Amy sounded indignant. 'Well, if you don't want to see your mum, then you'll have to come out with me. Come to The Fox for lunch, I'm going to meet Chris in his lunch break.'

No way. 'No, no, I'd feel a right gooseberry.'

'Don't be silly, we're not like that.'

But you are like that.

'Ask Paul too, then,' Amy suggested. 'You can't stay home all day on your birthday and feel sorry for yourself.' She laughed. 'Come *on*. You're only eighteen once and it's going to be sunny. Surely you can't resist a ploughman's in the pub garden?'

Olivia sighed. 'All right, then.'

It was a warm spring afternoon and all the tables in the garden were taken by the time they arrived. Chris found two empty benches at the front of the pub, flanked by large pots tumbling over in pink blooms. Amy and Chris sat on one of them, heads bent together, forcing Olivia to sit with Paul on the other.

After they'd eaten, Paul lit a cigarette and passed it to Olivia. 'Having a good day?' he said as he lit one for himself. 'I can't believe we've nearly finished college. Soon it'll all be over. No more exams, no more studying, no more lessons, just the freedom of summer – bring it on!'

Olivia had been so focused on revising, she hadn't put any thought into what she'd do in the months between exams finishing and university starting. She ought to have found a job for the holidays by now. Apart from needing to earn money, what the hell else was she going to do?

'When do you start your summer job at the pool?' she asked. 'They won't like your new nipple piercing.' She laughed and pointed at his T-shirt. She'd been surprised to learn Paul was a keen swimmer and had a weekend job as a lifeguard at the local leisure centre. She wondered, briefly, what he looked like in shorts and no make-up, sitting on the lifeguard's chair. Or perhaps he wore the make-up?

'Beginning of June. What about you? Have you got a job?'

She shook her head. 'I haven't even looked. It's probably too late now.'

'The café at the leisure centre needs people, why don't you apply? I could put in a word.'

'What, flipping greasy burgers and clearing tables?'

He shrugged. 'Could be worse.'

'Liv,' Amy called over. 'Where do you want to go tonight? You decide, you're the birthday girl.'

Olivia had already chosen a pub. The White Cross attracted a slightly older crowd – university students and the like – and she'd heard it had a good vibe on Saturday nights. She'd have no trouble getting past the bouncers now she was eighteen and had a genuine driving licence to prove it. 'The White Cross? You know, the one across town?' she said.

Amy shrugged and looked at Chris.

'Yeah, sounds good,' he said, standing and stretching. 'Got to get back to work.' He pulled Amy to her feet and leant down and gave her a long, lingering kiss.

Olivia looked away. Did they *ever* stop?

'Wait, it's such a beautiful day, let's take some photos.' Amy darted over to her bag and pulled out a camera. She handed it to Paul. 'Take a few snaps, will you?'

Olivia watched Chris wrap his arms around Amy's waist so she could snuggle back into his chest. He bent his head, inhaling the scent of her hair.

The camera clicked – and Olivia's stomach turned over.

Chapter 33

AMY

Now

What am I doing?

I watch Chris's chest rise and fall in the rhythmic pattern of his sleep. We fall asleep late and I no longer wake early. I'm pulled down into a deep cocoon of contentment and then, when the alarm shrills, I jump up, feeling a little guilty, yet strangely bright and lucid for someone surviving on so little sleep. Though it doesn't take much to be cajoled back by the lustful look in Chris's eyes. I fit into his arms like I used to, things are the same – but different. We might be worn around the edges but inside we're teenagers all over again.

What am I doing? As Bea's homecoming date marches closer – ten days and counting – the question shouts a little louder. Things have moved fast between Chris and I, but perhaps they haven't. Perhaps a little something has shifted each time we've seen each other this last couple of months.

I place my hand on his chest and feel his heart pulse against my palm. Panic clenches my belly when I think about what he might say when I finally admit *he has another daughter*. I could've told him that first night, out on the swing seat, when our bodies throbbed electric under the blanket and we filled in so many other gaps in our lives. He reminded me that memories of this place will always be in my mind and not lost in the demolition. They weren't new words, but they sounded real coming from him, and I can see a shard of light in my future.

Still, I didn't tell him.

But then he didn't tell me anything more about Gemma either.

I've become good at boxing off things I don't want to think about – does he do this too?

There's still so much unsaid between us. I run my fingers gently through the waves of his hair and he stirs a little. He's not had a haircut since he walked back into my life and the ends are tinged blond, reminding me of when I drew his portrait in art class all those years ago. He says he kept the picture. I laughed because I thought he was joking, but he insisted he had, and when I blushed, he smiled and kissed the heat in my cheeks.

I want to tell him how much I've missed him. How long I waited for him to follow me here. But I can't talk of these things until I've told him he's Bea's dad. But now there's *this* between us, I'm scared. Really, really scared. *I've hidden his daughter from him.* What kind of person does that? I see my crime in all its gory detail. But what do I do? Shouldn't Bea be the first to know? But even if I could call her, I can't announce this kind of news on the phone or in an email. I need to wait until I've picked her up from the airport. Tell her when I can read every nuance of her reaction and hold her tight.

Chris stirs again and reaches for me. I snuggle back down, breathing in the scent of sleep on his skin, and he spoons into me, arms reaching around and pulling me close. He's not asleep any more. There isn't time, I've got so much to do, but I'm liquid when I'm with him.

◆　◆　◆

Later, we rush down the stairs and I fling open the shutters and slide back the doors to let in the salty air to energise the café. Chris helps me shake out the tablecloths and they billow in the breeze as we lay them on the tables. We chat about my love of vintage and how I found the treasure box of fabrics all those years ago.

'I can see why you love the Boat Shed so much,' he says, putting his arms around my waist and pulling me towards him. Desire flutters once more. I'm reminded again of the photo outside The Fox and I have the urge to show Chris, to tell him I was pregnant all those years ago.

'What do you think?' says Chris and I realise I've not heard a word.

'Sorry – daydreaming!' I reply with a smile.

He laughs. 'This is a historic building and that's a really good reason to keep it. It'd be a travesty to knock it down.'

I look at the splintered shutters and the weathered wood cladding. A breeze gusts in and I'm reminded winter is not far away and I'm living on borrowed time. Shannon's right. This place *is* freezing in winter, even with heaters on – no wonder the customers don't come. *The memories aren't here*, I remind myself, they're locked in my heart.

'But it *is* only a building,' I say slowly. 'Perhaps it's time for a change.' I realise I actually mean what I say. I think about the modern industrial building on the other side of the harbour with the huge glass windows. Offices filled with people wanting a place to relax over breakfast and lunch where they can admire the views.

Yes, I can do this.

Chris crouches down to run his hands across the floorboards. 'The Boat Shed really ought to be preserved,' he repeats. 'Look at this wood, it's beautiful. What kind is it?'

'Kauri, I think. But it's scratched and scuffed.'

'Lived-in,' he says, straightening up. 'It's pure vintage.'

I hadn't thought about it like that. Pure vintage.

He goes over to the window and presses his finger into the decaying wood frame. 'You could repair these,' he mutters, and looks around. 'Add insulation to the walls and the ceiling. This place could be transformed.'

'There's just one small thing you're forgetting,' I say, folding my arms. 'I haven't got any money.'

'You could get a loan,' he says, taking my hands. 'Write a business plan, do it properly. You could make it work.'

I look around but I can't see what he sees. 'Really?'

'I've sketched you a design,' he says hesitantly. 'Look, I don't want to interfere, I just think it's such a waste to knock this old place down, especially when it means so much to you.' He pauses. 'Do you want to see the drawings? I've got them upstairs in my bag.'

I don't reply because I don't know what to say. He's thought about this? About me? I feel a flicker of hope. 'I'd like that.'

Chris disappears back up to my flat and I wander into the kitchen, excitement starting to bubble. I go over to the framed newspaper cutting on the wall with my five glowing gold stars and hear Shannon call out as she comes into the café. She catches me staring at the article.

'Hey, hun,' she says as she plonks a box of freshly baked bread on the worktop. She pulls me into a tight hug. 'Don't worry about the café. I promise, you'll be a great success wherever you are. I've told Grant I'm going to help you make a go of the next place until the baby arrives.'

I laugh. 'I'm fine,' I say, and for once I actually mean it. There's a thumping sound as Chris jogs back down the stairs and rushes into the kitchen holding the plans he's drawn. His face radiates pleasure, but he stops short when he sees Shannon.

'Morning,' she says and laughs throatily, making a deliberate point of looking at her watch. She's been on the school run all week and this is the first time she's caught Chris here with me so early.

I try to ignore the wolfish grin that shows off the gap between her teeth, but I'm feeling giddy and burst out laughing again. She knows I've seen Chris, but I haven't told her he's slept in my bed every night this last week. I've placed all thoughts of him and how I feel in another box in my head. I'm beginning to see a pattern, is this what I do? Box off the stuff I don't want to deal with?

I put my arm around Chris's waist. 'Chris thinks I should keep the café,' I say.

'*Really?*' Shannon leans back against the counter, her green eyes narrowing.

'Not as it is,' I rush on. 'A renovated version. A *restored* version.' I find myself championing Chris's corner even though I haven't seen the plans myself yet, worked out how much the project will cost or if there's a possibility of getting a business loan. 'Show us,' I say to him.

Chris unrolls the drawings and talks through his ideas about improving the fabric of the building, installing heating for winter and outdoor heaters on the terrace for the months when the evenings are cool. 'You might want to think about getting an alcohol licence and staying open later,' he concludes. 'You could be a café by day and a restaurant by night, but get a chef in to do the cooking – otherwise you'll be working all hours.'

'Sounds amazing,' Shannon murmurs as she scans the plans.

I stare at Chris's drawings, hand-drawn with pencil in bold, decisive strokes that remind me of his artwork at college. I feel the familiar throat ache that seems to arrive so easily these days. *He's done this for me?*

'I love it,' I say, turning to him, and the strange look on his face makes me think I've said 'I love *you*' by mistake, and I turn away, embarrassed. 'It looks expensive though.'

'I've put together costs for the project,' he says, handing me a sheet of paper and darting a look between Shannon and me. 'You can use them in your business proposal.'

I run my eye over the numbers. They're big and scary. But I look at them both and smile. I can do this, I really can.

Later, I'm clearing tables outside, daydreaming about Chris's drawings and what my café could become – then wondering how quickly I can close, to be alone with him again. I straighten up and my eyes automatically land on Bea's island family spiking up from the sea, and for the first time I feel a real burst of excitement about telling her that Chris is her dad. And he's *here*, right here in Auckland!

'What are you grinning at?' says Shannon, coming to my side.

'The islands. They remind me of Bea. I can't believe she's going to be home in ten days.'

'I know, I'm excited too, the kids are excited – we've all missed her.'

We stand quietly. I hear the rumblings of John's voice at one of the tables as he tells a silly joke to the children, then shrill laughter from Reuben.

'When are you going to tell Chris?' Shannon speaks softly, but I still whirl around to check he's not within earshot.

'I keep changing my mind,' I whisper. 'I hate the idea of him knowing before Bea – surely I have a responsibility to tell her first?

So she's got time to come to terms with this craziness before she meets him?'

Shannon doesn't reply and I bristle because I want her approval. 'What else am I supposed to do?' I demand.

'You're shagging him! Shouldn't the poor man know before she comes home? So *he's* got time to come to terms with it?'

Echoes of every other relationship I've had before ring through my mind – the moment where I have to choose between my daughter and my lover.

'I just want Bea home so I can tell her face to face,' I repeat stubbornly. 'No more half-truths and lies.'

Shannon sighs. 'OK, I hear you. Have you thought about what you're going to say to her?'

My mind is a blank, then rapidly fills with words and phrases that jumble over one another. What *am* I going to say? 'No.' My face constricts. 'She's going to hate me.'

Shannon smiles. 'No more than any teenager hates their mum from time to time.'

'God, thanks for the reassurance.'

'You've got to be realistic. This is going to be a massive shock and she's bound to be angry at first. Have you thought about writing down what you want to say? It might help you straighten things out in your mind.'

'Writing stuff down didn't work last time,' I mutter, thinking about Chris's letter.

Shannon shakes her head. 'That letter is old ground, Amy.'

'I know – but I've let Bea down.'

She squeezes my arm. 'It wasn't your fault and now you can put things right. Why don't you start by telling her about the letter you wrote to Chris? Explain what you told him and how he never knew. She'll understand.'

Tears blur the volcanic family. 'Will she?'

Shannon hugs me hard. 'Yes.'

I pick up the tray and, as I walk past Shannon's family, I think, what if Dad *had* delivered the letter? I'd never have known Reuben or Kira and their sweet little faces and funny words; Shannon's throaty laugh and dancing eyes; Grant's kindness and loyalty; John and Linda's love and support. I'd never have known any of them.

I wouldn't be here in my café on the beach. Or living in my flat with its amazing sea views. None of this would've existed in my world.

But I would have had Chris – wouldn't I?

Chapter 34

AMY

Now

Bea will be home in nine days.

My untruth is pressing on my glow of happiness and when I woke this morning, I rolled over each option again. I've swivelled around to stand in Chris's shoes – how would *I* feel? With all that's happened, I wouldn't want any secrets between us, I'd want the truth. I owe him the truth, and he needs time to digest my bombshell before his second daughter walks into his life. So even though I promised myself I'd speak to Bea first, I've decided I'll tell him.

Not yet, but tonight.

Out on the swing seat, the morning air is sharp with the hint of oncoming autumn and clouds wisp across a watery blue sky. I snuggle closer to Chris, savour every second – before everything implodes. I've not dared ask him anything more about Gemma, when all I want to say is, when's she visiting? When can Bea and I meet her? Surely he'll want her to experience a holiday here before he leaves? But that's jumping ahead to a different conversation, a muddling conversation about *this* – us – that I can't sink into until we've had the *other* conversation. I'm chancing my luck – he might hate me, refuse to see me again, be relieved to go home. The edges of my happiness wobble.

Chris pushes the swing seat gently with his foot, wearing a quiet smile of contentment as he gazes at the beach through sleepy, half-closed eyes.

It's agony.

Later, we'll walk along the beach and watch the sun sink down behind Bea's island family and I'll tell Chris what she used to say – *Mummy, Daddy, me* – and then I'll explain exactly what I wrote in the letter, to show him my intention was *always* for him to know he was going to be a dad. And then? I don't know. I have to accept this could be the end of *this,* whatever 'this' is between us. We might end up back where we started – or not. The choice will be in his hands.

'This place is just too good for you to leave,' Chris says, breaking my thoughts. He strokes the curve of my hip and my body tingles in excitable goosebumps. I press myself against him. I want everything to stop right here. Because isn't this what we all strive for in life? The simplicity of contentment. The simplicity of love.

Love?

I push the nonsense thoughts away and go back over his drawings for my new café in my mind. Now my eyes have been opened to this stylish café redesign, everything about my flat seems like a shabby embarrassment.

'If I decide to try and get the bank loan and take on the café, I'll need to do something about my flat,' I say, an idea forming in my head, even though such a huge project makes me feel giddy. 'Show me the business plan again.'

Chris gets up and comes back outside with the paperwork and I run my eye over the numbers. They're just as frightening as they were yesterday, but I'm not going to dismiss them until I've had a proper conversation with the bank. 'How much would it cost to renovate the flat too?' As I talk, my excitement grows. 'It could look amazing. I could save some money by doing some of the work myself. I'd have to close the café anyway to renovate so I might as well do the whole building.'

He smiles. 'Now you're talking. You'll easily see your money back. It'll be worth a fortune once it's been done up.'

I look at the numbers again. 'I'm probably dreaming. I've no idea if a bank would lend me the money to buy the building, let alone renovate it.'

'Your accountant could help you work it out.'

I laugh. 'I *am* the accountant!'

Chris looks surprised. 'Wow, you *are* busy.' He scratches his cheek. 'Have you thought about discussing the idea with your mum?'

I snort.

'Don't knock her, she's an experienced businesswoman. Don't let pride get in the way.'

I narrow my eyes and I'm about to make a smart remark when I realise this isn't Shannon I'm talking to and what Chris says are plain facts.

'I could, I suppose,' I say, trying not to sound grumpy. I can already picture Mum smirking when I show her Chris's business plan. 'She'll make me feel like an idiot,' I mutter. 'She already thinks I've made a mess of my life. She's never liked me running the café. She thinks it's a cop-out. She had bigger hopes for me and my life than . . . just this.'

'Really? When I saw her, she went on and on about how great it was you'd won the award and how much you deserved it.'

'Yeah right!' Then I realise he's serious. 'You must have heard wrong.' I make a face. A part of me wants to tell him he's wrong about Mum, but actually he's right, she *is* the best person to speak to about this project. I just need to figure out how to approach the conversation because, as Chris quite rightly points out, pride sits heavily on my shoulders.

Later, we go down to the café and into the kitchen where Chris sits on the worktop while I make a batch of scones to sell tomorrow. He chats to me about a project he's working on. I listen, ask questions; I enjoy hearing the passion he has for his job.

When the scones are in the oven, I ask Chris if he'll give the outside tables and chairs a wipe down while I mop the café floor. I need time to form the sentences in my head as to how I'm going to tell him about Bea. The more I say them to myself, the more convincing they sound, and I have a sense that everything is going to be just fine.

I'm just about finished and look up to see Chris staring out across the bay. His face is in profile and I regard the contours of his cheek, the curve that tickles the corner of his mouth – and laugh at my ogling. I'm about to go over and nestle myself into his back and ask him what he's dreaming about, but his jaw clenches: once, twice, three times. I hesitate. Perhaps he's thinking about Gemma. Perhaps he needs this private moment alone.

Chris must sense me watching because he glances over, and in that split second before he smiles, it's like he's thrown a bucket of cold water in my face. But before I can say anything, he strides towards me and plants a lingering kiss on my lips.

'Everything OK?' I say, pulling back, searching his face.

'Perfect,' he says, running his thumb over my cheek and staring at my mouth, then he kisses me again.

I'm imagining things. I'm imprinting my own emotions on him as the time moves closer for our walk and for me to tell him he's Bea's dad. My heart begins to thrum. 'Let's go for that walk now,' I say impulsively.

'Now?' he says.

'Why not? I'm pretty much ready for tomorrow. I can finish up later.'

'But I'm not done yet,' he says, stepping back slightly, eyes sliding towards the door.

'Let's not waste any more of our Sunday.' My voice has an edge to it as I realise how much I need to get this awful secret out in the open. I soften my tone. 'It's lovely outside.'

Chris looks at me strangely. 'What's the rush?' he says.

'Who's rushing?'

He glances at the door again. 'It won't take long and then I thought we might—' He brushes his lips over mine again, sparking a pulse of desire, and, just like that, my tension drains away.

I'm still smiling when he disappears back outside to finish off and I fly about the kitchen, emptying the bucket and loading the dishwasher. I'm flicking the cloth over the surfaces for a final wipe when I realise Chris hasn't come back inside. I pop my head around the kitchen door and I'm about to make a flirtatious remark when I see he's still on the terrace, talking to someone.

From this angle, I can't see Chris's face, nor the tall, slim woman who has her back to me. Then she shifts slightly and touches his arm. It's nothing, a light touch, but their voices are low, muted, and a slow thump begins in my right temple.

I walk towards them, my mind thick with sluggish thoughts that can't quite grasp why I'm feeling like this as I take in the woman's long flowery skirt, the plain black vest tucked loosely into the narrow waistband, her straw beach bag hooked over her shoulder. As I get closer, Chris's eyes jump to mine and his face flushes. The drumming at my temple intensifies as I stare at the waterfall of dark brown hair down her back.

The flat of her hand swiftly strokes the right side.

Olivia?

Chapter 35

Amy

Now

A jolt of electricity snaps through me and it's as though I've said her name aloud. She turns and the years peel away, then flicker back as Olivia's older-now-self smiles at me. I don't know what I was thinking. I'm alert and smiling, and I tuck a stray curl of hair behind my ear and wipe my hands on my shorts.

'Amy,' she says warmly, and draws me into an equally warm embrace. She smells of sun cream and sea air and I find myself hugging her back, thinking the old Olivia would never have been so intimate.

'Olivia . . . my God . . .' We draw apart and my eyes travel over her face again. Her olive skin has held back time longer than it has for me, and her cat-like eyes have a confidence that strengthens her gaze in a way it never did before. But I guess I'm not the same person either.

'It's so lovely to see you,' Olivia says, still gripping my hands and smiling. She's staring at me intently, and it feels a bit *too* intense. I glance at Chris. He's trying to smile but it looks fake, like something he's stuck on to his face, and he won't meet my eye. 'What an amazing place to live,' she continues. 'Such a beautiful beach and your café looks just wonderful.'

I gently tug my hands away and nod, feeling a strange mix of wariness and pride. 'What on earth brings you all this way?' I say, confused, and I look at Chris again. He's still wearing the weird grin and my own smile begins to falter as my mind whirs to catch up with this strange event unfolding in front of me.

This is no coincidence. Chris *and* Olivia? Here? Now? Together?

'Well,' Olivia replies, a little too brightly. 'I've come to see you. To . . . well, to have a catch-up, but I wasn't expecting Chris to be here!'

Her fingers touch his arm again. The gesture is simple but so *familiar* that the warning throb now stabs at my temple.

'He never tells me anything.' She laughs, but it sounds strained.

He never tells her anything?

The three of us stand in a triangle, with Chris at the apex. His mouth works noiselessly, then settles into a silent line. He folds his arms and stares at a spot over my shoulder. Olivia strokes her hair and darts looks between us.

'Seems like he never tells me anything either,' I reply coldly, and I move to stand in front of him so he *has* to look at me. 'Why is Olivia here?'

Chris's eyes slowly inch over to mine. 'I didn't know she was coming.'

He sounds imploring and suddenly I have an urgent need to get away from them both and I mutter 'I have to get the scones from the oven', even though I don't, and bolt back to the kitchen. I press my hot hands on to the cool surface of the stainless-steel counter. My skin's spiked in anxiety and that thing is still flickering and niggling and nagging at the back of my mind, and I can't grasp hold of it.

Don't be a victim. Wasn't that what I told myself when Chris first arrived? When I thought he knew about Bea? But why am I thinking this now? And yet . . .

I'm about to stride back out but I stop short when I see Olivia reach up and touch Chris's face with those butterfly fingers again. He doesn't brush her off, he doesn't pull away. I notice how easy they look together; her height a much better match to him than mine. She seems even taller than I remember; perhaps it's the long skirt that grazes her ankles.

She's tall, with long dark hair . . . she's beautiful . . . loves photography . . . no, I don't have a photo on me, I didn't bring my wallet out . . .

It's as though the curtain has been snatched away.

The niggle I couldn't pin down.

I surge forward and stumble across the café floor towards them. 'What are you really doing here, Olivia?' I call as I come back out on the terrace, because it makes absolutely no sense that she's just turned up at my café, out of the blue, all the way from England.

She smiles carefully and her eyes land on Chris.

'Olivia,' he says with a warning note in his voice. 'Don't.'

She turns back to me, her cat's eyes watching me closely. 'Like I said, I wanted to talk to you about something – in private. I didn't expect Chris to be here.' She laughs lightly. 'I mean, obviously I knew he was *here*, here in Auckland. Goodness, he might be living on the other side of the world, but he hasn't deserted us! What I meant was, I didn't expect to find him *here* – with you.'

Olivia's amused expression sends a shiver up my spine.

'What do you mean – *us?*' I say slowly, as everything sharpens. 'Do you mean Gemma?'

Olivia glances at Chris and I see a tiny shake of her head, in the kind of shorthand language couples use when they communicate without words. Couples who've been together forever. 'Yes, Gemma,' she says, a frown knotting her smooth forehead as she throws him another look.

Even though Olivia's dropped the bomb and cracked open his little secret, Chris doesn't look contrite, or sad, or anything. He just walks away to the edge of the terrace and stares at the sea.

What a shit.

Now Gemma's name is out in the open, the flickering memories in my mind shift and solidify into a collection of images showcasing the teenage Chris and Olivia, laughing together in a snapshot of scenes I thought I'd forgotten. Now I've heard the truth, I'm vaguely surprised I'm not writhing on the floor in agony, gnashing my teeth. The niggle, the flicker, the blur of Gemma's shadowy face I've never actually seen, has shaped into young Olivia – Gemma's mum – who's been waiting in the wings.

Chris's shoulders hunch and another shot of anger blasts through me. Why didn't he tell me? But I know the answer. I try to breathe evenly through the hammering in my chest as I toss over memories of Chris, Olivia and I, sifting through them all to make sense of what I'm thinking.

When . . . when did this happen? How could this happen?

'How old is Gemma?' I say softly, pushing at the corners of the conversation Chris and I had on the beach not so long ago, and at an answer I don't really want to hear.

Olivia's expression changes. She looks incredulous and patches of red begin to stain her neck. 'Chris, why haven't you spoken to Amy about Gemma?' she says.

He doesn't reply and somewhere in the distance I hear a child on the beach call for their mother. It's a drawn-out cry that I remember as indignation rather than fear. Probably time to go home.

'You didn't know about Gemma?' She sounds shocked but I'm not sure if this is part of some carefully planned act. 'When Chris said he'd seen you, I thought he'd told you that he and I . . .'

Chris spins around. 'Enough, Olivia,' he says, moving towards me. 'Amy, let me explain . . .' he begins.

But I step back. 'Just tell me how old she is,' I say, in a voice so bright and brittle it might shatter at any second.

Olivia wraps her arms around herself. 'Come on, Chris,' she says quietly. 'There's no point in being secretive, it's a long time ago.'

Liquid fills Chris's eyes.

Liar.

'She's seventeen,' he says quietly, and I catch a flash of myself strolling down the corridor at college with him, our arms wrapped around one another, blissfully unaware our future was about to change.

My brain scrambles to do the maths but the confession is here anyway, then I hear Olivia say, 'For Christ's sake, Chris, Gemma's nearly eighteen,' and I think of my lovely, beautiful, eighteen-year-old daughter coming home to me, and I'm ready for our lives to go back to how they were. Before she left, before Chris came, before Olivia, before Gemma. Before, before, before.

They stand next to one another – linked by their child and their marriage – and stare at me with disgusting pity. Has it always been like this? Has there always been a thinly veiled curtain hanging between me and them? Catching the breeze every now and then, giving glimpses of this moment, and I've not been able to see the full picture until now?

Chris and Olivia.

Their baby Gemma. My baby Bea.

Sisters.

My thoughts start racing again.

They want to show off their happy unit to Bea. To coax her into their family fold. Bea's an adult, she's old enough to decide for herself, and who wouldn't be wooed by the promise of a better life in England? Close to London, hours from Europe – not stuck out here on the thumb of the rest of the world.

Chris steps towards me again, his expression cleverly arranged into pain. But I'm cold. There never was *us*, just me the fool and he the con man, with Olivia standing in the shadows waiting for the moment to pounce. She strokes her hair and I see it's a languid, cat-like stroke: powerful, controlling and with none of the anxiety of years before.

I move towards the door, my home, the safe place where Bea and I live. 'It looks like you two have some catching up to do,' I say, forcing my voice to be level and strong. 'I need to lock up.'

'Amy, please . . .' Chris pleads, but I hold up my hand.

Olivia is about to speak and then lifts her hand to her mouth as if to silence herself. A diamond band slips loosely around her ring finger and I stare at it for a moment, then slam the terrace doors shut.

He took off his wedding ring. She didn't.

I turn the key.

Gemma's nearly eighteen . . .

I cross the café and climb the stairs to my home.

My Bea is eighteen . . .

I open my front door, walk into my bedroom and drag out the pink box from under my bed.

Chris and Olivia. Olivia and Chris.

I carry it back into the living room, snatch off the lid and turn the box upside down so the contents spill out on to the carpet.

I've been stupid, so fucking stupid. Not just once. But twice.

Chapter 36

Olivia

Then

'Are you sure you don't mind driving tonight, Livvy?' Chris called from the back seat.

The traffic lights turned red and Olivia looked in the rear-view mirror. Amy was snuggled into him, her arm slung across his body, clinging on as though he might run away. *Possessive.* They'd all had to listen to her recount a row she'd had with her mum earlier. Apparently, Susan had demanded Amy stay home and revise because she'd spent too long out with them that afternoon. But Amy had refused and stormed out, going to Chris's house where Olivia had picked them both up.

Clearly the argument had been forgotten. A dreamy smile played around Amy's lips.

'Don't you even want to have one drink to celebrate being eighteen?' Chris pressed. 'It's our last blow-out before the exams.'

She watched him tug absently at one of Amy's curls, unspiralling the ringlet and letting go: stretch, spring; stretch, spring.

'We don't all feel the need to get hammered when we go out,' muttered Paul next to her.

The lights changed and Olivia pressed her foot down on the accelerator a little harder than she meant to.

'She doesn't drink,' murmured Amy, 'so you don't mind, do you, Liv?'

'Yeah, but it *is* her birthday,' Chris persisted. 'She might want the one. You know, to celebrate being legal for once.'

'I am here, you know,' Olivia said drily. 'I do have ears and a voice.'

She pulled into the pub car park and they all got out. As the four of them sloped off towards the entrance, Olivia looked across to the bouncers, then back at Amy. She had to think quick.

'Hey, Paul,' she said, nudging him, 'show Amy your new piercing.'

Amy stopped in front of him. 'Another one?' she said, smiling. 'Where?'

Olivia fell into step with Chris, wishing she could link her arm through his. 'So are you going to buy me that birthday drink, then?' she said.

The bouncers eyeballed them briefly and Chris pushed open the door to the foyer. 'You just said you weren't drinking!'

She laughed. 'Well, you're right, it's my birthday, I ought to make an exception tonight. I can always leave the car here and we can get a taxi home.'

Olivia followed him through to the crowded bar and her heart began to beat a little faster. Paul and Amy weren't behind them, she was pretty sure; she just needed to hold her nerve.

'Where are the others?' Chris said, his eyes darting back towards the door. 'Shit, I bet the bouncers have asked them for ID. I'd forgotten, they're pretty strict here. Paul will be all right if he's got his driving licence, but Amy's fake ID is crap.' He thrust a note into Olivia's hand. 'Get the drinks in, I'll see where they are.'

Olivia pushed the money away. 'I'll go. I'm always invisible to bar staff, you'll get served quicker.'

Chris hesitated, then looked at the queue snaking along the bar and nodded.

Olivia nudged her way back through the crowd and into the quiet of the foyer, her heart booming in her ears. Through the glass door panel, she could see the two bouncers standing with their arms folded, eyeing Paul and Amy. Amy's arms gesticulated wildly, her voice raised but muffled, and then she marched forward. Olivia froze. Amy appeared to be staring right at her. Olivia stumbled back, then one of the bouncers sidestepped and barred Amy's way.

Paul gently pulled her arm, muttering something. Olivia exhaled. Could she? Could she just *go back inside*? She took another step back. She could. It was *her* birthday. They'd be all right, there was a phone box outside, they could call a taxi.

She sucked in her breath and turned away, pushing her way back inside – back to Chris.

◆　◆　◆

'I can't believe those bastards didn't let them in,' Chris repeated, well on his way through his fourth pint. The warmth of his thigh pressed against Olivia's as they sat jammed together in a booth. They were sharing the table with two guys, both with long straggly hair and fuzzy brown beards, giving them a biblical look.

Olivia took another gulp of her vodka and orange and squinted at the denim jacket one of them was wearing. He had a row of badges and patches neatly stitched on to the sleeve and she wondered hazily if he'd sewn them on himself.

'I just don't get why Amy would get a taxi home with Paul without telling me,' Chris muttered. 'She could have waited for me to come out and find her.'

Olivia patted his thigh. That first electric touch of his leg against hers had settled into a fiery warmth that heated her blood. To the guys opposite, they looked like a couple, didn't they? There was no one here they knew to say otherwise.

'Perhaps Paul *planned* to whisk Amy away,' she mused, swirling her vodka and orange around and around. It was funny really. Once you started drinking this stuff, you couldn't really taste the alcohol. It wasn't her fault Paul and Amy weren't allowed in the pub. So what if she didn't *exactly* see them climb in a taxi and drive away; they'd have got one soon enough. She hadn't lied, not really, just skirted around the truth. It was *her* birthday, after all.

Chris straightened up. 'What do you mean? Are you saying they didn't even *try* to come in the pub?'

Olivia smiled briefly and took another swig of her drink.

He stared at her. He really did have lovely eyes. A delicious hazel streaked in gold she'd never seen in anyone else before. Kind of molten, like caramel.

Chris slumped back in the seat and took out his cigarettes. 'Nah, Paul isn't like that. He wouldn't stab me in the back.'

He gave one to Olivia and lit them both. The guy with the badges let out a squeaky laugh at something his friend said. He sounded like a guinea pig and Olivia squinted at his hair and beard, but it was too much of an effort to summon up one of her animal caricatures.

'Has he said something? Has Amy?' Chris blew out a trail of smoke. His voice sounded small, and Olivia felt a tiny bit sorry for him and stroked his thigh. Silence was best in this kind of situation. He tipped back the last of his pint, clunking the empty glass down on the table. 'Not much of a birthday for you, is it? Stuck with miserable me!' He laughed drily.

Olivia twisted around to face him. The neckline of her black camisole slipped and his eyes momentarily dropped to the exposed lace trim on her bra. She pressed her hand firmly on his thigh. 'I'm having a *great* time.'

'At least we're celebrating,' he said, resting his forehead on hers.

Olivia's breath caught and she closed her eyes. She breathed in his heady scent of citrus laced with beer and cigarette smoke. Then he moved away and stubbed out his cigarette. 'Let's get another,' he said, clinking his empty glass against hers. 'You do want another? For someone who doesn't drink, you're making up for it tonight!'

Olivia smiled and stretched her arms high above her head. Her camisole rose a little, exposing a slice of bare skin. Perhaps she should have got that belly piercing after all. She put her hand back on Chris's thigh. 'Well, tonight's different, isn't it?' She stared meaningfully at him.

He was looking at the bar. 'Well, yeah, I suppose it is, it's your eighteenth.'

Olivia didn't say this was the first time she'd got a bit tipsy. She didn't want to sound naive or hear him tell her she'd had enough. The moment would be ruined. She took the last drag on her cigarette and watched him stride over to the bar, *Christ*, his bum looked amazing in those tight jeans.

'So why don't you usually drink?' he said as he returned. 'I mean, you can have a drink and not get pissed, so what's the big deal?'

Olivia felt something deflate inside of her. Images of her mum sprang into her mind: passed out on the bathroom floor after school; wobbling around the kitchen, waving a hot pan of burnt pasta; Olivia wrestling the car keys from her. Then, all of a sudden, the images turned into real words, and she didn't care if the two biblical-badged-bikers were listening because *Chris* was listening, and at some point, he took hold of her hand and held it tight.

She told him how her mum's drinking had grown. '*No little tipples before five o'clock*' before four o'clock, before three o'clock, and then a twitch of the net curtains to check her dad had gone to work. Then one day there had been a car journey to the shops. Olivia had clutched her seat, willing her seventeenth birthday to come around so she could be the driver. Her mum had pulled Olivia around the perfume counter, her sharp, minty breath like hot acid on Olivia's cheek, as she doused herself in layers of fragrance, demanding Olivia choose the most scented, the most viscous, *the most masking*.

Olivia glanced down at her empty glass and felt all hollowed out. 'Then Dad and I, we . . . caught her in bed with his best friend.' Tears sprang and Chris squeezed her hand. She looked down at his long fingers laced through hers: the missing piece of the jigsaw. And felt his calmness flow through her.

At some point in the evening, Chris excused himself to go to the loo and Olivia looked around her. The bikers had gone and music pulsed through the room. Tables and chairs had been pushed back to make a temporary dance floor and groups gyrated drunkenly together, laughing.

A pleasant giddiness enveloped Olivia. She reached for her drink and was surprised to find it empty again. She saw a spot at the far end of the bar where fewer people were waiting to be served and weaved her way through the dancers to reach it, eyeballing guys eyeballing *her* and matching their grins as she passed.

'Hey!' she shouted to the bartender, and elbowed her way forward. She waved a note high above her head, but he ignored her.

Someone muttered something that she didn't catch. She huffed and stood straight, glad of the extra inches in her heeled boots.

'I wondered where you'd gone.' Chris's voice sounded in her ear, and she felt the thrilling heat of his body pressing against her as the crowd pushed them together. 'Good thing you're easy to spot,' he murmured.

'Time for a shot,' she said, as two glasses were placed in front of them with slices of lemon and salt. She squinted – which first? Chris picked up the salt and she copied him, shaking some on to the back of her hand.

'Ready?' he said.

I'm ready.

Olivia locked eyes with him and slowly licked the salt. The tequila burned as it slid down her throat and she sucked hard on the lemon. For a second the room spun, then seemed to sharpen into focus. 'Let's have another,' she yelled. 'I'm only eighteen once!'

Two more tequila shots appeared, and it seemed perfectly natural for Olivia to press herself against Chris. She leaned in to see the caramel streaks in his eyes, but they didn't seem as clear now. Cigarette fog clouded her vision. It was hot in here, really hot. She grabbed his arm.

'You OK?' he said, peering at her.

She fanned her hand in front of her face. 'It's warm, let's get some air.' She tugged Chris away from the bar, into the corridor and through a door she'd seen earlier, leading into the garden. Cool air stroked her hot cheeks as she stumbled along the path, pulling him past groups huddled around tables, until they reached a picnic bench in the shadow of a tree away from everyone.

'So,' she murmured, tugging him towards her. His eyes widened a fraction, but this time she didn't bother looking for the caramel streaks. She didn't think about anything at all. She pushed herself against him, snaking her tongue inside his mouth and sliding her hands beneath his T-shirt to stroke his hot, silky skin.

It was *her* birthday. He was *her* present.

This was it. Now was *her* moment.

Chapter 37

Amy

Now

I tear through my box of scattered memories, looking for evidence that'll prove what I already know. Chris was never going to come looking for me – whether he got my letter or not – because of Olivia, because of *their* baby. Gemma. No wonder Olivia never wrote back.

I fall on the photo of Chris and me outside The Fox. I'm leaning into him, his arms wrap around my waist, holding me tight, my smile is dreamy. I think about us standing in the same pose downstairs earlier, mirroring time without realising, and I can still feel the imprint of his embrace.

I remember we'd gone to the pub for Olivia's birthday. We'd sat out front because the garden had been busy with customers enjoying the spring sunshine, like us. I look more closely at the photo. In the corner, Olivia's perched on the end of the bench, I'd not noticed her before; she's angled towards us, staring. At me? At *him*.

Was this where it all began? I was pregnant, was Olivia pregnant too?

Nausea rolls my stomach and I scrabble to my feet and run the kitchen tap until the water's cold. I splash some on to my face, fill a glass and drink greedily.

Back in the living room, I pull out the poems Chris wrote and reread the words that had stung my teenage heart when I realised he was never coming for us. Were they even meant for me? Were they for Olivia? Did I just assume they were mine?

I remember the first poem fell out of Chris's bag when we tipped it upside down to find the key to his house, the afternoon we lost our virginity. I'd picked it up and he'd laughed, embarrassed, and I'd tucked it into my pocket because I'd wanted something special to mark the moment. I'd found the second poem – a song, this time – a few weeks later, tucked under his pillow like a love note. We'd been curled in each other's arms, the afternoon sunshine pressing through the thin curtains, and he'd sung them softly to me, and every word felt like mine. Then there was another in his guitar case; one in the pocket of his leather jacket. I hadn't gone looking for them, they were just there, they belonged to me – so I'd thought.

Perhaps he *was* hiding them from me.

Because they were for *her*.

I stand up and go out to the roof terrace. In the distance, I see Chris and Olivia strolling across the sand. A handsome couple, people must think as they pass. A perfect match.

I run back in and throw myself on the sofa. Then I spring up again as I think about Chris and I tangled here, naked, not so long ago. My eyes flick around the room, he taints my flat, and I drop to the carpet and hug my knees.

When did they begin? I close my eyes and think back to the end, after Mum found out I was pregnant, and the horror that unfolded afterwards.

'You can't keep it,' she'd said tightly at the kitchen table, hands clenched. 'He won't want you if you keep it. You're both too young. You're bloody stupid.'

'Susan!' Dad had shouted, and we'd both looked at him in surprise. He never raised his voice, he never contradicted Mum. 'This is Amy's choice. This is her future. If she's old enough to . . . well, she's old enough to take on the responsibility.'

'Responsibility,' Mum spat. 'You don't know the half of it. You're in the middle of your A levels, for Christ's sake, you should be in your room studying, not standing here telling me your life is over! That boy isn't going to support you. He's going to disappear off to university and leave you. We'll be gone, living on the other side of the world, then what'll you do? How are you going to manage?'

I swear I felt my baby move right there and then. I could never have aborted her – my precious Bea – but the seed of doubt nestled its way in and took root. What if Mum was right?

I'd tried to bury myself in revision to concentrate on my future, my baby's future. I desperately wanted to tell Chris, to tell Olivia, to talk to someone. But Mum seemed to be everywhere. She escorted me to and from my exams and guarded the phone, leaving Dad to wind the business down and sell the house as they prepared to emigrate.

'It's not too late to change your mind,' Mum said one day, tossing an abortion leaflet on to my desk. 'We'll pay for it. But you need to work harder than you've ever worked, you can't mess up now.'

Her words sickened me and I remained stubborn. I don't know why. Having this baby was the most important decision of my life. It was the only thing I was sure about – and Chris. Then when Dad took me to the park that day and gently pointed out what life would be like as a mother, it cracked open a door to this other future, my future that's now.

He won't want you. He's young. His whole future is ahead of him. So is yours.

I rode a roller coaster of emotions, and being trapped at home without *him* calling *me* made me think Mum was right. He'd got bored. So I wrote him a letter to tell him I was pregnant. To give him the chance to say he loved me, he'd love our baby.

Now I understand. Whether he got the letter or not, the truth is alive in Gemma.

'Having this baby's your choice, you know,' Mum had repeated as we got on the plane. 'I don't know what you're going to do. Being a single mum will be no fun.'

Dad squeezed my hand. 'We'll look after you,' he said – and he was true to *his* word.

I open my eyes. *When did Chris and Olivia begin?*

Chapter 38

AMY

Now

'Amy,' says Mum, her face flickering into surprise as she opens her front door.

She's probably wondering why I've walked the long route via the street instead of cutting across the beach, but ringing her doorbell announces the formality of my visit. She steps back to let me in. I stalk through to the kitchen and for a moment I picture Dad standing at the cooker in the old kitchen that, of course, is long gone. A desperate pang of longing threatens to consume me before I've begun this emotional journey.

The doors are open and it's dusk outside. Streaks of orange cling to the edges of a purple sky, as though the sun doesn't want to give in to night. I spot Mum's half-eaten dinner left on the island when she came to answer the door. She eats alone most nights – like me. Why did Dad leave us like this? Our lives shouldn't have turned out this way.

'Sorry, I've interrupted your dinner,' I mutter, sliding on to the bar stool opposite her, a rumble in my stomach reminding me I haven't eaten in a while.

'Do you want something?' Mum's already at the fridge, putting salad on a plate, carving another slice of bread.

She sits back down and carries on eating, waiting for me to announce the intention of my visit. I want to tell her Olivia is here. But what good will that do? It won't change the past, it can't change the future – but I do want to know the truth about the letter.

'How's Chris?'

Mum's question catches me off guard, but then she's still living in the moment before Olivia arrived. No doubt the gossips would've filled her in, whispered that Chris has stayed over, not once, not twice, *but all week* . . . The bread turns dry in my mouth and I swallow a gulp of wine.

'Do you think he's going to move here for good?'

I stare at her. 'What? I don't know.'

'You've been spending quite a bit of time together. I just thought . . . perhaps he might have told you his plans.' Her beady eyes pin mine like a bird of prey. 'It might be . . . nice if he did. Would you like him to?'

'You've never had a good word to say about him,' I say tersely. 'You made it very clear to me a long, long time ago that you never wanted me to speak about him again. What's changed?'

Mum appraises me. 'Things are . . . different.'

I narrow my eyes. 'Are they? In what way? In that we're not teenagers any more? Because he's a respected architect and not a barman pulling pints?' *Breathe.* 'Why now? Why do you want me to rekindle everything?'

'I thought . . . you seemed to be getting on so well . . . I heard . . .'

'You heard wrong,' I snap.

Mum puts down her fork and I challenge her stare. I fight to stay silent but my temper jumpstarts again. 'Why do you still want to manipulate my life?'

She shakes her head slightly and takes a sip of wine. 'I'm not. I've had time to think.' She puts her glass down. 'What about Bea?'

'What about Bea?' I retort, slamming my hands flat on the worktop. 'Bea's my concern, not yours.'

'You have to tell her Chris is here,' she commands. 'She'll be home soon.'

Hot anger floods me. Mum wouldn't tell her, would she? I know she's capable of terrible things, but I'd never forgive her if she hurt Bea.

'Don't tell me how to parent! Bea's *my* daughter! What do you know about being a mother anyway? You dragged me to the other side of the world when I was vulnerable and forced me to leave Chris!'

Outside, the sky bleeds scarlet and I'm shaking in a heady mix of elation, fear and fury at the words I've never been brave enough to say out loud before. Tears scratch at my throat and my head is a muddle and something nags at the back of my mind . . .

'I didn't want you to throw your life away,' she says slowly.

'With the man I loved? You stole my future! You made it clear there were no choices.'

'I thought it wouldn't last, he was your first boyfriend. I thought I was protecting you and protecting your future. Surely you must understand that's what mothers do? But now I'm saying you need to give Bea the choice to meet her father. She's eighteen, for goodness' sake, she's an adult.'

'What, so you don't feel guilty any more?'

Mum's gaze falters. 'You're a mother,' she says quietly. 'What if Bea came back from her travels and said she was pregnant? That she was going to stay with whoever this man was and start a new life in Thailand or somewhere else far away? How would you feel?'

Her words burn. I know the answer. I couldn't live without Bea in my life. If she were to leave me – then? My world would end.

'This isn't about you, Amy. This is about Bea,' she presses.

I stand and stalk across the room. 'It isn't about you either! You telling me how to live my life and what I should do!'

Mum sighs and throws her napkin down. 'I'm saying I was wrong, Amy. Bea deserves the chance to meet her dad. What are you frightened of?'

A flash of *them* burns my mind. I don't want Bea to be seduced by their exciting life in the UK, because that's how she'll perceive it. I spin around. 'Because they'll take her from me!'

Mum frowns. 'You're not making sense.'

'Olivia's here!' I shout. 'It's a bit convenient, don't you think? I see neither of them for almost nineteen years and they're *both* here?' Mum's cheeks flush and the niggle in the back of my mind jumps into my conscious thoughts and my voice begins to tremble. 'You knew they were together back then, didn't you?'

Mum stares at me, but her eyes are glassy and distant. 'Olivia's here?'

'Have they always known about Bea?' I repeat, my voice like steel. '*Did* Dad deliver my letter? Don't lie to me any more.'

Mum snaps back to me. 'Yes, I knew about Olivia and Chris,' she says slowly. 'When you asked me about the letter a few weeks ago, I didn't give you an answer and for good reason.'

The shock of her honesty turns my legs liquid and I slide back on to the stool.

'Of course Dad told me you wrote a letter, why wouldn't he? He loved you, Amy, very much, but he loved me too.' Her lips tremble a little. 'We thought your letter was a good idea. We thought if Chris really loved you, he'd stay by your side. We weren't going to force you to come with us if you *both* wanted a life together with a baby, but we couldn't risk leaving you in England without any support. Dad planned to take your letter to Chris, then call in at Olivia's afterwards and invite her over to cheer you up.'

'You'd banned me from seeing her, though.'

Mum shakes her head. 'No, I didn't. You were awfully miserable – the pregnancy, all those hormones flying around – and I just wanted you to concentrate on your exams and get them finished. We were all shocked, it was a tricky time for everyone.'

'But you said I couldn't go out! You used to drive me to and from the exams!'

'Amy, you weren't even eighteen years old and you were pregnant! Getting good exam results was more important for you than anyone.'

I look over towards the disappearing glow of the sunset and think back to those weeks. Mum was right. After my jubilant discovery, I'd become scared of being pregnant – scared of what my parents would say, what Chris would say; I couldn't even tell Olivia. I couldn't cope with her scorn enforcing the deep shame I already felt.

I'd been naive and foolish. Despite being on the Pill, I'd taken antibiotics for yet another sore throat and had forgotten they could interfere with the contraceptive. Only dumb teenagers got themselves knocked up and everyone knew their boyfriends would ditch them the moment they found out. I'd seen those girls, pushing their buggies around town on a Saturday afternoon with listless eyes and lank hair. I'd plummeted from a bouncy future of fun-loving freedom into an abyss of unknown responsibilities. I spent hours shut away in my bedroom, lying on my bed, reading the poetic lyrics Chris wrote for me over and over, crying until my face was puffy and raw. Mum's harsh words had hit home and I couldn't be sure of anything any more.

'Tell me what happened,' I say quietly.

'Dad was on his way over to Chris's house and he saw them outside, they were kissing . . . so he turned around and drove home.'

'Kissing?' I repeat dumbly, and my thoughts swing back to them earlier, standing side by side on the terrace watching me.

'When Dad told me what he'd seen, I have to say I wasn't surprised. Chris had gone cold on you during your exams and I'd seen the way Olivia looked at him when you were together.'

'Cold on me?' I repeat again. 'He was studying. We were all studying.' But even as I speak, I feel the familiar wash of my teenage doubt and confusion.

Mum shrugged. 'That may be, but you were very upset. Olivia always looked . . . *pained*, I suppose, when you spoke about Chris. And then when they came to the house together to see you, they looked guilty as hell.'

It's the truth.

It's the same story Chris told me.

We were worried . . . We came to your house to talk to you but, God, I don't know, one minute you were there and the next minute you were gone . . . You went and moved to the other side of the world . . .

I imagine the scene that Dad witnessed: cruising up the cul-de-sac, his mouth slackening in horror as he sees Olivia's tall, willowy body curved against Chris, him sliding his hand beneath her glossy hair and bringing his lips on to hers.

How many times had this happened?

Why didn't I see this?

I want Mum to be lying, I really do, but there's nothing to be gained from her lying now.

'Dad was so shocked, he really liked Chris.' She threw me a wry smile. 'Chris had a lot of front, but I could see how happy he made you. We couldn't just leave you in England to find out he'd been cheating on you with your best friend.'

And he's cheated again. On me; on Olivia.

'We thought we'd done the right thing,' Mum continues. 'Neither of us wanted you to throw your life away. Then when Chris walked into my work meeting the other month and began showing an interest in you again, I wondered whether it was time to forgive and forget, for Bea's sake.' She pauses. 'But with Olivia here, it seems like we're back where we started.'

Tears fill my eyes. 'Chris has a daughter called Gemma,' I whisper.

Mum inhaled sharply, then comes to my side. 'And Olivia is Gemma's mum?'

I nod and I see sorrow in her dark eyes before she wraps me into a tight hug.

Chapter 39

AMY

Now

I leave Mum's by the back gate and as I turn to wave goodbye, I catch a sadness in her expression that I've never seen – or noticed? – before. I reach home and it's as though the imprint of Chris and Olivia sears the terrace. I can't stay here tonight.

I grab my bike and navigate the undulating coast road to Shannon and Grant's with a speed that burns my thighs. As I pedal, I think about how Olivia was always everything I wasn't. I bounced from one thing to the next, bursting with chatter and annoying giggles; she remained passive and cool. I admired her composure, I wanted some of it to rub off on me. She was also guarded and secretive – it had taken her months to trust me enough to tell me her mum was an alcoholic, and I felt flattered to be the friend she confided in. I wanted to be ultra-cool and ultra-sexy, I wanted to be just like her.

I never knew what she wanted from me.

But now I do. She wanted Chris.

She *got* Chris.

I never stood a chance.

Soon, I'm battering on Shannon and Grant's front door like a mad woman, gasping as I force air back into my overworked lungs.

'Mate, what's wrong?' says Grant, steadying me as he opens the door. He's holding a tinny and the distant sound of a chanting sports crowd filters through from the den.

I push a sticky curl away from my face. 'Just cycled a bit fast. Where's Shannon?' I stride past him down the hallway towards the kitchen before he can reply.

Shannon's standing at the island, pouring something pink and bubbly into a wine glass, and looks up in delight when I come into the room. 'Just in time,' she says, as if she's expecting me. She grabs another glass from the cupboard. 'Wine? Or do you want to join me in sparkling raspberry water?' She laughs and strokes the swell of her belly.

'Water's good,' I say, and down half a glass.

'You in training for something?' she says, eyeing my bike helmet and sweaty face. She touches her bump again and I follow her to the sofa that faces the garden.

'I've been at Mum's,' I say.

'With *Chris*?' Shannon smiles. 'What's all that about? I thought you'd be tucked up at home having some kind of weekend sexathon.'

Her throaty laugh annoys me, and I catch sight of myself in the reflection of the glass door. Deep lines drag down my mouth, a frown crimps my forehead, and my eyes are small and piggy from crying earlier. I look bloody awful.

Olivia still looks smooth and serene – as gorgeous as she's always been. Why did I ever think Chris was interested in me?

'Olivia's here,' I say, as if this explains everything.

Shannon's face is blank. 'Olivia?' she repeats. Then her expression clears. 'Oh! You mean the friend you went to college with.'

The innocence of her response makes me feel giddy and I sink down next to her on the sofa. There's so much she doesn't know, so much I have to explain. So I start from the beginning, the words jostling against the new bits of history I've only just heard, to piece together this new-old version of Chris and Olivia.

'Olivia turned up at the café today,' I say. 'I saw her talking to Chris on the terrace and I came outside and . . .' I pinch my eyes shut, remembering the sparkle of pleasure in our hug before I caught Chris's stricken face. 'For a moment, I was so pleased to see her.'

'Amy,' Shannon says carefully. 'What exactly did you see?'

My eyes snap open. 'God, Shannon, I'm not bloody naive. What are the chances of Chris rocking up out of the blue from the other side of the world, then a couple of months later Olivia trotting along? They both looked guilty, like they shared a secret I didn't know about.'

'Right,' she says, still studying me, 'a secret.'

I hear the double standard. 'All right, I *know*,' I retort, standing up. 'You're going to say I'm just as bad, having a secret of my own, but at least I didn't hurt anyone.'

She says nothing, which is even more infuriating.

'Turns out my secret is a good thing!' My voice becomes the petulant tone of teen Amy again. 'Olivia's Gemma's mum! She's nearly eighteen! The same age as Bea! Do the maths – what does that tell you?'

Shannon blinks and then rubs her belly in quick circles. 'Whoa . . .' she says quietly. 'So you think Chris was cheating on you with Olivia when you were teenagers?'

'Think?' I'm practically shouting now. 'I *know*. When I was carrying his baby, she was carrying his too, so quite clearly they had a lovely romance going on behind my back and were probably bloody delighted when I pissed off to the other side of the world and they didn't have to see me again. Problem solved!' My breath rasps. 'Once they discover Bea's Gemma's half-sister, they'll be desperate to bring her back to the UK to become part of their precious bloody family!'

Shannon stares at me. 'Is Gemma here too?'

I realise I don't know, and I shouldn't care – but I do.

'Chris is a two-timing shit and Olivia betrayed me,' I mutter. 'I feel like marching around to his place and asking her why she married such a bastard, he can't be trusted.'

'What? She's *married* to Chris? You mean they're still together?'

Hot anger dissolves into uncontrollable sobs. Shannon shimmies across the sofa and puts her arm around me. She lets me cry and as I draw in deep breaths to control myself, she murmurs, 'You know, I thought Chris was one of the good guys. I can't believe after all this time he was married. What a shit. I'm so sorry, Amy.'

I wipe my eyes. 'The most important thing now is finding a way to get Bea to stay away a bit longer. I don't want her coming home to— *this*.'

She watches me. 'If that's what you think is the right thing to do.'

I stay over and rise early, waving my goodbyes at the kitchen doorway while the children eat breakfast. Kira runs over and flings her arms around my waist as if to hold me hostage, but I prise her gently away and slip out of the door.

I cycle slowly, a gusty wind furrowing me along in fits and starts in tandem with my twirling thoughts. Visions of Chris and Olivia together with *their* baby; *their* child; *their* teenager, a family for all these years.

I turn into my street and see a familiar figure walking towards the café. He bows his head to the wind and I'm tempted to slam on the brakes and cycle away, but I know he'll find me eventually.

'Amy,' Chris calls as I reach the back of the café where I store my bike. 'Did you get my messages? I need to talk to you.'

My phone lies at the bottom of my bag, turned off since yesterday afternoon. I focus my gaze over his shoulder to where the road ends and the pōhutukawa trees grow along the edge of the beach. I can feel him looking at me. A cluster of words gathers sourly in my mouth and I press my lips tight. I have nothing to say.

'Can we go inside?' he says.

'No.' I'm careful to make my voice sound neutral. I'm not going to make a scene because that'd mean I care. And I don't. 'I'm busy, I've got to open up.'

I turn the handlebars to get past him and he steps in front of my bike. 'Wait,' he says.

My breath catches as we lock eyes and, for a second, I think he's going to press his warm hands over mine.

'I had no idea Olivia was coming,' he says quickly. 'She just . . . appeared, and it was a surprise. I didn't handle the situation properly at all.' He pushes a hand through his hair and it stays stuck up at the front.

Bed hair.

'OK,' I say with a shrug, because *I don't fucking care.* 'Can you move out the way, please?'

'She shouldn't have turned up like that,' he carries on, his voice rising. 'She should've told me she was coming. She thought you knew all about Gemma . . . and I should have told you . . . I'm so, so sorry, Ames.'

I don't want to listen, but I have to, and swallow hard. 'Told me what, exactly?'

'Olivia and I . . .'

Oh God, just the pairing of their names . . .

'We . . .'

I stare at the low, broad branches of the pōhutukawa trees bouncing gently in the wind; at the waves crashing on to the sand. Surfers might try their luck today.

'I should have told you Olivia is Gemma's mum,' he says, as though I don't already know.

'I have to open up.' I push past him, lean my bike against the wall and walk away. Away from his confessions that've come too late.

Chapter 40

Olivia

Then

The sun was doing its best to press through the heavy black curtains at the windows of the school hall, large golden rectangles that would have been almost heavenly if Olivia hadn't been sitting in the molten pot of hell. She stared at the English exam paper in front of her. The questions danced and perspiration spiked her hairline. The room felt like a furnace.

An invisible string tugged the top of Olivia's head again.

Don't.

Just one more time.

Slowly she looked up, careful not to alert the invigilator, and allowed her eyes to rest on the back of the person sitting in front of her. His neck had turned a honey-brown in the sun and she swallowed.

Skin like silk.

Olivia closed her eyes. She remembered running her palms beneath his T-shirt – and then? Fragmented memories of that night jostled, inconsistent, dreamlike, with chunks of black nothingness, as she tried to make sense of the chain of events once again. Did everyone have blanks when they drank? Or was it a hideous genetic thing she'd inherited from her mother?

What had she done?

Tears scorched her throat and she rested her hands in the lap of her long cotton skirt. She'd thrown the denim mini away. And the God-awful thigh-high boots. She'd looked like a hooker in them.

She'd *behaved* like a hooker – just like her mother.

So that's how life would be now.

Before. After.

She watched Chris's shoulder muscle twitch as he scribbled at the exam paper. How could he concentrate? Why did he have to be sitting right there when she'd successfully spent the last few weeks avoiding him, avoiding Paul, avoiding Amy? Though not *completely* avoiding Amy, that would've been way too obvious. Instead, Olivia had woken with a queasy hangover and fudged her way through a phone call with Amy, until Amy had seemed satisfied she hadn't missed any fun and believed the evening had been a total flop for Olivia and Chris too. Revision had been the perfect excuse to hide away and although they'd spoken a couple of times since, now Olivia came to think of it, Amy hadn't called in a while.

Olivia looked over to where Amy sat at the front of the hall. She, too, was bent over her desk, writing. Olivia would have to disappear quick-smart afterwards if she wanted to avoid her. She'd keep walking and say she had to get back to her revision. Amy wouldn't think it weird, they all had to revise.

Now concentrate.

She blinked hard and the questions on the exam paper swam into focus. What mattered now was getting the exam done and getting the hell out of there.

Olivia slipped away that day unnoticed, and a few more times after that; it was pretty easy to be absorbed into the surge of students leaving the building at the same time. Once, she'd been driving away and had seen Amy standing alone by the entrance, waiting for someone. Olivia had waved as she passed and Amy had lifted her hand in response. Her blank expression chilled Olivia. She'd thought about phoning to see if she was OK, but what if *she* was the reason Amy *wasn't* OK?

Olivia had decided to compartmentalise these dangerous thoughts. She'd taken to revising at the library to get away from her bedroom because the air felt clogged with stuff she didn't want to think about. Today, she'd been filling her brain with complex maths formulas and was so busy absorbing the specifics that she didn't notice Paul until he was standing right in front of her.

'Can I join you?' he said.

One of Olivia's carefully closed compartments sprang open. Seeing Paul meant thinking about Chris, and that meant thinking about *that night*, and about Amy, and she couldn't go there right now.

'No,' she muttered.

'No?'

She looked up. One black eyebrow arched the question and a smile flickered on his face. She sighed. 'Go on then, just don't talk to me.'

Paul slipped into the chair opposite. 'You're getting really stuck in then, or does it just look that way?' He smiled again, broader this time, pushing faint dimples into his cheeks. He'd gone lighter on the make-up today: just a touch of kohl that sharpened the blue of his eyes.

'It's going OK,' she replied. 'What about you?' She gestured at the books he'd dumped on the table.

'Boring,' he said. 'But got to be done. I really want to get my accountancy place at Leeds.'

Olivia looked down at the chipped black nail polish on his fingernails. 'I can't imagine you being a grown-up and wearing a sensible suit.'

'I've got years before I need to look sensible,' he replied. 'Anyway, you'll be wearing robes and a ridiculous wig if you become a barrister.'

She made a face. 'No chance. I'll be happy doing family law somewhere far, far away from here.'

His gaze settled on her. 'A worthy job.'

She shifted in her seat and picked up her pen. Why was he always so bloody intense?

Paul pulled out a sheaf of notes and for a moment didn't say anything. 'Why do you want to move far away? You running from something? Or someone?'

She threw down her pen and stared at him. 'I meant,' she said tightly, 'I'll probably stay in the town where I go to uni.'

'Right,' he said, still staring. 'Edinburgh.'

He'd remembered? 'Yes.'

'Cold.'

'It's pretty,' she shot back.

'You like tartan and haggis?'

'Ha, ha. Now shut up.' She ran her finger down the page to find her place, but the sentences kept jumping together. *Bloody Paul.* She'd never shake him off now. He'd be in here every day waiting for her and she'd have to go back to revising at home.

'Have you seen Amy recently?' he said.

Olivia's head snapped up. 'No, why?'

'She walked out of the geography exam.'

'What? How do you know?'

'Sticky Lips told me – with great delight.'

'Sticky Lips?'

'Yeah, you know—' Paul pursed his mouth, looking like a frog, and she smiled, mentally filing away the caricature for another time.

'You mean the frog who wears lip gloss.'

He laughed, a belly-deep sound, loud enough to make the librarian turn and frown.

'I call her Sticky Lips too,' she said.

'Do you?'

They looked at each other for a moment.

'*Anyway*,' she said. 'Why the hell did Amy walk out of an *exam*?'

Paul shrugged. 'I don't know. I thought *you* might know.'

'Chris will know.'

He shook his head. 'I doubt it. He's locked himself away to revise so I've hardly spoken to him.'

A hot flush crept up Olivia's neck. 'So? He just wants to get good grades. Speaking of which . . .' She tapped her book with her pen.

'But what about Amy? It's weird.'

Compartments. That's all I need to do. Stick to the compartments and everything will be fine. 'I'll phone her later,' she said. 'Perhaps she's got another sore throat.'

'It's a bit bloody drastic to give up halfway through an exam.'

'She doesn't want to go to uni anyway,' Olivia replied. She snapped the book shut and dropped it into her bag. 'Perhaps she's finally plucked up the courage to stand up to her mum and tell her she wants to go to cookery school. Perhaps this is her way of fighting back.'

'You could call round.'

'All right, who are you? My mother?' She swept the rest of her things into her bag. 'If I go around to her house and there's been some kind of drama, I guarantee you Amy's mum will answer the door and I'll never get past her. You know she's banned Amy from doing any socialising until the exams are over?'

'What – even speaking to you?'

'Jeez, Paul, what's your problem? Go round there yourself if you're so bothered! It's like you've got a crush on her or something.' She flushed again and snatched up her bag.

His eyes narrowed. 'I'm not the one with the crush,' he muttered.

Olivia was surprised to see her dad's car parked on the drive when she got back, then she remembered it was the afternoon and he'd obviously finished his Saturday game of golf.

'Hi, love, how's the revision going?' he said, coming in from the garden.

He looked tanned and relaxed in a polo shirt and, through the window, she could see washing twirling on the line. She hadn't put a wash on yet.

He followed her gaze. 'Love . . . I . . .'

'It's OK,' she said, holding up her hand. 'I get it, you listened to me.'

Not now. Keep the compartments closed.

'Right.' He looked sheepish.

She went over to the sink, filled a glass with water and took a long drink.

'When's the next exam?'

'Monday. Maths.'

'A tough one, but I know you can do it,' he said, smiling.

Does he?

She crossed to the fridge and opened the door.

'Shall I get us fish and chips tonight?' he said. 'We could choose a DVD to watch together.'

Olivia stared at the unfamiliar food on the shelves. He'd been shopping, too? Busy day. *Probably won't last.* 'Yes, that'd be nice,' she muttered, shutting the door. 'I'm going to get on with some work, still got some stuff I need to revise.'

'Yes, of course, love, you do that. Do you want a cup of tea? I can bring one up?'

She looked at him again – the sheepish expression was back – and nodded.

Upstairs, Olivia sat on her bed, mulling over the strange domestic scene she'd walked into. She reached for the phone to call Amy to tell her, then stopped. She couldn't, she couldn't just ring her like she used to.

Paul's words burned through her again. A crush? Had Chris told him what had happened? Whatever *had* happened. And why had Amy walked out of the exam? She thought about her blank expression the other day and picked up the phone again. But what if she was responsible for Amy's behaviour? She put the receiver down. But then what if she *wasn't* and there was something else going on? Olivia dialled Amy's number before she changed her mind. Amy's mum answered.

'Amy's revising,' Susan said, clipped and cold.

'Please can I have a quick five minutes, that's all?'

'No, Olivia. I'll tell her you called, though.'

Olivia paused, unsure what to say next. She could hardly say she was calling to find out why Amy walked out of her geography exam. What if her mum didn't know? She'd go nuts.

'Is she . . . OK?' she ventured.

'Amy will call you when she's ready.' The phone went dead.

Chris must have told Amy. *She knows. She's told her mum. It's all my fault.*

Chapter 41

Olivia

Then

Olivia had darted off to the loos after the maths exam, but as she went to leave, she saw Amy standing outside the main entrance with Paul – but no Chris. Fear clawed at her stomach. She couldn't avoid her forever.

Even from this distance, Amy didn't look her usual self. Her arms held her body like she was cold, though it was warm outside, and she angled herself away from Paul. Briefly, Olivia imagined Amy's expression when she finally came face to face with her. Would she explode in anger? Or stare her down in a cool, calculated way that somehow would be much, much worse?

'Olivia!' Paul called, catching sight of her.

'Hi,' said Amy, and then her eyes were back on the car park.

'How was the exam?' he asked.

'All right.' Olivia eyed Amy nervously, feeling the steady thump of her heart begin to pick up pace.

'Where's Chris? Didn't he have a DT exam today?' Amy directed the question at Paul. Lines tugged away her usual grin.

Was Amy blanking her? Olivia scanned her face. *She's not angry, she's sad.* She wanted to reach out and say something to reassure her, to protect her even, but from what? Herself?

'Amy!' A sharp voice rang out across the car park. Susan stood next to her smart red sports car, gesturing for her to come over.

'Better go.' Amy gave them both a watery smile. 'Did you see Chris leave?' Again, the words were directed at Paul.

Paul shuffled his feet and nodded.

'When? Why's he gone already?'

His eyes grazed Olivia's, then settled on Amy. 'He's revising.'

'He's acting weird,' Amy murmured. 'I've hardly seen him. And when we talk on the phone, he sounds odd . . . What's going on, Paul? Has he said anything to you?'

He shrugged. 'I think he's feeling the pressure. He really wants to get good grades. You know, it's hard to get a place to study architecture.'

'Amy!' Susan slammed the car door and began marching in their direction.

'Here comes the prison warden,' Amy muttered. 'I have to go.'

'Don't take it personally, I haven't seen much of him either,' Paul said quickly. 'Why don't we all get together after our last exam and celebrate? When do you finish? My last one's Friday.'

'I'll have to let you know . . .' Amy replied.

'I tried to phone you,' Olivia interjected. 'Your mum . . .'

Amy frowned and then Susan was there, pressing her hand on to Amy's shoulder. 'Let's not get ahead of ourselves and start planning celebrations yet,' she said, eyeballing them both. 'Amy needs to finish her exams first.' She frogmarched her back to the car.

'Call me!' Olivia shouted, but she wasn't sure if Amy heard.

Something wasn't right, Amy wasn't right. They watched Susan's car slip through the gates and disappear. But surely if Amy knew about *that night*, she'd have been angry with Olivia? She'd

302

have made it clear right there and then. But perhaps not. Perhaps that wasn't her way. Olivia didn't know if she knew her at all any more.

Paul turned back to Olivia. 'What went wrong, then?' His blue eyes bored into hers.

'Sorry?'

'In the exam. Sounds like you've been doing tons of prep, but you look – well, I don't mean to sound rude, a bit strained or something. I thought you'd have breezed it.'

He moved a little closer, reminding her of the way she'd thrown herself at Chris *that night*. Pressing herself against him, no better than a prostitute, setting off this irreparable chain of events that had led to the sorry mess they were all in now.

Paul reached out and stroked her cheek; his fingers quivered, and she closed her eyes for a moment. She thought he might kiss her and that might not be such a bad thing, and then her eyes sprang open. What was she thinking? Kissing Paul, kissing Chris, *fucking* Chris, whoring herself around.

'You're not OK,' he said softly. 'Is it your mum? Has she tried to contact you again?'

Olivia blinked. How did Paul know about Jeanette's problems? What had Chris been saying? She'd told him in confidence, she'd thought. Though that conversation was soft and blurry too. All because of alcohol. The poison that ruined lives.

'Sorry,' he said, raising his hands in apology. 'Chris said . . . perhaps he shouldn't . . . look, I'm worried about you, that's all.'

'I can look after myself,' she snapped, wiping her eyes with the back of her hand. 'I don't need your help.'

She stalked off towards the car and Paul watched her leave. Did he know about *that night*? There was something about the way he'd looked at her . . . and then there she was again, pushing herself on to Chris, running her palms up his back, tangling her hands in his

hair, pressing her lips on his and parting them with her tongue . . .
and then what? A big, black yawning hole. She'd woken up with
the residue of the night in her mouth and in her mind, like a
shamefully sexy dream. Which it was. It was a fucking nightmare.

Had they? Surely she'd *know?*

And if they had, what did she think was going to happen next?
Chris knocking on her door and telling her how amazing she was?
How he'd got it wrong and Amy wasn't the one for him? This wasn't
a fucking fairy story.

Olivia pulled on to the drive and slammed the car door, her
eye catching a car that had just pulled up. The window slid down,
revealing Jeanette behind the wheel.

Christ. 'What are you doing here?' Olivia shouted. 'How d'you
know where we live?'

'I followed you.' A pause. 'From college.'

They stared at each other for a moment. Jeanette looked like
she had when Olivia had bumped into her in the supermarket.
Styled hair, careful strokes of shimmery blusher, lips in a shade
of rose that matched her fingernails. Briefly, she imagined her as
a proper mum who she could talk to about what had happened,
and who'd give her a hug and say she hadn't betrayed her only true
friend, and that the kiss was just a mistake.

Assuming it *was* just a kiss . . .

'What do you want? I've got revision to do,' Olivia snapped.

Jeanette nodded. 'Of course, I'm not staying. I wanted to see
how you were getting on with your exams, but I don't want to get
in the way.' She pulled a scrap of paper from her handbag. 'Here's
my number,' she said, holding it out through the window. 'Give me
a ring when you're ready. You must be finishing your exams soon?'

Olivia edged towards her. Jeanette's hand wasn't shaking, and
she took the number and pushed it into her back pocket.

'I'll leave you to it,' she said with a careful smile. 'But I mean it, I do want to know how you're getting on.'

Loneliness scratched at Olivia's throat. 'I had a terrible exam today,' she said in a rush.

'What happened? Which exam was it?'

'Maths.'

'Not your favourite subject, right? That's art.'

Olivia looked at her sharply. 'What would you know?'

'You've been drawing since I can remember.'

'I'm surprised you remember anything.'

She held Olivia's gaze. 'I deserved that.'

Olivia thought about the long afternoon and evening ahead. Her dad wouldn't be home for ages. 'I've got time for one cup of tea and then you have to go,' she said, striding back up the drive to the front door.

In the kitchen, Jeanette hovered as Olivia moved around making tea. The silence pressed against her and she wondered why she'd thought this was a good idea. She had nothing to say.

'So what happened? In the exam?' Jeanette asked, spooning sugar into her mug.

Olivia's throat tightened. Could she tell her why it was so hard to focus? Could she say the words out loud?

'There's this guy . . .' she began, and squeezed her eyes shut as tears threatened. 'There's this guy . . .' she repeated.

Jeanette slid her hand across the table so their fingertips touched.

'We . . . I . . .' Snatches of the evening flickered again. Pieces frustratingly missing, the chain of events broken.

Booze.

Jeanette would understand.

She'd be disappointed.

Anger flashed through Olivia. It was Jeanette's fault she'd behaved like this. She'd inherited her messed-up booze gene. She sucked in her breath and smiled tightly. 'It's fine, I'm being melodramatic. There's so much stress with these exams, you know.'

Jeanette nodded slowly and pulled her hand away. 'Which universities have you applied to?'

'Law at Edinburgh if I get the grades, otherwise Durham or Newcastle.'

'Is that what you want to do? Law?'

Olivia frowned. 'What do you mean?'

'I thought you might have done something with art.'

'Art? That's just an indulgent daydream for a kid who thinks being a grown-up is all about having freedom and fun – not a fight for survival.'

Jeanette looked visibly shocked. 'Is that what your father told you?'

Olivia pushed back her chair. 'No!' she shouted. 'It's what I learnt from *you*!'

Jeanette's face paled, making her blusher look garish and streaky. 'I'm sorry,' she said quietly. 'I didn't ever mean to make you feel like that.'

She fiddled with her mug. 'This is such a big turning point in your life, and I want you to be sure you're making the right decision. For you. Not for me, not for Dad, but for *you*.'

'Law *is* my choice,' Olivia replied through gritted teeth. 'It's the best future I have.'

Jeanette nodded. 'You're right, it'll be a great career and you'll excel at it.' She swallowed. 'Look, I need to go, but I just wanted to say one more thing. The thing that happened with Pete . . .'

Olivia flapped her arms. 'I don't care. I don't want to know.'

'I just wanted you to understand that things hadn't been right between Dad and I for a long time. Years, in fact.'

'Is that your excuse?'

She shook her head. 'Of course not. I'm entirely to blame. Well, the alcoholic version of me is.'

'Convenient,' Olivia muttered.

'I'm taking responsibility, but I know I have years of making up to do with you.'

Before Olivia could reply, the phone began to ring.

Jeanette stood up. 'You get that. I'm going now.'

Olivia picked up the receiver. 'Hello?'

'It's me.' Amy's voice sounded tense and distant.

'Hi, can you wait a sec?' Olivia put her hand over the mouthpiece. 'It's my friend. I haven't spoken to her for a while . . .'

Jeanette touched Olivia's arm. 'I'll see myself out. Phone me soon?'

Olivia nodded and watched the front door close behind her. 'Hi, Amy, I'm back,' she said. Amy didn't reply; Olivia could hear cars swooshing past. 'Amy? Why are you in a phone box?'

A choked sob came in response.

'Amy?' Olivia's skin prickled. This was it. Chris had told her. This was the call when her friendship shattered into a million pieces.

'I . . .'

'Where are you? What's going on?' Her mind whirred. What could she say? Sorry wasn't going to crack it. It was probably just another one of Amy's dramas with her mum. Things had obviously reached a head. Since she'd started going out with Chris, the tension between her and Susan had stretched so tight it was only a matter of time before everything snapped. Amy was spending too much time with Chris; Amy wasn't revising; Amy wasn't helping around the house. 'Is it your mum? What's she said this time?'

Amy sucked in a shaky breath.

'Just ignore her, you know what she's like. She can't keep you locked up forever. We can celebrate finishing our exams soon.'

The roar of a motorbike masked Amy's reply.

'What? Say that again.'

'It's not that,' she repeated, and the phone started to beep, signalling the call would be cut off soon. 'Fuck, I've been so stupid, I've been so fucking stupid . . .' she howled.

She'd been stupid? 'Put some more money in! I can't hear you properly!' A scuffle sounded and then a clunk as Amy dropped in a coin. It must be something to do with the geography exam. Or perhaps she'd finally told her mum she didn't want to go to university.

'Mum's going mental,' she whispered. 'She won't let me see Chris.' Another sob swelled. 'She's told me I have to go with them. To New Zealand.'

Shock bolted through Olivia. 'What?' Amy sounded scared. Really, really scared. 'Why? Why would she do that?'

Because Susan knew. But Amy didn't.

Olivia's mind raced. How could Susan know? She scrabbled to line up her thoughts. She had to explain everything to Amy. She needed to speak to Chris first. She couldn't drop the bombshell now, not like this. They had to go and tell her together. To say they were both sorry.

Amy broke into a fresh bout of sobs.

Olivia pinched her eyes shut. No, they couldn't tell her. Amy would fall apart.

'I need to speak to Chris. Olivia, you have to tell him I love him, no matter what. I've written him a letter explaining everything.'

'Explaining what?' she said. 'What do you mean?' The phone sounded the warning beeps again. 'Put some more money in!'

'I can't . . . I haven't got any more change. I've got to get home before Mum notices I'm gone.' The phone clicked and fell silent.

Chapter 42

Amy

Now

I spend the early part of the morning in the kitchen furiously baking, punishing my batters with a wooden spoon and wishing Bea were coming home today. I've worked out a plan. When she gets back, I'm going to collect her from the airport and whisk her away to Linda and John's holiday bach in the Coromandel. We can be alone. We can catch up. And the horror can blow over.

The baked cakes cool on racks and, naked of icing, they look as ugly and as miserable as me. I have a fierce urge to pummel them into crumbs. Instead, I force a deep breath and stride back into the café because it's nearly time to open.

Before I reach the door, a flash of Chris's design springs into my mind. *Breathe.* I look around me like it's the first time I've come inside. Dust motes twirl in sunlight that pushes through holes in the closed shutters. The floral tablecloths are worn and faded, *so old-fashioned.* Cobwebs above me loop across the ceiling like a Halloween-themed party.

Breathe.

My eyes land on Chris's plans, still propped up on the counter, and I snatch them up, walk through to the kitchen and toss them in the bin. The tears I've been swallowing back rip up through my throat and I sob and thump my fists on the counter. Through the haze, I catch sight of my grinning face in the newspaper article on the wall. I suck in a deep, shaky breath and straighten up. I drag a tissue over my eyes. I make a decision.

It's time I moved on.

After work, I trudge across the beach towards Mum's. I frame the words I want to ask her, bending my head to shelter my face from sand that's being whipped up by the wind. The weather reminds me of the evening before Dad died. How I wish it was him I was going to see, instead of having this difficult conversation with Mum. But if I want to survive, I have to swallow my pride.

Opening a café in the port is my best option. It's my only option. It'll take time to get used to the sterile building, but I know I can build a successful business, I've proved myself before, I just need Mum's help with the numbers. I can't rely on Shannon and Grant any more, they've got the kids and their new baby to think about. A heavy feeling settles in my stomach. Of course I'm happy for them, I really am.

Despite the thread of understanding that brought Mum and me together last night, this conversation will still make me feel like a failure. I hesitate and the wind buffets around me, tugging at my curls. I could move further out, to the edge of Auckland, or further still. I could make a go of a small café where rent is cheap, find a room in a house share until I got back on my feet.

But what about Bea?

'Amy!'

Mum's waving at me from her gate. The wind flaps at her coat and she pulls it around her, walking as quickly as the sand allows, as though I might run away if she takes too long.

'Thanks for waiting,' she says, her breath ragged. The wind ruffles her dyed blonde hair and I see a chunk of grey lining the roots. 'I was just coming to see you. After you left yesterday, I came over as I had something more I wanted to say, but you weren't home.'

Her words sound accusing, but I scan her face and see concern. 'I stayed at Shannon and Grant's.'

Mum nods. 'Good,' she says, zipping up her coat. 'It's important to have company when you're having a difficult time.'

I'm taken aback. Mum's always on her own.

'I was coming to see you too,' I say. 'Come on, let's walk and talk, it's too blowy to stand here.'

We trudge down to the foreshore, where the sand is firm underfoot from the receding tide. Mum moves slowly and her breath is laboured. She isn't young, I ought to offer her my arm, but I don't want her to shrug me off.

'I've decided to open my new café in the port,' I say, trying to sound pleased with my decision. 'I'd really appreciate some help with putting together a business plan. I've got some ideas . . . but I need to get a bank loan because I want to give it my best shot.'

Mum gives me a funny look and then says, 'Of course.'

I'm expecting her to sound more enthusiastic – after all, the port was her idea – and I'm about to make a spiky remark when she grasps my arm.

'Of course I'll help,' she repeats.

I'm thrown. Am I seeing things differently? Or has something changed in her?

'But first, do you mind if I talk to you about something else?' She sounds anxious. 'I'm not dismissing what you said,' she adds quickly, 'this is important too.'

I nod, curious.

'I've been thinking about our conversation yesterday. I never wanted to punish you, though I can see why it might have seemed that way. Dad and I were sure we were doing the right thing by not giving Chris your letter.'

I'm shocked when Mum's eyes fill with tears. I don't think I've ever seen her cry. She'd stayed rigid and dry-eyed throughout Dad's funeral – and I hated her for it.

'You need to understand this,' she says fiercely, squeezing my hand painfully. 'You were never meant to be our only child. I had many, many miscarriages before you and each one seemed to send me further and further into a dark place. When I finally became pregnant with you, Dad and I were overjoyed. But the doctor told us there wouldn't be any more babies. Just you.'

She smiles briefly. 'It's ridiculous, but I've been frightened of losing you since you were first conceived. Then when *you* became pregnant, I wanted to keep you close to me. I was wrong, Amy. Despite what Dad saw, we should have given Chris the choice to know his child. God knows things might have been different between him and Olivia. We should have given you both the choice to make it work.'

Her hand still squeezes mine and the wind sprays salty water on to my face. I make no move to wipe it away. 'But it doesn't matter, does it?' I reply. 'Olivia was pregnant with Gemma. Chris would have had to choose between us.'

Mum sighs. 'I wanted Dad to throw your letter away, but he refused,' she says. 'When Chris didn't make contact, I assumed he'd given it to him anyway and Chris had made up his mind. But after Dad died, I was going through his things and I found the letter. It was such a shock. I said to myself I'd give it back to you straight-away, but I kept putting it off. I couldn't bear the thought of you discovering Chris never knew about Bea. You'd have left me and

312

taken Bea back to England to find him. I couldn't risk that – or for you to discover his betrayal. It became easier to pretend I'd never found the letter.'

She reaches into her pocket and pulls out a pink envelope. It flaps in the wind, but she holds it tight. I remember the matching pink notepaper inside with flowers around the border, a writing set I'd had since I was twelve, but had never found reason to use. Somehow, pretty paper had seemed important. 'This is yours,' she says.

I take the letter from her and turn it over. My handwriting loops joyfully around the letters of Chris's name. The blue biro hasn't faded and the envelope still looks clean and crisp.

It's been looked after.

'I should never have hidden it from you,' says Mum. 'It was wrong. *I* was wrong.'

Chapter 43

Amy

Now

The following morning, I wake late; sleep had taken hours to come. I roll on to my side and the cold, empty space next to me is a stark reminder of the new day. I fling myself on to my back and stare up at the ceiling. If I could be bothered to get up, I could pull back the curtains, open the window and flood my room with sea air and early autumn sunshine. I could drink in the sea view and feel blessed to be living here, but all I crave is grey skies and rain bullets hammering the glass.

Muffled voices float up from the terrace below and I glance at the clock. I picture a cluster of my early-morning regulars reading the notice I put on the door last night – *Closed? Unheard of!* – as they try to peer through the shutters. So what? I've taken a day off. Bea will be home soon, and I need to get stuff sorted out so we're ready to dart off to John and Linda's bach in the Coromandel as soon as she flies in.

But that can wait a little longer. I close my eyes; brightness dances on my eyelids, morphing into images of Chris and Olivia.

It's the past where I see them, sneaking a snog behind the big oak tree when my back was turned; Olivia gliding towards Chris's house in her sleek silver Mini, an overnight bag packed with black lacy lingerie – and those God-awful thigh-high boots she wore everywhere. I press my fingers against my eyelids and red splinters the images. He'll be lying next to her this morning – like he did with me every day last week.

Suddenly, my bed isn't my haven any more and I push myself up and out, slouching into the bathroom and then back to the living room, where I flop on to the sofa and drag Bea's purple throw around me. I breathe in her scent. I can't wait to see her run towards me as she comes through Arrivals, the feel of her in my arms, for us to sit side by side while she pours out her travel tales.

I still need a plan for afterwards, though. Mum and I ate dinner together last night and talked late into the evening about Dad. It wasn't the right time to carry on our conversation about my café. I must talk to her soon. I don't want Bea to notice the tight smile that hides my worries. I want it to be like it was before she left – Bea, me and my café.

A hammering on the café door downstairs makes me jump and I hear Shannon's voice calling my name. I step on to the roof terrace and lean over the railing. Thankfully, the customers have given up and gone, and it's just Shannon with Mum.

'What're you doing?' she says. 'Why haven't you opened? I could have come earlier if you needed me, you should have phoned.'

'I'm having a day off,' I reply, ignoring the fact I'm running a business that could do without turning customers away.

Mum looks concerned and Shannon roots around in her bag and pulls out a bunch of keys. 'I'm coming in,' she says.

I don't want them here, but I can hardly say no when she's got the keys in her hand and could've let herself in without asking. I'm making tea as they come through the door, which I leave on the coffee table, before dropping back into the comforting folds of the sofa. It's a weird scene. Mum and Shannon sit on the hard dining chairs opposite, Mum perched on the edge of hers in pressed navy slacks and Shannon sighing and shifting. I'd offer her the sofa, but she'd never get up out of the sagging cushions.

They assess me in silence as though they're visitors to a sick invalid and don't know what to say. I'm about to make a smart remark then realise, with shame, I don't want to say anything rude or hurtful to Mum. Our relationship has been toxic for too long.

'I'm having the day off to sort a few things out,' I say.

They glance at one another and I'm aware how lame I sound, aware of the thick scent of my sleepless night lingering on my pyjamas. I push myself upright. I don't want to be the kind of woman who sits around all day slumped in self-pity over a man.

'I've made a decision,' I say, standing up. 'I can't live here any more. The flat is a dump, the café's a dump. I've been sleepwalking through my life for too long. What the hell's Bea going to think when she comes home? She's not going to want to live here. I'm going to sign a lease at the port, rent a flat over that way and start again.'

Mum and Shannon glance at one another again. There's an edge of madness to my voice, I know, but I have this *urgent* need for change *now*, before Bea comes home, which is completely ridiculous. I think about Mum saying she needed to keep me close. I *want* her to want to stay with me for just a little longer before she flies the nest for good.

'I wanted to talk to you about that,' says Mum unexpectedly. She eyes me standing there in my pyjamas and I think she's about to demand I get dressed. For once, I don't jump on the defensive and she doesn't say anything, and the moment passes. 'I said I'd support you with your business plan and I meant what I said.'

Shannon throws me an encouraging smile, but I don't need persuading, I'm going to need all the help I can get. I lower myself on to the arm of the sofa and blow on my tea.

'This building – your home – it isn't for sale any more,' Mum says.

Despite my bold announcement, my stomach flips in anxiety. 'Sold?'

She looks levelly at me. 'I've been thinking long and hard about your business, and, well, I've begun to see things differently. When you won the award . . . You've worked so hard over the years to grow your business and I couldn't see all that just disappear. Look at you. You've brought Bea up single-handedly *and* you've been a success. I couldn't have done that. Without your dad, our business would have gone to rot years ago.'

I'm puzzled. 'How can you say that? All you've ever done is work, I can't remember you not working. And you've managed all right without Dad, haven't you?'

Mum's silent and I suddenly feel the weight of her sorrow, my burning shame for not noticing, for not supporting her. Dad would be so disappointed.

She shrugs. 'Too much time focusing on the wrong thing. I thought making money would give us stability and a future, but I should have taken more time to focus on you and Bea. And the future's now, isn't it? Bea's old enough to leave home, Dad's gone and without him . . .' Her voice chokes a little. 'I don't know, I haven't been able to do or say the right thing to you and all I wanted was to make things good.'

She takes a deep breath. 'Throwing myself into work was the only way I could cope without him. I couldn't sit in our empty home alone. I'd have shrivelled into retirement and old age. Anyway, this isn't about me, it's about you.' She leans forward and places her hand awkwardly on my knee. 'Amy, I'm really proud of what you've achieved, and you'll be a success wherever you have a café. Did you know that sometimes people stop me in the street to tell me how much they love coming to the Boat Shed?'

I laugh nervously. *What's she talking about?*

'I've bought the café,' she says quickly. 'I mean, the building.'

Shannon exhales loudly, making a noise that sounds like 'Jeez'. She rubs her belly.

'You?' I say, not quite believing what I'm hearing. I look at Shannon. 'Did you know about this?'

'Shit, no! But it's fantastic news!'

Mum winces at the bad language and somewhere in the back of my brain I can feel the hard arm of the sofa turning my bum numb. I stare into my tea, the mug warm against the palm of my hands. 'What're you going to do with the building?' I say, careful not to jump to conclusions.

Mum laughs and it sounds strange: light, happy. 'You silly thing!' she says. 'I bought it for you! You don't have to move or start again, you can keep the flat and the café.'

For me? She's bought the building for me?

Shannon lets out a throaty laugh. 'That's awesome!' she says.

They're both waiting for me to respond.

'I don't want it!' I shrill, jumping up and slopping tea on to the carpet. 'The building's horrible, it's old, it's tatty and outdated. I've made up my mind. I want to start again, somewhere new.'

I go over to the window and stare at the empty swing seat on the roof terrace. It's rusty and ugly. I'm aware I sound supremely ungrateful, but this new responsibility feels like a noose. 'It's freezing here in winter,' I mutter, running my finger around the damp timber frame. 'The flat's falling apart.'

Mum comes and stands next to me. 'I've thought the same, Amy, for years,' she says, placing her hand gently on my shoulder. 'Look, I know what happened between you and Chris is . . . awful, but what about his design? It's really good, isn't it?'

'No,' I say firmly as I realise what Mum's suggesting.

She sighs. 'I understand, I really do, so I was thinking I could liaise with him on the design, you don't have to have anything to do with him. You know, I've been wanting to help you for years, but . . . I don't know, I couldn't ever seem to find the right words without sounding like I was patronising you. So I'm just going to say it, before it's too late, and I apologise now if I get it wrong.' She takes a deep breath. 'Please let me give you the money and help you renovate the building, and you can create a new café and a much nicer flat to live in. And if you don't want to live here, you could rent this place out and have a second income. I'll help you buy somewhere else.'

Mum's offer is so wildly huge and generous, it's overwhelming and hard to absorb. 'Chris showed you the drawings,' I say, latching on to this instead of trying to get my head around her extraordinary gift. 'Why would he do that?'

'He was excited,' she says quietly. 'He told me that you and he . . . well, I think he hoped there might be a future. He really wanted to do something for you. His design is really something and brings out the potential of this place, doesn't it?'

Potential? I thought *we* had potential.

'What, so he came to you because he felt sorry for me? He thought I needed help getting back on my feet? Is that it? He thinks I can't manage to sort my own life out?'

Mum drops her hand. 'He didn't come across like that, he sounded honest.'

'Honest?' I say, rounding to face her. 'He cheated on me! There's no way I could use your money to renovate my home into his "dreamy design". Do you honestly think I could carry on living here after that?' I shake my head in disgust.

'Chris cheated on you over eighteen years ago,' says Mum levelly.

'He's still cheating on me!' I shout. 'Clearly our time together doesn't *count*. I was the one stupid enough to think this was something *more* and not just a holiday fling. Olivia and Chris are married, a fact that Chris neglected to tell me, until she turned up for a cosy family holiday with Gemma.'

Angry tears prick my eyes. 'Now I get why Chris didn't want to talk about Gemma. He didn't want me asking questions because he'd have had to admit that Olivia was her mum.'

'That may be true,' Shannon says wearily. 'But we don't know all the facts.' She rubs her back and drains the last of her tea. 'Isn't it time you ask the people who actually *know* the truth for answers? It'll be painful, but this nightmare's never going to end unless you do.'

I'm about to retort but Mum interjects. 'What do you want to do, Amy?'

Shannon pushes herself to standing and watches me carefully, green eyes glowing with sympathy. I know in an instant that I'm not angry with her and the heat of the moment evaporates, leaving behind a tight, empty space. Mum squeezes my shoulder and I feel bad about how swiftly the conversation has marched away from her unexpected and extravagant offer.

'I have to tell Bea about Chris and Gemma,' I say slowly. 'She needs to know who her dad is and that she has a half-sister.'

Mum and Shannon nod.

'OK, I'm going to open up,' Shannon says briskly. 'You get yourself ready for Bea coming home. You know where to find me if you want to talk.'

At the door, she wraps me in a tight hug and her bump presses against me. Without thinking, I turn and hug Mum too. For a moment she's rigid beneath my touch, then I feel her relax. I can't remember the last time I reached out to hug her. 'About before,' I say, 'I don't want you to think I'm being ungrateful, I'm not, I'm really *very* grateful, I just . . . I can't think . . . I need some time . . .'

'I understand,' she says. 'You need to sort this out first. We can talk about the café when you're ready and work out a plan that's right for you.'

The enormity of her gift comes rushing back and fills my eyes with tears. 'Thank you so much, Mum, it's . . . unbelievable really.'

'I'm not going anywhere,' she says, squeezing my hand. 'Just concentrate on doing the right thing. Have a shower, smarten yourself up and go and see Olivia and Chris, and hear what they have to say. Don't be like me and hold the secrets inside you – or you'll lose Bea.'

I close the front door and lean my head against the wood. My phone bleeps from where it's lying on the coffee table and I go over and glance at the screen. It's an email from Bea and I fumble to open her message.

Hi Mum! I was going to phone, I've got so much to tell you! But the time difference is such a bummer, you'll have opened the café by now. Sorry I've been off the radar, Shannon's been giving me grief about not contacting you, don't worry, I'm still alive!! And guess what? I'm coming home early – on Thursday!! I'll explain everything then! Can't wait to see you!!!!

B xxx

Ps. Have you seen Olivia yet? Isn't she lovely!

My eyes fall upon Olivia's name and my body begins to shake. I look again, I'm not mistaken, and a blast of terror and jealousy collide in my head. I try to make sense of what Bea's written. She'll be home on Thursday? It's Tuesday today. I need to speak to her *now*, but that damn phone she never took is still sitting on the coffee table.

How does she know Olivia?

I don't understand.

Isn't it time you ask the people who actually know the truth for answers?

Chapter 44

AMY

Now

Olivia stands by the gate at the foot of the coastal path where we've arranged to meet. I've chosen here, away from the city, where the path trails the edge of the clifftop, because I can't be anywhere near my home. She looks model-like, in stylish wide trousers and a belted jacket, one hand resting on the gatepost as though posing for a photo. Confidence blooms – of course it would, she won the prize! She got Chris; she had his baby.

She stole my life.

I touch my hand against my bag; the letter to Chris is inside. I grabbed it just before I left, thinking I might shove it in Olivia's face to show her how she'd turned my happy news sour all those years ago, and left *my* child without her father.

But I remind myself this meeting isn't about me, or her, or Chris, it's about Bea, and I push aside my teenage thoughts. I stride towards her wearing yesterday's clothes, curls pulled back into a hurried ponytail. I've rehearsed what I want to say, it's important I get the words right. I have to speak slowly and with care, otherwise the tide of emotion I'm struggling to hold back will burst out and I won't be able to get the information I need.

Where is Bea? Why does she know you? Why does she like *you?*

My instinct to protect my child is fierce.

Olivia tentatively lifts her hand to wave but drops it when she sees no reaction. As I get closer, I see she's plaited her hair into a long braid and the beauty in her heart-shaped face strikes me hard. I'd always envied her slim frame and long legs but now, it seems, graceful ageing is another jab in the guts.

'Hi,' she says, cat's eyes darting across my face. Then they settle confidently on to mine, in a way the old Olivia would never have had the courage to do.

Then I get it. *She* holds the power.

'Thanks for meeting me,' she says levelly.

I shrug and push open the gate. Sheep graze dumbly in the field and the footpath is empty of walkers. Far below, I can just about make out a curve of creamy sand edging turquoise sea. It's a bay only accessible by boat and looks like an advert for a holiday in paradise.

I start to walk and focus on the steady thrum of my trainers as they connect with the ground. I've walked this walk many times before. I know we can go for miles if we have to, or we can stop at the top when we reach the monument. The iron structure marks the highest point on the cliff for a reason I don't remember now – although I doubt either of us will care to admire the panoramic sea views.

Olivia's jandals flap behind me. I'm not afraid of the silence between us. I'll speak when I'm ready. But before I can utter a word, Olivia starts to say something, reminding me that the new Olivia is nothing like the old Olivia, who always waited for me to initiate conversation.

'There's something I need to tell you,' she says.

Her voice is different too, rushed, softer, the spikiness gone – how could I ever have thought she was my friend?

I spin around. 'No, *I* have something to say first – where's Bea?'

Shock jumps into Olivia's expression, then the jagged lines smooth back to neutral.

Neutral. *That* hasn't changed. She was always good at masking her feelings.

'Where the fuck is Bea?' I repeat with a snarl.

'She's at my house.'

I instantly leapfrog to Chris's home, where he's never taken me. I stop and stare blindly at the sheep, heads down, plucking at the grass.

Bea's home already?

'I . . . I don't understand,' I stutter. 'Bea's back already?'

Olivia frowns and shakes her head. 'Here? No, no. I mean she's in England.'

'In England?' The path tilts, this can't be right. She's with the elephants, lying on golden beaches, taking bike rides on dusty red roads. 'You're lying!' I shout, and I take off up the path, marching to put the space I need between us. The idea that Olivia knows where my daughter is and I don't, is just too much. Bea's almost as far from me as she could ever be on this planet. *Am I the only one who knows nothing about anything?*

'Wait!' Olivia calls, and her flapping jandals quicken as she runs up behind me. 'She wants you to know she's OK.'

'She's travelling!' I yell over my shoulder. I refuse to think about the email I read this morning. 'In Thailand!' I insist, because this is the truth I want to hear. It doesn't matter that Bea has told me she's met Olivia. It doesn't mean she's back *there*. Back in that horrible town with its shitty broken promises.

Olivia's flapping jandals come close again and her breath is short as she falls into step alongside me. I focus on the monument up ahead, but from the corner of my eye I see she's rummaging in her bag. She puts her hand on my arm to stop me walking and I shrug it off. She reaches again and grips hard.

'Hey!' I say angrily, but she's holding her phone up with the screen facing me. The sun bounces off the surface and I see nothing but my own angry reflection and push the phone away.

'You need to see this,' she insists, thrusting the phone in front of me again.

I snatch it out of her hand and shelter the screen from the sun. My eyes lock on to Bea straightaway and briefly I register her tan and the sun-bleached streaks in her wavy hair that remind me of Chris. She's standing with her arm around the shoulders of a young woman who looks so much like a blend of Chris and Olivia that my heart twists.

'I don't understand . . .' I shove the phone back at her like it's burnt me. 'Why've you got this photo?'

Olivia sighs. 'Bea came looking for her dad,' she says slowly. 'That's why I changed my plans and flew over earlier to see you. I wanted you to know she'd tracked me down because she hoped I'd be able to give her some information. By chance, she came to exactly the right place.'

I stare at the phone.

My Bea?

She never cared who her dad was!

She's travelled all the way to England on her own without telling me?

'How? How did she find you? How did she even *know* about you?'

'She said she'd found some old photos in a box of yours. You'd written our names on the back of some of them, so she guessed from our age that either Chris or Paul was probably her dad. I think she hoped it'd be Chris rather than a strange-looking Goth guy wearing make-up!' She tries to laugh, but the sound is shrill.

'She thought she'd find answers back in Hillgate and did a bit of googling and found me. It wasn't hard, I've got an art gallery on the high street.'

I stare and stare at Olivia as random thoughts jump around my head: *Bea found my box? She's seen all the photos.*

Bea *already knows* Chris is her dad.

'Bea's still there? At your house?' I manage to say. The thought makes me feel sick. She's been alone on the other side of the world with strangers. With a woman I don't really know, and now wonder if I ever did. *And Bea knows Chris is her dad.*

Olivia nods. 'She's been staying with us. She's flying home early, so she'll be back on Thursday – with Gemma. The girls are so excited. Bea's bursting to see you and tell you everything that's happened.'

I gaze blindly at the ocean. I know where Bea is, I should feel relieved, I should feel excited, she's coming home *in two days*. But instead, raw jealousy rips through me and I spike Olivia with my eyes. Right now, this *amazing* and *beautiful* woman knows more about my child than I do. 'Is there anything else of mine you want?' I say coldly.

Olivia turns away. I've scored a point. I don't wait for an answer because I know the answer and instead I up my pace again on the hill. This time she sticks with me, and I'm reminded how she used to do this. Stick to me like glue, making it awkward when I spoke to other friends at college because she'd be still and silent until I gave her my full attention.

A thought occurs and I spin around again. 'How did you know Chris was her dad?'

Olivia is so close behind me that she steps back, and I think she's going to stumble on the sloping path. 'Come *on*, Amy!' she says, almost cheerfully, and I detect a familiar hint of sarcasm. The old Olivia would've said, *Duh, Amy, who the hell else would Bea's dad be?*

Olivia knows Chris is Bea's dad. Olivia's met Bea. Bea's met Olivia. *Bea knows Chris is her dad.* My stomach churns. This isn't how I wanted things to play out, but there's absolutely nothing I can do.

'Bea looks like Chris, doesn't she? She's gorgeous.'

Olivia talks about Bea like she knows her so well.

'Please don't be cross with her,' she continues. 'She told me she'd fibbed a bit about her travels and hadn't been in contact for a while because she didn't want to keep lying to you. But I said you needed to know where she was. And . . .' She pauses for a moment.

'Long bloody way to come to tell me my daughter is safe in *your* house,' I snap.

'No, I don't mean I came all this way just to tell you that . . . Look, I understand now why you just upped and went without saying goodbye.'

Then a terrible thought swirls into my mind, making the bright colours of the fields and ocean blur together. 'You came here to tell Chris about Bea,' I say, trembling. 'You've already *told* Chris about Bea.'

Chapter 45

OLIVIA

Then

Olivia sat at the patio table and scribbled the last words of the letter. Grey clouds had gathered across the sun, leaving her shivering in a T-shirt and jeans – shaking as Amy's phone call played over and over in her head. Did her letter make her a coward? Probably. She forced herself to whisper each word out loud into the empty garden. They sounded like a story, a sordid story, and she imagined the echo in Amy's head when she read the words herself. Her expression would be disbelieving at first, her eyes widening as the truth sank in and then she'd . . . what? Olivia didn't know.

She screwed up the letter and flicked her lighter to it, dropping the ball of fire on to the patio, where it quickly turned to ash. How simple life would be if she could just burn away *that night* and pretend it never happened. She kicked at the ashes; she needed to speak to Chris. Because who the fuck else would have told Susan about *that night*? He needed to know what a fucking mess he'd made of everything now Susan had told Amy. And there was that other thing Amy had said . . . about her parents dragging her away to New Zealand, did he know about that, too?

Olivia jumped up and went inside, grabbing her bag before she changed her mind. Out front, she stood by her car, but the enormity of remembering how to press the pedals and push the gearstick seemed too big, so she set off on foot to Chris's house. She had no idea what she was going to say. She just knew she had to have it out. How dare he do this? Rip her friendship with Amy apart just because he felt guilty?

Three back-to-back cigarettes later and Olivia was ringing Chris's doorbell. She reached up to stroke her hair then stopped herself – *no, she wasn't a kid any more* – and lit another cigarette instead. If Chris's mum or dad answered she'd look like a right tramp, smoking on their doorstep, but then she was a tramp, wasn't she? What kind of friend teased their best friend's boyfriend, stuck her tongue in his mouth, and then . . .

The door opened and Chris stared at her. 'What you doing here?'

She dropped the cigarette. Her heart pounded as she stared into his handsome face, the anger that had driven her here suddenly vanishing and, to her utter horror, she felt her face crumple. She turned away, swallowing hard and wiping her fingers under her eyes. God, she didn't need to look like a hysterical wreck. 'Nice welcome,' she mumbled.

'Sorry.' Chris glanced over his shoulder and stepped out, pulling the door half closed behind him. They stood for a moment, almost eye to eye, and the closeness between them pulsed a shameful sweep of desire through Olivia again. *Christ.*

She stepped away from him. 'Why did you tell her?' she demanded.

'Tell her?' Confusion lined his face and then he paled. 'I haven't told Amy anything, why the hell are you asking me that? What's she said?'

Olivia watched him closely. Was he lying? He looked convincing enough. 'Did you tell Susan, then?'

'What the fuck?' Anger stained his cheeks. 'No! Did you?'

'Of course not! So why isn't Susan letting me speak to Amy?'

Chris exhaled. 'Is that what's happened? You know what she's like. She's a bloody pain in the arse.'

She narrowed her eyes. 'Have *you* seen Amy, then?'

'I can't,' he whispered furiously, glancing over his shoulder at the half-open door. 'Not yet, anyway.'

Olivia frowned. 'Why?'

Chris grasped her by the elbow and propelled her down the path towards the pavement, away from listening ears. His grip was firm, but Olivia didn't care, she didn't want him to let go.

'You know – the scratches?'

She looked at him blankly. 'Scratches?'

'For fuck's sake, keep your voice down,' he whispered. 'Your bloody nails! They were like talons on my back!'

Olivia stared at him, then a misty memory of his silky skin, so irresistibly smooth, drifted back to her. How she'd gasped when she'd felt him hard against her, and that dizzy urgency to drag her nails down his back.

And then . . . ?

Her face burned and she turned away. 'Sorry . . . I don't remember . . . well, I do, kind of, now you've said, but I don't remember anything else.' She looked up at the sky and drizzle dampened her warm cheeks.

Chris sighed. 'We were pretty hammered . . . It all happened so fast, one minute we were having a laugh and then . . .'

'It was my fault,' she muttered.

'Yeah, well, I didn't exactly push you away.'

Neither of them spoke for a moment.

'I feel bloody awful,' Chris continued. 'I've hardly spoken to Amy. I can't, I've got guilt written all over me. I don't know what we were thinking, we shouldn't have done it.'

Done It?

Something shrivelled up inside of Olivia. What a way to lose her virginity. She was just a meaningless shag, a meaningless *slapper*.

'Sorry,' he said, noticing her expression. 'I didn't mean . . .' He rolled back on his heels. 'God, this is so fucking awkward.'

'Well, I'm sorry I was an *awkward shag*, an annoying slag that got in the way of you and your precious Amy!' she yelled.

Chris stared, his mouth open, and as she turned to leave, he spun her back around. '*What?*' he said, gripping both her arms. 'What are you talking about? A shag?' He let out a squeak of laughter. 'It was kissing, Olivia! Kissing!'

His face was inches from hers, she could smell mint and cigarettes on his breath. She squeezed her eyes shut and tried to piece together the rest of the fragments. *He'd ground against her . . . she'd dug her nails into his skin . . . her mini skirt had ridden up, that wasn't her imagination, was it?*

'No.' She shook her head and tried to pull away from him.

'Yes,' he whispered, 'just kissing.'

An absurd surge of disappointment washed over her. Just kissing? That was a good thing, wasn't it? She swallowed. 'But my skirt . . .' she whispered furiously, not caring about the burning in her face any more.

Chris let go of her. 'Well, let's just say it was *some* snogging . . .' He coughed. 'Did you think . . . ?' He laughed. 'God, you really can't remember anything. I ordered us a taxi and I dropped you home. I'm not that much of a shit!'

Olivia straightened up. 'Of course,' she said, her head dizzy. *It was only kissing.* They looked at each other and, in a surge of relief, she reached out and cupped his face in her hands. Slowly, she touched her lips to his, breathing in the scent of him up close one last time.

For a couple of beats he didn't move, and then he prodded her away. 'What you doing?' He laughed, awkwardly.

It was nothing, just a kiss.

Olivia folded her arms. 'What are we going to do about Amy?' she said briskly. 'I've tried calling her and it's like Susan's guarding the phone, she won't let me speak to her. Then yesterday, Amy phoned from a call box, crying. I tried to find out what was wrong but she could barely speak, then she ran out of money.' She sighed. 'I thought it was about . . . you know . . . *our kiss.* I'm scared she knows what happened and hates me. Hates *us.*'

'Get a grip, Livvy, she wasn't hiding in the bushes at the pub watching and, anyway, what's there to tell? We had a drunken snog. It didn't mean anything.'

Olivia lifted her chin. 'Of course not.'

'I need to see Amy.'

'I'll come with you.'

He shook his head. 'I should go on my own. If we turn up together, then – well, if she *had* seen us snogging then . . .'

'You just said she can't know a thing!'

'I just don't want to make things any worse than they might be.' He patted his pocket for a cigarette. Olivia pulled hers out and passed one to him. 'Did she say anything else?' he said, lighting up. 'Anything that might indicate she knows?'

Tell Chris I love him, no matter what . . . She's telling me I have to go with them. To New Zealand.

'Something about her parents taking her to New Zealand,' Olivia said slowly. 'It didn't make any sense. I mean, why would she go with them? She's got you and her whole life ahead of her. Perhaps Susan's blackmailing her because she's finally told them she doesn't want to go to university. But they can't tell her what to do any more, can they? She'll be eighteen in a couple of months. She can do what she likes.'

Chris grabbed her arm, his face pale. 'Whoa, back up a minute. What do you mean, Amy's moving to New Zealand? This is news to me.'

'I don't know! It was just something she said. *That's* why I want to see her. To check she's OK.'

Chris opened his mouth to reply but his eyes widened on something behind her. Olivia turned to see a battered Ford parked opposite them. The window was down and Amy's dad was staring right at them. Fear prickled Olivia's spine. How long had he been there? Had he heard them talking?

Unsmiling, Geoff lifted his hand in greeting but, instead of getting out to say hello, he drove away.

Just kissing. That's all Olivia could think about as they made their way to Amy's house. That was forgivable, wasn't it? But how could a kiss be just a kiss when your friend trusted you? If this was why Amy had decided to chuck away her life and move to New Zealand, then they had to tell her it was a stupid mistake.

Olivia and Chris stood on Amy's doorstep together. Olivia wanted to feel the squeeze of Chris's reassuring hand, but of course that was ridiculous. She reached to knock and the door swung open as if Amy's mum had been watching them through the spy hole.

'Yes?' Susan looked odd in a pair of casual slacks and a man's shirt rolled up at the sleeves. Behind, packing boxes lined the hallway. 'The lovebirds,' she said, her voice like ice.

Fear shot through Olivia and she glanced at Chris.

He was staring at Susan. 'You're mistaken,' he said firmly.

Susan's dark eyes roamed over them both. She grimaced as if they were something disgusting, then her gaze settled on Olivia. It was like she could read the inner workings of Olivia's mind and she felt like curling into a ball.

Don't be fooled. She doesn't know a thing. She can't know any-thing. Do this for Amy's sake.

'Is Amy home?' Olivia said.

Susan didn't move an inch. 'That's not your concern.'

The house was silent. 'Can we see her for a minute? It's import-ant,' she pressed.

'Important?' Susan sneered. 'Important for who? You two, or her?'

Olivia glanced at Chris again, her courage wavering. What was going on?

She knows.

She can't. She's just being a cow.

Chris appeared to be staring Susan down. 'We've got revision to do too,' he said. 'We just need five minutes, that's all.' He pointed to the boxes. 'I can see we've caught you at a bad time and you're busy. We won't come in.'

'No, you definitely *won't* be coming in. And, yes, it *is* a bad time, particularly for poor Amy.'

Olivia sucked in her breath. 'Look, I don't know what's going on, but I think Amy might actually want to speak to us. We're worried about her.'

Susan laughed, a shrill sound that prickled Olivia's skin. 'You're *worried* about her? Isn't it a bit late to be worried? Neither of you seemed worried before. Worried wasn't a word I'd use.'

Olivia flushed. *Before?* What was she talking about?

Susan stepped down from the threshold, forcing Olivia to shuffle backwards. 'I know about you two,' she sneered. 'I've always known and now I have proof. If you think you can pretend nothing's happened, you're too late, Amy knows. She knows you're a scumbag' – she pointed to Chris – 'and you're a tart.' She jabbed a finger at Olivia. 'Get the hell out of here. Amy doesn't need people like you in her life.'

Susan slammed the door and a roar filled Olivia's ears. She swayed as the words rattled back through her body and settled into the recesses of her mind.

Amy knows.

I'm a tart. I'm a whore.

It was just a kiss!

Still a tart. Still a whore.

Just like your mother.

Chapter 46

Amy

Now

'No,' Olivia says firmly. 'I haven't come to New Zealand to tell Chris. Bea's *your* daughter and this is for *you* to tell him. I came because I wanted to see you. Chris phoned me to say he'd come across you by chance, but I didn't know anything about Bea until she turned up at my gallery.'

I imagine Bea standing in front of Olivia in clothes that probably needed washing and a grubby pack on her back. *She travelled so far. All on her own.* I feel a tiny swell of pride, mixed with relief that Olivia hasn't told Chris.

'Chris and I had always planned for Gemma and I to come to New Zealand for a holiday before he left. But once I met Bea and discovered Chris was her dad too . . .' Olivia's voice wobbles and she pushes her mouth into a watery smile. 'Well, it changed everything, didn't it? I needed to come and see you myself. I didn't think it'd be right for Bea to fly back, desperate to meet her dad, and for neither Chris nor you to have any idea she knew.'

She sucks in her breath. 'And I wanted to talk to you about . . . well, I assumed Chris had already told you about Gemma and you already knew Bea had a half-sister, but when I saw you at the café . . .' She looks up towards the monument, then back at me. 'I guess it wasn't ever going to be an easy conversation for him to have with you.'

A breeze ruffles hair that's worked loose from her plait. Tightness clamps my chest, but I breathe through it, I have to ask. 'When was Gemma born?'

Olivia moves off the path and sits down on the grass. She starts plucking at the daisies and a memory of her sitting on the college field threading daisy chains rolls into view. How easy life had been back then. Before this. Before we grew up.

She looks up at me, cat's eyes wary, and in our silent stare I hear the distant hum of the waves breaking on to the shore below.

'What you really want to know is when she was conceived,' she says at last. 'We – I made a stupid mistake.' She shakes her head. 'No, no, that's not right. Gemma definitely *isn't* a mistake, she's beautiful and we love her very much.'

The sound of the waves swell – or is it blood pounding in my ears? I fold my arms, then grip my elbows. I'm not ready to hear what she has to say, I want to scream, but an inkling of a memory leaps to the front of my mind. 'Was it your eighteenth birthday?' I demand.

Olivia's eyes widen. 'No.' She shakes her head. 'No,' she repeats more firmly. 'I thought . . . God, I was so naive . . . we kissed that night, nothing else.'

The sun feels warm on my cheeks, but a chill skates across my skin. It's the first time I've heard this confession but, buried beneath the years that've passed, this idea isn't new to me. I remember being stranded outside the pub with Paul that evening and seeing Olivia framed in the doorway. She stared directly at us then turned away and strode back inside. Paul didn't believe me. He thought I was being dramatic. Then, afterwards, the tight look Chris wore that he insisted was exam stress. The shock of learning I was pregnant, Mum's hideous words and the exams I knew I'd failed before I'd finished, all swimming together in a medley of confusion and paranoia.

'But it wasn't just the once, was it?' I press. 'You both . . . you were cheating on me. Dad saw you kissing outside Chris's house.'

Olivia looks shocked, then her eyes fade as if she's trying to remember. 'That's why she spoke to us like that,' she mutters.

'Who?' I say. 'Who spoke to you?'

Olivia shakes away the memory. 'Your mum and dad were mistaken, it wasn't like that. I went to see Chris that day because I was worried about you. Your mum had you pretty much locked up at home and you'd phoned me from a call box the day before, crying. I knew it was something important, which I guess now was probably that you were pregnant.'

I'd planned to phone Chris, but I couldn't. Mum's words still spun around my head and I'd dialled Olivia's number instead. I'll never forget the stench of piss and the sticky plastic handset, it's all so clear in my mind, yet also so far, far away. I feel a terrible wave of sadness. For me; for my teenage self.

'I *did* kiss Chris that afternoon,' Olivia continues quietly. 'I brushed my lips over his, like a farewell kiss, I suppose. I knew then I'd been deluding myself that there could ever be anything between us. We went to your house together, but your mum sent us away. She told us you knew about "us" – even though there was no "us" – and then you were gone.' She sighs. 'I'm sorry you've had to believe this shit for all these years. It's my fault, I should have replied to your letters, but when I got pregnant with Gemma . . . I was afraid of what you'd say.'

I wait for my anger to explode. Anger at Dad for making such a stupid mistake that set this monumental *fuck-up* that is my life into motion. But there's nothing. I'm defeated and utterly exhausted. I lower myself on to the grass next to Olivia.

'I didn't know,' I say. 'Mum only told me recently. She tried to protect me from what she thought Dad had seen. But looking back . . . Chris was behaving strangely, he didn't want to see me, so I knew something wasn't quite right between us.'

Olivia clutches both my hands. Her skin feels cool against mine. 'We weren't having a fling behind your back,' she repeats. 'It *was* only that one evening on my birthday. Chris felt terrible about it. *I* felt terrible about it. It was a stupid, naive, drunken teenage thing to do.'

'But you don't drink!'

She shrugs. 'Only the once and never again.'

Slowly, I unpick what she tells me. 'I don't understand,' I say. 'How does Gemma fit into this? You got married.'

Olivia nods slowly then stands up, gesturing for me to walk with her. 'Chris was devastated when you left without a word,' she says as we fall into step together. 'No phone call, no letter. *I* was devastated. We both really missed you and so we kept drifting together to go over it all. He'd tell me how much he loved you and how angry he was that he couldn't find you to explain that your mum had told you a bunch of lies.'

'And?' I look down at my feet, vaguely surprised they're still carrying me forward.

'We drifted into this weird . . . relationship that summer. We kind of found comfort in each other, I suppose. I'd told Chris I was on the Pill, but I wasn't. I had a warped way of thinking back then. I played a foolish game of roulette – will I get pregnant or won't I? Destiny would decide. I had this sick idea that it'd be a deserved punishment as it was my fault you'd split up and left. Have a baby. Ruin my life.'

Her hand flies to her mouth. 'I didn't mean . . . God, *such* a stupid thing for me to say. This was how I thought, back then. I was a miserable mess.'

Shocked sadness skitters over me. It's too much to fully understand yet.

Olivia looks at me and takes my silence as permission to carry on. 'I guess being pregnant gave me the negative validation I thought I deserved. Only trashy teenage girls had babies,' she says softly. 'I was caught in a downward spiral. I'd treated my best friend – my *only* friend – like shit. I had no faith in Mum's new-found interest in me, I'd got brilliant A grades, but I couldn't settle at uni – what would it matter if I had a baby? Who'd give a toss?'

Chris would. That's the kind of bloke he is. Why didn't I understand that back then? If I hadn't listened to Mum, if I'd believed in Chris, then I'd never have left. I look up at the big blue sky above us. *Because you were only seventeen. A child-woman. How could you have known these things?*

'I never imagined Chris would stand by me. Gemma came along about a year after you left. Chris wanted to stay in Hillgate with us, but I insisted he go to Manchester uni as planned, and he did at first, but the pull to spend time with Gemma was too strong and he transferred to London. We decided to try and make a go of it, become a proper family and . . . got married.'

And there it is: the ugly truth spread out in front of me.

You really did steal my life.

'The three of us lived with Chris's parents and he got the train to London every day. I could see the strain on him. He was working in the pub when he could to help pay for things that Gemma needed. In the end, it was easier for us to move in with Mum. She was brilliant. Having Gemma around really encouraged her to sort

341

her life out. She hasn't had a drink since Gemma was born. She looked after her, so I was able to go to art college.'

Olivia's story is a painful one, but I can't think about her pain just yet, only my own. My tongue feels thick. 'Despite everything, you and Chris made it work, you still love each other.' I point to her pretty wedding band studded with diamonds. I see everything now, like I chose not to before. She'd always adored Chris, sneaking glances when she thought I wasn't looking and hanging around us whenever she could. But it never worried me because he loved *me* – or so I thought.

Olivia glances down at her ring. 'Oh!' Then she stops and grabs me painfully by the hand. 'No, Amy! No, I don't *love* him, I *thought* I loved him. Years and years ago, in a completely different life, when I was a completely different person! There was no dramatic end. When Gemma and I moved in with Mum, Chris and I were both relieved to part ways. We didn't have to pretend any more. And we've stayed friends because that's the beauty of never being right together in the first place – there's no bitterness.'

My fingers are crushed in Olivia's grip, but I don't move an inch, I'm listening.

'Chris never loved me, Amy, and yes, once that hurt but now it doesn't. He's still Gemma's dad – *he's Bea's dad* – the three of us will always be tied together in some way.'

I stare at her pretty cat's eyes and her radiant face devoid of make-up – that Chris couldn't care less about.

'You're not married to Chris,' I repeat, slowly enunciating each word so I'm absolutely clear I've heard her correctly.

Olivia laughs. 'Technically, yes, but no, not in any real sense. Chris and I never got around to divorcing. Stupid really, but we weren't particularly bothered. Neither of us thought we'd ever want to get married again after making such a colossal mistake the first time. We didn't have assets to divvy up and we've always been happy with our parenting arrangements for Gemma. We spend Christmas together, for Christ's sake!'

I stare at the wedding band on her finger. 'But your ring . . .'

'Isn't it beautiful?' she says, holding her hand up to the sun so that shards of light splinter out from the diamonds. 'Paul has good taste, hasn't he?'

'Paul?' I repeat.

'You remember him, don't you? Paul the Goth! That was another good reason to come all this way. To tell Chris that Paul's proposed and to get him to sign the damn divorce papers. Didn't Chris tell you we met up again a few years ago? Bloody hell, he's *such* an idiot.'

Chapter 47

AMY

Now

Olivia suddenly stops smiling at her ring and snaps her attention back on me. 'So if Chris didn't tell you about Paul and I, nor the full story about Gemma, then when I turned up yesterday you must have thought . . . Oh God, Amy, I had no idea, I thought you were frosty because of the stuff your mum had said about us all those years ago, but of course you didn't know . . .' Her voice trails. 'What an awful mess.'

I can hear Olivia talking, but I'm not properly listening.

Chris isn't married. Chris isn't in love with Olivia.

I feel as though I'm having an out-of-body experience.

Chris is Bea's dad.

We're Bea's parents.

'Amy.' Olivia tugs my arm. 'What *is* going on with you and Chris? I meant what I said before. I came to the café to see you and I'd no idea Chris would be there. I knew he'd met up with you again, but he didn't say that you two had, well, got back together.

You have, haven't you? I mean, I know there's all this new stuff to get your head around, but I don't think he ever stopped loving you.'

I'm still staring at nothing, frozen to the spot. If I move, then I'll be back on the coastal footpath demanding Olivia tell me where Bea is.

Olivia must sense I need some time to absorb everything that's been said, and she pushes her arm through mine. 'Come on, let's walk.'

She begins to chatter about Hillgate and how it's changed over the years and slowly I find myself coming back to reality. The Crown is still there, she says, and our sixth-form college, but now at lunchtime the students favour the trendy cafés serving cappuccinos and lattes, or the wine bar on the corner that used to be the bakery. Her gallery is where the sewing shop had been and she tells me how much she loves her work as an artist and gallery owner, and that she can't really believe it's her job.

For the first time, I wonder if I should go back and visit my old home. I wonder what Bea's made of this funny English market town that's nothing like she'd have ever seen before.

'And what about Paul?' I say, finally finding my voice. She tells me how he slipped away as silently as me, devastated when Chris told him they were having a baby. He'd gone to uni in Leeds and stayed on after graduation, becoming an accountant, getting married and having two children. Then one day he appeared in the doorway of her gallery.

'God, he frightened the life out of me,' says Olivia. 'I was working on a painting and I looked up and he was just standing there, staring at me, in that intense way he always did when we were at college, do you remember that?'

I shake my head. I'd never noticed.

'At first, I had no idea it was him. He didn't look like the skinny Paul we used to know. Do you remember the black bob and make-up? His hair is short and blond now and he runs marathons!' She laughs. 'His eyes are still electric blue – I don't know how I forgot those blue eyes. Anyway, it was only when he smiled and dimples popped into his cheeks that everything clicked. I knew it was him. I really *knew*.'

I look sideways at Olivia's animated face and her expression amuses me. I don't ever remember seeing her look this happy. The thought makes me feel sad: poor, mixed-up Olivia who nobody really understood. I'm pleased she's made peace with her mum and I sense that Gemma is the reason Olivia is the strong and vibrant woman I see today. The parallels between our lives are uncanny – distance and time mean nothing.

'Apparently, Paul had been coming back to Hillgate with his family for years to visit his parents,' she says, her breath becoming short as we climb the stone steps that lead to the monument. 'I asked him why he didn't come to the gallery before. Turns out he was doing his best to avoid me – and Chris and Gemma. He's divorced now.'

Paul's life didn't go to plan either. But does life *ever* go to plan? Isn't that the point? To let life take its course, to ride the roller coaster of good times and bad? Even if Chris had got my letter, would we still be together now? We were so young. We had our lives ahead of us. We were only together for such a short time. As painful as it sounds, sharing the responsibility of Bea could have been too much for us back then.

I won't ever know the answers. But there's no point in dwelling on the past, it's done. The future is what's important now.

We don't say anything more until we're at the top of the steps, catching our breath. It's like we're on top of the world. The Pacific stretches out in front of us, a scattering of distant islands veiled in a haze of mist. To the right, I can just about make out Bea's island family, and a jolt of pleasure reminds me how relieved I am to know she's safe, and how excited I feel about wrapping my arms around her so soon.

Chris doesn't know he's Bea's dad – but Bea does.

My eyes fall on the bench facing the ocean, where a familiar figure sits with his back to us.

Chris?

'You've seen him then?' says Olivia, following my gaze. 'Look, I know I'm meddling, but no more secrets, no more lies, no more misunderstandings, you two need to talk.'

She steps forward and kisses me on both cheeks and I'm warmed by the fondness in her eyes. 'You and I have two beautiful girls. They're sisters of sorts, just like you and I used to be,' she whispers. 'Can we be that again soon?'

I nod and she turns and picks her way carefully back down the steps. I look back at Chris and my heart begins to pound. He still hasn't noticed me. He's wearing the same green T-shirt he wore when he first bounded back into my life, stretched across his lovely broad shoulders – tense today, rounded in guilt, I suppose, knowing the secret of Olivia and Gemma he's been hiding from me is now out in the open. But he doesn't know I have reason to be nervous too. To feel guilt digging into *my* shoulders because I'm still holding *my* secret inside.

I take a deep breath, walk over to the bench and slide into the empty space beside him.

He glances over, expecting me, his mouth a line, then he swivels around. 'Where's Olivia going?' he says, watching her retreat back down the steps. 'We agreed we need to talk to you. Together.'

His face creases in worry and I realise Olivia found a way to be alone with me for good reason. She knew how important it was to tell me Bea was safe. She couldn't have done that if Chris had been with us.

He frowns. 'What's she told you?'

347

Where to begin? I look across the sea towards a fleet of yachts, scudding along the waves far, far away, their triangular sails like a string of colourful bunting pinned to the horizon. My gaze travels to the coastline, following the weave of the cliffs where thousands of years of erosion have scooped out the sandy coves for our twenty-first-century selves to enjoy. 'You should have told me at the start that Olivia was Gemma's mum,' I say, my words sounding more accusing than the softness of my tone. But as I hear myself, I hear the echo of the secret *I'm* still hiding and I don't know who's right and who's wrong any more.

I'm not sure it even matters.

'She's told you everything, then?' I'm surprised at the bitterness in his voice. 'I wanted to tell you myself! I was going to, the other day, but you wouldn't listen. Shit.' He screws his fist into his palm.

I watch a kayak approach one of the coves, the two paddlers working in synchronised strokes. They reach the shore and tug their boat up the beach, leaving a furrow in the sand.

'I wanted to tell you myself,' he repeats, quietly this time. 'But I didn't know how. Gemma . . . Olivia . . . the whole thing was complicated, and then when you asked if I was married and had children . . . I didn't know how to explain. You already thought I'd been a bastard to you once. I knew I was responsible for your decision to leave.'

He punches his fist into his hand again. 'I promise you I was going to tell you – I knew Olivia and Gemma were coming over to visit at some point. But when we became . . . close, I couldn't see how telling you Gemma was Olivia's daughter was ever going to sound OK. You'd have thought I'd cheated on you all over again – when I hadn't.'

The kayakers have unclipped their life jackets and laid out a picnic blanket. They flop down and I imagine them snoozing in the sunshine, letting the warmth relax their aching muscles. 'I didn't ever think you'd cheated on me. Mum never told me – not until recently.'

Chris's eyes widen.

'She said she didn't want to tell me before because she wanted to protect me.' *And Bea.*

'Shit,' he whispers, scuffing the dirt with his foot. 'All those years, you never knew?' He swings around to look at me properly. 'But you were so . . . off with me when I turned up at the café that first time.' He sighs. 'If only I'd known back then, I'd have . . .'

'What? What would you have done?' It's like I'm watching the reel of this scene in which Olivia and Chris stand on the doorstep of my old house with Mum shouting at them. Except I'm watching them through the wrong end of a telescope, the figures are small and inconsequential. I feel strangely detached. It's as though now the truth is out, it's pushed all the regret and sadness back into the past, where it belongs.

Chris tips his head back and looks up at the sky. 'I couldn't have done anything, could I? I didn't know where you were.'

We're quiet for a moment. 'I'm glad you didn't tell me you married Olivia,' I say, and I realise how true this is. 'We had our chance again, didn't we? If you'd told me before, well, I'm not sure I'd have been able to . . . sleep with you.'

He catches my eye and we both smile a little. 'Sleep with me?' he repeats, his voice teasing. 'Don't you mean the hot sex we had?'

I flush slightly and turn my head away. The yachts have reached Bea's island family and I press my hand self-consciously against my bag. Chris scoots closer to me and I feel the heat of his body next to mine. He coils a finger through my hair and I tremble. I'm scared to look at him.

He tugs my curl gently. 'Hey,' he whispers, and his breath tickles.

Slowly, I turn and see that what I've been hoping is real is right here: waiting, hopeful and wanting.

'Then why did you leave me, Ames?'

My chest is tight, as if my words are bunched up together inside, pressing to come out. 'Do you remember I said I wrote you a letter? Dad never delivered it to you because he thought he saw you and Olivia kissing. But he didn't tell me. I didn't know about the kiss, I didn't know you didn't get my letter, I thought *you* had left *me*.'

Chris frowns. 'I don't understand. What did you write in the letter?'

My hand is already in my bag, my fingers are already clutching the envelope, and I thrust it towards him, my heart thumping.

He stares at my stricken face, then at the envelope. He traces his name with his finger. Then he tears at the flap and pulls out the words I wrote all those years ago.

To Chris, whatever you decide after reading this letter, you must remember this: I'll love you forever.

Epilogue

Olivia

Two years later

'Dad!' Bea's voice is distant but rolls clearly across the water to where Chris, Paul, Gemma and I are returning to shore in Chris's boat. He took us out fishing. Gemma's delighted with her catch – a shiny red snapper – but the engine keeps cutting out so we're bobbing up and down, drifting with the tide.

Bea's hopping up and down on the shoreline now, waving, but it's not a friendly, how's-it-going kind of wave, her long arms sweep the air in urgency. Then she must remember what Chris told her to do, because she stops waving and stands purposefully in the sand, placing one arm across the other above her head to form an X-shape.

'Shit,' says Chris, recognising the emergency sign Bea's made. 'I knew I should have stayed with Amy.'

Two summers have passed since we were last here. Bea returned home with Gemma and Paul in tow, and our funny broken and patched-together family circled one another until we found a way to forget the past and look forward to our future together. When it was time for the three of us to go back to England, the girls were devastated to part. Gemma hated leaving Chris – and Amy and I cried too. I promised we'd be back and so here we are – and right on time, it seems.

'There's time,' I say to Chris as he bangs on the motor to make it start.

Gemma stands up and the boat rocks precariously. 'Is Amy having the baby? Now?' Her face has broken into a delighted grin.

'Careful, Gemma!' Chris says sharply. 'Come on,' he mutters to the engine. 'Don't fail me now.'

Paul shades his eyes and squints in the direction of the beach where we left Amy and Bea earlier. Amy had wedged herself into a deckchair, her bump as firm and round as a melon, still a week away from being fully ripe. 'Not yet,' Paul says to Gemma with all the authority of a baby expert. 'Babies take ages to come.'

I open my mouth to say otherwise, and Chris seems to read my thoughts. 'Not Gemma,' he says.

I smile at our daughter, the memory of her birth so clear. Of course, Chris was there, but that was then and what's important is now. He needs to be there at *this* birth.

Paul has inched his way over to Chris, quietly observing what he's doing. I know he's calculating how he can help. 'I reckon if you pull *that* it might do the trick,' he says, pointing to something I can't see.

Chris mutters and the engine chugs back into life. He claps Paul on the shoulder and the boat leaps forward, knocking Gemma off her seat. 'Chris!' I shout and Gemma laughs, pulling herself upright. His eyes are fixed on the shore and the path he's cutting through the waves to reach Amy.

As soon as we're close enough, Chris leaps off the boat and wades to shore, shouting instructions to Paul on how to drop the anchor. Bea runs over to him and they stride across the sand, arms linked, long legs working in harmony. I watch them and think about the precious years he had with Gemma and missed with Bea. Years he won't ever get back. But with years ahead he can enjoy with her now – and, of course, with the new baby.

I look around at my family. Paul and Gemma work as a team to make the boat secure. Gemma's chattery and excited as she talks about the imminent arrival of her baby brother, and Paul nods and listens. It's like he's always been part of us.

He catches me watching and smiles his slow, sensual smile that moors me to him in all manner of ways that wouldn't be appropriate to be thinking about right now. We've not yet managed to tie the knot. We want Bea, Amy, Chris and their new baby to be part of our special day, so we've put our ceremony on hold until the baby is ready to manage the long journey to England.

Gemma climbs out of the boat and wades to shore. Paul stands in the water and holds out his hand to help me. Always a gentleman. I bunch up my long skirt and reach for him, and he pulls me from the boat and into an embrace.

Sometimes I allow myself to take a glimpse at what our lives would've been like in a parallel world where the four of us settled into our right relationships all those years ago. It isn't comfortable viewing – it's a life without Gemma. Though I know in my heart I wouldn't have been ready for Paul back then. And I think, if he was honest, he'd admit he wouldn't have been ready for me either. And Chris and Amy? I don't know. They probably don't know either – but they know the answer now.

Sometimes you need to let life roll before you take ownership.

'Mum, look, they're going!' Gemma shouts, pointing across the beach.

Bea and Chris have hauled Amy out of the deckchair and they're walking her carefully across the sand towards the roadside, where Amy's mum waits in the car.

'Hurry up,' Gemma says, rolling her eyes at us still standing in the water holding hands, my skirt now a soggy mess. 'We need to catch up with them.'

'No,' I reply. 'They'll be fine now.'

ACKNOWLEDGEMENTS

This book began with a germ of an idea conceived during the Creative Writing Programme in Brighton. In our first session we were asked to introduce ourselves and say what we hoped to achieve. My response? *'I want to find out if I'm capable of writing a novel.'* I am (hurrah! I'm still pinching myself . . .) so my first big thanks is to <u>you</u>, the reader, for choosing, buying and reading my book.

On the writing course I met talented writerly friends who've been championing my work ever since: Lisa Fransson, Pippa Lewis, Louisa Bell, Jane Branson – and my favourite tutor, Susannah Waters, for her inspiring teaching and unwavering editing eye. Thank you all for your support.

Jenn Hawkins (née Fryer). We've been writing together for decades – remember Saturday afternoons, aged twelve, holed up in my bedroom scribbling stories? Now we're side by side in our own writing group with the gang (as forementioned) – plus the delightful Rosie Pannett. Thank you all – particularly wonderful Pip, for being our chief organiser.

Thank you to my first readers for encouraging me to believe in this story and myself, you are all fabulous: Jane Whitehurst, Gwenny Whelan-Burch, Sarah Wright, Hannah Barratt, Sam Bailey, Paula Melis, Lisa Deeprose, Debs Quantrill, Jo Slack, Heidi

Phillips, Kate Crittenden. Also, to the support from Brighton's Westhill Writers with the magnificent Anna Burtt at the helm, whose advice and guidance are unparalleled.

Joanna Rees – aka Josie Lloyd – author extraordinaire, thanks for reading my first three chapters. Your uplifting feedback propelled me onwards and upwards.

My agent, Rufus Purdy at Two Piers Agency, a HUGE thanks, where would I be without your expertise? And to my editors at Amazon Publishing, Victoria Oundjian, Celine Kelly, Jenni Davis and Sadie Mayne for helping me shape the final edits into the best read this book could be. Emma Rogers – I love my front cover!

Mel Watson and Donna Smithies, you've been brilliant with my (many) Kiwi questions. And, of course, there is Auckland, my muse. You are a beautiful place to live, the inspiration for this story, and I hope the residents can forgive me for moulding their city (just a little) in my imagination.

Last, and the *most* important, are my family. You know who you are. You are the best. Mum, you are an amazing listener. Xanthe and Kenzie, there's a whole world out there waiting for you, just look at what you can achieve if you keep exploring.

Never to be forgotten, my Ian. You are my one and only.

ABOUT THE AUTHOR

Jane Crittenden is a homes and interiors journalist, who writes regularly for magazines such as *25 Beautiful Homes, Grand Designs* and *House Beautiful,* and finds that writing about house projects is the perfect excuse to meet people and ask (lots of) questions. She has had stints of living in Canada, Greece, Spain, Ghana and New Zealand. Nowadays, she lives by the coast in Hove with her husband, two children and labradoodle, where she enjoys the beach and reading and writing in local cafés (often giving into the temptation of a homemade brownie).

Follow Jane on Instagram @janecrittenden and Twitter @crittenden_jane.

Follow the Author on Amazon

If you enjoyed this book, follow Jane Crittenden on Amazon to be notified when the author releases a new book!
To do this, please follow these instructions:

Desktop:

1) Search for the author's name on Amazon or in the Amazon App.
2) Click on the author's name to arrive on their Amazon page.
3) Click the 'Follow' button.

Mobile and Tablet:

1) Search for the author's name on Amazon or in the Amazon App.
2) Click on one of the author's books.
3) Click on the author's name to arrive on their Amazon page.
4) Click the 'Follow' button.

Kindle eReader and Kindle App:

If you enjoyed this book on a Kindle eReader or in the Kindle App, you will find the author 'Follow' button after the last page.

Printed in Great Britain
by Amazon